THE
MERVYN
STONE
MYSTERIES

THE MERVYN STONE MYSTERIES

2

DVD EXTRAS INCLUDE: MURDER

NEV FOUNTAIN

First published in November 2010
by Big Finish Productions Ltd
PO Box 1127, Maidenhead, SL6 3LW

www.bigfinish.com

Project Editor: Xanna Eve Chown
Managing Editor: Jason Haigh-Ellery
With thanks to: Matthew Griffiths and Lisa Miles

Copyright © Nev Fountain 2010

Geek Tragedy
978-1-84435-530-3 (numbered edition) 1-84435-530-6
978-1-84435-513-6 (hardback) 1-84435-513-6
978-1-84435-531-0 (paperback) 1-84435-531-4

DVD Extras Include: Murder
978-1-84435-532-7 (numbered edition) 1-84435-532-2
978-1-84435-514-3 (hardback) 1-84435-514-4
978-1-84435-533-4 (paperback) 1-84435-533-0

Cursed Among Sequels
978-1-84435-534-1 (numbered edition) 1-84435-534-9
978-1-84435-515-0 (hardback) 1-84435-515-2
978-1-84435-535-8 (paperback) 1-84435-535-7

A CIP catalogue record for this book is available from the British Library.

Cover design and photographs by Alex Mallinson.

Printed and bound in Great Britain by Biddles Ltd, King's Lynn, Norfolk
www.biddles.co.uk

Secret passcode: 4J

For Nicola

Thanks to...

Nicola Bryant, for her creativity. She knows what I mean. She knows which murder she was behind. Not mine, thank God. Thanks to her for squandering a romantic weekend in Tylney Hall by talking through the knottier plot points in this book. Thanks for listening to me read out the whole thing even when she had a raging toothache. Thanks for being Nicola.

Big Finish Towers. Jason Haigh-Ellery, for buying a drink and three novels, David Richardson, Nick Briggs, Paul Wilson and Alex Mallinson for being so positive and for their attention to detail.

Jonathan Morris, for getting me a very interesting book for my birthday.

The police guarding David Cameron, parked on our street corner covered with guns and flak jackets, for their invaluable advice on police procedure.

Andrew Beech, for showing me a DVD commentary being recorded, and Lis Sladen, Barry Letts, Terrance Dicks, John Leeson, Linda Polan and Eric Saward for allowing me to sit there while they talked about old television shows. No one got murdered that time, thank goodness.

Simon Brett and Jon Culshaw for their encouragement.

John Banks, Tom Jamieson, David Tennant, Rob Shearman, Peter Ware and Ann Kelly for their help and time.

Xanna Eve Chown and God, for their patience.

Foreword by Jon Culshaw

Vixens from the Void stays with you.

Like the aroma of fly spray.

I'll never forget the first episode. You remember on *Top of the Pops* where Legs and Co danced to *I Lost My Heart to a Starship Trooper?* It was like that, with slightly more acting, and a lot more Bacofoil.

In fact, I am indebted to *VFTV* for making Bacofoil more interesting. Sunday dinner stopped being 'just' Sunday dinner. Now that joint sizzling inside the oven had been transformed – into an imprisoned space chicken. Bringing jeopardy to Sunday beyond *Bullseye*. I liked the ingenious way the programme created the feeling of a multi-dimensional universe, which you could cheaply recreate at home, simply by sticking your head in an empty Rover Family Circle biscuit tin. Ah, the pleasant hours I whiled away in the Kwik Save car park, whose trolleys reminded me of the dreaded Styrax sentinels (they would have invaded the whole of Ormskirk with their deadly cargo of peach halves, Crunchy Nut Cornflakes and Um Bongo, if their wheels aligned for long enough). Those little devils were no trouble but the Styrax superior (Mr Prescott's Reliant Robin) was far more of a challenge. Those sinister headlights seemed to follow you all around the garage.

It wasn't just the shiny monsters that left an impression. Vanity Mycroft was a name which certainly awakened my teenage self. That was, until I discovered that there was a shop on the way to Preston called Vanity Myerscough, which sold UPVC replacement windows and skylights. It was never the same again. It closed the door on my adolescent fantasies with a secure soundproofed 'clunk'.

The psychological effect of the theme tune too! Rather haunting, even though the cost of recording it must have been around 45 pence. It was my second favourite tune, next to the *Wildtrack* theme - Tony Soper's eulogy to Mother Nature.

Yes, the theme tune, the monsters, the girls. One way or another, *VFTV* kept you hooked. As I look around my palatial London apartment, tastefully adorned with Kelly Hoppen taupes, Fritz Hansen chairs and Helmut Newton prints, I note with approval my own contribution to the décor: a silver figure resting on my shelf... a home-made tribute to the *Vixens* robot Babel-J, which has never left my side. Many's the time one of my international supermodel girlfriends has screamed 'It's me or the silver Action Man', and the answer is always: 'There's the door luv, don't shake Babel-J off the shelf when you slam it...'

See what I mean? Once you get hooked, for good or ill, it never leaves you.

Jon Culshaw. London, August 2010

AUTHOR'S NOTE

I love murder mysteries, and I love ploughing through entire ranges of murder mystery books. There's nothing more satisfying than discovering one grisly murder and knowing there are plenty more bodies piled up just around the corner.

There's one thing I don't love. One thing that pulls me out of a story is that clunking artificial line that inevitably occurs in crime book ranges. You know the line. It usually goes something like: 'Hastings! Do you not recall the case of the Silent Parrot we solved last year? When that murderer whom we both knew, but shall not name or attach a masculine or feminine pronoun to, did all those notorious murders? What an unforgettable unspecific murderer that person was!'

To this end, I am warning you, fluffy reader, that you will not get anything like that here.

This book takes place one year after *Geek Tragedy*. Because it had such a momentous effect on Mervyn's life and the ripples are felt within this book, the identity of 'Geek Tragedy's murderer is discussed freely.

If you haven't read *Geek Tragedy* yet... Well, I wouldn't want to be a spoiler...

Extract from the *Vixens from the Void Programme Guide,* originally printed in the fanzine *Into the Void #49.*

THE BURNING TIME (Serial 4J)

Transmitted: 9 November 1989
Recorded: Studio: BBC Television
                  Centre 6-7 March 1989
                  Location: Betchworth
                  Quarry 13-16 February
                  1989

Medula:	Tara Miles
Arkadia/Byzantia:	Vanity Mycroft
Professor Daxatar:	Brian Crowbridge
Tania:	Suzy Lu
Velhellan:	Jennifer McLaird
Elysia:	Samantha Carbury
Excelsior:	Maggie Styles
Yelack:	Sid Needham
Vizor:	Roger Barker
Officer Tovey:	Vicky Bacon
Acolyte Guard:	Amanda Kyle
Archaeologists:	Robert Frend
	Malcolm Smith
Production Design:	Paula Marshall
Writer:	Marcus Spicer
Script Editor:	Mervyn Stone
Director:	Leslie Driscoll
Producer:	Nicholas Everett

Synopsis:

PROFESSOR DAXATAR is excavating some ruins on the legendary planet HERATH, the Origin World, when he finds a book that dates from before the Burning Time. It alarms the religious head of Vixos, EXCELSIOR, and attracts the interest of ARKADIA.

...cont

Arkadia lands on the planet with ELYSIA (unknown to Arkadia, Elysia and Daxatar are lovers). Daxatar shows Arkadia the book and they both investigate the excavation site further, discovering an underground crypt. Its contents have the potential to turn the whole belief system of the Vixen culture on its head. Arkadia toys with releasing Daxatar's findings and risking a religious war with Excelsior.

Ultimately it is decided that the cost of destroying their civilisation is too high, and it is Elysia who kills Daxatar, burning his research along with him.

But the precious book (called 'the Bible') survives...

Notes:

- This story is notorious for being the most controversial episode of *Vixens from the Void*. On the night of broadcast the BBC switchboard was jammed with complaints from Christian groups.

- The idea of the Vixens' religion being an inversion of the Christian faith was a neat one, the premise being that all trace of Christianity was burned away by some kind of atomic war, leaving only statues of the crucifixion and the Virgin Mary behind. It gave the shattered survivors of the war the distorted impression that women were meant to be dominant over men, and men were there to be punished - essentially creating the Vixens' culture and empire.

- The concept would have probably passed without comment had not the director made quite so much of the visual imagery in the script. One scene outside the Vixens' spaceship, where men were sacrificed to the Allmother by being strapped to crosses and whipped by leather-clad women until they passed out, was particularly graphic and seen by many as blasphemous.

- Questions were asked in the House of Commons. Conservative MP Michael Barnet was particularly vocal, demanding that the licence fee be removed, because encouraging such behaviour was not part of the BBC's public service remit. He would have gone further, had it not been revealed that Mr Barnet enjoyed being strapped to crosses and whipped by leather-clad women until he passed out as well.

- The fact he claimed for these experiences as expenses sealed his fate, as his words were gleefully repeated back to him in the press about such practices 'not being a public service'.

- Writer Marcus Spicer defended the episode stoutly on radio and television, and his robust exchanges with outraged Christians sparked a long and successful career as a prominent humanist writer and polemicist. His books *The Serpent on the Mount* and *The Last Sucker* sold millions.

- He has to date become the only *Vixens from the Void* writer to make a name for himself in an area other than science fantasy. Even though Spicer has argued he is still writing 'science fantasy' to this day.

CHAPTER ONE

It was a glorious September morning in Shepherd's Bush. The leaves on the trees were curling and transforming themselves into a blazing orange. The windows of the buses were misting up with the heat of the passengers inside. Shutters rattled upwards as the few shops that didn't stay open all hours prepared themselves for the first custom of the day.

Mervyn emerged from Shepherd's Bush tube station and headed off towards Television Centre. White City tube was much nearer, but he fancied a stroll. He felt very virtuous, forsaking the padded comfort of a BBC car for a tube ride and a bracing walk; a chance to smell the morning air, stiffened by the exhausts of a thousand badly-maintained minivans; to hear the innocent laughter of the drug dealers as they played in the park.

And, of course, to look at girls.

September was Mervyn's favourite time of year. It was warm enough for young, attractive women to persevere with their skimpy clothes for a few more weeks, unwilling to pack away the summer for another year, yet cold enough for nipples to punch enterprisingly through thin T-shirts and fragile cotton blouses, bulging unfettered from their bra-less bosoms in much in the same way as Mervyn imagined his eyes bulged as he beheld them.

Mervyn didn't think of himself as a dirty old man. Oh no. In his book, a D.O.M. was the type of bloke normally found on park benches or shopping centres, fiddling furiously in his pockets whenever a luckless woman of any age, size or description went past. He wasn't nearly dirty or old enough for that.

Yet.

Perhaps there was a reason he hadn't ended up as a grunting old geezer waiting in Hyde Park for a shapely pair of tracksuit bottoms and a sports bra to chug past. Fortunately for him, he'd managed to find a less furtive way to enjoy the female form in all its wobbly glory.

There was certainly a murky and libidinous corner of his mind that prompted him to propose *Vixens from the Void* to the BBC in the mid 80s. It was an idea for a science fiction TV drama that depicted an intergalactic empire with females as the dominant gender. It heavily featured nubile young women wearing skin-tight lycra and thigh-length leather boots, striding through spaceships and ordering people about. To his delight, the BBC fell for it, and for eight glorious years he script-edited and wrote for the show; inventing more and more implausible planets, monsters and ways for the cast to get their costumes torn off during torture.

His time working on *Vixens from the Void* was the reason why he was striding along Shepherd's Bush Green. He was on his way to BBC Television Centre to record a DVD commentary for that very show, an episode from season four called 'The Burning Time' – a notorious episode that many fans thought the finest example of *Vixens* and that even many self-confessed 'TV experts' found a thought-provoking piece that straddled the line between television melodrama and proper, 'literate' drama. It had even been shown at MOMI one year. More importantly, it was 50 minutes of shouting, spaceships and very tight costumes.

Yes, it was going to be a good day.

As he turned into Wood Lane, he noticed a small crowd of people clustered around the Television Centre entrance. From this distance they looked very excitable, huddled together in a tight group and talking animatedly. They seemed familiar to him... Were they autograph-hunters?

For moment an insane notion frolicked round his head. Were they waiting for him? But then he remembered he was a script editor of a long-gone and profoundly dead cult TV show, and the notion stopped frolicking, clutched its chest and collapsed with a terminal coronary.

Silly man. Hero-worship of a deluded old fool like him only happens inside the confines of science fiction conventions. They had probably got a tip-off that Robbie Williams was appearing on the National Lottery or something.

When he got closer he heard the chanting. He saw placards. He heard angry words crackling through loudhailers.

That's more plausible, he thought. *Another loony pressure group trying to claw its way into a news bulletin by picketing the BBC...*

It was only as he got nearer that he was able to read the placards. 'Original Vix-sin' was one. 'Worship, not spaceships' was another hilarious effort.

With a shock, he realised they *were* waiting for him – or, to be more precise, they were there to protest about 'The Burning Time' and its imminent release on DVD.

Mervyn toyed with the idea of slipping in one of the side entrances, but he knew it was futile. His BBC pass had long expired. There was only one way into the building, and that was through the wall of sensibly dressed protesters.

Grimly, he braved the god-mob and entered the solid wall of duffle-coats and scarves, meeting the chanting head-on. He was brushed, rubbed and jostled from all sides. It was like going through a knitted carwash.

'NO DVD! NO BLASPHEM-EE!'

Not bad for a protest chant, thought Mervyn. *It even scans.*

CHAPTER TWO

He found himself on the other side of the protest and inside the huge revolving doors with surprising ease. Once he'd taken a leaflet they left him alone. He went up to the front desk and announced his presence to the chirpy girls on reception.

In the reception area, there were banks of TV sets showing the myriad channels the BBC chucked on to the airwaves with gay abandon. Mervyn noticed that one had News 24 on it and was covering the mêlée outside. He sat down to watch. There was a BBC correspondent gabbling urgently into the camera while the protesters stomped behind, waving their placards over his shoulder. It switched to a studio, and to a newsreader. Well, Mervyn assumed she was a newsreader. She was young, heavily made-up and insanely pretty, with 'Look at me, I'm supposed to be clever' glasses, and a blouse that gaped open a perilously long way down. All in all, she looked to Mervyn like an actress from an adult movie unconvincingly made up as a news presenter.

Mervyn's fast-coalescing fantasies withered when the camera cut to a wide shot, showing the news presenter joined at her desk by a man with a smiley moon-face, shiny slicked-back hair and unblinking eyes which darted around the studio. It was obvious that he wasn't used to being on television; he was dressed conservatively in brown tweed with a handkerchief poking primly out of his pocket. His hands were balled into fists and looked welded to the tabletop.

The BBC had put CEEFAX subtitles on, so word-by-word, the interview slammed across the bottom of the screen in fat black blocks.

Lewis Bream, chairman and spokesman for Godbotherers UK, joins me. Mr Bream – it is a rather unusual name for your organisation, isn't it? Most people would think that Godbotherers is a rather derogatory name for Christians.

When any group is oppressed and spat upon, as we in the Christian faith are, they tend to appropriate terms of abuse and use them as a weapon against the oppressor. Just as the word 'nigger' was embraced by rap groups in America, so we embrace this term too, we are Godbotherers. We are right to bother God and he is right to be bothered – about the way we live, the way we behave, the sin we immerse ourselves in –

So you took the term for yourself and made it your own.

Yes, that's right.

In much the same way, of course, the word 'queer' was adopted by the gay community.

The man rose about a half-inch in his seat, as if his buttocks had suddenly locked in the 'clench' position.

Well I wouldn't put it in those terms like that, exactly. We do not regard homosexuals as an oppressed minority, as such –

Why not?

Well, as a Christian... Well... Obviously we believe that homosexuals – as you call them – have free will, and encourage us to judge them by ignoring the word of God. It is their free will to be... what they are... So they can hardly call themselves oppressed – any more than a burglar can call himself oppressed by the law.

But you choose to be a Christian? So by your logic you're not oppressed either.

To not choose the word of God is a sin. There is no choice in the matter.

Some argue that no one chooses to be a homosexual.

Well, 'some people' are mistaken. I'm sorry, I thought I was here to talk about our grievances.

The news presenter had enjoyed poking Lewis Bream with a stick in the hope he'd say something outrageous, but the fun was now over. The BBC Trust members were watchful, and might take a dim view of an 'oppressed minority' being hounded out of a BBC studio. The presenter reluctantly steered the interview back on course.

So why are you demonstrating outside the BBC?

The BBC is planning to release on DVD a piece of drama which we deem unacceptable and blasphemous.

This is the 80s BBC sci-fi series *Vixens from the Void*?

That's correct.

What's wrong with it?

The episode in question depicts Christianity as a joke. I'd say that's offensive in anyone's book. Particularly the good one.

The BBC have released a statement saying that

The presenter glanced down at her notes.

'The episode in question was making a satirical point about how religion can get misunderstood and distorted by its own worshippers. By no stretch of the imagination can it be seen to be a specific attack on one religion.'

Well, that's nonsense isn't it? It's a specific attack on Christianity.

But the protest today – what's the point? It was shown back in the 80s. Haven't millions of people already seen when it first went out on television?

That's true, but those were less enlightened times back then. It was the era of Dennis Potter and so-called 'alternative comedy'. The BBC didn't think twice about insulting the Christian community. We think that two wrongs don't make a right. There is no need to rub decent people's noses in it by making it freely available in our high streets.

But surely, the only people who are going to buy this release are a few thousand fans? Your public protests will only ensure that more people will buy it to see what the fuss is about.

It's the principle. We've got to make a point. If this sort of trash gets released by the BBC without comment, then the BBC – which is publicly funded with our

money, let's remember – then they'll think it's business as usual when releasing blasphemy into our shops. Were this a Muslim play I'm sure the attitude of the BBC would be very different...

Lewis Bream, thank you.

Mervyn slumped lower and lower in his chair, disappearing inside the folds of his jacket. He always knew that 'The Burning Time' flew close to the wind (indeed, there were complaints at the time) but he sort of hoped that no one would mind the DVD release, that it would slip out on the nod because it was an episode of a trashy, inconsequential piece of sparkly nonsense. Obviously he was being too optimistic.

News 24 moved on to another story, and Mervyn didn't find much of interest on the other screens (an Australian was shouting at another Australian on one, and an unrealistically happy girl was singing a song with a puppet on another).

Pulling his attention away, he saw a familiar face. Brian Crowbridge, tomato-cheeked hell-raising actor of the old school was embedded in one of the chairs that dominated the reception area. He was a large, shaggy beast with thick grey hair and pale watery eyes. He looked like an Old English sheepdog in a suit and tie, dressed up and ready to play snooker with all the other anthropomorphic dogs.

Brian had looked very different in the late 80s, when he played a stubble-cheeked boffin called Professor Daxatar, a galactic archaeologist who was excavating a site on Herath; the planet where 'The Burning Time' was set.

He had been handsome in a roguish way, more inclined to be cast as a bit of rough than square-jawed hero. More Lady Chatterley's Lover than Casanova. He was a bit stocky by the standards of leading men these days, but nevertheless had been deluged by letters from lascivious housewives. However, as Mervyn knew, if you took anyone with eyes, a nose and some of their own teeth and put them on television with enough frequency, they were bound to become a sex symbol of some description. Mervyn gave a rather self-conscious wave to gain Brian's attention, but Brian was also transfixed by the television screens.

Mervyn groped in his pockets, pulled out some scrunched up sweet wrappers and threw them at Brian. After being hit on the ear a few times, Brian finally got the message, looked up, grinned delightedly at Mervyn, and ambled over.

'Brian!'

'Hello Merv. Haven't seen you since... Well...'

'Well...'

'Well, it must be... since we did the telly.'

'Oh yes. It must be...'

Shortly after appearing in *Vixens*, Crowbridge had had a very public breakdown. He left his wife, was outed in the tabloids as gay, confessed to a debauched lifestyle involving drink, drugs and a young Conservative named Tarquin, dried out, found God, lost God, got drunk again, crashed two cars and went back to his wife. It was quite a fortnight.

Since then, things had never quite settled. For Brian, life was like a snow-smothered mountain during the spring thaw. It didn't take much to set off an avalanche and sending everything plunging back into the abyss. The last thing that prompted the ritual of drugs-booze-tearful apology was Tarquin's AIDS related death a few months back. Brian started drinking at the wake, and never really stopped. The last time Mervyn saw Brian, he was on the front of a Sunday newspaper, half-naked, covered in vomit, having been thrown out of a restaurant at one a.m. for screaming at the staff, demanding a good Chardonnay and scallops in Madeira. Whether the good people of Burger King managed to provide him with such things, the article didn't say.

'Madness, Merv.' Brian twitched his head.

'Beg pardon?' Mervyn was mystified.

'Madness, Merv. Out there. All that nonsense.' There went the head twitch again. A bigger one. His left eye spasmed in sympathy.

Mervyn stared, then realised with a flood of relief that the twitch was in the direction of the protesters outside. 'Oh, them! I thought...'

Brian caught the look in Mervyn's eye. 'Don't worry about me, Mervyn. I feel much better now. Went straight into a loony bin for a good long rest. The head doctors had a right old rummage up here,' he tapped his head. 'I'm just as sane as I ever was.' As if to punctuate this, his head and eye twitched again. This time it was not a 'look over there' twitch. Definitely a good old-fashioned mad twitch for its own good old-fashioned mad sake.

Before Mervyn had a chance to dwell on the horror of Brian being restored to his usual level of sanity, a huge roar of rage went up from the crowd outside. The sea of protesters had suddenly been whipped up into a typhoon.

The main attraction had arrived. A sleek black chauffeur-driven limousine had glided up to the entrance. The number plate read 'GOD L35S'.

'Good grief,' muttered Brian. 'What the blazes is going on?'

CHAPTER THREE

Brian and Mervyn half stood, craning their necks to see what was happening, but the crowd had surged forward, blocking their view. Nevertheless, Mervyn had a pretty shrewd idea of who was emerging from the car.

Of course, thought Mervyn. *It all makes sense now. That's why they're all making a big deal out of this. It's all part of their vendetta with Marcus.*

The huge revolving doors spun and a man glided smoothly into reception, like a magician emerging from his sparkly cabinet. An expensive coat hung about his shoulders, as did two heavily made-up personal assistants and a thuggish looking minder.

Marcus Spicer. Millionaire, ex-TV scriptwriter, and now an energetic proponent of blasphemous propaganda (as the Godbotherers would put it) using his provocative novels.

He brushed some imaginary dust off his shoulders as he was greeted by an insanely tall, thin man, with a queasy, panic-stained smile on his face.

'Mr Spicer?'

'The very same.'

'Lovely to meet you, sir.' The man started to blurt out apologies for the protesters, but Marcus waved him silent with a regal hand.

'Bit of a fracas outside, eh? Well it gets them out of the house. Can't say I'm not used to it. Goes with the territory.'

He was in the process of being ushered to the inner doors when he caught Mervyn's eye. Marcus's face blossomed with delight and he made a beeline for him.

Mervyn didn't know who was more intimidating; the protesters, or Marcus bearing down on him with his flunkies and assistants flanking him like an advancing rugby team. Mervyn found his hand engulfed in a warm handshake. 'Mervyn, me old mate, how the devil are you?'

'I'm fine.'

'How wonderful to see you again.' He flashed a winning smile at Brian. 'And Crowbridge, too! The gang's all here, I see. Great! I can see this is going to be *loads* of fun...'

They were about to dip into small talk when Marcus spotted a famous actress on the other side of the foyer. He changed direction at once. 'Marjory! How the devil are you! How wonderful to see you again...'

Mervyn and Brian watched him go, minder and personal assistants scuttling after him. There was a certain amount of undignified struggling at the internal revolving doors, but a side door was quickly opened to let them all through.

It was only after they dispersed that Mervyn could see a formidable-looking woman taking up the rear. She was in a plain, off-the-peg trouser suit and simple blouse. Her pale milky face had a calm neutral expression, which contrasted with her severe hairstyle; a bob so businesslike it probably concealed a zip-up pocket to keep important documents flat. It was Joanna Paine, the ball-buster who was Marcus's agent. And used to be Mervyn's.

She sauntered past Mervyn and Brian and arched a playful eyebrow in Mervyn's direction.

'Mervyn,' she said with a slight grin.

'Joanna,' Mervyn said, coolly. She didn't even slow down.

'Well that was short and sweet,' said Mervyn, looking after Joanna's retreating rump.

Brian hadn't seen Mervyn and Joanna's exchange and thought he was talking about Marcus. 'Well, after all, he *is* a leading man now,' grinned Brian. 'I've seen his type before when I did the theatre. Always on duty. Always performing.'

'Great,' muttered Mervyn, transforming himself into a very passable impression of Marcus. 'I can see this going to be *loads* of fun...'

'Mr Stone? Mr Crowbridge?'

The spindly man who had guided Marcus in had returned.

'That's us.'

'Good to see you. Sorry you were kept waiting,' he said, proffering a translucent collection of bones which passed for a hand. Mervyn took it cautiously, afraid he might snap it.

'No problem... Robert isn't it?' said Brian, checking his sheet of paper.

'Trevor, actually. Trevor Simpson. Sorry.' He flinched, and blushed. 'Robert's upstairs. He's dealing with a problem. Sorry.'

'Is that why we're running late?'

'Sorry, no. That's me. I had to organise passes for Mr Spicer and his staff, and show him to his dressing room. Sorry.'

Dressing room? Thought Mervyn disbelievingly. *We're recording a bloody DVD commentary, not doing* Strictly Come Dancing.

'I thought it best to get them in and settled before I attended to you.'

'Naturally.'

'Sorry about the circumstances. Glad you managed to run the gauntlet.'

'Oh, that lot out there?' chortled Brian. 'One or two of them recognised me, and one came at me with a sharpened leaflet but... Thankfully, no paper cuts.'

'Oh God, I'm sorry.' Trevor seemed mortified. He looked at Mervyn. 'Were you bothered?'

'There are very, very, very few advantages to being a writer. One of those very, very, very few advantages is relative anonymity.'

'Sorry?'

'They don't know I'm me.'

'Of course. Sorry. Sorry. Of course.' *Trevor never stopped apologising,* Mervyn remembered. *He was a machine powered by perpetual cringing. It's no wonder when I first met him and tried to store his name in my head, I nicknamed him 'Simpering' Simpson.*

'Not every writer is as anonymous as you, Merv,' said Brian, pointedly nodding his head in the direction of Marcus Spicer's exit.

'No. Not every writer. That's very true.' Even though Mervyn fought hard to keep it out of his voice, his words were seasoned with irritation.

The conversation lulled, and Trevor leapt mindlessly in. 'Anyway, really glad you could find us...'

'I have actually been here before,' snapped Mervyn.

Trevor 'Simpering' Simpson paled and almost shrivelled into his suit as he realised what he was saying. 'Oh sorry. Of course you have. Stupid of me. You've done some commentaries for us before.'

Mervyn kept snapping. 'And I made the show here. And I worked here for 11 years. I had an office and a wastepaper basket and everything.'

'Oh God. Of course. You made the show here. Sorry. Of course you did. Sorry. What an idiot I am. Sorry. I'll organise some passes for you.'

After a few seconds with the cheery ladies on the front desk, they were granted access to the inner sanctum. The shiny steel and glass décor gave way to grubby white corridors stretching away into the distance, adorned with pictures of shiny shows, shiny stars and shiny awards.

As they walked, Brian sidled up to Mervyn. 'Bit tetchy, Merv?'

'Who me?'

'I thought you and Spicer were old drinking buddies.'

Mervyn really didn't want to talk about it – especially not to a crazed old ham like Crowbridge. 'Oh it's nothing, Brian. All in the past. Old scars never completely heal. You of all people know that.'

That was uncalled for, Mervyn admitted to himself guiltily, *but at least it shut Brian up.*

There was a long wait, as only two of the four lifts were working (Mervyn remembered that two lifts were being repaired the day he left the BBC in 1994. He wondered if they were the same ones). They eventually headed up to the floor where the recording suites were located, through another set of long winding corridors; left, right, through doors, past a Costa Coffee, through more doors and more even narrower corridors. Mervyn whiled away the time negotiating his way around the building by conjuring up a meeting between the head of the BBC and the architect.

Head of BBC: *The thing is, Mr Architect, we haven't a hope of competing with these ITV chappies. They'll wave their chequebooks, poach all our talent and they'll all be off to the independent sector before you can say 'licence fee'.*

Architect: *I see, and what can I do about it?*

Head of BBC: *Just make it impossible for the buggers to find their way out of the building, won't you?*

Mervyn glanced uneasily at Brian, whose face was blooming into a beautiful shade of magenta.

There was certainly a hint of the laboratory experiment in the way the BBC was laid out. Mervyn half expected to arrive at his destination and find a piece of cheese waiting for him. Or, more likely, to get punished for arriving at the wrong destination by finding some nasty surprise waiting for them.

A few more turns, a few more doors, and finally, the end was in sight. And there *was* a nasty surprise waiting for them.

CHAPTER FOUR

Just when the corridors couldn't get any narrower, their way was blocked by two figures having a very animated discussion that was teetering on the edge of a stand-up row.

One was the short, stocky and bald form of Robert Mulberry. Mervyn could see the distinctive goatee beard that sprouted out of his chin, a useful metaphor for Robert's famously bristly temper.

Mervyn had already done quite a few DVD commentaries with Robert. Many of the less personality-challenged *Vixens* fans had managed to get jobs where they could live out their fantasies. Mervyn found them everywhere: magazine editors, actors, writers, special effects technicians and, in the case of Robert, DVD producers. Mervyn wondered why, with so many fans in powerful jobs in the media, he still couldn't get any work.

The other man towered over him. He had a huge bald head and a big greying beard, like an angry Father Christmas. It was a very familiar form. Like Robert, he was another 'professional' fan. And a far less welcome one.

Oh God. It's Graham Goldingay.

Graham was a superfan; an odd character who'd managed to inveigle his way into the lives of ex-members of the *Vixens* production team. A founder member of VAS (the Vixens Appreciation Society), he turned out to be a shrewd businessman, starting a small production company. Soon he was making all manner of *Vixens*-related merchandise: cheap videos comprising interviews with the stars and low-budget dramas, all featuring actors from *Vixens*. When he was on his uppers, Mervyn had been persuaded to write a few. A decision he deeply regretted.

The problem with Graham was, once he'd got a celebrity's name safely in his Rolodex, the phone never stopped ringing; requests to attend dinners, appeals for old scripts, demands for interviews. The word 'No' wasn't in his dictionary; neither were the words 'perhaps', 'maybe' and 'possibly'. In fact, the word 'yes' barely counted – unless it was coupled with the word 'now'.

As the years passed, Graham's tinpot operation grew into an impressive media empire. Now he had money and time to pursue his first love in grandiose ways: hosting celebrity auctions, celebrity dinners and celebrity cricket matches – all *Vixens*-themed, and all for charity. The demands on Mervyn and other fading stars grew ever more extravagant, and ever harder to turn down.

Now it looked like Robert was on the receiving end of Graham's brutish and demanding personality. Graham was throwing words out like fists, punctuating his argument with a meaty finger, which he jabbed in Robert's shoulder.

'You need me Robert, I am essential personnel, and only I am qualified to host this,' he said, in his trademark Irish brogue. 'I personally saved the studio edits in '93 from the cutting room floor and successfully bought the shooting scripts from Nicholas Everett last year.'

'Graham I don't –' Robert tried to reply, but Graham mowed into him, chopping Robert's words into little pieces.

'I can recite the words, not only to the broadcast version but the unedited non-broadcast version, the three drafts before that *and* the original spec proposal where Professor Daxatar was originally called Professor Dexadin, before it was changed because it sounded too much like a prescription pain-killer.'

Graham was always angry about something or other. When he first met him, Mervyn was reminded of the old out-of-date atlases he used in school – the pink bits denoting the British Empire perfectly matching the colour of Graham's furious complexion. In fact, once Mervyn started to think of him in geographical terms, he found he couldn't stop. Every time he met him, Graham's face seemed to look more and more like an Ordnance Survey map of England and Wales.

Just as the Pennine mountains bisect the north country, Graham's forehead was split in two by a craggy frown, meandering down from the top of his huge bald cranium to rest between tiny murderous eyes nestling close together; or, as Mervyn thought of them, Manchester and Sheffield. His swollen nose grew out beneath them in a way that could only be described as Birmingham, and all three features were sandwiched between huge damp cheeks; East Anglia on one side and Wales on the other.

Completing the effect was a huge hairy mole that squatted on the left side of his mouth – exactly where London would be. Ironically, just as the country's capital sucked attention away from the regions; so too did Graham's mole. When talking to him, your eyes were inexorably dragged away from his face and towards his large brown growth.

As they reached them, Graham Goldingay broke abruptly from arguing with Robert and proffered an outstretched hand to Mervyn. Quite *why* Graham picked him out to greet wasn't clear, and that mystery alone caused Mervyn to flinch slightly, before reluctantly resting his hand in the middle of Graham's slab-like paw.

Graham immediately started firing off meaningless sentences in all directions, like a local radio DJ terrified of leaving dead air.

'Greetings. I'm Graham Goldingay. Pleasure to meet you, we have met before several times but you probably don't remember, I do though.

I loved Andrew's book about you, you must sign my copy. Terrible about Simon, I never liked him, but you never wish that on your worst enemy, and I suppose he was my worst enemy, so there but for the grace of God go I. As you're aware, there's been some kind of mix-up. We're in the process of sorting it out, I'll be conducting the commentary for today.'

'You will not!' said Robert hotly, his shiny head blushing into a beetroot-coloured fury.

'As you can see, there's been a bit of a mix-up, but I'm sure we can sort it out.'

'Graham, I told you that you're not conducting the commentaries. We don't *need* anyone to conduct the commentaries. We only do that if we're doing programmes from the 50s and 60s where the guests have gone a bit...' He realised he was in polite company. 'Where a lot of time has passed, and the guests might not have *complete* recall of events, and don't have sufficient grasp of all the details of the original recording.'

'Look, Robert, you are producing an inferior product without me because I have expert knowledge that will turn this DVD into one of your best-sellers of all time. I will complain to the BBC.'

'Graham, this is a Zappp! production. I am managing director of Zappp! The only reason we're here is because I, as managing director of Zappp! have decided to hire BBC facilities. Complaining to the BBC will do you no good.'

'I am offering my services for free and for gratis here and you are being deliberately and wilfully incompetent by passing this up.'

Robert had had enough. 'Trevor! Will you put a call down to the front desk, and ask them to send up a couple of security people? We have an intruder here who is interfering with a recording session.'

Trevor started to move but Graham held up his huge hands in surrender. 'All right, all right, you've made your point Robert, but let me tell you, you might be king of the castle in this bit of corridor, but out there, there will be repercussions, mark my words.' Graham lumbered off in bad grace, giving a final booming response. 'You will be hearing from my blog in due course.'

Robert glared at his retreating form. 'Trevor, will you escort *Mr* Goldingay to BBC reception, and makes sure he safely gets out of the building?'

'Certainly. Sorry. I don't know how he got up here. Sorry about that...' Apologising all the way, Trevor pursued Graham along the corridors.

It was Robert's turn to grovel. 'I'm sorry about that. Trevor's not the only one with no idea know how he got in here. He must be able to fly in windows like a vampire bat.'

'Don't worry about it,' said Mervyn. 'I know Graham only too well. The advantage of being pugnacious to the point of obnoxious means that he usually manages to bully his way into places he shouldn't.'

'Oh crikey, yes,' added Brian. 'Do you remember when he managed to find his way into the green room after we recorded one episode? He pestered everyone he could find, and talked the ears off the producer with some mad idea about him becoming the series continuity adviser – even made himself a badge with "continuity adviser" written on it – talked to Nicholas for hours until he was strong-armed and evicted by one of our rougher cast members...'

Mervyn grinned. 'Wasn't that Vanity Mycroft?'

Brian tried a nonchalant 'Cheeky? What me?' expression and failed miserably. A grin sneaked across his face. 'As I said. One of our rougher cast members...'

'I'm sure Graham knows dozens of people here,' Mervyn assured Robert. 'Any one of them could sign him in if he asked them.'

'You're quite right,' sighed Robert. 'Doesn't stop him being a majorly bloody nuisance, though. Please, come through.'

CHAPTER FIVE

They were ushered into a tiny green room dominated by a large window, beyond which Mervyn could see the recording suite. There were dinky little bowls of chocolates and crisps and bottled water by the gallon arranged neatly on low tables. The edges of the room were lined with squashy squared-off chairs in delicate shades of corpse grey, with just a hint of asphyxiation purple.

Languishing on one of the chairs was a hippyish woman flicking idly through a newspaper. She was wearing a frilly shirt, a brown Hessian waistcoat and faded jeans with a swirly, vaguely Chinese pattern stitched on to them, running from thigh to ankle. Her round face was swamped by a pair of huge spectacles which had fallen out of fashion in the late 80s and wild yellow hair, black at the roots, with authentic nicotine highlights. She was late 40s, dressed like she was 20, and looked almost 60.

She was surrounded by rubbish; sugar sachets, showbiz magazines, a half-eaten sandwich in its plastic shell. Her bag had disgorged most of its contents on to the floor, vomiting lipsticks, pens, books – two obscure historical romances by an author Mervyn had never heard of – and a dog-eared script. Detritus had gathered around her feet, as if she were building a nest.

Mervyn remembered that Samantha Carbury never so much arrived in a room as crash-landed. It was said that you could tell how she was, how her day had been and whether she was seeing anyone by simply inspecting the floor around her ankles and reading it like tea leaves. As Mervyn and Brian entered she looked up, gave a girlish smile, and the years fell off her face.

'Oh gosh, chaps, lovely to see you, haven't seen you in ages!' Her voice was floaty, distant; like talking to someone through a pane of glass.

Brian gushed fulsomely, as actors do. 'Samantha, darling! You look marvellous! My gracious, you haven't changed a bit, how do you do it?'

'Hello Samantha, lovely to see you again,' said Mervyn.

Mervyn and Brian dutifully stood with their cheeks out so Samantha could graze them with her lips.

On *Vixens from the Void* Samantha Carbury played Elysia, sadistic henchperson, sidekick and dogsbody to the Princess Arkadia. Mervyn remembered that she looked particularly good in studded leather. Elysia was an interesting character for most of the series run, but in this particular episode her part had been unusually meaty.

'This is very exciting,' she gushed, gesturing around the green room. 'But I'm not absolutely certain what I have to do here. I mean, what does one *do* in a commentary?'

Behind the nibbles and bottled water there were two big chrome cylinders. Being a writer, Mervyn was a natural scavenger and made a beeline for anything that was available for free; coffee was his main weakness. He grabbed a polystyrene cup, pressed the button on the top, and the nozzle gushed; hot coffee splattered into his cup, on to the table and on his hand.

Sucking his fingers, he looked over at Samantha. 'Didn't Robert or Trevor explain anything to you?'

'Well yes... The thin one did try to explain it...' She absent-mindedly twirled a lock of her hair around a little finger, like a distracted child. 'But I didn't quite understand what they were driving at; I mean, aren't we talking about this episode in front of an audience, like we do in the conventions?'

'It's not quite like that,' said Mervyn gently. 'What happens is, we watch the episode in the studio, and while we watch it, we talk about our memories, impressions, anecdotes; anything that comes to mind. Robert and Trevor record us, and they put our comments on the DVD so people can hear us while they watch it.'

'But... Won't the people who buy the DVD get all distracted with us chuntering away all the time?'

Mervyn grinned. 'Don't worry Samantha, our chuntering is optional. They can watch the episode without the commentary, and if they want to hear us talk about it, they can press a button and hear it with us.'

'Ohhh... I see.' Samantha said, slowly and cautiously. Mervyn wasn't 100 per cent certain she *did* see, but she was too polite to admit that his explanation failed, and he was too polite to raise the possibility that she was too stupid to understand his explanation. When they were filming the series, she'd always managed to take every piece of information and lose it somewhere inside her pretty head. It was a small miracle she'd managed to turn up to the studio on time, in costume and make-up, with the lines at her fingertips.

'Where's Marcus?' said Brian suddenly, to the room in general. 'Didn't he get in here ahead of us?'

'Is Marcus here?' Samantha sat up pertly, like a sixth-former waiting for a particularly dishy supply teacher to enter the classroom. 'How lovely! Where is he?'

'Ah!' Brian slapped his forehead. 'He must be in his *dressing room.*'

'Oh? Have we got dressing rooms?' Samantha clutched at her bag, ready to leave.

Robert looked uncomfortable. 'Um. Not exactly...'

Mervyn realised that Brian – the mischievous old bugger – had waited for Robert's entrance to mention Marcus's preferential treatment in front of Samantha.

Brian piled on the embarrassment. 'Don't worry. I imagine yours is right next to Marcus's, Sam.'

'It's just that...' Robert blustered. 'The thing is... There's normally lots of shows on and they take a lot of the available dressing rooms. And there weren't that many rooms free in the first place. So as a precedent, we don't actually supply rooms, as we're pretty much in and out in a few hours...' Robert sank slowly up to his neck. 'However, as Marcus's agent asked specifically and as there was one going begging... We didn't think anyone would particularly... Oh! I think there's a problem. Trevor's gesturing me through the glass.' Robert vanished with great relief to join Trevor, who hadn't gestured at anyone.

'Hello playmates!'

Marcus poked his head round the door, causing Samantha to emit squeals of delight.

'Marcus! Marcus, Marcus, Marcus!' She rushed to him, shuffling on platform heels, draping her arms over his shoulders as she half hugged, half fell on him.

'Sammy! How are you doing, my darling?'

'All the better for seeing you. My gosh, what have you got on? You smell so scrummy!'

Marcus's hands almost grabbed her bum, but realising he was surrounded by loose-tongued actors and staff, overrode his instincts. He stopped them about an inch from her body, one hand hovering over each buttock. He gave Brian and Mervyn a mock-exasperated 'What can you do?' look. He released her, and disentangled her arms from his neck. 'So... How have you been? I saw you on that documentary about the 80s last week. You were great!'

'Oh my gosh, I was so dreadful on that. They edited it to make me sound like some sad druid from the loony society, or something. I couldn't bear to listen to the rubbish I was coming out with.'

'Who said anything about listening? I couldn't take my eyes off the screen. "Wow," I thought. "Sammy looks even better now than she did then!"'

Samantha blushed.

Marcus glanced at his ferociously impressive watch. 'Oh flip, am I really 20 minutes late? Sorry all, had to liaise with the staff – Siobhan and Carlene, my PAs, and Aiden my minder. Told 'em to get a proper coffee from Costa and collect me in an hour and a half. This won't last longer than that, will it?'

Mervyn shook his head.

Samantha raced back to her seat, tucking her knees underneath her and patting the chair beside her. 'Sitsitsit... You must tell me everything that's happened to you in the last five years.'

Marcus stepped gingerly over the mess on the floor and sat by her. 'Oh, the usual boring stuff. Telly interviews, book tours, heading back and forth across the Atlantic, radio interviews, more book tours...'

'Oh, that sounds so fantastic!'

'It sounds more exciting than it is, believe me. I spend my life eating airline food for lunch and hotel food for dinner.' He realised that his hand had found its way on to one of her knees, and slowly withdrew it. 'So how about you chaps? Mervyn – how's life treating you?'

'Oh much the same as you. Planes and hotels. Back and forth to the US. It never stops...'

'Oh yes. Science fiction conventions?'

'That's right.'

He didn't assume I was flying to America to discuss a film script or a book deal, thought Mevyn. *Not even for a second.*

Marcus steered the conversation back to all things Spicer. 'Good stuff! Keep the old *Vixens* flame alive, eh? The Yanks need a culture injection now and again. They keep asking me to do conventions, but of course, I'm too damn busy. The minute I finish a book these days the pre-publicity gets under way, the book tours get planned... and off I go on the merry-go-round all over again. Yes, it would be nice to go one day, particularly as the money they're offering goes up each time the phone rings. I'll do one, one of these days, when I'm old and decrepit.'

Mervyn remembered that Marcus was always one of those types who didn't ask about other people's lives with any sincerity; he did it to demonstrate he was interested in people, and then he used what they said as a trampoline to bounce back on to his favourite subject: himself. He used to do it when he was a struggling writer, but his shabby charm conjured up forgiveness from most people. Now he was sleek and successful, it prompted raw and unvarnished irritation from Mervyn. He never did it as shamelessly as this, surely? Perhaps Mervyn's memory of Marcus had yellowed with age until it had transformed into a beautiful, sepia-tinted photograph.

'And how's it going with you, Crowbridge?' Marcus asked with mock severity.

'Oh, good, Marcus. Very good.'

'Great.'

'Not to say I haven't had a few pile-ups on the road to recovery, but the head doctors helped push me off the hard shoulder and on to the motorway...'

Nonsensical metaphors started to flow thick and fast from Brian. It was obvious that he had enlisted every 'professional' he could find to sort himself out, from doctors to psychiatrists to life coaches; probably mediums and horse whisperers too.

'It took a while but they convinced me I have a compulsive self-hating personality which causes me to destroy anything good that comes into my life. I've done a lot of group therapy and one-to-one sessions that have helped me find myself...'

Never ask a recovering alcoholic or drug addict how he's doing, thought Mervyn. *Not unless you're prepared to bed in for the long haul.*

'It's been a long and difficult process. Dr Lewis took me by my hand, and she's helped me enormously. She's metaphorically held my clothes and watched while I paddled; then slowly but surely, I waded in up to my waist, and then I finally kicked off my shoes, dived in and swam out from the coast of denial and into the ocean of me...'

Marcus's eyes had glazed by the fifth word, and were flipping around the room by the tenth.

'Yes, well, madness is what madness does. I do get a lot of crazies myself, as you'll have noticed – the Jesus freaks outside. They do tend to follow me around on my tours. Luckily, my fans keep them at a distance. Not that they're any saner. Have you met them? Oh boy, now *that's* a kooky bunch...'

But Brian wasn't to be deflected that easily. 'Yes, she's told me that, just because I share myself with others, it doesn't mean I'm not being selfish, it's actually the most selfish thing you can do, in many ways. I had to learn to just share myself with me, and only share either of us to others when they want it...' From the frozen smile on Marcus's face, it was obvious that he wasn't keen on Brian sharing any bits of himself, but Brian wasn't taking any hints. 'Anyway, you know all this. When you were in rehab she probably did much the same with you.'

The sunny smile disappeared as a cloud passed over Marcus's features. It was clear he wasn't best pleased to be reminded of his alcohol-fuelled past. Or was he just annoyed to be reminded that he had anything in common with 'ordinary' people? Mervyn thought that was more likely.

'Well I don't remember anything about that. It was a long time ago...'

'Not really, Marcus. Time's different for people like us. One day or five years, it all feels like an age when you're on the wagon. And when you fall off it feels like no time at all.'

Brian had obviously realised Marcus's discomfort, and was starting to enjoy rubbing it in.

Robert's shiny head popped in from the doorway. 'Hello gents and lady, we're ready for you. Can you make your way into the studio, please?'

CHAPTER SIX

Mervyn, Brian, Marcus and Samantha were in the recording studio clustered around the screen; headphones hanging around their necks, BBC passes dutifully pinned to lapels and shirts. They swivelled on their chairs to face Robert Mulberry, who lounged on a desk, one foot on a chair, the other dangling aimlessly beneath him.

Briefing time.

Trevor 'Simpering' Simpson scuttled in and handed out a crib sheet, detailing some facts about the episode they were about to see. Nothing that was new to Mervyn, but Samantha and Brian examined them like there was going to be a test later. Marcus slipped his sheet under his coffee. Robert waited until 'Simpering' Simpson scuttled out, and then cleared his throat.

'Okay, thanks everybody for getting here so promptly and managing to get past the demonstration out there... I know some of you have done this before, but for the benefit of those who haven't, I'll just go over a few points...'

Mervyn, who had done this kind of thing many times before, tuned himself out. The others all leaned forward attentively.

'While you're watching the episode, try not to just describe what you're seeing. The viewers can see what's on the screen. Use what you see to remind yourself about the show. They want you to talk about the production, any memories, funny stories, interesting anecdotes, stuff like that. We like to keep the commentaries relaxed and informal, like people chatting in a restaurant, so keep it light and friendly.'

Mervyn didn't feel very light and friendly at the moment. He started to tear his crib sheet into little strips.

'Our microphones are very sensitive, and can pick up most noises in the studio, so try not to fiddle with pens or glasses...' He looked meaningfully at Mervyn. 'Or bits of paper...'

Mervyn stopped tearing his crib sheet into little strips.

Robert tugged at the tuft of his beard. 'When it comes to the story, don't worry about revealing how it's going to end. You're not spoiling it for the viewers because they've probably all seen it many, many times before. Our market research shows that most of them already own a video copy, and are buying the DVD for a better picture and for the extras.'

'Oh, absolutely,' said Marcus. 'Out of the half-dozen or so television adaptations they've done of my books, these days it's always the DVDs with the most extras which sell the best.'

A little bit of Mervyn died inside him.

Robert continued. 'But on the other hand, try not to get too far ahead of yourselves. Talk about each bit as it comes on screen. If you have something interesting to say about the last five minutes, try and wait until then.' He looked at his notes. 'Some commentators start to watch the show and forget to speak. It's a very easy thing to do, but try to resist. There's not much use in a commentary without comment.'

Samantha laughed, slightly too hysterically.

'So keep the chat going, keep the energy up, and don't swear or make defamatory remarks about your colleagues. You are being recorded, remember.'

Samantha put a hand up. 'What happens if you, um, you get confused, and you think you just said something a bit silly or not very nice about someone who doesn't deserve it?'

'If for any reason you stumble over your words or say anything strange, we'll stop the recording and let you take it again. The same goes if you sneeze or have any coughing fits. Just because we want spontaneity doesn't mean all of it has to be "as live". We might shift anecdotes around to fill up gaps in the commentary when you're not speaking.'

Robert left the studio. Mervyn could see him through the glass, taking a seat just behind Trevor, who was obviously the sound engineer. Behind them both stood Marcus's agent, Joanna Paine, staring intently through the glass. She had her arms folded, head jutting forward, like she was auditioning to be the Genie of the Lamp in a pantomime.

Trevor started to tweak things on the dizzying array of knobs and slides arranged in front of him. None of them said anything. They exchanged uneasy smiles. For all Robert's enthusiasm for a 'chat in a restaurant', it didn't feel very friendly. More like getting ready for the first night of a play.

Robert's voice barked out of nowhere, making them jump. 'Just one more thing – for logistics. When the episode starts, could someone start us off? We just need someone to introduce everybody, so the viewer knows who's talking.'

'Marcus should definitely do that, he's got such a lovely voice, and he is the most famous,' gushed Samantha.

Marcus spread his hands apart in an 'Aw, shucks' way. 'If you want me to...'

Robert's voice crackled again. 'Actually, we usually ask the senior production person. A producer. If not a producer, a director. If not a director...'

All eyes gravitated to Mervyn.

'Me?'

'Great,' said Robert. 'Thanks. No need for a script, just do it in a relaxed off-the-cuff way.'

'Hello, this is the commentary for "The Burning Time". I was the script editor for this show – also here is Brian Crowbridge who played Professor Dax–'

The intercom came on. Again.

Stopping them. Again.

Weariness was leaking into Robert's voice. 'You didn't say your own name, Mervyn.'

'Didn't I? Damn. Sorry.'

Mervyn was on his fifth take. There was a barely audible sigh from the others. They'd been in the studio for ten minutes and hadn't got past the opening credits yet. Mervyn knew this was going to happen. He didn't do off-the-cuff very well. It was one of the many things that he never seemed to get to grips with, like being spontaneously witty when a recording device got shoved in his face. He'd managed to escape most occasions where recording devices featured by cunningly not getting married, not encouraging women to give birth to his child, and not winning any major awards. Then technology cursed him by making itself smaller and lighter. For a writer who made his name through science fiction, it was ironic that his nightmarish dystopian future had already arrived – in the form of digital cameras inside phones and laptops.

'Marcus, perhaps you should do it,' rumbled Brian.

Marcus raised his voice a notch, shouting to the invisible spirits that were listening in. 'I don't mind, really. If Mervyn doesn't.'

'Don't worry about it, sorry,' this time the voice belonged to Trevor. 'He's already said all the bits we need. We'll just edit them all together later. We'll start after the introductions. Just let the opening titles roll for a few seconds before speaking so we can slip it in at the beginning.'

The atmosphere relaxed. Mervyn let go of the desk, which he'd been gripping like a drowning man clutching a piece of driftwood.

The opening titles rolled; cheesy, faux-*Dynasty* credits, with all the exciting bits of the episodes chopped up and stuck together. It was a tapestry of fist fights, spaceships, snogging and explosions.

Remembering it was important to talk, even though he had nothing to say, Mervyn started off: 'So, here are the titles. All very exciting and jazzy... All very 80s...'

'Oh gosh!' exclaimed Samantha. 'Is that person running from that explosion really me?'

'I don't think so,' said Mervyn, suppressing a smile. 'I think you'll find that was our resident stuntman: Duggie "Don't lean against that window" Fletcher. You remember.'

'Are you sure?' she squinted through her glasses at the screen, but the tiny clip had long gone, replaced by a cluster of hairdryers glued together and sprayed silver blowing up.

'Oh yes, I'm quite sure. It's verrry subtle, but if you looked at that bit again... You'd notice the muscly arms...'

'Oh I –'

'*And* the height nudging six foot four. And the five-o'clock shadow. And the broken nose. And the scar across the broken nose. And the glass eye. And the tattoo that says "Mother".'

'Oh yes! Him! Why was he my stuntman? He doesn't sound much like me.'

Mervyn pulled a mock-incredulous face. 'You mean you don't have a tattoo that says "Mother"? And we did so much research.' Samantha exploded with laughter, and Brian and Marcus joined in.

Mervyn looked through the glass. Robert and Trevor were also laughing. Robert caught his eye and gave two thumbs up. Mervyn sighed with relief.

The DVD commentary had begun.

CHAPTER SEVEN

Mervyn wasn't sure what went wrong, exactly. It all started amiably enough.

The first sight they were greeted by was a scene shot on location: the stark and primitive alien planet Herath (Betchworth Quarry). The indigenous people, the primitive jabbering Ukks (extras in wigs, furs and sandals) were digging in the dirt with picks and shovels; the whole effect was an intentional echo of the great archaeological digs in 1920s Egypt.

'Ah. On location I see. No expense spared...' drawled Brian.

Marcus leapt in, interrupting him. 'I suppose I first got the idea for this story when I read about the Dead Sea Scrolls...'

Brian carried on like Marcus hadn't spoken. 'Where did we film this, Merv? Surrey was it?'

'I think so.' Samantha's voice.

'Betchworth Quarry, I think.' Mervyn gave a good pretence of sounding spontaneous, but he was reading from the notes.

Samantha again. 'I remember it being very cold.'

Brian laughed, suddenly loud. 'That's right! Betchworth Quarry. There was a lovely little pub in Dorking, I remember, where we all stayed...'

Marcus breezed in with a typical Marcus comment: 'I didn't stay in the pub. I stayed in Hambley Hall, up the road. Far nicer.'

Samantha made a 'Brrr' noise. 'I had two layers of thermals on and I still ended up completely blue.'

'Still,' Mervyn heard himself, 'it does look good as an alien planet.'

'What was it called?' wondered Brian.

'The planet Herath.'

'No, the pub.'

'The Dog and Duck?'

'No, that wasn't it...'

'So cold.' Samantha made another 'Brrr' for extra emphasis. 'You got out of the car, and your fingers went numb in minutes.'

'The Dog and something,' Mervyn suggested.

'That rings a bell.'

'The Dog and Ferret.'

'Hmm... No.'

'I remember waking up in that bed and breakfast, opening up the curtains and finding ice on the inside of the windows,' said Samantha. 'I was so glad to get warm in a nice big stately home for a change, wake-up in those lovely sheets, and have a hot bath...' She realised what she was saying and added quickly: 'It was so nice you let me use your room to have a snooze and freshen up, Marcus...'

Marcus just glared at her.

'That was it,' said Mervyn suddenly. 'The Dog and Monkey.'

'Are you sure?'

'Oh yes. One of those revolting 80s novelty names. Now I remember. It was called the Millstone before. Yes, the Dog and Monkey. Nice little pub. Lovely big barmaid.'

'Oh yes, Merv. You were very friendly with her.'

'Well it was *very* cold...'

Laughter from Samantha and Brian. Marcus had seemingly switched off from the conversation.

'Her name was Brenda, and her opening hours were –'

'Oh my goodness!' Brian interrupted Mervyn. He had seen something on the screen that interested him. The thing that was closest to the heart of every actor. 'Look at me!'

Brian, in his role as Professor Daxatar, had emerged from the quarry with a box of samples and a pickaxe from the future (a pickaxe sprayed silver with redundant buttons glued on the side). He was looking very dishevelled. Not as quite as dishevelled as his photo in *The Sun* after he attacked the Burger King, but dishevelled enough.

Samantha laughed too. 'I love the overalls, Brian, very fetching.'

'I look like I'm off to work in a garage. Crikey, I look so young.'

'That's because you were, Brian,' said Mervyn.

'Do you know, I haven't seen this since it went out, and even then I'm not sure I saw it when it *did* go out...'

The scene cut, not too subtly, from location to studio. 'Professor Daxatar' climbed into his scientific dome, laid out his samples, and started examining them.

'Hey,' said Marcus suddenly, loudly, excited he had something to contribute. 'I had that thing on my mantelpiece! That thing there, right in shot! That statue of Mary!'

In among the 20th century artefacts on Daxatar's table (a digital watch, a walkman and a running shoe) there was a small statuette of the Virgin Mary holding the infant Jesus; an ugly, crudely painted thing, the type bought by tourists outside the Vatican, desperate to find any souvenir small enough to stick into hand luggage.

'It got stolen last month – bloody burglars. I've been searching high and low for the damn thing.'

'Why on Earth would anyone want to steal it?' growled Brian.

'More to the point, why on Earth would you want it back?' quipped Mervyn.

'Well I use... well, I use it.'

'Gosh. Whatever for?' said Samantha, and gave a huge laugh.

Marcus didn't laugh at all. 'Novelty paperweight...' he mumbled.

There was a pause, during which someone in Marcus's headphones asked him if he could avoid swearing during the commentary.

'Oh, okay...' Marcus's mumbled, to the unseen voice. 'Sorry.'

'Hmm. Marcus – you call your wife Cheryl your "Little Mary", don't you?' said Brian, slyly. 'I recall you mentioned it once... During one of our AA meetings.'

That was uncalled for, thought Mervyn.

'Yes I do, thank you Brian,' seethed Marcus through a fixed grin. 'It's because she once rode on this mangy old donkey during a holiday in Greece, and I thought she looked just like –'

'Oh my gosh, look!' shrieked Samantha.

There was an explosion of laughter. On screen, Maggie Styles made her entrance, waddling through an opulent spaceship, and as usual her hugely affected style of acting reduced everyone to giggles.

'What has Maggie got on her head?' said Samantha, gulping and fighting to breathe.

'A sort of traffic light meets plant pot ensemble,' Mervyn suggested.

'Probably was a plant pot, knowing costume,' muttered Brian. Then, realising he was being recorded, he tried to cover himself. 'Sorry costume, if you're listening! They did wonders, didn't they?'

'Oh yeah, definitely,' said Samantha. 'I was very grateful to the costume people for my outfits.'

'We all were,' quipped Mervyn. More giggles.

'It's a great get-up,' said Brian, directing his attention once more to Maggie's outrageous costume.

'It's what all the best-dressed high priestesses were wearing that year,' said Mervyn. More laughter. 'Dear old Maggie. She loved doing this part,' added Mervyn, trying to find something nice to say.

'She didn't seem to like it at the time,' muttered Brian. 'Always saying the script was a load of rubbish.'

'How dare she say that!' Mervyn feigned mock-indignation and was rewarded with more titters. He patted Marcus's shoulder. 'Seriously, Marcus – don't be offended if she said your script was rubbish.'

'I'll try not to,' said Marcus, in an unsteady voice.

'I'm really not surprised she said that,' Mervyn continued. 'All actresses of the old school used to say that kind of thing when they did telly. It's their way of saying to the director that they're used to better, and they'd like to be kept in mind for "proper work". It was the mature actresses' way of touting for business.'

'And what did immature actresses do to tout for business?' Brian piped up, wickedly.

'I'd rather not say. Can you remember, Samantha?'

More gales of laughter.

'Oh, stop it you two!' said Samantha, choking on a giggle.

Mervyn was becoming increasingly aware that Marcus was very quiet. He tried to calm everything down and bring him back into the group. 'Perhaps we'd better talk about the story a bit. Marcus how did you go about writing "The Burning Time"?'

'Quite right, good question,' said Marcus, with an edge in his voice. 'Yes, my story was inspired by the Dead Sea Scrolls, and the Council of Nicaea and all that jazz. Well before Dan Brown came along. I'd read *The Holy Blood and the Holy Grail*, read about all those bits that were chucked out of the Bible. It amazed me how bits of a religion, a disciple's entire role in events, could just get negotiated into oblivion.'

'Hmm...' Mervyn said, with the merest flavour of irritation. ' I think, for the record, it actually all started when the producer and I read *The Holy Blood and the Holy Grail* and wanted to explore the Vixens' religion, which we'd already featured in quite a few episodes – in a minor way, granted – and we approached you to see if you wanted to do it...'

'Oh absolutely, Mervyn. Of course. And I used that vague brief as a springboard for my own ideas...'

'This is all very talky,' said Samantha, plaintively, directing her comments at the episode. Marcus's face stretched in outrage as he briefly thought Samantha was referring to him.

'Well it had to be,' said Brian. 'In those days, TV was practically made like theatre. Rehearse, rehearse, run-through and record in the evening. It was an absolute nightmare some evenings. I mean, look here, we've been on this two-shot for what, for more than a minute? It seems like it, anyway. Multi-camera studio, you see, so not a lot of movement, no big effects. These days it's all far easier, but very choppy. I find it very hard to watch a lot of telly drama these days. All that hacking away at the scenes with extreme close-ups. Not to mention all that wobbly documentary-style stuff they do.'

Mervyn agreed, abandoning Marcus to keep the commentary going. 'I know. They have Steadicam now. Even documentaries aren't filmed like documentaries these days. It feels so self-aware and artificial.'

Marcus wedged himself back into the conversation, desperate to steer it back to something he knew about. 'I like the filming on the adaptations of my books. They're pacey, but they don't use a lot of trickery on them.'

There was a huge dead silence. Nobody knew how to respond to that. Eventually they chose not to.

Mervyn reluctantly turned his attention back to what they were being paid to discuss. 'What's going on now?'

'Ah, well that ship's she's on?' Marcus dived in again. 'That's about to blow up.'

Samantha was confused. 'I don't think it does, does it? Not this episode...'

'Oh you're right. It blows up in episode two, doesn't it?'

'This hasn't got an episode two.' Mervyn's voice was now threaded with weariness.

'Oh,' said Marcus. 'I should have watched it before I came here, shouldn't I?' He laughed, but he was on his own. 'That spaceship looks like one of my wife's dildos,' he said suddenly.

The comment crashed head-first into another wall of silence.

'Oh,' said Samantha, finally.

Robert must have said something on the headphones about the word 'dildo' being unacceptable, because Marcus suddenly said to no one: 'Well my nephews know what a dildo is.' There was more silence, as Robert patiently explained the concept of certification to Marcus. 'Seriously?' said Marcus at last. 'You've got women stomping around with their tits hanging out, flagellation, an angry mob outside ready to burn us... and me talking about my wife's dildos could mean you have problems getting your PG certificate?' More silent comments from Robert. 'Oh very well. I will insert no more dildos into the conversation,' said Marcus, trying to make light of it.

The commentary limped on. Every time Marcus opened his mouth to talk about the script – names, plot points, in fact the whole basic storyline – he got it woefully wrong, and Mervyn felt duty-bound to correct him. Soon, Marcus was glaring at Mervyn like an admonished puppy, told off for something he didn't realise was a Bad Thing.

Then he suddenly blurted out: 'Hey, wait a minute. I remember the Dog and Monkey. Fucking awful pub. And the barmaid. Ugh!'

'She was a very nice woman,' said Mervyn, hurt.

'She was a complete dog! And she watered the beer! What a penny-pinching slack-titted old boiler,' hooted Marcus.

There was another embarrassed pause, and Marcus was given another talking-to through his headphones. 'Oh fine,' he said testily. 'Fine. She was a lovely woman, and gorgeous to boot. How much longer have we got to go on sitting in this bloody sweatbox?'

The episode chose to cut back to another scene shot on location. 'Professor Daxatar' was shouting at another, younger actor. 'Here we are, back at the quarry,' said Brian unnecessarily. 'Shouting at Yelack. I do a lot of shouting at Sid. Poor boy.'

'"Yelack." What a funny name! How *do* you come up with them, Marcus?' twittered Samantha.

Marcus sounded pleased to be asked a question. 'Yes... It is a funny name, isn't it? There's an interesting story about how I came up with it. It's a derivation of "Yashmak", the Muslim veil – I called the character that because he symbolises a "religious cover-up" in more ways than one.'

Samantha gave an 'Ooh'.

Mervyn snapped. 'I think you'll find that "Yelack" is an anagram of "Lackey".'

There was a long, terrible silence.

'Oh yes! So it is,' Brian chortled.

'I think I must have renamed your character in a later draft, Marcus,' said Mervyn – apologetic now, but the damage had been done. 'I did it quite a lot. Remember Gildernun the assistant scientist?'

'That snivelling little character played by Gregory Symes?' said Brian.

'It's an anagram of "underling",' said Mervyn.

'Oh yes! So it is. I'm thinking of other words that might be anagrams now. Herath... Could that be "hearth" as in "hearth and home..."?'

'That's a good observation, Brian,' said Mervyn. 'It sounds like it could be. But no, it's just a phonetic corruption of "Earth"...'

Marcus was having none of it. He was in a bad mood now. He'd stopped caring what anyone else wanted to talk about; he wanted to talk about himself. He crashed into the anagram conversation. 'Come to think of it – that thing on the table. That bloody statue. I don't want it back at all. I don't know why I kept it in the first place. Bloody fans, forcing rubbish on me and filling my house with crap.'

'What was the director's name again?' said Samantha, uneasily.

'Horrible bloody thing. Ugly as sin. Stuck on the mantelpiece for years. Makes her look like a whore. Thought I'd sell it to the highest bidder if I ended up on hard times. Perhaps they could use it as a suppository, or an anal sex toy or something. Never had to sell it of course. Never been that desperate for cash. How about you, Mervyn? I expect you've sold off most of the stuff you got from the set over the years...'

Mervyn was annoyed. Such an obvious back-handed insult – such a clumsy attempt to use the commentary to make a distinction between Marcus The Success and Mervyn The Failure. His hands balled into fists.

Marcus was being told off through his headphones again.

'Well it does look ugly. It's not my fault it looks like something you could stick up your arse. I don't see why you're so squeamish about me saying it would make a good sex toy?'

Right, that's it, thought Mervyn in fury. *He's had this coming for years. I'm going to punch him right now.*

CHAPTER EIGHT

He was saved by a little voice in his ear.

'Right. I think we'll take a break.'

It wasn't his conscience. It was Robert. The screens fluttered and died. Robert entered the studio, cheerily holding a thumb aloft.

'That was great, majorly good,' he said, lying through his teeth. 'There was lots of majorly good stuff in there.'

'I think we were starting to flag in the last five minutes,' said Mervyn apologetically. *That's the understatement of the millennium*, he thought.

'Not to worry. That normally happens. That's why we normally take a break every 20 minutes.'

Mervyn knew that they normally did nothing of the sort, that they normally continued right through, but he could see Robert was anxious to let things calm down. Samantha pulled off her headphones and looked around her dazedly, as if she'd come up from a deep sea-diving expedition. 'Golly, was that really 20 minutes? It just flew by, didn't it?'

'Thanks everybody. We'll have a break for ten minutes and crack on with the next bit.' Robert's head disappeared.

Marcus leapt to his feet and left the studio without a backward glance and without saying a word. He wasn't pleased.

Brian shook his head, grinning. 'It's amazing isn't it? You go in thinking you won't have anything to say, and it all comes flooding back.'

'Yes, it's funny like that.'

Samantha looked at Mervyn with an awestruck expression, as if he were some wise old sorcerer. 'You were really good. Did you do lots of homework for this?'

'Oh, I used to do loads. The first time I did one I went through my original scripts, looked up reviews on the internet, I even bought a reference book – but I found that they give you all that stuff anyway.' He waved what was left of his crib notes.

Brian grunted. 'They are fans, after all. That's what they do best.'

'Exactly. Nowadays I just watch the tape through once, the night before.'

Samantha looked at the screen. 'It's amazing how well it holds up. I mean, it's obviously "of its time", but you could easily see it on BBC1 now, couldn't you?'

From the expressions Mervyn and Brian pulled, they were unconvinced.

The door opened again. This time it was Trevor 'Simpering' Simpson.

'Everything all right?'

There was a chorus of 'Yes's.

Samantha stood and picked up her bag. 'Could I have some water please?'

Trevor looked confused. 'There's water over on the table outside...'

'No, could I get some different water? I did say before. Um, I don't like the brand. I'm sure you understand...'

'Oh sorry. Of course. I'll have a look in the canteen for you. Sorry about that.'

'Thank you. I sound a bit loopy don't I? It's just water, after all.'

'No problem. Still or sparkling?'

'Still please. Sparkling feeds my cellulite.'

Mervyn got slowly to his feet, prompting his joints to crack like bubble-wrap. 'Talking of water...' He always drank too much coffee at these things.

Now he'd calmed down, Mervyn was doing a very Mervyn thing. He was feeling guilty. He was starting to blame himself. Perhaps he'd surrendered to temptation and allowed a few misplaced comments to fly in Marcus's direction, and Marcus had only become insufferable in return? *I'm sure they'll work around that unpleasantness in the edit,* thought Mervyn.

He arrived at the gents. Joanna Paine was already there, her hand resting on the door of the ladies, opposite. She smiled at him, a slow cold smile. 'I'm hearing good things about you, Mervyn. Your name is coming up in quite a few meetings.'

Mervyn's ears pricked up. Was his writing career starting to create ripples again, after all these years? 'Oh really?'

'Really. I'm representing Andrew Jamieson now. He's looking for a sequel to his best-seller. Thinking of solving any more crimes?' She gave a sly grin.

'I doubt it,' muttered Mervyn.

'Keep at it, Mervyn. Don't let your writing get in the way of searching out more juicy murders.' She disappeared into the toilet.

Mervyn was uncomfortably aware that his former agent had just told him to give up his day job. He entered the toilet, only to find Marcus already there, leaving one of the cubicles and heading to a sink.

'Mervyn.'

'Marcus.'

Marcus washed his hands vigorously, his eyes fixed on his reflection in the mirror. Mervyn headed swiftly to the urinal, glad that he had a reason to turn his back on an awkward moment.

'I guess I should have watched the tape they sent me,' Marcus said. He tugged some paper towels out of the dispenser.

Mervyn grunted.

'Look, I am grateful, really. I've always been grateful. You know that, Merv.'

'Of course I do.' Mervyn wasn't very convincing. He sounded vaguely non-committal at the best of times, but 'tepid' had given way to 'cool'.

'Of course you do.' Marcus said vigorously, trying to convince himself more than Mervyn. 'There's no need for things to get awkward. Certainly not now, not after all these years.'

'I don't know what you mean.'

'Awww. You do.'

'No. Seriously. Please tell me, Marcus.'

'Oh come on! I know the joke's on me, and it's all big yuks, etcetera, and I know you're having fun trying to trip me up on things, but it's hardly sporting, when all's said and done.'

'Trip you up on things?' Rare anger flared in Mervyn's voice. 'It's you who doesn't even know whether it's a two-part story or a one-parter! The only person "tripping you up" is you!'

'Yes, but you don't have to correct me all the time. It's embarrassing.'

'Marcus, this DVD is bought by fans. They know these things. The first thing they're going to say is "Why does the writer think that character is named after a Muslim veil when we all know that's utter nonsense?"'

'They'll just think I'm an absent-minded old sod. Lots of writers can't remember the names of their characters.'

'I know! I've done it myself! So what's your problem?'

Marcus kept glaring at Mervyn, but didn't answer. Mervyn's voice softened. 'Look, It's perfectly natural for a script editor to correct a writer on a few points. After all, he might have changed the character names in a later draft.'

'I suppose... Yes, that could be true.' He looked like he was assessing the plausibility of the story, as if they'd cooked it up together. Mervyn didn't like feeling complicit in any imagined scheme involving Marcus, but at least it gave him some leverage.

'It would look far weirder if I sat there and didn't correct you on things that every fan knows backwards.'

Marcus dipped his hands in the water and threw some on his face.

'Ok. Fine. You're right. I'm sorry. It's just that... I feel a bit of a fraud doing this.'

Mervyn said nothing. Marcus expected some noise of conciliation from Mervyn. When none came, he became petulant. 'All right... I *am* a fraud. You know it. I know it.'

Mervyn sighed. 'No. No you're not. It's not your fault. It was my responsibility and my decision to make. I would have done it again...'

'Mervyn...'

'And anyway, those books of yours... They've made you millions. You're no fraud. Just next time. Please. Just watch the damn tape the night before you do a DVD commentary.' He banged the door open with the flat of his hand and was halfway down the corridor before it swung shut.

On his way back to the studio, he realised he hadn't washed his hands. Mervyn never liked to see a job half-done (apart from the uncompleted novel in limbo inside his computer, of course). Well, he certainly wasn't going to go back to the toilet while Marcus was still in there, he was rather pleased with his dramatic exit and wasn't going to spoil it. He knew from his time in the BBC that the toilets were situated in the same place on every level, so he decided to go down a floor. Opening the door to the stairs, he immediately heard a loud voice echoing up the stairwell – someone was talking to himself.

Peering carefully over the banister, Mervyn saw Robert. He wasn't talking to himself; he was on a mobile, and he was very angry with whoever he was talking to. He was curled into a corner with his hand cupped round his mouth, as if by holding the conversation inside his palm he could avoid being overheard. No such luck.

'I don't care, you're not, and that's that... No... No... You know damn well why... Cos they'd have my guts for garters, that's why! Lionel, listen to yourself! Lionel! There is no way. *No*! Because I don't want the police called in again, that's why! You heard what the police said, you disgusted them. Listen, Lionel – you disgusted *me*! Look, your things... Yes. The tapes have all been confiscated. Yes – all of them. Well, what did you expect? Anyway, what's left is in a box on my desk, and you can collect it today. Whatever, the laptop too. Yes... Fine. No! Don't even think you're coming up! I'll come down to you. See you at one. I'm – no! I'm finishing this call now, Lionel. I want you out of the flat. I never want to see you again. Yes I'm sure you are. So am I.'

Robert snapped the phone shut, sighed wearily and started up the stairs to where Mervyn was eavesdropping. Mervyn hastily ducked behind the banisters and hurried back the way he'd come.

CHAPTER NINE

Mervyn arrived back at the green room, grabbed some bottled water from the table and went into the studio.

The others had already taken their places, laughing and joking and nudging each other. Marcus was particularly jovial, back in life-and-soul-of-the party mode. He greeted Mervyn with gusto, behaving like their little altercation had never happened.

Robert popped in, rubbing his hands. 'So, that was a great rehearsal. Everyone ready to go for a take?'

Brian, Samantha and Marcus laughed. Mervyn chuckled too, even though he'd heard the joke before. Robert said it during every commentary recording.

'Seriously though, you're doing great. Majorly great. Try not to repeat yourselves too much...'

'You've said that once already,' quipped Brian.

'Keep your energy up... and one more thing. Marcus and Mervyn. Perhaps during the next part, you'd like to touch on the controversy this episode generated? Obviously, we're making a documentary about the whole religious angle to go on the DVD, but a few comments from your points of view would be good, just so they're there. Don't worry about duplicating information – we can always cut it down.'

'Will do,' said Mervyn.

'No sooner said than done,' said Marcus.

The episode started running again, and after two minutes, Mervyn dutifully kicked things off, talking as if it had just occurred to him.

'One thing that sticks in my mind about this episode is the amount of my time and energy it took up after it went out. Normally you sign off a script and forget about it, get on with the next one. I had to talk about this story at length to people I was theoretically answerable to, people who I'd never seen before in my life. Heads of this, and Senior that... The trouble this story caused!'

'Tell me about it!' Marcus started to join in. 'The BBC's switchboard jammed didn't it? All Thursday evening, all Friday, Saturday and all through Sunday.'

'The producer was very supportive though. Nicholas said –'

Marcus chopped him off. 'Odd really. All the complaints flooding on that Sunday morning. You'd expect them all to be at church. Obviously the happy clappers and tambourine tappers weren't as devout as they made out.'

Mervyn winced. 'Though looking back at it, in some ways I think we went too far. The scene outside the spaceship, particularly, when the men are whipped on those crucifix-like structures. Yes, in hindsight, I think we sailed too close to the wind...'

'Oh, nonsense Mervyn,' erupted Marcus vigorously. 'I've been through this time and time again, "The Burning Time" was fair comment about how religions can distort their original message over time. All that business in the Council of Nicaea. This was just like that in reverse. It's all completely fair comment.'

'Even so. We were just making adventure stories for telly after all; with hindsight it might have been a little provocative...'

'It was intended to be. Take that whipping scene. All we did was glorify a method of torture in exactly the same way Christianity does; why else do they wear their rinky-dinky little crosses round their necks?'

Brian instinctively moved his hand to the crucifix around his neck. Mervyn wished that Marcus expressed himself in slightly less pugnacious terms.

Marcus was building up a head of steam. He was now in his element, declaiming on the subject that had earned him a place in *Who's Who*, two PAs, a bodyguard and a house in the country.

'Christians glorify an instrument of Roman torture and suppression by erecting it in their houses and genuflecting to it! How appallingly tasteless can you get? Mohammed told his followers not to make images of him because he didn't want to be worshipped like a god, and that message becomes so twisted, so corrupted, that images of him can't be made on pain of death *because* they think the mere depiction of his face desecrates his name... so he's worshipped like a god anyway! It's *diametrically opposite* to what Mohammed intended, and are we allowed to say this? Are we hell!'

'I know all that,' Mervyn was starting to get testy. He was becoming annoyed at being painted as some craven apologist, and was sure that this was Marcus's revenge on him for embarrassing him before the break.

Marcus wasn't going to be deflected. 'Being an honest writer takes courage, Mervyn. There's no point acting like a dormouse, hiding in your teapot and hoping the nasty men with their swords and placards and burning effigies don't notice you. There's an idiotic mob outside this building trying to curb our free speech, and there's nutters out there threatening murder over doodles, and it's about time we spoke out. I think it's brilliant that this episode is being released now, perhaps it should be repeated on BBC1 as well, to give a sense of perspective to all the bloody madness going on out there. Mark my words, we're heading back to a new dark age, where people are once again put to the sword for simply saying the world is round, and it was created a few thousand years ago; those are the stakes we're playing for... And I for one don't want to be tied to one just yet.'

His well-rehearsed diatribe finally over, Marcus leaned back triumphantly and groped in his pocket.

KLAK-LAK-LAK-LAK-LAK.

'Can we stop there?' crackled Robert. 'We heard a noise in the studio.'

'Sorry, just opening my water,' said Marcus, and raised his water bottle to the figures behind the glass in an ironic toast. He took a deep, triumphant swig

'I know all that, I wouldn't have... commissioned the story if I didn't believe that,' said Mervyn coldly, watching Marcus glug away. 'But there are plenty of moderate people of faith in the world who despair of extremism just as much as we do. Being thoughtlessly provocative doesn't help anyone's case. All it does is leave a nasty taste in the mouth.'

'Oh!' Marcus suddenly shouted. 'This can't be what I...' He got slowly to his feet, stared at the water bottle curiously, and then he started coughing and gasping, retching noisily.

'Marcus? Are you all right?' Samantha's voice had dwindled to that of a frightened little girl's.

Marcus spun round in an odd, almost graceful way and collapsed to the floor. The bottle flew from his fingers, hit the wall and lay in the corner, its contents bleeding into the carpet.

CHAPTER TEN

No one moved.

Robert was listening through his headphones at the desk. Wondering what was happening, he looked through the glass, gaped, clapped his hands to either side of his shiny head as if trying to unscrew it then rushed into the studio, closely followed by Joanna.

'Oh my God...' Robert knelt over Marcus and touched his neck.

Joanna took charge. 'Jesus Christ. He looks like he's choking. Lie him flat on his back and open his mouth.'

Robert didn't do any of those things. He straightened up and stepped back, his mouth hanging open. He shook his head disbelievingly.

'Is he all right?' asked Brian.

Robert's voice was a dry whisper. 'No. I think he's dead.'

There was a 'whump' noise behind Mervyn. He turned. Samantha had crumpled to the ground in a faint.

CHAPTER ELEVEN

It was obvious that they couldn't stay in the green room. They knew that Samantha would only have to catch a glimpse of the body in the studio and she would dissolve into hysterical whimpering.

They were ushered into the BBC club, where Robert provided free whiskies and coffees to steady everyone's nerves. All around them, TV types drank, ate, jabbered and hooted with laughter, oblivious to what had just happened.

Joanna paced near the doorway, her severe bob fluttering slightly in the air conditioning. She had a mobile phone clamped to her ear, having one intense call, then another, and another. Mervyn was no lip-reader, but he knew after each call she made she said 'Fuck' to herself, before sighing and starting to dial again.

She eventually stopped phoning and turned her attention to Marcus's minder (*Adrian. Was that his name?*). He didn't look happy either. She talked to him in a low intense voice, in a swift rat-a-tat-tat delivery which wasn't conducive to conversation; the minder started a lot of sentences which he wasn't allowed to finish, and he said 'Ma'am' a lot. Despite his big muscles and his shiny sunglasses, the man looked diminished.

It didn't seem fair to Mervyn. Here they were in the BBC club – a place packed with employees whose jobs thrive on self-defined measurements of success; where 'Failure' is a word never spoken, and poor old Aiden (*Aiden! That's it!*) was the only one here with a job where there wasn't a lot of wiggle room to massage the performance targets. He was a bodyguard, and the body he'd just been guarding had just keeled over and died. He couldn't point to the very favourable audience appreciation figures, or show how well he'd done with the elusive 18-24-year-old demographic. He'd failed, and he was now being informed of the fact in no uncertain terms by Joanna.

Everyone had clustered around Samantha, cooing like maiden aunts around a newborn. She was making a striking recovery; all the way from hysteria, to smiling-through-the-tears in the space of 20 minutes.

Mervyn found himself an alcove to nurse his coffee, and he'd barely had a sip when Brian slipped in to join him. He dipped his head so it was close to Mervyn's. Mervyn wasn't surprised to see that Brian's twitch had returned. It was dancing a jig all over his cheek and his left eye. 'Merv. What the hell happened?'

Mervyn shrugged. 'You tell me.'

'But how? Was it a heart attack?'

Mervyn gave another shrug. 'It looked like it.'

'But he was so healthy. Pounding the Kensington pavements in his sweats every day... All the newspaper photographers used to run after him on his morning jog. Used to leave them standing.'

Mervyn shrugged. 'He was acting very oddly in the studio...'

'Yes he was, wasn't he? Perhaps he was on drugs? Or the booze again? He used to be a pretty heavy drinker, like me; Cheryl even made him go to the same AA meets as me, but booze doesn't make you keel over like that. Not dead. I don't think he was on coke or heroin. Not now, anyway.'

'It doesn't matter if he wasn't on it now. You know that stuff does lasting damage to the system, even if you give it up later and lead a blameless life. It's not a coincidence that a lot of popstars and TV celebrities suddenly drop dead from heart attacks when they hit their 50s.'

Brian rolled the thought around his head. 'You're right. You're absolutely right. That's what must have happened.'

'Yes. That's what happened,' repeated Mervyn, trying to convince himself as much as Brian.

Brian chuckled to himself. 'I'm 52 you know. I suppose I've got all that to look forward to.' He stared into the middle distance for a very long time (so long, in fact, that Mervyn was about to snap his fingers in front of his eyes) and then sighed. 'It's at times like these, when you finally see your own mortality staring you in the face... well, you do start to think; is my house in order? And I don't mean just possessions and the like. I mean one's metaphorical house...' he thumped his chest. 'One's immortal soul.'

Mervyn was intrigued. 'And have you put things in order, Brian?'

'I hope so, Merv. I hope so. But once you've done that, it's just the start. You realise there are always others who need help to find their way out of the murky forests of doubt...'

'And into the designated picnic area of enlightenment?'

'Exactly, Merv. I have a friend I'm working on at the moment, for example. Putting him back on the right path to God.'

'Like who?' asked Mervyn

'Can I show you this leaflet?' he said, pulling a sheet out of his pocket and unfolding it.

Trevor 'Simpering' Simpson came across. 'Sorry to interrupt, Mr Crowbridge, sorry. But did you want another whisky?'

'Oh, I should say so!'

Brian leapt up, all thoughts of everything else forgotten.

The leaflet was left on the table. Mervyn picked it up.

It was one of the Godbotherers' leaflets.

The Godbotherers?
Surely Brian wasn't a member of that crowd?

A thin bald man called Inspector Preece arrived with three uniformed constables. They took Marcus away, they took notes, they took statements, addresses and then they took their leave.

Finishing off the commentary was out of question; Robert was very solicitous – he all but pushed them into the best cars he could find.

Brian was poured into his. No one had noticed he'd been knocking them back until it was too late. The driver assured Robert that Brian would get to his front door safely, checked on him lying in the back seat (with a pain-stricken glance at the upholstery) and then inched out of the car park.

Samantha disappeared into a shiny Merc and pressed her frail little face to the window, waving as it drove away. She looked like she was a World War Two evacuee being packed off to the Cotswolds before the bombs arrived.

Once again, Mervyn refused a BBC car, intending to take the tube from White City. After everyone had been packed off home, he found himself standing, alone, outside Television Centre. The protesters had gone. The only evidence that they'd ever been there were brightly-coloured leaflets lying on the ground; the damp pavement had made them limp and transparent.

Now what?

The first time he'd seen a corpse, it affected him deeply; he remembered that he could barely stop shaking and his teeth chattered like castanets. Just last year, but it seemed a long time ago.

Marcus was the fourth body he'd witnessed in two years, and all he had now was a curious empty feeling in the pit of his stomach.

He walked to White City. There were the *Evening Standard* boards outside, with their enticingly vague headlines, designed to intrigue those not au fait with Teletext, radio, the internet and 24-hour rolling news into buying a paper.

The headline was "FAMOUS WRITER DIES".

Mervyn wondered, when he finally failed to meet his last deadline and floated up to the Writer's Room In The Sky, whether he'd merit a vague "FAMOUS WRITER DIES" from the *Evening Standard*.

Probably not.

CHAPTER TWELVE

Things carried on, as they inevitably do.

Mervyn spent the following day with his head buzzing about Marcus's demise. He bought all the papers and spread them out across his living room floor, scouring the obituaries (he was mentioned once, or rather someone called 'Melvin Stone' was). But the day after that, the grind of trying to write his book, trying to write his radio play, and making cups of tea so he could avoid doing either, put the events out of his head.

There was another DVD commentary being recorded three days later, less controversial; just the usual type of episode with silly cheap monsters and sexy young girls with guns, thank heavens. Mervyn was invited to attend this one, too, as were a fresh gaggle of actors ready to groan about their 80s hair and get confused about which quarry they filmed in. As usual, he used public transport to get there.

He heard the sound even before he even left the tube station. It reminded him of a medium-wave radio left on late at night, oozing static and occasionally fastening on to the gibber of a foreign radio station. It ebbed and flowed like waves, a hiss of noise surging into a bubbling roar and back again.

He knew what it was, and the sound made his neck itch. There was a large crowd somewhere outside. Sure enough, there was another mêlée at the entrance of Television Centre, but this time it wasn't Christians. Quite the opposite.

Journalists.

There were hundreds of them, dwarfing the Godbotherers' protest by a factor of fifty. Six-deep, they covered the entrance like maggots seething at the bottom of a dustbin. Stepladders were erected and photographers hung from them like gibbons, trying to snap away at the startled people inside the glass-fronted reception.

What was going on? This time it was *definitely* Robbie Williams appearing on the National Lottery. *Must be.*

Mervyn pulled out his mobile phone and called the contact number he'd been given. It must have been Robert Mulberry's number, because it was Robert that answered. 'Yes?'

It was scarcely a word, more of a hysterical squeak. Robert sounded very harassed.

'Oh, hello Robert, it's Mervyn, I'm outside Television Centre. I can't get in because there's some kind of hoo-ha outside, can someone come round and let me in another way?'

'Mervyn? God! I'm sorry. Didn't you get my message?'

'What message?' Even as Mervyn asked the question, he could see a flashing in the corner of his eye. He moved the phone from his ear and saw a little icon winking in the corner of the screen. 'I've been on the tube.' No signal, of course. 'What message?'

'I tried to get you before you left, but you'd gone. Everyone else got BBC cars, so I was able to contact the drivers and turn them back. I'm really sorry about this Mervyn, but the session's been cancelled. Something big has come up.'

'What's going on?'

Mervyn was pacing, as he usually did when he was even slightly agitated. He was moving in a small circle on the pavement, and at that moment he turned so he was facing White City station again, and the *Evening Standard* boards by the entrance.

One read: "FAMOUS WRITER MURDERED INSIDE BBC."

Another read: "POLICE BAFFLED BY 'PERFECT MURDER'."

Mervyn's arm went slowly limp, allowing the phone to sink down to his waist. All he could hear was Robert's distant squawk. He recovered himself, and brought it back to his ear.

'Mervyn? Mervyn? Are you there?'

'Yes, I'm here.'

'Did you say "You didn't know?"'

'Yes.'

'Have you not seen the papers?'

'No...' he said slowly. 'I have now.'

There was no point trying to get access to TV Centre; Robert and Trevor were far too busy to talk to him. He got the distinct impression that they were cordoned off by 'Police – do not cross' tapes even as Robert spoke to him.

Mervyn grabbed a *Standard*. There was talk of Marcus dying from foul play – poison was mentioned – but it was infuriatingly vague when it came to the actual details of this 'perfect murder'. He guessed that most of the facts of the case were legally sensitive.

He was crazed with curiosity. It was so annoying being out of the loop on this; he only wished he could think of a way to –

Oh. Oh of course.

Him.

He was forced to admit that there was only one person he could contact; someone who might have the inside track on the information. Unfortunately for Mervyn, he'd resolved to have as little contact as possible with this 'someone'.

He flicked open his phone, scrolled down the phonebook, stared at the little glowing screen, and pressed the 'Call' button.

CHAPTER THIRTEEN

'Mr St– Mervyn!'

On seeing Mervyn, Stuart's face exploded in delight. He was being guided by a flint-faced prison guard to a table where Mervyn sat. Mervyn had spent an anxious ten minutes in the visitors' room, throwing nervous smiles of acknowledgement at the other visitors and inmates.

Stuart was wearing a T-shirt, jeans and an eye-rupturing fluorescent green bib. With his ruddy complexion and tidy muscles (arranged on his shoulders and arms like kitchen shelves full of the best china), he looked like he'd just bounded in from a friendly game of basketball.

Stuart was an ex-Special Constable and *Vixens* fan. He had helped Mervyn with the investigation of three murders at a science fiction convention last year. In the end, he had proved a little over-helpful because he'd committed the murders himself. The police hadn't quite caught the distinction between murder and murder for moral support, and Stuart had ended up here.

'How are you, Stuart?'

'I'm great, Mr St– Mervyn. Just great. I'm settling in nicely. There's some really nice people here.'

'Really.'

'Oh yes. You know, when I got sent down, all my old friends in the force said that prisoners hate bent coppers, and I'd be choking on broken glass and pooing out razor blades before my second night in prison... But I'm more popular in here than I ever was in the police force! Can you imagine that?'

'Yes, Stuart. I can imagine that.'

'I wish I'd done this ages ago. Oh yes. Everyone thinks I'm great in here. And do you know why?'

'No.'

'It's because I've organised video weekends themed around sci-fi in general, and *Vixens from the Void* in particular! How funny!'

'Hilarious.'

'I tell you Mr – Mervyn, I bet you can't believe how many psychopaths, murderers and rapists are *Vixens from the Void* fans.'

Mervyn shifted uncomfortably in his seat.

'I'm so glad you're here.' He pulled out a collection of empty cigarette packets from inside his top, which cascaded on to the table. 'Can you sign a few of these? The boys in the library would just kill me if I didn't ask.'

Normally, Mervyn wouldn't sign anything without getting paid an appearance fee, or if it was official merchandise. But he needed something from Stuart. Sighing, he got out a pen from his pocket. 'All right. Who are they for?'

'One's to Psycho Billy, this one's for Hammer Barry, this one's for the Scorpion King – but could you make it out to "Bitch face"? It's for his mum.' Stuart grinned happily, as Mervyn signed the cigarette packets and handed them back.

'Hey!' A guard was pointing at Mervyn. 'Hey big nose! Don't pass cigarettes to the inmates!'

'But I wasn't. I was just...'

'Shut up. Stay there.'

Everyone in the visitors' room watched as the cigarette packets were inspected and Mervyn was vigorously searched. Nothing dubious was found (apart from a Styrax key ring) and the guards returned to their places.

'Just watch it you. And next time, don't be clever.'

Stuart watched the whole thing like it was a game and carried on as if nothing had happened.

'Actually, talking of *Vixens from the Void* – and I talk about it a lot – I was thinking of organising a convention in here. Perhaps you could help out? Nothing big, perhaps a few panels, a handful of guests... H-wing is really keen to meet Vanity Mycroft. Do you think you could persuade her to make an appearance?'

'I think that might be a bit dangerous.'

'Oh gosh, H-wing are lovely. Don't worry about Vanity.'

'I was more worried about H-wing.'

Stuart giggled like a girl, and despite himself, Mervyn joined in. Here he was, chuckling companionably with a mad multiple-murdering superfan. His job had finally sent him round the twist.

'Perhaps I can help you. But I need your help first.'

'What can I do for you, Mr Stone?'

'I need some details on a crime.'

'In here?'

'No. There's a friend of mine...'

'Marcus Spicer.'

'Yes, Marcus Spicer. You'd know that, wouldn't you?'

'Can't keep anything from us fans, Mr – Mervyn. You know that.'

'Well, anyway. The papers say he's been murdered. They're calling it a "perfect crime", but they're a bit short on facts. I wondered if you still had any contacts in the police who might be able to help get me the details? You know, keep me informed about the investigation.'

Stuart's eyes glowed. 'Oh. Wow. Gosh. Mervyn Stone on a case! I'd be honoured to help you again. Let me think... Oh. There is someone who might help you. Someone on the force. Another fan. Mick. We nearly went to a convention together.'

'Okay, do you have his number?'

'Wow this is so great. Just wait till H-wing hears about this. You're on a murder case, and the only person who can help you is the criminal you helped to put in prison. What a scenario! Gosh. Very *Silence of the Lambs*, isn't it? Am I Hannibal Lecter to your Clarice Starling?'

'Hardly.'

'Can you hear them, Mr Stone? Can you hear the screaming of the fans?'

'Okay Stuart. I'm threading my shoelaces back in my shoes, and I'm going now.'

'Hey, sorry, I'll help you. I'll give you my contact. Mick's going to be thrilled. Mick's such a fan.' He closed his mouth and tapped his chin with a finger. 'Hmm... I have to warn you though –' said the cross-dressing triple murderer.

'What?'

'About Mick. Well... She's a little weird.'

CHAPTER FOURTEEN

'All this cloak and dagger stuff is very exciting,' Mervyn said. They were in a motorway café that was made entirely of moulded green plastic.

But Mervyn was nervous. He pulled sugar sachets out of the pot on the table and started absent-mindedly tearing them open, pouring the contents into a little pile on the table. 'So is this the place where you coppers meet all your "narks" and "grasses" and "stool-pigeons"?' he asked, sipping the scalding cup of brown water that for some reason was given to him when he asked for coffee.

Mick gave him a dispassionate glare. 'No. This is the place where we coppers can afford to eat.'

Mick was not what Mervyn expected. For a start, she was a woman. Secondly, she was an incredibly tall woman; Mervyn just about came up to her shoulder. Everything about her was big; hands, arms, shoulders – her head was enormous and her huge slab-like features jutted out of it in all directions. She looked like a woman wearing a Disneyland costume of herself.

She was looking at him with a cold appraising gaze; Easter Island statues looked jollier. Her mouth was a thin line, hiding under a large nose, and one of her eyes was a bit off-beam, which made her look slightly crazed – or was just the fact she *was* slightly crazed that made her look slightly crazed? She had scrappy bottle-blonde hair that sprouted out of her head like charred crop stubble. If Glenn Close had ever been accidentally subjected to gamma radiation and was able to turn into her own version of the Incredible Hulk, she would become Mick.

He wondered fleetingly if she used to be a man, but no. There wouldn't have been enough anaesthetic in the world to put her to sleep for an operation like that.

'So... Mick. Is it Mick?'

'Short for Michaela. Michaela is a shit name, so I'm Mick. I won't change my name because my mum gave it me, and she's dead now. She fell out of a van. So in her memory I keep it, even though it's shit.'

'Well Mick, I'm sorry for bothering you. Stuart gave me your number.'

'Stuart's a pussy,' she said. Her voice was deeper than Mervyn's. 'He wasn't even a proper copper, just a "Plastic Policeman". I should never have given him my number.'

'Oh, I'm sorry. I sort of gathered that you were his friend.'

'Fuck no. I just saw him at one convention. The mincing little queer parades around in girl's clothes. I kept telling him; "Just cos I like *Vixens from the Void*, it don't mean we should like each other. Cos I don't. Like you. At all." But he never listened. I wouldn't dream of consorting with a wet little girlie like him. No spine. No backbone. No balls.'

'But he did murder three people in cold blood.'

'A fanboy, a midget and a fat retard. Was I supposed to be impressed?'

Mervyn felt that the meeting with this odd woman had reached the end of its natural life, and stood up. 'Well, nice to meet you "Mick", I'm sorry to have wasted your time, so I'll bid you good day. I'll go and put our trays away...'

'Sit down.'

Mervyn sat.

She leaned forward, covering the table.

'Do you know I live my life by the codes of the Vixens?'

'I didn't know there were any codes.'

'Oh yes. There are codes. There are always codes. Treat men like shit, use the power of your body to get your own way and keep the empire intact.' She pulled open her police-regulation blouse to reveal a sparkly bra. 'I made it myself. Obviously it's not much use under my blouse, but I wear my whole costume whenever I'm off duty. And you know why?'

'Why?'

'Because I *am* a Vixen.'

Oh hell...

'I am a Vixen, and you... You are my God. You created me. Formed me with your brain. I have sworn allegiance to you in my mind every day since I was 15. I am now 38, and my loyalty to you remains intact. My body is yours to command. And there's not many old, overweight geezers like you can say that.' She plonked a file on the table. 'Strictly speaking, we're not allowed to discuss ongoing cases with members of the public. Let alone with potential suspects who were in the room when the victim karked it. So giving them a look at the files is a definite no-no.'

'Okay, I'm sorry to have put you in a difficult position.'

'But fuck that. This is Mervyn fucking Stone here, and his wish is my command.'

Uncomfortable with the naked hero worship radiating from Mick, Mervyn ripped open a sachet of pepper and added it to his pile.

'So, are what the newspapers saying correct? Marcus was definitely poisoned?'

Before Mick could tell him, a waitress in a grotesquely unflattering uniform appeared at Mervyn's elbow. 'Please don't do that,' she snapped, indicating the growing pile of sugar, pepper and salt. 'I have to clear that up after you've finished.'

'I can't help it,' said Mervyn helplessly. 'I have to fiddle. It's a nervous trait. I have to do something with my hands.'

'Then don't.'

Mick rose to her feet, like a cowboy in a saloon bar. The waitress looked the policewoman up and down, as if judging the effort required to throw her through the window. Mervyn could feel the phrase 'Awkward Scene' encroaching.

'I'll be willing to take any suggestion that stops me seasoning your table,' gabbled Mervyn. 'Believe me.'

The waitress held Mick's glare for a second longer, said 'Hang on,' and set off in the direction of the till. She came back with a sheet of paper and a box of crayons.

'That's perfect,' said Mervyn.

Mick watched impassively as Mervyn scribbled intently on the Kidz Klub fun page the waitress had brought him. Mick waited until Mervyn finished a particularly difficult bit (the flower on a clown's hat) before saying: 'Yeah. He was poisoned.'

'I see.'

'No doubt about it.'

'It wasn't a heart attack or anything like that? I was hoping for a heart attack.'

'Definitely poisoned. The bottle was filled with cyanide solution.'

A sudden thought thrust its icy hand up Mervyn's shirt. He froze, the fat red crayon in his hand poised a centimetre above the clown's nose.

'The other water bottles?'

'Only his had poison in it.'

Mervyn relaxed. 'I see,' he said, taking a green crayon from his box. 'The next obvious question is, how did the poison get in the bottle... Were there any puncture marks on the top?'

Mick flapped through the file. 'No puncture marks. Someone must have slipped the cyanide into his water beforehand.'

'No.' Mervyn rubbed his forehead wearily, leaving green streaks across his eyebrows and down his cheek. The effect was already more elaborate than the make-up of most of the *Vixens* aliens. 'Absolutely not. Impossible. It couldn't have been planned.'

'Why not?'

'There were at least a dozen other water bottles on that table.'

Mick folded her massive arms. 'Fifteen, including his. Fifteen bottles found in the studio and the next room, twelve of them unopened, two half-drunk. One of them was a different brand.'

Mervyn's ears pricked up. 'Marcus's?'

'No.'

Mervyn slumped, disappointed.

'They all had ordinary water in – apart from the dead bloke's of course.'

'Right... And they were just left on the table for anyone to take, and we all just picked one at random.'

'Could be the caterers. I found a pubic hair in a meringue at my sister's wedding.'

'Is that really the same as finding poison in a bottle?'

'Not really.'

Mervyn finished off the clown's bow-tie in a cheery mix of yellow and purple. 'Perhaps someone in the room handed him the bottle?'

Mick pulled some A4 pages from the file, attached at the corner by a paperclip. 'We've got a statement from Robert Mulberry, the producer. He said he was right beside him when Marcus picked a bottle up.'

'He could be lying. He could have given Marcus the bottle himself.'

'Yeah, but there were other people in the room. His story got backed up by some guy called Trevor.'

'They could both be lying. It could be a conspiracy.'

'Maybe. Maybe not.'

'Can I have a look at that file?'

'Anything for my God.'

'Erm... Yes. Thanks.'

She slid the file over to Mervyn's side of the table. Mervyn picked it up, and flipped it open.

'Let's see. Here we are, Robert said: "All the bottles were placed in two clusters on both ends of the table. Marcus took one from the cluster nearest the recording booth, from in the middle somewhere, when we broke for ten minutes." When asked if anyone broke the seal on the lid for the victim, he said: "No, Marcus definitely opened it himself, I even heard him break the seal on the bottle."' He looked up from the file. 'Yes I heard that too. Everyone did. We had to stop recording it was so loud.'

Mervyn stretched out two fingers and thumb. 'Okay, let's say Robert's telling the truth. That leaves us with three possibilities. One: it was a mix-up in the bottling plant. Pretty unlikely, I would think.' He curled his thumb into his palm, leaving two fingers outstretched. 'Two: it was placed in the bottle, sealed, and placed in the whole batch of water bottles before or after it got delivered to the BBC, and in that case it must be some crank with a grudge out to get any one of us in the studio, or anyone in the BBC for that matter, or just anyone in the country who drinks bottled water. Anyway, that's also pretty unlikely because that kind of mischief comes with blackmail notes and threats and phone calls to national newspapers... I assume there's been none of that.'

'No. Not that I've heard.'

He held up one finger. 'So that leaves us with the last possibility. Someone specifically wanted to kill Marcus. And did it in a very, very clever way.'

'Yep.'

They finished their foul drinks and levered themselves out of the tiny plastic chairs.

After they left the café, the waitress noted sniffily that Mervyn had coloured over the edges and had crayoned on the table.

CHAPTER FIFTEEN

'Well,' sighed Mervyn, as they stood in the car park. 'As Arthur Conan Doyle wrote, if you eliminate the impossible then whatever remains, no matter how improbable, must be the case.' He sat heavily on a low wall. 'It's obvious Arthur had a premonition about what it was going to be like to script-edit *Vixens from the Void*.'

Mick unlocked her police car. 'Want a lift anywhere?'

'No, it's all right. There's a bus stop just down the road that takes me near the Metropolitan...' He dribbled to a halt, perplexed, as a heavy rock version of the *Vixens from the Void* theme tune ripped through the air. 'Where's that coming from?'

Mick took out her mobile, and the sound of the theme suddenly rose to deafening proportions. The phone was juddering alarmingly in her hand.

She took the call. 'Yeah? This is Vixen One to Spaceport Central. Well fuck you too, Terry. What do you want? What? Yeah?'

Mervyn was about to wave goodbye and back away, but something in Mick's tone stopped him. An expression finally found its way on to her face. Total surprise.

'You are joking? You're not serious. You are serious. Fuck. Okay, I'll be back in ten minutes.'

Mervyn was frantic with curiosity. 'What? What's happened?'

'We've just had a call. Claiming responsibility for the murder. It's the Godbotherers.'

Mervyn exploded with incredulity. 'The Godbotherers have claimed responsibility for murdering Marcus?'

'No. They're claiming responsibility on behalf of God. They claim God killed him.'

Mervyn took his leave of Mick, and headed for the bus stop. Suddenly, there was a bellow behind him.

'Mervyn Stone!'

Mervyn turned; Mick was waving her file, flapping it in the wind as if she were training an angry falcon. 'You've coloured in all the "o"s on the confidential file!'

Mervyn waved, pretending not to hear, and started to run.

CHAPTER SIXTEEN

'I'm so sorry Cheryl.'

Cheryl's face trembled for a second, as if she were about to sneeze, then it gave up the fight and collapsed into tears.

Mervyn knelt down in front of the wheelchair. She leant forward and fell in his arms, burying herself into his armpit. They stayed there awkwardly like that, on the porch of 'Earthly Delights', Marcus and Cheryl's ivy-smothered country retreat, for several minutes; Cheryl trying to regain her composure and Mervyn trying to lose his spontaneous erection.

Cheryl's muffled sobs eventually lost their intensity, slowing and quietening to such an extent that Mervyn wasn't entirely sure she hadn't gone to sleep. Finally, she disengaged herself, wiping her nose with the sleeve of her cardigan. 'Would you like a cup of tea?' she asked with a raw croak, her voice scraped clean of emotion.

'Yes thanks. That would be lovely.'

Dutifully, he followed her in and sat on the settee, listening to the reassuring tea-making noises coming from the kitchen.

'Help yourself to food.'

There were plates of sandwiches on the table, bowls of crisps and nuts, and a tin decorated with flowers. Mervyn levered the lid off the tin, found shortbread, absent-mindedly helped himself to a piece and paced the room, inspecting the décor, for want of something more positive to do.

'I appreciate you coming all this way,' she called out. 'I know you don't drive. I wouldn't wish the train journey on my worst enemy.'

'It was the least I could do,' muttered Mervyn, lamely.

'I've had all sorts of calls from Joanna, from Aiden, publishers, producers offering their sympathies and sorrow. You're the first person I've seen that I can honestly call a friend.'

'I'm honoured you think of me like that.'

Mervyn's eyes roved around the walls. They were festooned with Marcus's triumphs. Certificates, cabinets filled with gold and silver trophies the shape of inkwells, pens and typewriters, framed cuttings and photos that archived the life that had ended five days ago, on the floor of Recording Suite 4.

Marcus's face was everywhere. There were pictures of him pumping the hands of the great and the good; side-by-side grins with Tony Blair, a respectful nod in the direction of a smiling Prince Charles, a matey hug with Mick Jagger on the stage of some fund-raiser. Ironically – and in typical Marcus fashion – the arch-atheist had turned the room into a place of worship; a shrine devoted to himself.

There was one item in the room that didn't pay homage to the many successes of Marcus's career. It was perched on a bookcase by the kitchen door, almost invisible, a small picture in a simple silver frame.

Marcus and Cheryl on their wedding day.

There was a simple sunny smile on Cheryl's lips, a beaming grin on Marcus's. Mervyn looked at the tiny figures in too-bright colours; he was decked out in tails and a blue flowery waistcoat, she in a scarlet dress. They were both unmarked by time, scrubbed clean until their innocence shone, and he felt weak with misery as he looked at them. His eyes prickled, and a lump of sadness sat in his throat. They looked beautiful.

Shame about the grinning vicar behind them, who was doing rabbit ears behind Marcus's head and a cheery thumbs-up in front of Cheryl's décolletage. *He was a very odd vicar*, Mervyn thought.

Cheryl's wheelchair whirred and glided into the room with agonising slowness, the tray perched on the armrests. Mervyn was torn between watching her wrestle the tea things to the table, and taking it off her completely. Would that violate her independence?

'Don't just stand there gawping. Take the bloody tea things off me.'

He carried the tray and placed it on a low table in front of them. Cheryl hauled herself out of the wheelchair and lowered herself limply on to the sofa. She reached down and perched her cup on her lap, making no effort to drink from it.

'You were there.' It was a statement, not a question.

'Yes. Yes I was.'

'Did he suffer?'

'When you say "suffer", do you mean how much of the episode did he have to watch before he... ahm...'

As inappropriate jokes go, it certainly went. It ran screaming from the room with its hair on fire. Mervyn wished he could follow it.

'It was very quick,' he added hastily. 'One minute he was standing up, the next minute he... wasn't.'

'What do you believe? Do you believe these "people"...' She faltered. It was obvious that she was controlling herself with enormous effort, and 'people' was the most neutral word she could muster without screaming and raging and cursing their existence. She scratched her ear vigorously, causing her wig to edge across her forehead. 'Do you believe these "people" killed him using some kind of voodoo?'

'Voodoo? I don't think they'd thank you for calling it that.'

'Sod what they think!' she barked with anger. With sudden energy, she put the cup down, pulled herself back into her wheelchair and scooted across the room. She pulled open a bureau and slammed a ragged pile of letters and packages on the table. Mervyn didn't need to inspect them; he instantly knew what they were. In his time in the *Vixens from the Void* production office, he'd seen crank correspondence on many occasions; the crabbed handwriting, the green ink, the long, rambling letters composed in capitals, the ominous Tupperware containers containing human and animal excrement. It was all too familiar.

'Marcus used to keep them all. For publicity,' she said with distaste. 'He liked to bring them out when journalists came to call for interviews. There's a cutting hanging in the toilet, from *The Observer,* that has a large photo of him by this very table, piled high with these things.'

She picked up one and sniffed it.

'Sometimes we got 20 to 30 a day, particularly after he'd been on some television show, showing off. They're all of a type. Quoting Bible chapters, usually from the Old Testament, telling him how he's going to be judged, he's going to burn in hell, he's going to be struck down by His wrath...' She gestured to the empty mantelpiece. 'I wouldn't be surprised if they were the ones who broke in and stole his precious statuette of the Virgin Mary, liberating it like it was some battery chicken.' She held up the flowery biscuit tin. 'Just look at these,' she said, levering off the lid. 'I got these this morning. Every month this stupid old Catholic bat sends us biscuits, and she hasn't even stopped now he's dead!'

'Those biscuits are from one of your... religious nutcases?' Mervyn's stomach plummeted into his boots.

'Yes, every month we got them, always with letters going on about sin and salvation and forgiveness and confession, mostly about transubstantiation. "This is my body," and all that. She makes the biscuits herself and mixes in her own dandruff. The crazy old bird thought if Marcus consumed enough of the body of good God-fearing Christians, he would begin to see the light.'

Mervyn looked at the hand at where the stick of shortbread had been. His mind was just starting to catch up with his body. His mouth seemed to want to turn itself inside-out. 'Oh God...' he said in a tiny voice.

'Yes, exactly. It's God this, God that...The very last crank letter he got was from one of that lot, telling him after what he said about God on some discussion programme he should have someone wash his mouth out.' She swivelled round and looked into his eyes searchingly. 'Do you believe it?' she asked again. 'Do you believe they had something to do with it?'

'That's a good question. Hold that thought. I'll think about it while I use your toilet.'

In the toilet, Mervyn sluiced his mouth out vigorously, seeking out bottles of mouthwash to consume.

The *Observer* article was indeed hanging above the toilet. The cutting was headed 'The Faith of Hate', and the photo was of Marcus, posing in the sitting room. Marcus had a cheery 'Wot, me guv?' grin, and was leaning irreverently on the mantelpiece. The piles of hate mail lay before him, surging towards the camera like the Biblical flood.

By Marcus's elbow was a statuette of the Virgin Mary and Child, a cheap gaudy thing made of plaster and daubed with primary colours.

Mervyn stared at the statuette in the photo for a good few seconds. Something was starting to click in his head.

Mervyn returned, after much gargling and spitting.

'I saw the article in the toilet,' said Mervyn. 'Good photo of Marcus.'

'He was very pleased with it. It took them two hours to arrange the hate mail. He wanted to lean on his statuette of Virgin Mary, just to be cocky.'

'Did you say that that statuette got stolen?'

'Yes. We had a burglary a couple of months ago and it was among the things that got taken. It was a prop from "The Burning Time". A fan gave it to him at a literary festival, years ago, and it amused him to put it in pride of place on the mantelpiece. He said he was being ironic.'

Mervyn snapped his fingers. 'Of course! He mentioned it on the commentary. He was talking about it being stolen just before he – well, just before...'

'Do you believe it?'

'Of course I do. I hardly think you're hiding it for the insurance money.'

'I'm not talking about who nicked the bloody statue. I'm talking about my husband's death.'

'Oh.' Mervyn sat down, exhaling minty freshness. 'Oh,' he said again.

'About God striking him down.'

'That's a curious thing to ask. You're a devout atheist. You don't –'

'I'm asking *you* what *you* think, Mervyn.'

'Oh. I'm not a believer either, as a rule. Give me a convincing argument and I'll go along with it. Until the next convincing argument comes along.' He knew he was sounding flippant. 'Probably. Possibly. But they didn't do it through the power of prayer, I'm sure of that. As sure as I ever get.'

She smiled humourlessly. 'Looks like God was short of thunderbolts that day. Had to make do with Estuary English sparkling mineral water.'

Her eyes flipped around the room, focussing on everything and nothing. Then she looked down at the tea cup on her lap. 'Andrew Jamieson came by a few months ago for a cup of tea.'

'A cup of tea?'

'There's only tea in this house now. Marcus and Andrew always kept in touch. They got on well, even after all these years.'

'Well he would. Marcus was the only writer in the world lazier than him...' He realised he was being tactless. 'Sorry.'

'No. No. You're right. I know it and you know it. Marcus wasn't the best at deadlines and drafts. He was always a stinker at avoiding the writing bit. He hated writing. He loved everything that went with being a writer... Just hated the writing part of being a writer.'

'Most of us do.'

'Not like Marcus, believe me. Oh, he liked all the other things that went with it, the book tours, the autographs, the talks at the literary festivals...' She brought out a grim smile. 'Oh, definitely those. Oh, how he thrived on parachuting into a tweedy English village, dazzling the Mrs Tiggywinkles and the Mr Toads...'

She moved his picture, carefully angled so she couldn't see him. Then she changed her mind, and picked it up. 'Truth to tell, even with all the ups and downs, our marriage was stronger than it had been in those early days back in the 80s. Marcus had even given up drinking, would you believe.'

'Seriously?'

'Oh yes, I was very proud of him. Hence the tea.' She stopped fiddling with the picture, and slapped the arms of her wheelchair in a 'Let's to business' kind of way. 'Anyway, when Andrew came round he was raving about you and your detective skills.'

'Well he would. He got a best-selling book out of it.'

'Yes, he gave us a signed copy. I think he only did it to annoy Marcus.'

'That sounds like Andrew.'

'I read it. Is it right you solved all those murders at that science fiction convention last year?'

'"Solved" is a bit strong. More like I bumped into the solution.'

'Don't dazzle me with false modesty, Mervy, I was married to Marcus, remember.'

'All right, it's true. Took me three murders before I did, but yes, I sort of worked it out in the end.'

'Good. I hoped it was true.' She leaned forward so their noses were almost touching. Her hand clamped itself to his knee. Mervyn didn't look down, but concentrated on looking directly into her eyes, hoping that his erection wouldn't make an indiscreet return.

'Find out how they did it, Mervy,' she hissed. 'Find out how they did it and get the bastards.'

'Okay,' gulped Mervyn. 'I'll have a crack. Is there anything you can tell me about Marcus's final days? Anything that might give me any clues?'

'Like what?'

'Um... Any threatening phone calls, letters, stuff like that?'

Cheryl considered this. 'Nothing unusual. Just the same three nutters with their daily deliveries of first-class poo. Phone calls? None to speak of. Well, there was one call he got, and he walked out of the house and into the garden when I came in. That was odd. We didn't have a lot of secrets from each other. He seemed to be talking about the statue. He was desperately trying to find it.'

CHAPTER SEVENTEEN

The hooded man watched Mervyn as he left the house. He had been watching Mervyn ever since he'd gone inside. He had been sitting in a car across the street from Earthly Delights for two days now, watching, waiting for someone to turn up. And up popped Mervyn.

Interesting.

Perhaps Mervyn was the man.

The hooded man had been doing a lot of thinking since Marcus's death. He wondered about his orders. Were they still relevant? Marcus was gone. But his legacy lived on.

He had to do something about that.

CHAPTER EIGHTEEN

Mervyn left Earthly Delights with grim resolve. He was determined to find out what had happened to Marcus. For Cheryl.

And, to be brutally honest, for himself as well.

In truth, he was propelled by one-third loyalty (to a woman he'd always admired and shamelessly lusted after) and two-thirds guilt. There was no denying it. There were a few brief times he'd nurtured ungenerous thoughts toward Marcus. Sometimes he'd wished him dead.

They'd been friends ever since their radio days, when they'd both been regular contributors to Radio 4's *Afternoon Play*. They'd once had a friendly competition as to who could put the word 'wistful' the most times in a single play (Mervyn won, with the simple and ingenious solution of calling one of his characters Inspector Wistful).

Many was the time they'd bump into each other in Broadcasting House and saunter down to the Yorkshire Grey pub in Langham Street – a regular haunt for radio types – to bitch about how thick producers were. When Mervyn got *Vixens from the Void* off the ground, he wanted to help his friend, and he asked if Marcus would like to write an episode.

Mervyn had just read *The Holy Blood and the Holy Grail*, and gave Marcus a vague idea of a plot where the Vixens uncover a dark secret that questioned the whole basis of their (up until that point) vague religious orthodoxy. He left it up to Marcus to fill in the blanks and work it up into a 50-minute script.

Unfortunately, Marcus's life chose that particular moment to fall apart. His drinking got out of control, and his attention span crumbled. Two months later and all Mervyn had squeezed out of him were a few rushed scenes and anguished promises left on the production office's answering machine. When a draft finally came in bare weeks before shooting, it was barely coherent.

Mervyn did what every script editor had to do at some point; he gritted his teeth, put another filter in the coffee machine and did a 'page one rewrite' – a technical term describing a process where the only evidence left of the original writer's presence is the title and the lingering desire to kill him. Mervyn didn't know that this particular rewrite would prove so controversial.

He realised later that, as he was in such a caffeine-addled hurry to finish the episode, he'd taken the brakes off a bit, and put in a lot of stuff he wouldn't normally have done while in a sane state of mind.

When the story aired there were enough letters and phone calls to plonk Mervyn on *Biteback*, the BBC's pat-on-the-head-and-go-away programme for angry viewers. Mervyn toed the usual BBC party line, defending free speech and apologising for using it all at the same time and making a stout defence of the 'writer' of the episode.

Mervyn knew that journalists might seek out Marcus and he warned him about that possibility. What Mervyn didn't expect was for Marcus to step into the controversy, defending 'his' script with such flair and gusto, browbeating reporters who came to his door and accusing the accusers of wasting everybody's time.

His lively quotes in the newspapers led to knockabout interviews on the *Today* programme and *TV-am*. With every performance, he warmed to the theme of anti-religion, becoming so impassioned that Mervyn was sure he'd forgotten it wasn't him who caused the controversy in the first place.

It wasn't long before Marcus had become a reliably controversial talking head on *Newsnight* and *After Dark*. He inhabited the role of crusading atheist with gusto, and his newly-found anti-religious attitudes crystallised themselves in his best-selling novels, the first of which was *The Serpent on the Mount* a spoof retelling of Jesus's life in which the Messiah was portrayed as a cynical confidence trickster. Marcus became, in quick succession, a celebrity, a celebrity author, a best-selling celebrity author and a best-selling millionaire celebrity author.

Mervyn knew that life was a random series of events designed to baffle the unwary; that the idea of destiny was a crutch for the desperate, the poor and the weak-minded. He knew that, by and large, it was people who created their own opportunities. He knew that if it had been his name as writer on the credits of 'The Burning Time', he wouldn't have capitalised on the sudden notoriety with the skill that Marcus achieved. He probably would have run and hid.

He knew all that. All the same, he never quite shook the feeling that Marcus had stolen a life from him.

And of course, there was Cheryl too.

Dear sweet Cheryl, a former production assistant who'd joined a BBC scriptwriter's course, and had been attached to *Vixens from the Void* to see how the words got thrown together. She was barely 20, and so fresh-faced and shiny she almost squeaked when she smiled; and she smiled often.

Mervyn instantly took a shine to her, and (he hoped and believed) she to him.

During the end-of-series wrap party back in '89, he'd licked her neck in the production office and made her giggle. Then he pushed her against the photocopier and somehow managed to slam her hand in it, fetching up a very nasty mark.

Mervyn was full of apologies and hunted for a plaster, ice, or a shovel to dig a hole and bury himself, but to his surprise, when she finally finished sucking her fingers and hopping around the room, she was still giggling. She wiped the tears of pain from her eyes and replaced them with tears of laughter at the silliness of it all.

She kissed his nose, still giggling. And then he kissed her giggling mouth, and the giggling stopped.

They were together for a few blissful months. She wore lots of tight tops which were quite unsuitable for the autumnal weather. Perhaps *that* was why he walked across Shepherd's Bush Green to record the DVD commentary that morning? Perhaps he was seeking out the sight of cold-hardened nipples, because on some subconscious level he wanted to remember her too, not just another old episode of *Vixens*? There was no 'perhaps'. He was sure of it.

And then the year ended, Cheryl went inter-railing and the series started up again, and then, somehow, she never came back. The *Vixens* treadmill began, she slipped out of his memory, and the 80s became the 90s. Then a year or so later he saw her name by chance – on a writing credit for an episode of *Brookside*.

A golden opportunity.

In his capacity as script editor, he contacted her agent to see about the possibility of Cheryl writing an episode for the new series. (It was hardly nepotism, he'd reasoned to himself. She was a professional writer, wasn't she?) Over the phone, she sounded just as lively and fresh, and incredibly excited to be asked – and was that also a bit of relief in her voice? Mervyn wondered why she, a young writer, hadn't done the obvious and contacted Mervyn earlier.

Then a day later, the card arrived.

It came in a smooth cream envelope, crinkled around the edges like an apple pie made by a sweet grey-haired grandmother. Mervyn almost missed it amid a pile of bills, junk mail and trade magazines. It was laid out in a jokey mix of television and radio script:

```
GRAMS:    FANFARE!

          MARCUS:   You are invited by TV and
          Radio scriptwriter MARCUS SPICER...

          CHERYL:   And TV scriptwriter
          CHERYL LIMB...

          BOTH:     (CONT'D) To their
```

forthcoming WEDDING, which will be set in...

1. EXT: THE VILLAGE OF DORKING, SURREY. DAY.

(AND...)

2. INT: ST MATTHEW'S CHURCH. DAY.

(ON SATURDAY, FEB 14TH AT 2PM. THE GUESTS ALL EMERGE FROM THE CHURCH GETTING INTO THEIR CARS AND DRIVE TO...)

3. INT. HAMBLEY HALL. DAY

(FOR THE RECEPTION, WHERE THEY EAT AND DRINK LARGE AMOUNTS.)

(THE GUESTS ARE NOT INVITED TO...)

4. INT: MARCUS AND CHERYL'S HONEYMOON HOTEL ROOM. NIGHT

THE END.

Mervyn went to the wedding with all the enthusiasm of a condemned man climbing into the electric chair, and managed to put a smile on his face that would have disgusted a corpse.

He was greeted by Cheryl after the service. She was a vision, a radiant smile in crushed red velvet, like the happiest pair of curtains he'd ever seen, and full of the giggles that tickled his neck and excited his earlobe that night in the production office.

She gave him a huge bear hug, and touched his cheek. He noticed the same mark by her thumb he created with the photocopier lid. She breathlessly told him how glad she was that he was able to come, and how glad she was that he'd contacted her agent. She'd taken it as a signal, some blessing from Mervyn that he'd 'come to terms with it', and that 'things were okay' between them – 'After, y'know, me and Marcus and all...'

Of course, with Marcus never choosing to tell him, Mervyn never had a chance to come to terms with anything. Mervyn merely turned his sickly grin up a notch and said yes, things were never better between them.

At the reception, Marcus was surprised to see him, and seemed almost to be avoiding him – odd behaviour for a mate who'd often descended into drunken speculation as to whether they would be each other's best men when the wedding bells tolled for them.

Mervyn thought he was being paranoid. *Grooms have to spend all day glad-handing distant relatives. He's too busy to stop and chat*, Mervyn thought to himself. Convinced himself.

Then, as Marcus and Cheryl were gliding round the ballroom floor to 'Dancing Queen' by ABBA, accompanied by wolf-whistles from the more thuggish looking pageboys, Marcus's eyes locked with Mervyn's.

Mervyn saw a cold calculation in them. And despair, too. And in that split second, Mervyn knew.

Marcus knew about him and Cheryl. He bloody knew.

What happened, Marcus? Was it an accident that you two got together? No, of course not. Ah, but the most important question really is...

Was it sincere on your part, or just a silly little game like in the old radio days? Did you see her with me and think 'Let's have a "Who can bag the pretty lady writer?" competition with me old mate Mervyn'?

Thanks for firing the starting pistol without telling me, you bastard. I bet you even told her that I knew you two were an item, and that I was sulking. I can see you now, puffing your post-coital ciggie and saying, 'Oh, don't get in touch with him, Cheryl. He's hurting. I know old Mervyn. He'll work it through for himself, and just when you think he's disappeared for ever, then he'll contact you out of the blue. Just you see.'

And then I did. That was a shock for you, wasn't it?

It all bloody makes sense now. No wonder I haven't heard from either of you for the best part of a year.

But it's all got a bit out of hand, hasn't it? Didn't expect to end up in the morning suit with a carnation in your lapel, making speeches and cutting cakes, did you? Was it her parents? Did they subtly twist your arm into matrimony? No, of course not. Cheryl's more than capable enough of worming the right responses out of a feeble, spineless man like you. Probably got you when you were flat on your back, weak from booze, desperate for your new nurse not to leave you in a puddle of your own piss and vomit...

And, from what he saw of them in the years after, he knew he was right. About everything.

Mervyn remained at the reception for an hour or so. His heart wasn't in it, but there was always that sense of duty one felt when personally invited to a birthday or a wedding or christening; to leave too early would feel like a betrayal. He hovered around the edges chatting to the vicar, who seemed to have used the hour after the service to get blind stinking drunk.

'Thish is great,' he kept saying, punching Mervyn playfully on the shoulder. 'Besht gig ever.' After a few more ladles of fruit punch, the vicar was using Mervyn as a lamp-post, draping himself around his shoulders. 'Itsh jusht you and me guy, jusht you and me againsht the world.'

'Just you and me against the world?'

'Yeah.'

'What about God?'

'Yeah, him too.' The vicar leered glassily up at him. 'Jusht you and me againsht God. Bashtard. We'll short him out.'

And then he vomited into the punchbowl. Mervyn assumed he was a vicar in one of the more progressive churches.

He slunk away shortly after. If it wasn't for the untidily-wrapped wok hiding behind a set of bathroom towels and a Kenwood mixer, there was no evidence that he'd even turned up.

He went back to work. The next two years of *Vixens from the Void* weren't going to script-edit themselves. Cheryl's writing career slipped quietly away and died peacefully in its sleep, in the shadows behind the lengthening autograph queues for Marcus Spicer: Raconteur, Blockbuster Novelist and God-Knocker in Chief.

The discussions about a Cheryl-penned episode of *Vixens* dribbled away to nothing; just as, after opening that cream envelope, Mervyn's heart had dribbled away through the gaps in his ribcage.

CHAPTER NINETEEN

Mervyn went on to the internet, found the Godbotherers' website, got their contact details and rang them up. He arranged a meeting with Lewis Bream on the following day. The whole thing took about 40 seconds.

That was odd. And slightly weird. The man on the other end of the phone seemed excited. Why were they so keen to meet him?

It was easy to find out where the Godbotherers were based. Their headquarters was slap-bang in the middle of Soho, on the top floor of a place off Berwick Street, located right between a darkened sex shop and a newsagents (which might as well have been a sex shop, judging by the contents of the magazine shelves). The Godbotherers' building was modern and glass-fronted, and it gleamed like a shiny crucifix dangling between two sinful-looking bosoms.

The foyer was overwhelmingly white; white doors, white walls, white floor. Even the chairs were covered in white leather. When he sat down he half-expected an alarm to ring and for someone to come up to him and tell him he wasn't allowed on the furniture. The Godbotherers shared the building with several other companies, but he couldn't help suspecting they had a hand in the décor.

He felt like he was sitting in heaven's waiting room, and that God had decided to spruce things up and bring a touch of corporate hospitality to the afterlife – put in a few pot plants, a magazine rack, replace St Peter with a smiley blonde lady with a name badge. It was a very consumer-friendly purgatory.

Sprouting out of each side of the reception desk were two lifts. Two pointless lifts. Lifts of unique pointlessness. Lifts so pointless that they were only to be found in large swanky foyers of shiny corporate buildings. The lifts were able to hold about two-thirds of a person at a push, moved at about three inches an hour, and only went up 30 feet. They also had glass walls, so as they rose into the air with arthritic slowness the occupants could smile sheepishly at those left on the ground; the lucky ones who had suddenly decided to take the stairs.

One of the pointless lifts was coming down.

Like a glowing angel descending from the heavens to scare the shit out of some shepherds, Lewis Bream's beatific smile shone through the glass. He was still smiling when the lift doors glided open and he glided out.

He was dressed in a herringbone suit (complete with handkerchief in breast pocket) that looked like he'd only just tried it on; it looked stiff and flat, like a doll's outfit cut out of a girl's comic. Lewis looked slightly less sweaty and odd than on the BBC bulletins (he could hardly have looked *more* sweaty and odd) but he still had that bug-eyed serenity in his face.

He was very warm and courteous to Mervyn, and offered his hand. 'Mr Stone, it's a pleasure to meet you.'

'I'm very glad you could find time to meet me.'

'Not at all,' grinned Lewis. His eyes glowed like bicycle reflectors. 'I'm so glad you could come to us.'

Mervyn couldn't cope with the creepy smile any more. He turned away to avoid the glare, and looked out of the lift. He was treated with the stunning views of the tops of people's heads.

'All the way up,' Lewis said. 'When I have guests, I say: "Get in the lift and head towards the light." Just one of my little jokes.'

The lift doors pulled open, and for a moment Mervyn was indeed dazzled by an explosion of light. After he got used to the glare, he could see why. They had walked into a bright, airy floor with glass-fronted offices and huge windows, designed to catch the natural light from every direction. Mervyn could literally see a 360-degree view of the London skyline, so clear it seemed like a diorama.

A sturdy round-faced man with a spotty tie, horn-rimmed glasses and huge mane of sculpted grey hair was seated at reception. He leapt up, brushing crumbs from his shirt, staring at Mervyn with frank awe, as though he were a film star.

'Cary, could we have some refreshments for my office? Mr Stone has come an awfully long way. He must be parched.'

'Certainly Lewis.'

Mervyn watched him waddle away. *The devil has all the best tunes,* he thought, *and he looks like he kept all the sexy receptionists for himself, too.*

'I'm surprised to find your centre of operations around here. It's hardly the most spiritual of neighbourhoods.'

This was obviously an observation frequently put to the head of the Godbotherers, because his response was smooth and rehearsed. 'Jesus did not preach in churches, nor did He keep the company of holy men,' beamed Lewis. 'He sought out the sinners, the unbelievers and the unworthy, and he preached to them where he found them.'

'Yes, I thought that's what you might say,' said Mervyn, flatly.

'Yes, there are traders in sin all around this area. The sinners are at our gate... And there are sinners within.'

'The sinners within? Right, well, that shows great humility to admit you're not perfect.'

'Oh, I'm not talking about us.' He chuckled. 'When I say "within",

I mean within these walls. We share this building with a video editing facility, two management consultancies, a PR company and the headquarters of a magazine aimed at the dedicated sodomiser. Truly, we walk amongst the godless.'

'What's so godless about a video editing facility?' said Mervyn.

'Need you ask? All manner of pornographic and pagan material is fed into their machines for processing, so that it can be broadcast into our homes.' He sighed. 'But I dwell on the lost souls within this building too much. All will be swept away when our saviour returns to us.'

'The landlord?'

Lewis didn't dignify that with a response. 'The benefits of sin are fleeting and fickle. They will come to nothing. I am pleased to say that the magazine ceased trading last week.'

'Well if the strapline on their cover is "For the dedicated sodomiser", I can't say I'm surprised,' snapped Mervyn.

'It is hoped when they are cast out, we will expand our offices and commit the rest of this building to good works. We will prevent this building becoming a house of iniquity'

'The House of Iniquity. I think I've seen their autumn catalogue. Apparently, whips and chains are the new black.' Mervyn was using the full force of his acerbic nature to prompt a response. Nothing.

They reached Lewis's office. Like the rest of the building, it looked just like an office in any successful corporation; there were posters on the walls advertising company products, photos of celebrity endorsements and awards. The only things that set it apart were pieces of scripture dotted around the walls and a large cross fastened behind the desk, tastefully made in cedar wood and varnished so Mervyn could see his face in it.

Lewis took a seat behind the desk and gestured Mervyn to sit. 'Now, Mr Stone. I trust this is about the miracle?'

'The what?'

'I knew it was only a matter of time before one of you came to me. What was it like? All my years of worship and I have never been in the presence of His Work. Was there a shining light? A mighty wind? Did you hear His voice? This is so exciting.'

'What miracle?'

'The miracle. The smiting of the blasphemer.'

'I think you mean the murder.'

Lewis smiled and threw up his hands expansively. 'You say potato...'

'Well his *widow* calls it murder.'

'Yes of course. Tell her I'm sorry for her loss, but the Lord's will...'

He allowed the rest of the sentence to float away. Lewis began to stare out of the window. Now he realised that Mervyn wasn't here to talk about a shining light, or about bearing witness to a miracle, he had completely lost interest.

Mervyn ploughed on. 'Unsurprisingly, the *widow* doesn't think that the Lord had anything to do with it. She doesn't believe there's an invisible deity waiting to "smite" anyone who happens to criticise him.'

'I'm sure *she* wouldn't like to think that the Lord punishes those who doubt him. Hmm. Mrs Spicer... Correct me if I'm wrong, but she is the one with cancer isn't she?' Mervyn didn't answer. He was too shocked and outraged at the obvious implication to even speak.

He scrambled for a question. 'What do you know about a statuette, Mr Bream?'

For the first time, Lewis was unsettled. 'A statuette? What statuette?'

'Yes, a small statuette of the Virgin Mary and Child. About so high. It belonged to Marcus. It was stolen from his house. He was looking for it in the weeks before his death.'

'I'm surprised a man like that owned such a thing.'

'Well he was being ironic.'

'Ah. Ironic. Ironic like a blasphemer looking desperately for Jesus. Albeit only in the form of a statuette, of course.'

'Would you be interested in such a thing? The statuette?'

'Why would I be interested in the man's statuette? We have many. We even make our own, and customise them according to the wishes of the buyer. You can have a Jesus for any occasion; you can have Him standing by a facsimile of yourself, Him with arms wide open in welcome to you, Him laying hands on your own likeness, Him kneeling with anyone you wish...'

'Is that the one sold to the dedicated sodomiser?'

Lewis didn't take the bait. He just smiled indulgently. 'Just keep digging that hole, Mr Stone. You'll find yourself in a deep, dark, hot place before long. The statues sell very well. It is one of the ways we raise funds for our good work.'

'So you've not come across this statuette, then.'

'Ah. Refreshments! Thank you Cary.'

The door opened and the round-faced man entered slowly, clinking as he came. He was bearing a tray laden with tea things, plates of biscuits and bottled water.

Mervyn took a biscuit, and leaned back in his chair. 'You seem much more relaxed now than you were during that BBC interview.'

The smile flickered – only slightly, but it definitely flickered.

Got him.

'After the trial of that interview... I gained strength from the Lord. His actions in striking down the unbeliever showed me I was chosen, transformed me, I became reborn in his love.'

'Well, I saw the interview. You certainly got crucified and no mistake.'

The smile drained off Lewis's face. 'Have you just come here to blaspheme?'

'No,' said Mervyn, munching away. 'I'm actually here on behalf of Mrs Spicer to find out what you actually meant when you said –'

'Do you like the biscuits?' Lewis said abruptly. He took one and held it up. Etched on it was a tiny face of Jesus. 'It's another thing we make. This is our post-Lent selection.'

Mervyn looked down at the tray. The other biscuits had other designs on them; crosses, fish, the Virgin Mary, and some quotes from the Bible.

'Isn't sticking him on a biscuit a bit... Blasphemous?'

'We are not Lutherans or Islamists, Mr Stone. The way we see it, it's good public relations; the more places He is seen, the better our "reach" with potential believers.' He proffered a tray. 'Try another one – they're very tasty. The face is cinnamon. Oh, but would you like some water?' he said, gesturing to the bottles on the tray. 'Please, pick any one you like.'

There were just two bottles of water on the tray. It was Estuary English, the same brand the BBC had given them for the commentary.

The same water that Marcus Spicer was intending to drink, just before his last moments on earth.

Mervyn wasn't thirsty, but he still stretched his hand out, hovering between the bottles like a man invited to play Find the Lady.

'Thanks.' His hand reached to the bottle on the right, moved away at the last minute, picked the left one up, broke the seal on the cap with a muted *click-click-click* sound and defiantly swigged from the bottle.

He drank it all, plonking the bottle down and wiping his mouth with an exaggerated gesture, using the back of his hand.

'Very refreshing,' snapped Mervyn. 'I didn't realise how thirsty I was.' He picked the other bottle up. 'You don't mind if I have this one as well? For later.'

'Oh of course.' Lewis spread his fingers on the wooden table, as if trying to heal the dead tree within. 'Water is the greatest of God's gifts to us, don't you think?'

He's playing with me, thought Mervyn. *He knows something or he might know nothing; there's no difference. Whatever he knows, he's planning to squeeze every bit of mileage he can possibly get from this. And do you know something? I don't blame him.*

He stowed the bottle away in his satchel, and stood up.

'I'm sorry to have wasted your time,' he said. 'No – on second thoughts, I'm not sorry to have wasted your time. I'm sorry to have wasted mine.'

Lewis accompanied Mervyn to the lift.

'Manufacturing miracles is hardly easy, Mr Stone. That's why they're called "miracles". If they were easy they'd be called "parlour tricks".'

'Oh... I don't know if manufacturing miracles is *that* hard. I thought seeing Christ's face in food was meant to be a miracle. If you sculpt it in in cinnamon using a machine in a ruddy great factory. Well... isn't that cheating?'

'Seeing His face in nature is a miracle to some, perhaps, those that crave evidence of His existence, and that's fine for them... But for those of stronger faith, who do not need such things, He manifests himself through us and for us. He rewards us with His divine love, and punishes our enemies with divine retribution.'

'That wasn't some divine retribution, Mr Bream,' said Mervyn sharply, munching on another biscuit. 'This was murder. A man was killed because he drank water that had been poisoned.'

'But how was this done?' The grin brightened. 'How was the water poisoned? How? How on earth could a random water bottle find its way – of all the places it could have travelled to – into your studio? With your blasphemous subject matter? And into the throat of the worst blasphemer of all?'

'I was hoping you could tell me.' Mervyn was very angry now.

Lewis looked like a triumphant chess player; he had obviously been waiting for Mervyn to ask that very question.

The lift finished its painfully slow ascent, and the glass doors slid open.

'Well... Let's not forget shall we?' said Lewis. 'It was He who showed us the miracle of turning the water into wine...' He leaned forward, his eyes aflame, and hissed in Mervyn's ear. 'It would hardly be beyond Him to turn the water into something else entirely, wouldn't it?'

Mervyn stepped into the lift.

'Goodbye Mr Stone. It's a slow journey from us, but at least it's down all the way. Just another little joke.'

CHAPTER TWENTY

Despite the brightness of his surroundings, Mervyn was in a black fury. He felt that Lewis either knew something or was just using Marcus's death as a PR opportunity. He couldn't decide which was worse.

To exhume the cliché, some of his best friends were deity-worshipers. He knew and respected people of many faiths, even though he was a devout non-believer in everything – even himself.

As an ex script-editor, Mervyn knew there was no place in a writer's life for concepts that were fixed and immutable – he only had to see how his writers ignored the fixed and immutable deadlines he used to give them to know that was the case. Most writers thrived under a comfort blanket of vagueness, and knew that most problems in life came from people who were Certain. Those with fixed views and who Knew They Were Right; censors, programme commissioners, producers, directors, critics, actors, awards judges... The list went on.

He never knew how to cope with people who were Certain. He believed that because they were so certain about things, they were probably wrong. But as he was so uncertain about the things he believed in, he never believed with any certainty that they were certainly wrong.

Damn them and their certainty.

As if on cue, an angelic voice fluted in from nowhere, and told him something with incredible certainty and with no room for doubt.

'Third floor.'

Mervyn was incandescent with rage that he'd forgotten to press the lift button. He pressed 'G', and the voice told him in no uncertain terms that he was going down. The pointless lift began its long and tedious journey down to the ground floor.

On the other side of the foyer, the other equally pointless lift began a stately journey to the top of the building. The two lifts inched slowly past each other, and he almost came nose to nose with a very familiar face.

Wait a minute... Wasn't that?

Mervyn pressed himself into the far corner, burying himself into the sleeve of his jacket so the occupant of the other lift wouldn't notice him; and, more importantly, wouldn't recognise him.

As his lift touched down, Mervyn leapt from it and ran to the middle of the foyer, looking upwards, but the man had disappeared. *Now why was he here?*

Why on Earth would Brian Crowbridge be here?

As he walked down Berwick Street, dodging punters furtively scuttling out of sex shops with their heads low, and circumventing a drunken group of lads laughing and pushing each other into the doorway of Raymond's Revue Bar, Mervyn remembered the conversation he'd had with Brian in the BBC club.

He remembered the leaflet Brian had produced out of his pocket.

He has to be.

Brian's a Godbotherer.

He decided to go back and wait for Brian to leave the building. He retraced his steps, found a handy coffee shop to monitor the comings and goings at the Godbotherers' building, and sat in the window, dipping his lips into the froth of a cappuccino and nibbling a jam thing with almonds on it.

Twenty minutes later, and the coffee and its froth had gone, and a second and third coffee had followed it. They'd gone on a tour of his intestines, seen the sights, had a lovely time, and were queuing up by the exit. The coffee shop was too small to have a toilet, and the waitress was eyeing his empty cup, ready to snatch it.

Mervyn gave the Godbotherers' building a final anguished look. It had either been a very short meeting and Mervyn had missed him leave, or a very long meeting and still ongoing. And Mervyn hadn't the bladder control or the inclination to sit there and drink another coffee.

Either way, an opportunity missed. Damn.

He nipped into a McDonalds to have a pee, and was contemplating going back into the building and asking Lewis straight out what he had to do with Brian. It went against every cringing instinct he had, but he felt fired up about things.

His mobile phone rang. The screen read 'Unknown number'. Expecting it to be some bank asking him if he was happy with his bank account, he warily pressed 'Accept'.

'Hello, is that Mr Mervyn Stone?'

'Um... yes. I think.'

'I'm Tim Parsons of Stoneleigh, Parsons and Williams. We represent the estate of Mr Marcus Spicer.'

'I see.'

'We would like to commiserate with you on the loss of your dear friend Marcus, and ask you if you would be prepared to attend the reading of his will on Thursday week.'

'Well, I am awfully busy...'

'It would be incredibly helpful to us if you could attend. The conditions Mr Spicer laid out in his will were very precise, and your presence was specifically required. The will cannot be read out until all stipulated parties are present.'

'Well, if you put it like that, I'd be glad to come.'

CHAPTER TWENTY-ONE

The hooded man watched Mervyn get up from his table. It was very easy to watch him; Mervyn was staring intently, refusing to allow his eyes to move from the Godbotherers' building.

The hooded man watched Mervyn in the café for a long time. It was getting boring. He entertained himself by flicking the button on his tape recorder on and off.

Mervyn's voice erupted from the tiny speaker.

'Did you say that that statuette got stolen?'

'Yes. We had a burglary a couple of months ago and it was among the things that got taken. It was a prop from "The Burning Time". A fan gave it to him at a literary festival, years ago, and it amused him to put it in pride of place on the mantelpiece. He said he was being ironic.'

'Of course! He mentioned it on the commentary. He was talking about it being stolen just before he – well, just before...'

'Do you believe it?'

'Of course I do. I hardly think you're hiding it for the insurance money.'

'I'm not talking about who nicked the bloody statue. I'm talking about my husband's death.'

The hooded man clicked it off, pressed rewind, allowed the recorder to gabble for a few seconds, then switched it on again.

'Did you say that that statuette got stolen?'

'Yes. We had a burglary a couple of months ago and it was among the things that got taken.'

CHAPTER TWENTY-TWO

Mervyn went home, making the agonising crawl back to Uxbridge along the Metropolitan Line.

London was the place where Mervyn had worked for the best part of three decades. He didn't particularly mind the city. So, it was unfriendly, untidy and haphazardly designed? Well so was he.

But he resented having to shelter under its petticoats in order to eke out any kind of career. His token rebellion was to live as far out as he possibly could while still having access to the capital via public transport. This was why Mervyn was pacing the carriage of a filthy tube train that ambled through about 183 stops, making a journey in the same amount of time it took bearded English eccentrics to hike to the South Pole and back.

Finally, he reached what he loosely called home. Anyone visiting his modest little house would understand what 'loosely' meant. Mervyn didn't move into any place with any degree of conviction; he doubted his commitment to places as much as he doubted his commitment to people. This flat was a prime example; eight years he'd inhabited this place like a rat in the wainscot, and he hadn't even redecorated.

The flat was filled with echoes of the previous occupants; a well-to-do Indian family who'd moved up to Birmingham to look after their parents. Their past lives mingled with his. The deep red wallpaper was theirs, as was the heavy bead curtain strung up between kitchen and living room, the sturdy pine furniture and the heady smell of exotic spices.

He liked it this way; he felt it gave his home a different, unknowable dimension, as if he lived with creatures that hid in the walls and cooked and took tea and loafed around the house while he slept. He reasoned that, if he'd decided on every last thing that went into where he lived, the wallpaper, furniture and carpets and ornaments, it would be so predictably *him*, and he'd wake-up every morning feeling hemmed in by his own extremely narrow tastes in things.

The small things, the knick-knacks were his; the certificates and photos on the walls; the odd, cheap-looking awards designed and dreamt up by fans to give to him at conventions and a huge bookshelf that dominated one wall, filled with DVDs, volumes of reference and an impressive collection of books (liberated from Oxfam and waiting patiently to be read) – Agatha Christie, Leslie Charteris, Ian Fleming, Ellery Queen and Dan Brown were just some of the names the eye glided across.

On one sideboard, the two worlds of the flat's different occupants collided in a multi-coloured accident. The Indian family had left it burdened with shelves of beautiful ornamental plates that had birds etched on them; they hadn't even contemplated trying to take these, probably assuming that the plates were very unlikely to survive the journey. Their delicate designs alternated with Mervyn's own more utilitarian crockery, which he kept in the gaps; cheap yellow plates from a warehouse clearance and bowls decorated with the Rice Krispies goblins displaying evil grins, waving their spoonlike weapons menacingly. The whole effect looked like an ad hoc draughts game where the players had lost most of the pieces.

Mervyn went straight into the living room and placed the spare bottle of water on the table. He plonked himself down in his favourite chair, and stared at it.

It was a symbol, he decided. The bottle of water was a symbol. It stood for all that was rational. It stood against hysteria and superstitious nonsense. He would drink that bottle of water when he solved the case; and when he did there would be no choking and falling to the floor; no agonising death, no vengeance from some supernatural power.

Six hours later, he went to bed. The bottle of water was left on the table, intact. Mervyn was determined to prove the death of Marcus was no miracle. It had to be a trick; he just had to find out what it was.

There was an obvious place to start.

CHAPTER TWENTY-THREE

'Gus?'

'Yes? Who is this?'

'It's Mervyn. Mervyn Stone.'

'Mervyn? Really? How are you, Mervyn?'

'I'm great.'

'I can't believe it. It must be, what – at least four years?'

'Nearly five.'

'Wow. Has it?'

'I've got a meeting in Hammersmith with someone from Endemol. I wondered if you fancy a drink this afternoon in the BBC club?'

'That sounds great.'

'Excellent. It's a date.'

'But let's not go to the club. It's a place where depressives go to die.'

'Erm...'

'Seriously, there's a nice little pub near Shepherd's Bush Green, it's much nicer. Good food, too.'

'Well... I was just thinking of you, Gus. Aren't you working on that new daytime panel game at the Beeb?'

'*Litterbuffs,* that's right. It's a show where people are asked questions about the contents of their own rubbish bins.'

'Thing is, I'm afraid I can't see you before two...'

'Oh.'

'... And I imagine you've got a technical rehearsal in the afternoon.'

'You're dead right. Best to have a quick one in the club.'

'Look forward to it. How do I get in?'

'Call me on my mobile when you get to reception. I'll sign you in.'

'Will do. See you at two.'

'Looking forward to it.'

CHAPTER TWENTY-FOUR

Mervyn felt quite guilty about using Gus just to get a guest pass into the BBC.

Even though that was his prime objective, he liked Gus, and enjoyed the half-hour they shared, recalling horror stories about shows they'd worked on; laughing about inept scene-shifters, mad make-up ladies, incompetent producers who didn't realise they were in charge and cocky production runners who thought they were. As the alcohol hit his brain, Mervyn felt very warm and fuzzy towards his friend, and convinced himself he would have probably met up with him even if he hadn't needed to slip furtively into TV Centre.

Probably.

Eventually, they waved each other goodbye; Gus to go back to Studio 6 and *Litterbuffs* and Mervyn to sneak back to Recording Suite 4 to have another poke around the scene of the crime.

The recording suites were all quiet and empty, but crumpled crisp packets and polystyrene cups of cold coffee suggested that it was being used. Someone had gone to fetch some tapes or to get a snack. Whatever the reason, he didn't have much time.

Everything from the other day had been taken away, of course. The bottles of water, the nibbles, the chocolates. Mervyn got down on his hands and knees to examine the spot where the poisoned bottle had landed, but there was nothing to see.

It wasn't a completely wasted journey, because it certainly refreshed his memory. He looked at the table, and his mind conjured up phantom bottles of water standing in regimented rows. He remembered that they were divided into two clusters, still and sparkling. Had that helped the murderer? Did the killer know that Marcus liked his water with or without bubbles in it? Was that how he or she steered Marcus's hand to the Drink of Death? Mervyn couldn't see how it was possible, but then he was rubbish at seeing how magic tricks worked.

He left the studio and went into the adjoining room that housed the mixing desk, where Joanna had scowled with arms crossed, Trevor had sat and twiddled his knobs and Robert had offered his encouraging thumbs-up.

He didn't know why it was worth looking in there; but he hit the jackpot.

There was a CD on the table, labelled 'Burning Time commentary'.

He couldn't believe it. Of all the things to be sitting there – in plain view!

He put it in the player, and heard himself say: *'Hello, this is the commentary for "The Burning Time". I was the script editor for this show – also here is Brian Crowbridge who played Professor Dax–'* A pause. *'Didn't I? Damn. Sorry.'*

Mervyn struggled on, and Mervyn cringed with him. 'Come on Mervyn!' he hissed at the CD. 'Turn it around...' Thankfully, they moved on.

'And we did so much research.'

There was laughter from the others, and Mervyn could feel palpable relief washing over him, even a week later. Mervyn listened to the commentary unfold, his hand poised over the 'Off' switch.

He couldn't help himself; he had to keep listening. He told himself he was investigating. Examining the conversation on the CD was just as important as examining the carpets in the recording suite. Both contained vital evidence.

Probably.

'Hey, I had that thing on my mantelpiece! That thing there, right in shot! That statue of Mary! It got stolen last month – bloody burglars. I've been searching high and low for the damn thing.'

'Why on Earth would anyone want to steal it?'

'More to the point, why on Earth would you want it back?'

'Well I use... well, I use it.'

'Gosh. Whatever for?'

'Novelty paperweight...'

Somehow, he couldn't bring himself to turn it off. He realised why these DVDs sold so well, skating on half-remembered anecdotes about tiny events from years past. He was already nostalgic for a time one whole week ago, a few minutes before his world went strange and mysterious and complicated. Again.

'Come to think of it – that thing on the table. That bloody statue. I don't want it back at all. I don't know why I kept it in the first place. Bloody fans, forcing rubbish on me and filling my house with crap.'

'What was the director's name again?'

'Horrible bloody thing. Ugly as sin. Stuck on the mantelpiece for years. Makes her look like a whore.'

It was funny how listening to the commentary brought into sharp focus things that were only dimly apparent at the time of recording. He remembered it started as a lot of fun, and he was having fun most of all, but at the back of his mind he was vaguely aware of Marcus saying less and less, getting increasingly isolated and uncomfortable and aching to drag the conversation back to something he could talk about with confidence. Something Marcus Spicer-related.

'What do you think you're doing?' Robert's voice was suddenly audible; loud inside the studio. That was a shock. 'Mervyn?'

That wasn't on the CD!

Mervyn turned round. Robert Mulberry was in the doorway, his face a collage of confusion and outrage.

CHAPTER TWENTY-FIVE

Robert rushed across to the desk and switched off the CD.

'What do you think you're doing here?'

Mervyn slipped effortlessly into his 'confused old buffer' role. Or was he really a confused old buffer and he just slipped out of that role sometimes? *Best not to think about it.*

'Oh hello Robert, I'm sorry, I thought I'd just pop in. I'd lost my phone. I was thinking I might have left it here during the commentary.' He pulled it out of his pocket and waggled it. 'Found it! Phew! Lucky me!'

'You left your phone here?'

'That's right.'

'The police pulled this place apart. They didn't find a phone.'

'Well no. It was tucked behind a... thing. One of those tall things in the studio. They must have missed it.'

'Didn't you phone me last week on your mobile?'

Mervyn couldn't answer.

Robert went to the internal phone on the corner of the desk. 'Right. I think you'd better leave. I'll get security to escort you out.'

'That's hardly necessary.'

'Hello? Can you put me through to the front desk?' He paused with the phone tucked under his neck, waiting for a response. 'Just how did you get in here, anyway?'

Mervyn decided to take a chance. 'A friend let me in the building. Just like you let in Lionel.'

Robert froze. He turned and looked at Mervyn like he'd just been slapped in the face.

'What do you know about Lionel?'

'You signed Lionel in last week. You remember. The day Marcus was murdered?'

The phone in Robert's hand was emitting an irregular buzz as a tiny voice tried to speak to him. 'What? Sorry, false alarm. Sorry. Bye.' He put the receiver slowly on to its cradle. 'How did you know I talked to Lionel?'

'I know lots of things.'

'You haven't... Have you mentioned this to anyone?'

'Should I?'

'Well, there's nothing to tell.'

'Isn't there?'

'I have nothing to be ashamed of.'

'Haven't you?

'You won't get out of this by just putting a question after everything I say.'

'Won't I?' Mervyn decided to blink first. *Let's try honesty – it might work.* 'Look Robert, truth to tell, I got myself in here to look around because I want to find out the truth about Marcus's death. I'm not being prurient or ghoulish; he was my friend and I want to do it for him – and his wife. She asked me to look into it, and here I am. I know it sounds stupid –'

Robert frowned. 'No, it doesn't sound stupid. I heard about what happened at the convention last year. I heard how you solved those murders.'

'Of course you did. Can't keep anything from you fans.'

Robert was still cautious, but he'd dropped the hostile glare.

Mervyn perched uncomfortably on the console, trying to look as casual as his nerves would allow. 'So that's why I'm here. You can ring up security and put me out if you like, and I won't tell anyone about Lionel because I don't even know who he is. All I did was hear you on your phone talking to him. I don't know what he's done which was so bad, but it's your business and if it's nothing to do with –'

'You don't know what Lionel did?'

'Um... No.'

Stark bewilderment stretched Robert's face into interesting shapes.

'Seriously? You'd not seen it in any of the papers?'

'No.'

'Or television?'

'No.'

'You seriously don't know?'

'No, I don't. I just said.' Mervyn looked confused and embarrassed. As usual, the Great Detective didn't know something that was common knowledge to the rest of the world.

Robert slumped down in the sound engineer's chair and started swivelling it aimlessly, back and forth. 'I can't believe you don't know.'

'I don't know. So tell me.'

'I'll do more than that. I'll show you.'

CHAPTER TWENTY-SIX

Robert took Mervyn to a computer in the corner and switched it on. There was a comforting chime and the screensaver swam into view. *Vixens from the Void*, of course – a rather nice ensemble shot of the Vixens posing and aiming their guns.

Robert went to Google and searched for websites. He wasn't having much luck. Time after time, he came across unhelpful little signs that said the website wasn't available, or the URL wasn't found. 'Nope. That one's been taken down... And that one... That one too.' He went through website after website, each one murkier and shabbier than the last. 'I'd better wipe my browser history after this...' he muttered.

They finally ended up looking at one in a lurid pink, called Peek-a-Boob. There was a huge exaggerated cartoon of a large-breasted woman lying on the logo, and running down the side of the screen were adverts for dating sites, featuring grim-looking women from Basildon and Norwich lying on cheap sofas with their legs open.

'Here we are.'

'Where exactly?'

'Peek-a-Boob.'

'So I see. Why? Is this what BBC employees do during the day?'

Robert grimaced, slightly embarrassed. 'This site collects candid footage of stars; basically the operators are a bunch of sad acts who trawl through daytime television and take screen-grabs of celebs when they're showing more flesh than usual; extra cleavage, erect nipples, flashes of knickers... you get the idea.'

'I get the idea. Why are we looking at this?'

'I'll just put a name in the search. Um... Okay. Vanity Mycroft.'

Another screen came up, hundreds of tiny pictures of Vanity Mycroft; star of *Vixens from the Void*. The makers of the site didn't exactly have to scour the world for candid photos of Vanity's body; she was happy to supply them herself.

There was a collage of nipples, cleavages and bottoms; a mixture of alluring publicity photos and screen-grabs of her on *Vixens*, taken while she was bending over or crossing her legs in very short skirts. He leaned to one side so Mervyn could see the picture he selected. It looked like a still taken from CCTV footage.

It was shot from high up, looking down on a tiny bare room, with only one piece of furniture. A toilet. It was a toilet cubicle. A woman was sitting on it, knickers round her ankles.

'Who's that?'

'That's Vanity Mycroft.'

'I don't understand.'

Robert sighed. 'This is what Lionel did. Let's say he abused his position.'

'How so?'

'Lionel Bickerdyke was a security officer in the BBC. He mainly worked nights.'

'Okay.'

'He was also my flatmate. I didn't know him well. He just answered my ad in *Ariel* for someone to share the rent.'

'Go on...'

'So... One night he took audiovisual equipment from the flat. Stuff I'd signed out to film interviews for a DVD extra.'

'Well I've put a few pens in my pocket myself over the years...'

'Oh, he didn't steal the stuff.'

'Oh, that's good.'

'He took the cameras and secreted them in the hollow ceilings of the cubicles of both women's and men's toilets in this building, on the third floor.'

'Oh. That is a bit...'

'And he took recordings of celebrities on the toilet. He filmed them while they were making commentaries for *Vixens from the Void* and they'd just popped into the loo.'

'Oh my God...'

'And he made DVDs of them, and sold them to several unscrupulous fans who put them up on anonymous websites.'

Mervyn boggled. 'He did that?'

'I'm afraid he did.'

'How many celebrities did he... um, film?'

'The police don't know for sure, but about a dozen.'

Mervyn gave a silent whistle. 'Who did he record?'

Robert sucked his cheeks.

'Come on Robert, you just said it was in all the papers.'

'Well we did a commentary about three months ago – and we contacted Liz O'Rourke to take part –'

'Oh my god! "BAFTA Betty"?'

Elizabeth O'Rourke was an esteemed actress who'd made a huge name for herself in heart-warming ITV dramas about lone women struggling against cancer, or arthritis, or MS, or just generally being a struggling lone woman struggling against stuff.

Every time she strapped on some callipers and donned a surgical gown she got another wheelbarrow full of awards. Like many esteemed actresses, she'd had a brief shameful role in *Vixens from the Void* before she'd got properly famous.

'She's nearly 70!'

Robert held his hands up helplessly. *Vixens* fans want to know how stars look naked. It doesn't matter what age or shape they are. Or even if they're that well known. It's a curiosity thing.'

'It's a sick, prurient thing, you mean.'

'I'm not arguing, Mervyn. I think it's horrible too.'

Robert continued. 'Liz is talking about suing the BBC for millions; talking about loss of dignity and damage to her reputation as a respected doyenne of stage and screen.'

'She should have worried about that when she did that insurance ad with the cartoon rhino. All right. Who else from *Vixens from the Void*?'

'Race Keynes came into to do "The Bride of Krell" commentary.'

'Race Keynes? The silicon enhanced seductress and footballer's friend? The one with that fly-on-the wall show on Channel Five? She was in *Vixens*?'

'Oh yes. You probably won't remember her. She played a tiny part in the last series, one of those cloned child geniuses you created in the episode "Children of the Revolution".'

'Really? One of those kids? My, she's a big girl now.'

'She's majorly pissed off about what's happened. In fact, she poured out her story of how her body's been violated over at least eight pages of the *News of the World*.'

'Complete with pictures no doubt, in case the readers can't remember what her violated body looks like.'

'You got it.'

'I would have thought she's the kind of person who wouldn't mind being filmed like that.'

'It because she's "that kind of person" that she's so annoyed. She's already done an "on the toilet" webcam for the website of *Jazz* – the lads mag? – which hasn't been streamed yet.'

'Streamed?'

'On the web. That's what they say when they put things on the web.'

'Not the most fortunate of terms.'

'Anyway, *she's* worried they're going to cancel the exclusive contract she's got with *Jazz*, so she's suing too. The whole thing's an utter mess. The BBC is going to get tied up in legal knots for years, and everyone is going to be looking at us and pointing fingers. We'll be lucky if we're allowed to record messages for our own answer machines after this.'

'Who else?'

'Well...'

'What?'

Robert sucked his pen. 'Now don't get agitated.'

'What?'

'I did say he put cameras in both toilets...'

'Oh no.'

'Men and women...'

'Oh God, no. Don't tell me...'

Robert found a photo of Mervyn sitting on the toilet. Mervyn was there, pen in mouth, reading his crib sheet for a previous DVD commentary. He was actually making notes on the toilet roll. Thankfully his shirt-tail hid his embarrassment.

'How come I didn't *know* any of this?'

'I'm surprised you didn't.'

Mervyn stared at the screen. 'This is a bit of a shock to me.'

'You're lucky you found out from me,' said Robert grimly. 'Liz O'Rourke found out about it when a fan stopped her on the street and gave her a sitting-on-the-loo screen-grab to sign.'

'Was he a number-one fan, or a number-two fan?'

'I wish I could find it funny, Mervyn, I really wish I could.'

'Actually,' said Mervyn dryly, looking at the screen. 'It's not a bad picture of me. I'm wearing my good socks, and at least he's put the camera high up, so he didn't get my double chin.' Not for the first time, Mervyn marvelled at fans' sinister creativity, or their ability once they'd taken their pound of flesh to slice off a couple more ounces. All thoughts of the murder investigation had predictably flown out of Mervyn's brain. 'So what's happened to Lionel now?'

'He's out on bail pending trial, hiding in a friend's flat. He was just ringing up last week to collect his stuff from my house. We're not flatmates any more, of course. I don't ever want to talk to him again. I'm majorly mad.'

'And that's what you were giving him that day. A box of his stuff?'

'Yeah... Well, no. I didn't give it to him in the end, the events of that day put the kibosh on that. He rang me back when we were in the BBC club after Marcus's death. I told him I didn't have the time to bother with his nonsense.'

'So you've still got his stuff?'

'Yep. Right here.'

Robert disappeared behind a desk, and reappeared with a sad-looking cardboard box that had 'LIONEL' scrawled on the side in crayon. It was filled with CDs, books and a laptop. A furry, smily creature on a spring poked out of the top of the box and nodded at Mervyn with a knowing grin. Mervyn peered into the box and picked up a CD with distaste, as if it were coated with something sticky.

'You were just going to give all that back to him, just like that? Did you check through it?'

'The police did,' said Robert defensively. 'There was nothing on those disks.'

'What about the laptop?'

Robert looked at the laptop doubtfully. Then he scratched the tiny toilet-brush-like bristle on his chin.

'The police haven't looked at the laptop...' he slowly said at last. 'I borrowed it off him six months ago when my Powerbook went kaput. I've been using it in here, in my office ever since. He hasn't used it in ages.' Robert's phone rang. He looked at the display. 'Speak of the devil. It's Lionel.' He took the call. 'Hello. Oh. You're here? Yeah I've got your stuff. If you want to wait ten minutes I'll be down...'

Mervyn shook his head vigorously, mouthing the word 'No.'

Robert stared at him in irritation, but said: 'Hang on a minute.' He put the phone on hold. 'What?'

'Don't you think you'd better check that laptop before you give it back?'

'But I've told you. It's just been on my desk.'

'Yes, but it's possible to download files on to it, even while it's been sitting on your desk. And he'd have the password, wouldn't he?'

'Yeeeesss...'

'Wouldn't that be safer for him – to keep all that stuff on your desk rather than at home?'

Robert just looked thoughtful.

'... And there's no telling what else is on there. Who knows, you were flatmates. Did you check your bathroom for surveillance equipment recently?'

Robert looked unnerved. 'I'm not famous.'

'Wouldn't you count as a bit of a minor celebrity to fans?'

Robert picked up the laptop, held it up to the light and examined it, as if by staring hard enough he could see toilet-related celebrity pictures inside.

'I think you might have a point,' he said. He pressed a button on his mobile. 'Hey Lionel, I'm sorry, but I'm busy. You'll have to come back tomorrow.'

There was a squeak of agitation from the phone.

'Look Lionel, that's the way it is. I can't help it. Something's just come up. I'm sorry. You're bloody lucky I'm doing this for you at all.'

He paused, listening, his chin bristling with impatience.

'Call them if you like,' Robert snapped. 'I'm sure the police would be very sympathetic, not to say intrigued by this laptop I've got in front of me. I'm not sure it won't be *me* calling the police.' Robert pulled the phone away from his ear and looked at it. 'He hung up.'

'Sounds like a man with something to hide.'

'Sounds like it.'

CHAPTER TWENTY-EIGHT

Mervyn got up to go, shrugging on his jacket. 'Well this has been fascinating and horrifying at the same time. But I have to make a move. I think I have to visit the gents soon; you'll forgive me if I wait until I vacate the BBC before I go.'

Robert looked at him in surprise. 'Wait a minute. Where do you think you're going?'

Mervyn tensed. *Is he going to hand me into security after all?*

Robert nodded to the CD. 'Aren't you going to listen to the rest of the CD?'

'Oh, of course.' Mervyn sat back down, grinning. 'I forgot about the commentary.'

'Some detective you are. So which bit had you got to?'

'Near the end. Marcus had started to get aggressive, saying stupid and nasty things.'

'Oh yeah, he was doing a "gooseberry fool", wasn't he?'

'A what?'

'That's what I call it. It sometimes happens during DVD commentary recordings. It's when one person becomes very aware that they aren't saying anything and overcompensates for it. They end up blurting out all sorts of nonsense that isn't even remotely related to the story.'

'Oh right. Yes, I'm very aware that I do that.'

'You're very good, Mervyn. You've never done it on a DVD commentary to my knowledge.'

'I wasn't thinking of DVD commentaries. I was thinking of what I do at parties when I talk to women half my age.'

'So... Do you want to finish listening to it?'

'Is that okay?'

'Sure. This suite isn't booked this afternoon. I was just here to edit up the commentary. I know it's very unlikely we'll do anything with it, but, you know, what he was saying was pretty unacceptable.'

'Yes, Marcus did like to be controversial...' Mervyn said wearily.

'I can't believe he compared that statuette to a suppository and a sex toy. There's no way we'd get that past the censors.'

Mervyn looked thoughtfully at the CD player. 'How much longer have we got to go?'

'A couple more seconds, then you all break for ten minutes, then you come back, then Marcus... Do you want to carry on?'

Mervyn nodded.

Robert turned the CD back on.

There was another ominous silence, broken by the sound of the studio door opening. *'That was great, majorly good. There was lots of majorly good stuff in there.'*

'I think we were starting to flag in the last five minutes.'

'Oh,' said Robert, frowning. 'Trevor must have left the tape running. That was naughty. I'll have to have a word with him. After Lionel we have to be super-careful...'

The CD continued. *'It's amazing how well it holds up. I mean, it's obviously "of its time", but you could easily see it on BBC1 now, couldn't you?'*

'Everything all right?'

'Yes.'

'Could I have some water please?'

'There's water over on the table...'

'No, could I get some different water? I did say before. Um, I don't like the brand. I'm sure you understand...'

'Oh sorry. Of course. I'll have a look in the canteen for you.'

'Thank you. I sound a bit loopy don't I? It's just water, after all.'

'No problem. Still or sparkling?'

'Still please. Sparkling feeds my cellulite.'

Mervyn switched the CD off. 'Now that's very weird.'

'What?'

'I remember thinking that was odd at the time, but I just forgot about it, what with one thing and another.'

'What?'

'Samantha asked for some water, even though there were already a dozen bottles on the table.'

'Yeah, she did, didn't she? She said she didn't like the brand of water we'd got. Trevor got her a different brand from the canteen.'

'A bit feeble isn't it? "I don't like the brand"? Who on Earth demands someone go two floors down and halfway round the BBC to get a different type of bottled water?'

'Um... Vanity Mycroft?'

'Apart from Vanity Mycroft.'

'Well, not Samantha. She doesn't have a reputation of being a prima donna...'

'So why would she do that? Unless...'

Robert looked puzzled. 'Unless?'

'Unless she knew one of the bottles on the table was poisoned...'

'I can't believe it. Not Samantha.' Mervyn found himself back in the BBC club, sharing a coffee with Robert. Mervyn hoped Gus didn't decide to pop back in, or he'd have some explaining to do.

The CD of the commentary was on the table. They were both staring at it, like chess players studying a miniature board.

Robert was still swilling the idea around his head. 'No way. Not Samantha.'

Mervyn sipped his coffee. 'Well, let's talk about Samantha. In fact, I want to talk about all of the other people who were in that DVD commentary. Samantha *and* Brian.'

'Okay...' said Robert cautiously. 'But I can't let you have confidential information about them. I can't tell you their fees for example.'

'That's not important. What I'd like to know is why they were there.'

Robert frowned. 'I don't understand. They were there to record a DVD commentary. Just like you.'

'All right, I'll phrase it in another way. It sounded from the way Samantha was talking that day that it was her first DVD commentary.'

'It was.'

'But you'd asked her to do them before.'

'Of course we had. Elysia is a major character, and she's in loads of episodes. She'd always turned us down... Oh, I see what you mean.'

'So she'd turned you down on many occasions...'

'At least a dozen times.'

'But not this time. Why this time?'

Robert shrugged helplessly.

'And Brian. Is this his first commentary?'

'No,' said Robert firmly. 'He's done at least three for us.'

'Oh,' said Mervyn, disappointed. 'Recently?'

'No. About three years ago.'

'So he stopped doing them.'

'Yes. He picked a bit of fight with us regarding his fees. He wanted a lot more money, and we pointed out we couldn't pay him substantially more than other main characters; not only would it break our budget, it would create a dangerous precedent. Can you imagine what would happen if Vanity Mycroft found out Brian was getting paid more than her?'

They both shuddered, instinctively.

'So he asked for more money, you refused to give it to him, and he stopped doing them for a while.'

'That's about the size of it.'

'So he was there in that studio. That means you sorted it out. He's getting paid more.'

'Well no, actually. It's out of the question. We can't pay more.'

'So even though he'd fallen out with the BBC contracts department, and refused to do another commentary for years, he agreed to do it? Doesn't that strike you as sort of... odd?'

'Well... Not really. That kind of thing does happen all the time. We just assume the guest has run out of cash, and needs the money.'

Mervyn looked uncomfortable. He was sure he was blushing. 'Well of course with Brian, that's a distinct possibility. But let's assume that's not the reason. What's the common denominator here? What's the unique thing about this DVD commentary?'

Robert smiled. 'Of course. That's easy. Marcus Spicer. This is the only one he's ever done.'

Mervyn reached out cautiously, like a teenage boy edging forward to take a girl's hand. His hand clamped round the CD containing Marcus's last hour of life. 'Can I have a copy of this?'

Robert looked pained.

'Is that a problem?' Mervyn asked.

'Well, me making and distributing copies of a recording of a man's death. It doesn't make me much better than Lionel does it?'

'This is important, Robert.'

'Well... Would it help?'

'I think it might.'

Robert sighed. 'Give me a few days and I'll make you a copy.'

CHAPTER THIRTY

Mervyn made the journey back to Earthly Delights where he was greeted by Cheryl. She looked tired and drained. As soon as they made it to the sitting room she flopped on the sofa, exhausted, her eyes fluttering as she skated around consciousness. Mervyn watched her, his fingers twiddling the levers on her empty wheelchair, which squatted in the room like a clumsy metaphor.

He decided to make tea. By the time he clattered in with cups and saucers she had fallen fast asleep. The knot of worry that had bunched between her eyebrows had disappeared, and there was almost a faint smile on her lips. Her face had been wiped clean of worries.

Mervyn looked around for a blanket, found one, and delicately pulled it over her form. She stirred softly, moving her head. Her wig stayed behind, and Mervyn could see a fine fuzz of downy hair on her scalp. He felt a bit seedy, like he was spying on her naked, so he gently eased it back on to her head. This time she didn't move.

Mervyn decided to let her sleep. She must have been in sore need of a rest after the stress of the last few days. After staring at her sleeping form for about five minutes, he felt intrusive, so he turned his attention to the rest of the room. He wandered around, idly looking at the books: all first editions of Marcus's own novels, of course. Hefty hardbacks with flyleaves, the type Mervyn could only afford at the local charity shop.

He flipped one over, and was immediately faced by a sombre black-and-white photo of Marcus in a studious pose, chin resting on a knuckle, head tilted down and eyes staring into the camera. Behind him was a lawn you could land a plane on, and a house you could store the plane in after it had landed.

A part of him whispered instinctively, *That could have been me.*

As he turned the book he heard a tiny *clunk*. He opened the book. Inside, a hole had been cut into the pages. Nestling in it, like an engorged silver-plated bookworm, was a hip flask. Inscribed on it in a fruity copperplate were the initials 'M.S.'. He looked at the publication date. It was a recent one, only last year.

He shook the flask. It was half-full. Marcus had been up to his old tricks – hiding his secret supply.

Far more creative as an alcoholic than he ever was as a writer, Marcus used to hide bottles all over the house in the oddest of places. Mervyn was surprised at how Marcus delighted in his secret drinking, even when he was supposedly 'on the wagon'; proudly and loudly ordering an orange juice in the BBC club to prove his virtue, only to spike it with vodka secreted in a flask under the table.

So Marcus had still been drinking. He'd been lying to Cheryl.

Mervyn had always known that Marcus was a habitual liar, to others and to himself, but now the secrets were only starting to come out; and Mervyn felt he'd only just begun to uncover the truth.

'Are you all right?'

Cheryl was awake. Wide awake. She was sitting upright and looking directly at him. 'What are you doing?' she said sharply

Mervyn had a choice. His back was to her, so she couldn't see what he was holding. IIc could turn round now and show her what he'd found; show Cheryl her dead husband had lied to her.

No. That was too cruel.

He could quietly slip it back in the book, and leave it for her to find in her own time. Maybe in a day, a week, a month, she would open the book and find out Marcus's lies.

No. That was cowardly *and* cruel.

There was only one thing for it. He slipped it in his back pocket. He'd get rid of it later.

'I'm fine, I'm just looking at Marcus's books.'

'Oh, which ones?'

'This one.' He opened the book, the flask-shaped hole away from her, hoping she wouldn't ask to read it with him. 'It's very good.'

'That was his last book – *The Last Sucker*. It's due out in paperback next week. It's already shifted 100,000 copies in this country alone.'

'Really? 100,000 copies? Amazing.' He slammed the book shut and examined the back cover with exaggerated interest.

'Yes, it's the story of Jesus using Doubting Thomas as a fall guy to get crucified instead of him. Did you know that his name meant "twin" in Aramaic? The Gnostic texts suggest that Thomas and Jesus were twins. My... Marcus thought that they swapped places, and Thomas's famous "doubting" was a literary joke played on the reader...'

Mervyn turned the book in his hands, careful not to let it fall open again. 'How fascinating. Perhaps I can borrow it.'

'Certainly you can.'

Mervyn stowed it away in his satchel.

'So Mervyn, my ace detective. Have you found out anything since yesterday?'

'Not really. But I have had a few thoughts.'

'Great.'

'After I re-listened to the commentary.'

'The commentary?'

'The DVD commentary.'

'Okay. That commentary.' Cheryl's voice grew strained. 'How did you hear it?'

'Robert Mulberry. He's producing the extras for this DVD.'

'Yes, I know Robert. He's been badgering Marcus for years. It was a major coup for him when Marcus finally agreed to do it. Marcus was not a big fan of the BBC.'

Mervyn made a tiny 'Hff' noise. He had enough of hearing about how special Marcus was.

'So what were your thoughts?'

'Nothing specific. But the thing is, Marcus... Well... he didn't seem himself.'

'How so?'

'He was rude, aggressive. He swore a lot.'

'Marcus could be aggressive.'

'Yes, he gets aggressive when he talks about religion – he did during the commentary, but he's not – he wasn't – normally rude for no reason. It wasn't like him.'

'How so?'

'It was only after he mentioned that statuette. The one that used to be on your mantelpiece. He pointed it out when he saw it on-screen, mentioned it being "used" for something, and then he stopped, like he'd said too much. Then he started talking very oddly; rude aggressive nonsense, off-colour comments, swearing and the like.'

'And you think...?'

'What strikes me is he mentioned that statuette, then regretted it, and he was doing everything he could to make the commentary unusable for DVD release. I think he was trying to get the whole thing scrapped.'

Cheryl's eyes widened. 'What makes a man so scared of mentioning a cheap statuette on a DVD commentary?' Her hand moved over her mouth. 'Oh my God...'

'What?'

'Do you know what?' she said angrily. 'I think you've got a point. I can see it. I can see what you're getting at. It never occurred to me before, but Marcus *did* say something about that statuette a few days before he died. Right after he took that phone call in the garden. Something weird. I didn't think much of it at the time, but I remember now.'

'What did he say?'

'He said something like "This might look like a piece of crap, but it's much more than that. This is the most valuable thing I own."' She looked up at Mervyn, face set with determination. 'That statuette holds some secret that somebody, the Godbotherers or whoever, didn't want uncovered, and they killed Marcus for it.' She tried to get out of her chair, failed and slumped back in her seat. 'We've got to find that statuette. Mervyn – *you've* got to find that statuette.'

CHAPTER THIRTY-ONE

They continued, and the hooded man listened.

'So you've no idea why it might be important?'

'None. No idea at all. Sorry. It was just a horrid, cheap little thing. I thought he kept it on the mantelpiece as a joke.'

'Well, I'll see what I can do. I'll find it, don't you worry.'

'But how?'

'I have contacts. I have a friend in the police force. I'll see if she can turn up anything.'

'If you can... You must get it back. I can't bear the thought of it falling into the wrong hands. Oh God, I can't believe that old thing could be so important.'

The hooded man switched his recorder off.

He was right; Mervyn was definitely the one to watch. Who knows, perhaps Mervyn would do his work for him.

This could turn out all right after all.

CHAPTER THIRTY-TWO

'There's another thing,' said Mervyn.

Cheryl rubbed her eyes wearily. 'Another thing?' She didn't look ready for Another Thing.

'Samantha Carbury. On the commentary she asked to be given a new bottle of water. Like she knew one of the bottles was poisoned.'

'Are you suggesting that Samantha...?

'I find it hard to believe, but Marcus and Samantha had been... friends, once. I remember them being very pally on the shoot for "The Burning Time".'

'Yes, but that was nearly 20 years ago. They hadn't even exchanged Christmas cards since then.'

'You're sure?'

Cheryl met his gaze defiantly. 'Mervyn – give me some credit. I knew my husband had affairs from time to time, and I was able to work out the guilty party in every bloody one – from the runner in his last movie adaptation to Joanna Paine. Samantha Carbury, no matter what history she shared with Marcus in the dim and distant past, was not on that list.'

'Fine.' He knelt down by her chair, nose to nose. 'But why on Earth would she ask for another bottle of water? On the commentary she distinctly says she...'

'Forget the commentary. I'm sick of the bloody commentary. I'm also sick of editors ringing up, fans camping out on the front garden and shit being pushed through my letterbox. The only good thing about now is... Just for a few days I don't have to think about them.'

Suddenly Cheryl leaned forward and grabbed Mervyn in a bear hug. He wondered if she was having some kind of attack, until he found his face being pummelled by Cheryl's lips, her mouth mashing into his.

His mouth opened in shock, and Cheryl's tongue found its way past his teeth and slithered into his mouth. Her arms curled around his neck, slipped down his body and rested on his bottom. She finished exploring his fillings, and nuzzled round his neck. Mervyn prayed that he'd done a half-decent job of shaving that morning.

'Mmm...' she said. 'I've been wanting to do that for some time...'

Mervyn's voice was quiet, reverent. 'Thank God you finally did.'

'God had nothing to do with it, Mervyn.'

He picked up her tiny form, removed it from the wheelchair and took her into the makeshift bedroom that had been set up in the front room after she had started to struggle with the stairs. He pushed aside dormant machines and trolleys laden with empty cups and sample bottles, and lay her down on crisp, starched sheets.

His hands were working furiously, trying to undo her blouse and his shirt at the same time. It wasn't working. Cheryl obliged, tearing open her blouse with surprising force and sending buttons pinging into space. Mervyn concentrated on his shirt now, and as soon as the buttons came loose, her hands moved inside, gripping his spare tyre urgently, squeezing his back, pulling him on to her.

'I'm not hurting you, am I?' he asked.

'Just kiss me, you sad old bastard,' she laughed.

Mervyn was happy to oblige. Her spindly hands scuttled down his waist and grabbed his buttocks. Grabbed them with surprising force.

... And then her hands were gone. She disengaged her lips from his. Her expression was puzzled, almost upset.

'Are you all right?' Mervyn didn't know what had happened. He felt like an astronaut counting down and facing the sky only for a little voice to tell him that there was a problem and he'd have to undo the straps and leave the capsule.

'Get off me, please.'

She moved her hands up to her face. She was holding the flask that Mervyn had stuffed into his back pocket.

Oh dear.

She examined the flask, read the initials on the back, and her eyes closed wearily. 'A monogrammed flask? Oh Mervyn...'

'Look, don't be too judgemental...'

'Not you too.'

Mervyn was confused. '"Not me too" what?'

She folded her arms, a bleak look on her face. 'I'm sorry. I just can't go through that again. Not with another man. Not the lies, the secrets, the hidden bottles... You'll have to sort out your problem by yourself. I know that sounds harsh, but... I'm sorry. I'm really sorry.'

'But you don't understand, I don't have a problem. It's not mine.'

'*Don't lie to me Mervyn!*' Her voice was suddenly angry; it was so raw and dry it was barely a scream; more like a furious rasp. 'Get out! Get out of here! I never want to see you again!'

Mervyn's mouth opened and closed, guppy-like. It was still flapping bonelessly when he found himself on the other side of the front door of Earthly Delights. She thought *he*, Mervyn Stone, had a drink problem?

Yes, she thought he had a drink problem. He had a hip flask in his back pocket with M.S. inscribed on it. Of course she thought he had a drink problem. It was funny, but in all the years he'd known Marcus, it had never struck him that they had the same initials.

CHAPTER THIRTY-THREE

'I was just wondering if there were any developments with the Marcus Spicer murder?'

'He's still dead.'

'Thank you for that, I was talking about the investigation. Do you have any leads?'

'Oh, we think we've definitely got our murderer.'

'Really?'

'Oh yeah. God is still our top suspect. We have attempted to contact the gentleman in question, but he seems to have made himself scarce. His next of kin seem pretty hard to get hold of as well. It's all very suspicious.'

'Oh, I can see you lot have been having fun down at the station.'

'We have had some information about his movements; apparently he's recently moved in mysterious ways. Combine that with the fact he's already got form with murder, manslaughter and wholesale destruction of property, and the circumstantial evidence is overwhelming.'

Mervyn was trying to look anywhere but in the direction of Mick's naked bottom. Their latest rendezvous was not in a motorway café. Mick's head was close to Mervyn's, but while Mervyn was sitting in a chair, Mick was leaning across a table with her trousers round her ankles. A large man with a drooping moustache and a spider's web on his cheek was crouching between her buttocks, staring intently at her bum and emitting a low buzzing noise.

'So you got to see Mr Godbotherer himself? Fuck. I'm impressed,' said Mick, not sounding impressed at all.

'Yes,' said Mervyn.'

'Amazing. But then that's you. You are amazing. You are Mervyn fucking Stone.'

'Thanks.'

'What did he say?'

'Not a lot. He was a bit... odd, as you might expect. Unctuous, superior, smug...'

'Sounds like a killer to me. It's always the smug ones.'

'I'm not sure. He seemed to want me to think that he did kill Marcus, or at least his God had a hand in it. I really don't know if he was capable or not. He seemed pretty fanatical.'

'I know the type. They can do pretty strange things.'

'How's your buttock?'

'It's fine.'

'I didn't hurt you, did I?'

'Nah.'

'He's not hurting you either?'

'Yeah he is, but I like pain. I used to draw pictures on my arm with a compass when I was bored at school. How's he doing?'

Mervyn allowed himself a quick glance at what was happening on the other side of the table. A quick glance was all he was prepared to make.

'How are you doing?'

The hairy man gave a cheery wink. 'I've just started on the "S".'

Mervyn turned to Mick, as if translating. 'He's just started on the "S".'

'Brilliant.'

Mick and Mervyn were in a tattoo parlour in Soho. The interior was intimidating, like any tattoo parlour. Pictures of skeletons, snakes, motorbikes and naked women decorated the walls, sometimes individually, sometimes in an exotic combination of two or more. One picture was of a flaming skeleton riding a flaming motorbike out of hell, with a naked woman riding pillion holding a snake.

Mervyn, being well into middle age, immediately wondered how much motorcycle insurance the skeleton would have to pay on his bike. Certainly quite a lot. The premiums must be huge. *He couldn't just take out third party, fire and theft*, Mervyn mused, o*n account of his bike being on fire already. And it won't help the premiums if the naked lady refuses to wear a crash helmet. But if she* did*, she wouldn't be naked, I suppose...*

'That's great. Thanks Judass.'

The tattooist had finished inscribing Mervyn's autograph on Mick's bottom and supplied a mirror for Mick to inspect it.

Mervyn looked at it out of the corner of his eye. Judass had stencilled over Mervyn's original signature in a fetching navy blue.

'Are you sure you want my autograph on your buttock?'

'If I'm not sure, then it's a bit fucking late. Judass just has to put your phone number under it so they know who to call if I get killed in the line of duty.'

'What?'

'Joke.'

A bandage was applied, and Mick pulled up her trousers.

'There. Your name is on my body. Now you own me.'

'Right... So... Shall we go somewhere and talk about the burglary?'

'Not yet. Take your shirt off, Mervyn Stone.'

'You are joking.'

'No.'

'I thought you were joking.'

'1 wasn't.'

Judass pointed a stubby finger to the back of the shop. 'If you can just hang your shirt on the chair and stand next to that wall – that would be great. And pick up that big sword.'

Mervyn slouched miserably to the wall and untucked his shirt. He slowly undid the buttons with the enthusiasm of a 50-year-old stripper trapped in a cheap Soho nightclub at three in the morning. 'I'm not sure about this.'

Mick shrugged. 'This is important. We had a deal. I tell you about the burglary at the Spicer house, you get your top off and hold that sword up.'

Mervyn took his shirt off and shielded his nipples with his left arm, pressing tightly and giving his emerging cleavage a bit too much definition. He picked up the exotic bejewelled sword from where it was leaning against the wall, and held it half-heartedly.

'Okay?'

'Could you look a bit more aggressive?'

'Not really. I've tried "aggressive" in the past and I always look constipated.'

'Okay... Could you give out a cry?'

'Give me ten more minutes and I'll burst into tears.'

Judass picked up a camera and started taking photos, prodding Mervyn into a variety of almost-aggressive poses. Meanwhile, Mick was dipping into a briefcase and pulling out a yellow cardboard file.

'So... the burglary. It happened eight weeks ago...'

Mervyn flicked his eyes across to Judass, who was happily snapping away. 'Are you sure you want to discuss this here?' he asked.

'Judass is very discreet.'

Judass nodded. 'I have to be. You wouldn't believe what the stars say when they're getting Chinese dragons burnt on to their boob.'

'Other than "Ow"?'

'Nice one. I like you, Mervyn.'

'Is that really your name? Judass?'

'It is now.'

'It's an interesting name.'

'Well, it sort of chose me, you know. I got a Judas Priest tattoo, and the twat spelt it wrong. I got Judass Priest, with two "s"s. So to save myself any grief and suchlike ridicule, I changed my name from Bernard Brook to Judass Priest. With one stroke, it went from embarrassing to cool.'

'You're a genius, Judass.'

'Ta. Can you raise the sword a little higher?'

'With my back? Not really.'

Mick had finished rifling through her notes and found the relevant sheet of paper. 'It was reported at six o clock on August the 3rd by a Mrs C. Spicer. Stuff that was stolen: assorted cash and jewellery, two tellies, one ghetto blaster, one DVD player, one laptop, one computer, one ten-inch figurine of the Virgin Mary plus the infant Jesus, one iPod. All the stolen goods have some resale value, electronic stuff that gets fenced every day. The usual British currency which can be exchanged at the Bank of Chavland.'

'All easy to sell on– *apart* from the statuette.'

'You're thinking someone broke into the house just to get the statuette and made it look like a burglary. Or the burglar just happened to know how collectable *Vixens* memorabilia was, realised its value when he broke in, and threw it in with the other stuff.'

'It makes sense, doesn't it?'

'It's more than sense. It's brilliant, Mervyn Stone.' She looked at the notes. 'The laptop and telly were recovered, but the other stuff... not yet.'

'Can I put my arm down now?'

'In a sec.' Judass was still clicking away, furiously dancing around Mervyn's semi-naked form. 'Can you do a stabbing pose with your legs apart? And open your mouth like you're screaming?'

'If I must. Do you think it's likely the statuette might turn up?'

Mick shrugged. 'Bit of problem with that – the Spicers didn't mark their stuff, so it's difficult. I can do some checks, but it's like looking for a needle in a tattoo parlour. Maybe I'll check the police auctions.'

'Also, I think it would be good idea to –'

'Keep your mouth open, Mervyn mate. If you move your mouth you'll blur your face.'

Mervyn obliged, keeping his mouth hanging open. 'A'so, I 'hnk, i' wi' be a gu' iea hoo kek o' rian a' hananka...'

'They're already checking out Brian and Samantha. Believe it or not, they're suspects. Like you.'

'Oh. I huhoh e ar. Ho-hay.'

'Why do you ask?'

'Weeee e' hing a'out...'

'I'm done now Mervyn,' said Judass, packing his camera away. 'You can put your shirt on.'

Mervyn scrabbled to retain his dignity, diving for his shirt and struggling to put it back on. 'Well the thing about Brian is, I saw him enter the Godbotherers building.'

'He's not on their records as a member. I'll check that out.'

'... And Samantha refused to drink the bottles of water on the table. She asked for a different brand of water to be sent in.'

'Yeah, she did, didn't she? The officers in charge of the case noticed that when they heard it on the CD. I wondered about that. You've got an amazing memory, Mervyn Stone.'

Mervyn hesitated. 'It just came to me.' He slipped on his jacket. 'I seriously think we should find that statuette. It just seems important somehow.'

Mick folded her arms and looked even grimmer than usual. 'Yeah, well, I've got a few suspicions about where it went. I'll see if I'm right.'

Mick paid Judass, and Judass handed Mervyn a card with a heart, a sword, a snarling tiger and 'Snakes and Ladettes Tattoo Parlour' on it.

'Thanks,' said Mervyn. 'You will let me know how it turns out?'

Judass grinned, stretching the cobweb on his cheek. 'Well, it's Mick that will have to show you. It will be on her body, you know.'

Mervyn cast a furtive glance at Mick. 'Yes... whereabouts, exactly?'

'I'll show you,' she said. 'You see this dragon?' She suddenly undid her belt and yanked down her trousers again. Mervyn was completely unprepared for that; his eyeballs dived for cover, and peered at the picture from behind the relative safety of half-closed eyelids.

A huge angry dragon crawled across Mick's torso; the front claws extended down her hips, the tail curled upwards until it wrapped around her left breast. Her belly button was disguised as a lizard-like ear on the side of its head. The head itself was on her abdomen, partially obscured by the thin elastic of her knickers, and Mick obligingly yanked it aside to show him the rest. This time, Mervyn closed his eyes completely, but not before he realised what the tattooist had used to represent the dragon's reptilian mouth.

'You'll be down here on the inner thigh, pointing your sword at my dragon's salivating maw.'

CHAPTER THIRTY-FOUR

Mervyn didn't know when the police were going to question Samantha, so he thought he'd get in there first, so to speak. He reasoned he'd probably get more out of her than some grim-faced copper.

He thought long and hard for a plausible reason to call her, but in the event he didn't need to. She phoned him.

'Hi Mervyn, guess who? It's me.'

'Hello Samantha. How funny, I was just thinking of calling you.'

'Really? You were going to call me? How lovely! You were thinking of calling me... and I called *you*! That's pure ESP! Have you tried using Zener cards?'

'No I haven't.'

'Because we really should! Fancy you thinking of calling me! My gosh, that would have been so super if you had! I never get any calls during the day! Except for cold callers. Aren't they annoying? But some of them sound so sad, you just want to buy their bathroom or their insurance to cheer them up, don't you? Or is it just me? So they ring me up, and that's about it... Though sometimes the salon rings up to remind me when my peel is due... Oh yes, and my psychic calls when she senses my aura isn't in balance, and my life coach...'

Apparently, many people phoned Samantha during the day. Mervyn was told about each and every one, until the muscles in his arm cramped and his ear turned red. He would have to stop her soon or his brain would get microwaved into guacamole and start leaking out of his ears.

Mervyn cut through the flow. 'So Samantha, what made you call me?'

'Well it's been on my mind since Marcus... passed over. The guilt. I do feel a lot of guilt about it all. I do feel guilty about Marcus...'

'There's nothing to feel guilty about.'

'Well there is, because... well, because of what I did. Because I think I killed Marcus.'

'You *think* you killed him?'

'Yeah, well, I'm more, sort of, sure I did. I need someone to talk to about it, if you're free. Would that be okay?'

'I'll be right over.'

'Oh gosh, during the day? I never get visitors during the day...'

Her house looked a lot like Mervyn expected it to look; a badly maintained Georgian monster in the unfashionable end of a well-to-do London borough – in this case, Richmond – sandwiched between a laundrette and a Chinese restaurant.

The outside of the house was grim and anonymous, save for a coat-hanger-type thing made of bells, wires and feathers that dangled by the porch, tinkling in rather a forlorn fashion.

He knocked and waited, more out of politeness than any need to be let in because the front door was ajar.

A cat was sitting at the window. Its fat form was shrouded by dusty net curtains, a hairy Alfred Hitchcock glaring at him in silhouette. He tried to stare it out, but the cat either couldn't see him, or wasn't interested in lowering itself to his level. He tapped on the window to get its attention, but the cat didn't want to know. It just kept staring, immobile as a buddha, behind the curtains. Giving up, he stepped back – right into the new-age mobile behind him. It jangled at him angrily and the hooks caught in his hair. He set about trying to free himself, flapping like a panicked seagull in a fishing net.

He was still flapping impotently when Samantha appeared. She wore a baggy T-shirt; reds and blues and greens were scattered across it in a crazy paving style. It was bunched in at the waist by an orange leather belt, clashing with her floaty mauve paisley skirt and large stripy yellow and green socks pulled up over the knee. Her whole body was a battleground of colour, locked in an ugly war for domination.

At first, Mervyn thought she'd done something nasty to her face. Then he realised she'd put make-up on it.

'Oh my gosh, what's happened to you?' She rushed to help him, inspecting his hair. 'You have been in the wars haven't you?'

Mervyn nodded, and his head jingled sadly. With the wires sprouting out of his head, he looked like a dejected *Thunderbirds* puppet.

She started to tenderly unpick him from the evil wire thing, hook by hook. Her face was practically touching his; Mervyn caught a blast of smoky breath and the sickly odour of wet clothes left in the washing machine slightly too long. His eyes self-consciously roved across her face, unable to avoid inspecting every little wrinkle and blemish. He became strangely fascinated by her fine hairy lip which, even bleached, was quite impressive; not a bad piece of fuzz – for a teenager trying to grow a moustache for the first time.

'This is my home-made dream-catcher,' she said, poking her tongue out in concentration and licking her moustache. 'It's not meant to catch writers. But I suppose, when you think about it, writers are dream-weavers aren't they?'

'I suppose that's true.' Mervyn talked through gritted teeth. This was like trying to sustain a conversation with his dentist, trying to juggle discomfort, politeness and the need to please the person inflicting the pain.

'Oh it's definitely true. They're the ones who spin dreams and make them reality.' She poked his nose with her finger, as if he were an adorable schoolboy. 'You're a dreamer, and my dream-catcher caught you. Isn't that funny?'

Mervyn smiled, uncomfortably.

'Come in. My door's always open.'

'Very welcoming.'

'No, sorry, I mean, my door *is* always open. I keep it open so that chi can flow into me.'

'Aren't you worried about burglary?'

'There's a lot of crime about here, but I never get burgled. I protect my space with white light and sea salt.'

When Mervyn went inside, he realised why she never got burgled. The place was a mess; there was nothing inside that would have excited any discerning crack addict who would want to ransack his way to a better neighbourhood.

From the outside, the house could have belonged to anyone, but the inside was distinctively Samantha. The décor was a collision of exotic cultures, fantasies and bottom-drawer philosophies, as confused as Samantha herself. Every piece of market-stall bric-a-brac – if it featured a unicorn, a dragon, a crystal or an erect penis – ended up on Samantha's overladen shelves and windowsills. A full-sized dream-catcher with a Yin and Yang sign hung batlike from the ceiling, and faux-Hindu tapestries were pinned to every wall. The floors were covered with shiny scatter cushions, making movement somewhat difficult. Mervyn had to stretch his legs far apart and place each foot delicately in the tiny areas of available floor space, as though he were picking his way across a muddy field. The unmistakable smell of joss sticks hung round the house, impregnated in the fabrics and wallpapers. Fat coloured candles were littered around the hearth in various stages of decomposition, from full stick to flattened splat. Dominating the fireplace was a huge, jagged sculpture made of pieces of coloured glass. It was shaped a bit like a trident.

'That's impressive.'

'Oh do you like it? I made it myself in my evening class. That's my tree of life. Would you like a tea?'

'Love one.'

'I only have herbal. That okay?'

Ack.

'Lovely.'

'Blackcurrant, raspberry leaf or peppermint?'

'Blackcurrant sounds marvellous.' He dearly wanted builder's tea, but he wasn't going to get it. Not in this house.

Samantha bustled in and gave Mervyn a mug with a smiling bumblebee on the front and 'Happy Daze!!!!' written above the bee's head.

As she clinked about the kitchen brewing her own strange concoction, Mervyn perched uncomfortably on a futon, sipping something that tasted like Ribena mixed with cough drops. Samantha brought in her own drink in a glass mug and sat near him, her eyes scorching his face.

'It's lovely to have visitors. I don't get to see many people since Toby left me...'

'Toby?'

'Yes. He departed. He – well, he crossed the veil and departed to the spirit world...'

'I'm sorry.'

'Oh, it's not too bad. He's very happy. I still talk to him, with the help of Megan and her guide Raging Water. He's about the only one I talk to these days.' She slurped at the greenish-yellow liquid. It could have been peppermint, but it could equally have been heated urine.

'Do you know, I haven't even talked properly to anyone about how I killed poor Marcus? The police don't want to listen to me about the way I killed Marcus. No one wants to talk to me about anything. Hah. Story of my current incarnation... I didn't get a lot of work after *Vixens*, well, not good work, anyway. I did have a couple of lines in an *Inspector Morse*... and I played a nasty yuppie in *EastEnders* for a week and a half. And it didn't seem the same, really. It was fun, you know, working my way up, playing bit parts in the background, gradually being allowed to get lines and put some clothes on...'

Mervyn listened awkwardly, waiting for the monologue to meander back to the subject of how she had killed Marcus.

'But after *Vixens*, well, going back to non-speaking weeny parts didn't really hold a lot of excitement for me. So I gave up the business, travelled a bit, then I opened a restaurant in Soho, jumping on the vegetarian bandwagon.' Her face fell almost comically. 'But I think I must have jumped on it too early, cos it went bust. Took all my telly money with it. Never mind. It was fun, you know? And I got to learn how to make beanburgers. And I'm a qualified reflexologist now.'

'Qualified? I see.' Mervyn's reaction would have been identical if Samantha had just claimed she was a qualified wizard. 'That's interesting.'

'It used to be called "zone therapy", it's all to do with the idea that most parts of your body are connected to the areas on your hands and feet. Manipulate the zones in those areas, and your whole body will feel the benefit. You can cure anything from headaches to infertility.'

The expression on Mervyn's face was a picture, an impressive watercolour showing a landscape of scepticism. Even Samantha noticed.

'Hey, I'll show you.'

'I don't think I'm infertile. And I probably wouldn't want to be cured if I were.'

'No, no. You'll feel the better for it, even if you haven't got any specific aches and pains to speak of. Take off your shoes and socks.'

Mervyn recoiled.

'I'd rather not...'

'Go on. You'll thank me. You'll feel so much better.'

Humour her, for God's sake. You're investigating.

'I'll just take one off, if that's all right...'

'Okay.'

Mervyn shrugged off one of his Chelsea boots and peeled off his sock. The Englishman inside him cringed slightly, but he knew he had reasonable feet – no odd lumps, funny yellow toenails or strange clumps of hair where there shouldn't be.

Samantha patted a spotty bean bag, inviting him to sit. He stretched out his leg and placed his foot between her legs, as though she were a blacksmith shoeing a horse. She pummelled his heel.

'Do you think a shock, or a shared tragedy can bring people closer together?'

'Oh, certainly.'

'I've always seen you as a caring sort of man.'

'Me? Oh no. Hardly.'

'Oh yes. A quiet, caring man. The sort that you don't notice. Well, I noticed you. I was always very fond of you.'

Alarm klaxons sounded in Mervyn's head.

'I was reminded how much I was fond of you when you talked so eloquently about your work during the recording, before Marcus... before I killed him –'

'Yes. Marcus. About killing him...'

'I have talked to his spirit about it, and he does understand. He's a bit cross, naturally...'

'And what else did he have to say...?'

She put her finger to his lips in an irritatingly melodramatic fashion. 'Plenty. But he's crossed over now. He's joined Toby. They're both happy. We won't help his spirit's passing by dwelling on the circumstances of his earthly demise.'

'Oh. Right, of course. Fair enough.'

'The thing is Mervy...' She twiddled her fingers and looked up at him. She looked like she was going to confess to not doing her homework. 'I believe in the life force, and I can only discuss the departed when engaged in a ritual of spiritual sharing.'

'You mean... Like drinking tea?'

'Not really, no.' To Mervyn's considerable surprise, she pushed him back on the bean bag, unzipping his trousers and pulling his penis out in one smooth motion. 'I'm quite a lonely spirit.' She kneaded it between her thumb and forefinger, and then started tugging at it urgently, like a bird trying to get a worm out of the ground. The penis was just as surprised as its owner, but it was no slouch; it was already starting to realise what was going on and was flexing its muscles ready for action. 'Really lonely.' She sat on him, and was already trying to insert him into her, one hand pulling the gusset of her knickers to the side, the other still squeezing him with an intensity that bordered on frenzy. It was all happening a bit quickly for Mervyn's taste, like a desperate first-time teenage fumble.

'No one treats me seriously, you see. They see some mad old mare who was quite kooky and endearing when she was young and attractive, but kooky and endearing doesn't last Merv... In a couple of years, I'll be a bonkers old trout, and then who's going to look after me?'

He realised that Samantha was the kind of actress – the kind of *woman* – who could only be honest when she was being physical; the ones who assumed conversation was artifice (usually they were the ones treated disgracefully by silver-tongued thespians who lied to them each and every day) and who only associated the carnal act with the baring of the soul.

She pulled her shirt over her head – no bra. Her boobs were brown and shapeless; age had deflated them, and they dangled above him like giant tea bags. Builder's tea bags, not herbal tea bags, at least.

His body was pressed low, sliding down the beanbag until only his head was left on it, embedded deep in its folds until he could barely hear. *If I get pushed any deeper in this thing, I'll suffocate, and in a million years time I'll be discovered as a tie-dyed fossil.*

He rocked his shoulders, and used the momentum until his body dispersed the polystyrene nuggets inside the beanbag and his head was practically flat on the floor.

He'd put his mug and his untouched tea on the carpet, and now he was nose-to-nose with it, the bumblebee filling his vision, leering at him, its cheery bee face distorted into that of an evil mutant insect.

Then he realised he was in danger of losing his focus. His penis was starting to soften and dwindle; it wasn't penetrating her like some tree-trunk-sized battering ram, it was nuzzling her crotch like a senile old dog. *If it deflates, there are two things that could happen*, Mervyn thought grimly. *Either (a) She'll blub about being old and ugly, she'll expect you to put your arm around her and comfort her and tell her she's a wonderful person for the next three hours, and she'll tell me how she 'killed' Marcus...*

Or (b) She'll just go into some masochistic frenzy about being old and ugly, accuse you of taking advantage of her like everyone else does (conveniently forgetting that she initiated this), probably throw a few things, and you'll end up pushed out of the front door with your cock still hanging out of your trousers. Bad thing. Won't learn anything that way, except the ambient temperature of the street outside.

He couldn't take the risk of (b) happening. Samantha was going to notice sooner or later. She could ring Megan and Raging Water, and they could all hold hands and get in touch with his dead penis and bring it back to the world of the living. He had to keep things going. He had to do something.

So he did a bad thing. He thought of Cheryl.

He filled his mind with memories of her tongue probing his mouth, and the soft caramel smell of her hair as she nuzzled his neck. Of making love in Hyde Park behind a bush. Of her slight gasp as he penetrated her in the darkened production office of *Vixens*.

Oh forgive me, Cheryl. Just understand what I'm doing here. I'm doing it for you.

Instantly, his penis woke from its extended nap, sprang upright, and slid smoothly inside Samantha like a well-oiled piston.

Samantha grabbed his shoulders and let the air out of her lungs very slowly, forcing it out between clenched teeth and making a hissing sound like a steam train arriving at a station. She threw her head back, shaking her hair out so it sashayed along her back, then she slumped forward so the hair pooled around her shoulders and almost covered her face. She opened her eyes, and fixed Mervyn with a fractured grin. The effect was part crazed seductress, part rabid Afghan hound. The rabid Afghan hound aspect was enhanced when she started making low growls in her throat, gnashing her teeth and snapping at the air. Then, eyes fixed like lasers on Mervyn, she started pushing up and down very slowly, like a fairground ride just starting to move.

'So,' he gasped, 'Marcus... he was a bit annoyed you killed him?'

'Oh... oh... oh, he was a little miffed, but he understood.'

'Oh... good.'

'If only he could have seen what I could see. Dark forces. Negative karma. It was everywhere in the room. Couldn't you feel it? It was in the water.'

'Was that why you asked for a different bottle?'

'Yes, of course I... Oh yeah... Of course I did. I couldn't have... uh, I couldn't have drunk any of the water on the table. The water was bad.'

'Bad?'

'Oh... Yes. Oh... Oh yes...'

There was something on his foot. Something furry and quivering. Tickling. Claws grazed his heel. Obviously Samantha's cat fancied himself as a bit of a reflexology expert too. *Get off*, he pleaded in his head. *Get off you hairy bastard.*

The cat was trying an experimental nibble of one of his toes. Right. That's enough.

He twitched his leg, catapulting the animal... somewhere. In amid Samantha's moans, he heard a distant crash and a squeak of indignation.

'What do you mean, the water was bad?'

'I mean, oh, oh, oh! I mean it was ah... Estuary English water. They say it's from a tributary of the River Severn, but I read on the internet that it's from a spring in Tanzania, where people are dying for want of clean water. It's completely unethical. I had them get me some other water that was ethically sourced to escape the bad karma... I do so hate to make a fuss, but when it comes to something like that I have to make myself... ah... oh... ah... heard! Oh! Oh! OH! AH-HURRGGGHHHHHH!'

She started hooting and hollering, and ground her hips into Mervyn's pelvis as she came, her eyes scrunched into slits and her hair plastered with sweat. She tightened around his penis, and despite the discomfort and his preoccupied brain buzzing with this new development, he felt himself empty into her.

She fell off him, and lay gasping on a futon.

'I should have told him about the bad karma,' she said breathlessly. 'But I didn't. If only I'd shared my knowledge of the unseen energies...'

'So the fact you didn't...?'

'Meant I killed him. I'm so sorry about it all. But Marcus forgave me. He was so lovely to me...'

'Oh, good.' Mervyn made the fatal mistake of sounding disappointed right after sex.

She gasped. 'You did enjoy that? Our spiritual sharing?'

'Oh yes. Lovely,' said Mervyn, smiling hastily.

'You did, didn't you?' her eyes widened and her bottom lip trembled like a toddler.

'Oh definitely,' Mervyn tried to sound enthusiastic.

'You look like your karma's slipped.'

'Well... Your cat was a bit of a distraction.'

'What, Toby? Surely not! He's harmless!' She rushed to the window, and pulled out the cat. He was rigid as a board, his face frozen in bug-eyed puzzlement, his paws stretching in mute surrender.

She waggled the stuffed creature in his face. 'Say hello to Toby! Hello. Toby!' she growled. Then she moved her voice up an octave. 'Hello Mervyn!' she squeaked back.

Mervyn remembered a time many years ago when he was invited into his girlfriend's bedroom. Instead of, as he expected, a fumble on the quilt, she introduced him to each and every one of her dozens of cuddly toys. This was not like that. This was a hundred times freakier.

Samantha tickled Toby under the chin. Toby was unmoved by the show of love. 'Awww! I was very sad when he passed through the ethereal veil, but he does visit me. I still leave food down and he always eats it...'

Wait a minute. If that's Toby – then what was nibbling at my...

Impaled on the tree of life, where he'd propelled it with his foot, was the biggest, nastiest, hairiest rat Mervyn had ever seen.

Mervyn staggered from her flat, shuddering with the memory. Not the memory involving the rat. The other memory. The sadness of Samantha as she bore down on his helpless form unnerved him.

Well that was frustrating, and an utter waste of time.

And it didn't help the investigation either.

CHAPTER THIRTY-FIVE

Mervyn had experienced a lot of strange things that week, but even he, now battle-hardened against the unexpected, was utterly unprepared for the phone call from Robert Mulberry.

'We're going to re-record "The Burning Time" commentary.'

'What?'

'We're doing it at BBC TV Centre, the day after tomorrow. Can you make it?'

'You're not serious. How the hell did you get permission to do *another* DVD commentary, after all the protests? Not to mention the *murder*? Have your bosses gone completely mad?'

'I pitched it as a tribute to Marcus Spicer. The BBC is scared of protests, but they're equally determined not to look like they give into pressure groups. "The Burning Time" DVD is coming out, whether the Godbotherers like it or not.'

'The timing is in shockingly bad taste. For goodness' sake, couldn't you have waited a couple of months?'

'It's in the schedules. It's been announced.'

'I'm not doing it Robert. Absolutely not.'

'It's going to be very special. You as his friend, colleague and script editor should really be there. We're going to have Marcus's widow there, too, to share her memories of Marcus and how he wrote "The Burning Time".'

Cheryl?

'All right, Robert. You win. I'll be there.'

Once again, Mervyn emerged from the tube and crossed the road to TV Centre. He'd been in and out of the building more times that month than he had in the past decade.

This time, the protest outside was bigger, noisier and more television-friendly. A huge easy-to-read banner had been unfurled adorned with the words 'JUDGEMENT DAY IS AT HAND'. Some of the more attractive female protesters had dressed up in sexually provocative *Vixens* costumes (complete with added horns and forked tails) and hung 'This Is Against God' signs around their necks; a breathtaking example of Cake-Having-And-Eating that could nestle comfortably in the pages of any national newspaper willing to evoke moral outrage while still featuring pictures of near-naked women. Not surprisingly, the photographers were snapping away at them with gusto.

The Godbotherers were obviously energised by the press coverage. This time it wasn't just the BBC covering what was happening on its own doorstep. Cameras from every major television network were there. At the centre of it, basking in the limelight, was Lewis Bream. He was in his most tightly pressed, cardboard-looking suit, and his smile was so fixed and broad it looked like he'd bought it from a joke shop. He was talking to two journalists. He saw Mervyn approaching, and gave a cheery wave.

'Good day, Mr Stone. This gentleman is from the *Evening Standard* and this lady is from *The Star*. Would you like to help them with their articles? They're interested in eyewitness accounts of Mr Spicer's demise.'

'You were there?' said one. 'You were in the room when Marcus Spicer died?'

'How did it happen?'

'Was it like *The Omen*? Did he claw at his neck or scream like he'd swallowed holy water?'

They looked at him expectantly, like cartoon vultures holding knives and forks and tying on their napkins. Lewis hovered by them, waiting.

'I believe one of the commandments is "Thou shalt not bear false witness",' said Mervyn darkly. 'In other words, "No comment".'

The reporters realised they weren't going to get anything from Mervyn, and drifted away to get a few quotes from a near-naked dominatrix screaming about sin.

'Quite a turn-out,' Mervyn shouted at Lewis over the din.

'Our flock grows,' said Lewis, surveying his empire. 'With every passing day the miracle brings more disciples to our cause.'

'You've managed to get rid of all the old disciples with the knitted hats and the cardigans. Are they back at HQ making miracle biscuits?'

Lewis simply smiled. 'Are you sure you wouldn't like to join us? Joy will be in heaven over one sinner that repenteth.' He handed Mervyn a flyer. It had lists of chants and protests on it, complete with lyrics. Mervyn looked at it with ironic approval.

'You've even organised the hecklers. Good to see you're all shouting from the same hymn sheet.'

'We're about to pray. Would you like us to pray for you?'

This unnerved Mervyn. 'No thanks.'

'Are you certain? This may be your last opportunity for redemption.'

'What do you mean by that.'

'Well you may have noticed... Sinners who enter this temple don't come out of its doors alive.'

Mervyn smiled coldly. 'This is the BBC, Lewis. The reason sinners don't come of those doors alive is because they leave from the back in chauffeur-driven cars.'

As if his words were able to conjure up a chauffeur-driven car, one hove into view, but instead of scooting into the side entrance, it pulled to a halt outside the front.

It was very big and very shiny. The tinted windows only hinted at the occupants within. The number plate read 'GOD L35S'.

There was a roar from the crowd; they instinctively knew who was in the car, and they were right.

Aiden emerged from the driver's side, ran around to the back and opened the boot. He pulled out a wheelchair and unfolded it in one smooth motion. Then he reached into the back seat and scooped up Cheryl's frail form, depositing her in the chair. There was a low hiss from the crowd.

Cheryl looked beautiful; dignified in a pale grey shirt and white jumper. A simple patterned skirt fanned across her knees. Mervyn wondered if the surges of passion he felt for her were nostalgia for who she used to be, or a masculine reaction to her obvious vulnerability.

The crowd continued to hiss, slowly metamorphosing into a low 'boo'. Cheryl didn't do anything. She didn't acknowledge the crowd or activate her wheelchair. She did nothing.

Joanna left the limo from the back and sauntered around the boot, watching everything dispassionately. Watching Cheryl's baptism of fire.

How could she be so callous?

Aiden pushed Cheryl's chair slowly to the BBC entrance, walking with silent and sombre dignity. Mervyn wondered why Cheryl didn't just push one of her levers and power into the building under her own 'steam'... and then he heard the catcalls.

That's the problem with demonstrations, he thought with horrified delight. No matter how well-drilled, no matter how Lewis organised his troops, there were always one or two who went too far. The murmurings were low and menacing at first, incoherent; but when Cheryl didn't acknowledge their presence, they were goaded into shouting.

'You're next, woman.'

'God came for the sodomites, he came for the Egyptians, he came for your husband and he'll be coming for you.'

'Anybody want a second-hand wheelchair? Hardly used.'

'You've not got long to go, blasphemer. Thou shalt not suffer a witch to live.'

And the cameras recorded it all.

Mervyn could see Lewis's face. It was the same, queasy panicked expression he wore when he had been interviewed on the BBC news channel. It was the expression of a man who knew the situation was getting away from him. He'd over-reached himself. Mervyn could also see the grim satisfaction on Joanna's face. She knew this was going to happen.

The fact that Cheryl was pushed bodily into the BBC made her look even more frail and vulnerable than she was already; she seemed the ultimate victim, a defenceless woman set upon by the mob. As graceful and innocent as the Madonna herself. It wasn't just the religious who knew the power of imagery.

Cheryl and Aiden vanished inside the BBC, still moving slowly and deliberately on their short journey to the reception desk. Once they had disappeared behind the glass, the cameras and reporters immediately turned their fickle attention back to Lewis, but this time the questions were along the lines of 'Do you defend the comments of your supporters?' and 'Is it Christian for a sick woman to be taunted in public?'

Lewis was getting crucified by the press again, thought Mervyn with some satisfaction. *He'll need another miracle to get out of this one.*

Joanna walked briskly into the building after Cheryl and Aiden. There was another low hiss from the crowd, and they surged forward; but now the cameras were all pointing away, Joanna didn't feel any need to look dignified and meek like Cheryl. She felt no need to turn the other cheek. One Godbotherer (dressed in a plastic crown of thorns and a T-shirt with 'Suffer the Vixens' written on it) leaned over a barrier as if to grab her, and she turned on him, a stubby gunlike device suddenly in her fist. 'Touch me and that's assault,' she snarled. 'This taser's got your name on it – let's see how close to heaven you can jump.' The Godbotherer dropped his hands, and Joanna walked inside. The door swallowed her up, then it spat out Aiden, emerging to park the car.

Mervyn waited until the crowd lost its hysterical edginess, and then followed the others in.

CHAPTER THIRTY-SIX

Cheryl was waiting inside, parked near the reception desk. When she saw him she turned her head away.

Joanna Paine was hovering behind her chair, arms tightly knotted into her chest. She didn't notice Cheryl's hostility to Mervyn, because she was pretty angry herself.

'Do we have to hang around in full view of those freaks?' she said, jerking a finger at the crowd outside. 'Where's Robert? Or Trevor?'

A rock clattered against the glass, prompting a pushback from the police and a roar of protest from the crowd.

'It seems they found someone without sin to cast the first stone for them,' quipped Mervyn.

'Shut up Mervyn,' said Joanna, giving him an incendiary glance. She looked at her watch. 'This is intolerable,' she snapped. 'If they're not down in two minutes then I'm hailing a taxi and going.'

'You didn't have to come,' said Cheryl.

'I'm here for Marcus. I look after his interests whether he's here with us... or not. Unless you'd like to dispense with my services. You do have the right...'

Cheryl and Joanna glared at each other, a hostile silence growing between them. Mervyn threw himself in its path like a reckless bodyguard. 'Well we all know where we're going. We don't really need anyone to collect us. Has anyone got a pass who can sign us in?'

'I *had* a BBC pass,' scowled Joanna. 'I present *Booking the Trend*, the Radio 4 series about the publishing industry. But I lost it and didn't get a replacement.'

'I don't think you need the pass,' said Mervyn. 'They can look you up on the computer and make you a temporary one.'

Joanna went off to the reception desk, leaving Cheryl and Mervyn alone. Mervyn sat down. He smiled feebly and cleared his throat.

'Cheryl about the other day, I hope you don't think –'

'I don't want to talk to you.'

'Okay.' He decided to let it drop.

But he couldn't.

'Because I didn't want to –'

'Stop. Really.'

'I mean I didn't mean to create an awkward situation.'

'You mean like this one?'

Mervyn shut up.

Oh well, he thought. *This is getting embarrassing.*

There was a shrieking noise from outside the building, which Mervyn assumed was a mad protester shouting 'Murder! Murder! Murder!' Then the sound joined them inside the BBC and he could hear it was someone shouting 'Mervyn! Mervyn! Mervyn!'

Samantha Carbury had arrived. She clattered towards him, knees pinned together by a tiny skirt, big noisy shoes clonking on the tiled floor. She fell on to him, hugging him and sitting on his knee.

Oh, he thought. *This is getting really embarrassing now.*

The green room was much busier than before, but much quieter. The atmosphere was distinctly muted.

Cheryl's wheelchair was surrounded by sympathy. She was flanked by Joanna Paine, Brian Crowbridge and Aiden the minder. Robert was also there, apologising for Trevor's failure to collect them. He had no idea what had become of him.

Samantha was alone, on the other side of the room, a lost little figure. Cheryl had lost her husband, and needed to be looked after; Samantha never had anyone to begin with, so it went without saying she was supposed to take care of herself.

Well, Samantha was not quite alone. At least she had Mervyn.

Mervyn couldn't get rid of her; every time he entered the room he could see her in his peripheral vision, delivering a cracked, longing gaze. Every time he stayed still for a moment, standing or sitting, she was magically there, close by him, brushing imaginary lint off his jacket, draping her hand across his thigh, laying her head on his shoulder.

'I'm so sorry about Marcus, Cheryl.' Brian shook his head sympathetically and immersed his head in his hands. 'But I'm sure wherever he is now, he's at peace.'

'He's not anywhere now, Brian,' Cheryl snapped. 'He's dead. There's no afterlife, there's no heaven, hell, Elysian Fields or Nirvana. Whatever's left of him is lying on a table, then he'll get put into an expensive box, the expensive box will then be buried, and they will both be eaten by insects, worms and maggots.'

'Oh Cheryl!' gasped Samantha, clutching Mervyn's arm. 'How horrible to say that. The body may pass away, but I can tell you, because I know it, his spirit is definitely still here, very near to us.'

Robert was standing in the doorway, arms folded, watching the scene play out. Was it Mervyn's imagination, or did Robert's mouth twitch in amusement when Samantha said that?

Samantha was still gripping Mervyn fiercely; hard enough to leave a bruise. She was obviously expecting some sort of comfort so Mervyn patted her arm awkwardly. 'There, there.' Joanna watched his feeble efforts at reassuring Samantha with wry amusement.

Robert cleared his throat, and Mervyn sprang to his feet with obvious relief.

'Hi everyone. We'll be ready for you in five minutes.'

Mervyn followed Robert into the recording suite. It was empty save for the two of them, so Mervyn took the opportunity to find out what the hell was going on.

'I can't believe you're doing this. I can't believe you dragged Cheryl into this. She's a grieving widow. We haven't even buried Marcus yet.'

'I have my reasons,' said Robert, and his eyes flicked across to Joanna Paine, who he could see through the door. Marcus's ex-agent was flicking through a magazine with frank uninterest. 'I *know* she's the grieving widow. That's why I brought her here.'

'What do you mean by that?'

Robert moved Mervyn over to a corner. 'I mean, there's more to this commentary than meets the eye. I'll let you into a little secret; you're not the only detective around here, Mervyn.'

He walked off to the console to twiddle some knobs, leaving Mervyn to pick up his jaw from the floor. 'What do you mean by that?'

'You know what we were talking about the last time we were here? About Samantha and the bottles of water?'

'Yes.'

'Well I've discovered evidence. I know Samantha Carbury killed Marcus.'

'What?'

'And, furthermore, I know how she did it, too.'

CHAPTER THIRTY-SEVEN

'I don't believe you.'

'Oh yeah, she did it, all right.'

'Well... How?'

'Ah-ah-ah, Mervyn, that would be telling! You're not the detective this time. I'm going to unmask her today in front of everyone.'

'You're mad.'

Robert's eyes narrowed as he demonstrated one of his trademark flashes of anger. 'And you're jealous. Go and sit down. I'll call you all through in a minute.'

Mervyn turned to go.

'Hey, Mervyn,' said Robert.

Mervyn turned.

'Here you go. I made you a copy.'

Robert threw a CD over to him. 'COMMENTARY' was written untidily on the case.

'Not that it matters any more, because I've solved the case, but I said I'd give you your "evidence". I hope that puts you in the picture.' Robert winked and gave a wicked grin. 'I'm sure you'll end up with the same deduction as me... Eventually.'

Mervyn realised he wasn't going to get anything out of Robert, so he walked back into the green room, fidgeting nervously with the case as he slipped it into his pocket. He was filled with a premonition that something unpleasant was going to happen. He wandered over to the refreshments table and picked up a bottle of water.

Then he realised what he was doing, thought better of it and put it back. He went to the far corner of the room to sit. Samantha immediately moved to be near him.

'You're the third person to do that, pick up a bottle of water and put it down,' said Joanna, without looking up from her magazine.

The bottles of water were arranged exactly as they had been that fateful day. Everyone was casting nervous glances at them. No one was drinking.

'Oh, for God's sake,' snapped Joanna. She got up, picked up a bottle, broke the seal...

click-click-click-click

... and took a swig. She slammed the bottle down, half empty, and stomped off to the recording suite.

Everyone followed her back. Cheryl, Samantha, Brian and Mervyn sat at the desk with their headphones. Samantha sat uncomfortably close to Mervyn. Aiden and Joanna glowered through the glass, both with arms crossed, expressions fixed, like stone lions guarding the gates to a stately home. Aiden had his eyes fixed on Cheryl. Obviously, his job had transferred from guarding Marcus's body to looking after Cheryl's.

Robert entered, perched on the desk, and pulled his most solemn face. 'Now I don't need to point out that this is going to be a somewhat sadder occasion than last time.' Everyone nodded thoughtfully. Brian reached across and patted Cheryl's knee. Samantha hugged Mervyn's shoulder.

Robert abruptly changed tack, trying to inject some life into the room. '... But I don't think Marcus would have wanted us to stop having fun, so... have fun! Remember, don't repeat yourselves, don't get ahead of yourselves, don't just describe what you're seeing, and keep it light, just like Marcus did.'

'And don't go quiet, like Marcus,' said Mervyn.

Everyone looked at him. He wondered why. He also wondered why the room had got so cold. Then he realised.

'Oh God, I didn't mean that. I mean during the *commentary*... He went quiet during the commentary. During the part of the commentary before he...'

'I'm just going to start the tape,' Robert said hurriedly, and he disappeared into the studio.

Mervyn avoided looking at Cheryl. Brian avoided looking at Mervyn, for some reason. Cheryl didn't look anyone in the eye. Samantha stared at Mervyn, waiting for the sympathetic smile that Mervyn was determined not to give.

'Do you want me to introduce the episode at the start again?' said Mervyn nervously.

'No, Mervyn,' Robert crackled over the headphones. 'We've got Richard Dawkins to record a special intro telling the listener how important it is.'

Everyone looked relieved, but no one looked more relieved than Mervyn.

'Aww, that's a shame,' said Samantha, 'you have such a lovely voice, darling.'

Mervyn would have taken issue with that observation, which was about as wrong as it could get; he knew his voice was nasal and fringed with hopelessness, like a man apologising for still having a head cold three weeks after catching it. But he was far too alarmed by the 'darling'.

Mervyn knew how actresses said 'darling', and Samantha had not said it like that. She said it how ordinary people said 'darling'. They'd had sex, and as far as Samantha was concerned, they were now a couple. Mervyn hated himself for it, but he was really starting to resent Samantha.

The credits rolled once again, and once again, they were treated to the same bright jazzy clips; all the loudest and most expensive bits of the series glued together with music.

Once again, Samantha said: 'Gosh, is that woman running from the explosion really me?'

'Yes,' snapped Mervyn.

'Well Marcus was very fond of this episode...' Cheryl spoke suddenly, in a clear authoritative voice. 'But fond of it like he was fond of the runt of a litter, or an injured bird. He saw it as his early work. He always looked back on it and thought it a bit clumsy...'

Mervyn bristled.

'Ooh look, there's me, looking young,' said Brian, brightly.

Cheryl carried on, ignoring him, speaking like a bored lecturer. 'As you can see from the objects on the table, the statuette of the Virgin Mary...'

Brian chipped in. 'Didn't Marcus call you his "little Mary"? When I went to the AA meetings with him, he always said how his "little Mary" was so supportive.'

Cheryl shrugged. 'I once had a blue headscarf, and he thought I looked like Mary. That was Marcus for you. Always into his religious imagery, as you can see here. But at this early stage of his writing, the imagery is thrown in quite crudely. I think by the time he got on to writing his books his work had become a lot more mature...'

Brian didn't speak much after that. He didn't want to interrupt her. Samantha stayed silent too, save for an occasional 'Oh', or 'That's very interesting, Cheryl'.

Cheryl spoke largely uninterrupted for 20 minutes, and every time she opened her mouth she pulled the script apart in new and clinical ways. Moreover, she was right. About every detail. She correctly pinpointed everything that was rubbish about 'The Burning Time'.

And Mervyn could not defend it; he couldn't shout down a freshly-minted widow. He couldn't say anything.

He was in hell, if such a thing existed.

They stopped for a break, and Brian disappeared into the BBC to get refreshments. Mervyn instinctively guessed he was going to buy water from the café, because he was never going to touch the bottles on the table. Not in a million years.

Samantha hung back, looking at Mervyn imploringly. 'Are you coming, Mervy?' Once again she was the sixth-form girl pleading for her dishy teacher to come and eat lunch at her table.

'No, I'll think I'll stay here, thank you.'

With one last anguished glance, Samantha disappeared.

Joanna grabbed hold of the handles of Cheryl's wheelchair and spun her towards the door.

'Come on,' she said. 'I'll take you to the bathroom.'

Aiden interposed himself between Joanna and the wheelchair. 'I'll do that, Miss Paine. My job, I believe.'

'I think your job stops at the door of the ladies, Aiden sweetheart.'

Aiden glared at her. He looked like he was about to take a gun out of his jacket and shoot her stone dead.

Cheryl grabbed her wheels and propelled herself out of their grasp. 'I'm quite capable of going for a piss on my own, thank you very much.' And off she trundled.

'Bitch,' muttered Joanna under her breath, and stomped out. There was obviously some tension there. *Did Cheryl say Joanna had had an affair with Marcus? Or did I imagine that?* thought Mervyn.

Aiden stayed, moodily picking at the bowl of chocolates.

Before Mervyn could talk to Robert, he dodged past him and out of the door. Mervyn poked his head into the corridor. 'Robert, wait!'

But Robert was already running down the corridor.

'Can't stop Mervyn,' he shouted. 'The game's afoot!'

CHAPTER THIRTY-NINE

There was a self-service restaurant on the second floor, smaller and cosier than the white-walled BBC canteen. Mervyn decided to make the journey and pick up a baguette. He kept a watchful eye out in case he accidentally bumped into Samantha, but thankfully she must have gone to the canteen.

Sitting on a metal chair and munching on a cheese ploughman's, he stared at the television fixed to the restaurant wall. It was on News 24, and Mervyn couldn't help letting his eyes gravitate towards the screen. The BBC was once again covering the demonstration at its gates. The sound was on, and an on-the-spot reporter (who must have walked all of 50 yards from his desk to get on the spot) was talking into the barrel of the camera.

'... Somewhat good-natured, but there is an undercurrent here. After Marcus Spicer's unusual death last week, there's almost an expectation that something is going to happen, some divine intervention...'

Mervyn knew what he meant. Ever since Robert had told him he was playing detective and declared Samantha the murderer, he had a sick feeling that something nasty was waiting just around the corner.

The camera cut to the newsreader in the studio. This time it was a grey-haired man who looked very serious.

'And is Lewis Bream encouraging this expectation?'

'Oh certainly. He's been working the crowd all morning. Leading the chants, reading from the Bible...' The reporter craned his neck round 'But after the crowd turned ugly against Marcus Spicer's widow, he made himself scarce. He seems to have disappeared...'

Brian entered the restaurant and claimed a jacket potato for himself – as well as a bottle of water, of course. Mervyn waited until he ambled from the till and then waved.

Brian walked up to Mervyn's table, his eyes fixed on the television. 'There they go again,' he sighed. 'Those Godbotherers, eh? At it again. They do go on, don't they?'

Mervyn smiled.

The television cut to a sea of protesters, a melange of angry people with sandwich boards and semi-naked women.

'I don't know how they've got the nerve, shouting and screaming like that. It's hardly Christian is it? It's hardly turn-the-other-cheek stuff, is it?'

There was another close-up of a pretty young Godbotherer in stilettos, fishnets and a corset, with a jerry-built placard saying: 'I am a Vix-Sin from the (spiritual) Void'.

'I don't know about that... If she turns around, we'll see her other cheeks.'

'Be serious, Mervyn.'

'I am being serious.'

'It's hardly right is it? Dressing like that?'

'Well you can bring it up the next time you speak to Lewis Bream.'

Brian flinched. 'What do you mean?'

'Nothing.'

'No... You meant something. I want to know what you mean.'

'I know about your little secret, Brian.'

'What are you talking about?' Brian's eye started to twitch again.

Gotcha.

'I saw you entering a certain building in Berwick Street.'

Brian's fried-egg eyes sizzled in surprise. 'You saw?'

'When did you join the Godbotherers?'

'What? I wouldn't have anything to do with that lot!'

'But... you are a Christian.'

'What a thing to say!' growled Brian, suddenly angry. 'Are you the kind of person who thinks everyone in a hijab is a terrorist? I don't count the Godbotherers as Christian. My God is a God of love, of grace. Not a homophobic hate-monger who smites anyone who disagrees with him...'

'I'm very sorry I assumed you were a Godbotherer, but it wasn't just because you were a Christian. I saw you enter the Godbotherers' building.'

Brian's expression crumpled in puzzlement. He thought for a while and then his expression cleared as he realised. 'Oh, I wasn't going to see them! I was going to *Dorothy*, on the second floor. The gay magazine. Well, I thought I'd "Put my house in order," so to speak. I thought they might want to print my story of failure and redemption in their magazine. I wanted to tell my story without having to garnish it with some tacky tabloid sensationalist froth. And they're very interested. It looks like they're going to publish it in the new-year edition.'

'Well, congratulations.'

'Thanks.'

Mervyn slapped Brian warmly on the back, toasted him with his bottle of apple juice and looked very pleased.

But it was just pretend. Brian was lying. If what Lewis Bream had said was true then the magazine had folded. There was going to be no edition in the new year.

Why was Brian lying to him?

Mervyn reached in his pocket (his fingers brushed the CD he'd been given by Robert) and found his phone. He had forgotten to switch it back on, and as soon as he did so, it sprang into life and rumbled across the table. He'd got a message.

Mervyn listened. It was Robert.

'Hello Detective Stone,' he said, his voice small and echoey, like he was sitting in a giant bucket. 'Robert here. Yes, just thought I'd call you and tell you everything's under control. You don't have to get your magnifying glass out for Cheryl, I've sorted everything for her. I'm just going to push –'

There was a terrific scream, and a split second later an unearthly voice came on the line. 'Sorry your call has been disconnected. Please try again later. Sorry...'

Mervyn looked at his phone, then at Brian. 'Something's happened to Robert.'

'Like what?'

'I don't know. It sounded serious.'

'Well... where is he?'

'I don't know.' Mervyn redialled and listened. 'I'm just getting the answering service.'

'Shall we go back to the recording suite? He might be there.'

'It didn't sound like he was in the recording suite. It sounded echoey. Like he was in a stairwell, or...'

'Or what?'

'Let's get back. I've got a suspicion...'

CHAPTER FORTY

Robert was in the men's toilets near the recording suite. He was lying on the floor. Quite dead.

He was stretched out, palms upraised, like a man holding up an invisible door that had fallen on top of him. His phone was lying near him, a black smudge of molten plastic.

Brian stared in disbelief, leaning over the petrified figure. 'My... my God... My sweet Lord... Look at his hands.'

Mervyn looked at what was on Robert's hands. It was difficult to miss them.

Brian knelt down to look closer. 'Do you know what they look like?'

'Oh yes.'

'They look like, well they do...'

'I'm way ahead of you.'

'They look like *stigmata*...'

Mervyn had to agree. There were two circular red marks in the centre of Robert's palms. Angry little dots. Dead centre. *Exactly where nails penetrated the palms of a certain religious figure,* Mervyn thought.

'Jesus Christ,' muttered Brian.

Exactly.

Brian straightened up and joined Mervyn, as though if they both looked at Robert's body from the same angle it might make some kind of sense.

'We'd better do something,' said Mervyn hollowly. 'Raise the alarm, get the authorities, just... do something.'

'Yes,' said Brian, dazed. His head was convulsing. His left eyelid was fluttering like a wounded insect.

Neither of them seemed able to move their legs.

Brian finally spoke. 'Well... the business with the water bottles might have been a clever trick... But this...'

'... This is something else,' Mervyn finished Brian's sentence for him.

'Indeed. I think the Godbotherers are going to make a meal out of this.'

'*A meal?* It's going to make the incident with the loaves and fishes look like an open sandwich.'

'Absolutely, Merv. This is bad. It's difficult to see how it could be worse.'

'Can you smell something?' said Mervyn suddenly. 'Like cooking, or a barbecue, or...'

Robert's body erupted in flames.

CHAPTER FORTY-ONE

Brian screamed in pure unvarnished terror and his body crumpled to the floor, cowering by the sink.

Robert's shiny bald head was engulfed in fire and became shrivelled and blackened like a spent match. His torso was a fountain of flame that leapt angrily into the air, as if the devil was manifesting right in front of them, surging towards them with hot clawlike fingers, tickling the hand-dryers and igniting the paper towels inside the dispenser.

Brian didn't seem to have any intention of moving. He looked paralysed. The flames weren't near enough to do them harm, but the smoke was filling the toilets, making the air smudgy. Mervyn looped his arms around Brian's waist and dragged him to the door. He pulled Brian through it (not without difficulty, because the door opened inwards, and Brian wasn't helping at all) and deposited him on the floor. Then he ran along the corridor, found a fire alarm and smashed the tiny window pane in the front.

Nothing happened.

Mervyn's brain gibbered. *More bad luck? Or does God not want me to raise the alarm? Does he want the entire BBC to burn to the ground? Is this his comeback tour? Sodom, Gomorrah, Shepherd's Bush?*

A security guard appeared.

'What's happened?'

'There's a fire,' said Mervyn. *And a murder too, but one thing at a time...* 'The fire alarm won't work.'

The security officer punched another one and alarms blared out.

'You have to break two,' he yelled. 'Nothing happens if you just do one. It's designed to stop troublemakers and accidents.'

'Have you told anyone about this?' Mervyn screamed.

'No.'

'Well I think you bloody well should!'

The security officer gave Mervyn a look, as if to say *Don't be a troublemaker.* 'Where's the fire?'

'In there.'

The security officer ran into the toilet, and ran out against almost instantly, clutching the wall for support. 'Jesus!' he shouted. 'Did you do that?'

'We just found him like that. Well not like that. He was dead, but he wasn't on fire.'

'He was just lying there on the floor!' shouted Brian, both eyes twitching. He was screaming himself hoarse above the noise of the alarm, but he gave the impression he'd still be screaming even if the alarm weren't ringing. 'He had marks on his hands! Stigmata! The crucifixion wounds of Jesus! And then he just started burning... like... like... like a *bush! Like a burning bush!'*

'Brian, get a grip,' shouted Mervyn. 'He's not a burning bush! The burning bush stopped burning eventually, and it was completely unaffected by the flames... I doubt the same thing's going to happen to Robert!'

The security officer was goggling at Brian. 'I think you'd better sit down and take a breath, mate.'

But Brian had snapped. It was all too much for him. He was already starting to whimper.

The evacuation of the BBC couldn't have come at a worse time. As the staff assembled out the back of TV Centre, which adjoined the entrance to the BBC car park, a couple of the more wily protesters were hanging around the area. The car park was protected by a flimsy gate which opened and closed with arthritic slowness.

When some BBC employees, inevitably bored by standing around and waiting for the all-clear, decided to nip across the road to the shopping centre, the Godbotherers were ready for them.

Half a dozen of them squeezed through the gate as it was opening, and before anyone realised, they'd clambered over the inner gates and into TV Centre. They dashed into the building, pursued by angry red-faced security officers, already harassed by the evacuation.

By the time they were caught, they'd run security ragged by sheer force of their numbers. The walls inside the BBC had been spray-painted with chapters and quotes from the Bible. Godbotherers pamphlets adorned every desk. They'd even managed to crawl out to the broken BBC clock and hang the banner ' JUDGEMENT DAY IS AT HAND' under it.

Mervyn and Brian went back to their fellow DVD commentators who had gathered outside the BBC. None of them were aware that the fire alarm had anything to do with their DVD recording, or that Robert was a greasy spot on the toilet floor. Cheryl, Joanna, Aiden and Samantha were waiting patiently by the gate. Trevor had managed to join them at last, and was of course apologising profusely for being so late.

Mervyn broke the news of Robert's death and spontaneous posthumous combustion, to horrified gasps of disbelief. Aiden groped inside his jacket towards a non-existent shoulder holster. Mervyn was sure that he wasn't allowed to carry a gun, but there was still that instinctive reaction that betrayed the training of an ex-soldier. Or ex-policeman?

Mervyn wasn't sure.

'One of these days, we're going to finish this bloody DVD commentary,' muttered Joanna, in typical brutal fashion.

Brian leaned against the wall, looking queasy.

Cheryl stayed silent in her wheelchair.

Mervyn looked at Samantha closely. She seemed just as horrified as the others; her hands twisted the strap of her bag, she bit her lip, and a few tears oozed down her cheeks. She looked at him as if to say *Comfort me please.*

But Mervyn didn't. Not this time.

The police turned up, and Mervyn made himself known to them. He explained that he'd discovered the body with Brian, and what had happened when they entered the toilet.

And then the police arrested him.

CHAPTER FORTY-TWO

Detective Inspector Eric Preece wasn't a science fiction fan. He found the names confusing, the costumes ridiculous, and the guns effeminate and unsatisfactory. He preferred late-night cop shows and movies, where everyone dressed in sharp suits, unless they were drunk, and were called Steve or Jim or Harry. He liked shows with guns that went 'bang' instead of 'zap', and you could see the blood flying when the baddies were shot.

He was not impressed by Mervyn's CV. He did not care that Mervyn was Script editor for *Vixens from the Void* from 1986 to 1993.

Not one bit.

Mervyn looked insolently around the interview room. 'So, this is nice. I like the grey walls. They really set off the grey ceiling, and they complement the grey floor nicely. Why am I here?'

'Just general enquiries, sir.'

'It doesn't feel very general. You're recording me for a start.'

'Recording you is just normal procedure.'

'That's probably what Lionel Bickerdyke said.'

From the expressions on the faces of Preece and the constable, they did indeed read the papers, and they knew about Lionel.

Preece looked frosty. 'We are talking to you because you happened to be present when two murders happened. Funny that.'

'Well I wasn't the only one. I want to know why I'm here and Brian Crowbridge isn't. Or Samantha Carbury. Or Joanna Paine. Or that bodyguard, Aiden, for that matter.'

'We've already talked to them, sir.' Preece didn't bother addressing Mervyn directly. Pen-pushers the world over were taught to inspect things on their desks, to exude a too-busy-for-the-likes-of-you attitude. Mervyn suspected that when the policeman had talked to the others, it wasn't in a room like this with a tape recorder humming. This treatment had been reserved for him.

'And what about Lewis Bream? He's the one who's claimed credit for the death of Marcus, and I'm willing to bet he couldn't wait to add Robert to his list of credits.'

'We take his "confession" as seriously as we possibly can sir, but it's difficult to reconcile his admission with the fact he had no access to the crime scene on both occasions.'

Preece flipped the case file open. Mervyn noticed with a little amusement that the 'o's and the 'e's were all filled in using brightly coloured crayons.

'Insurance companies may accept "acts of God",' he droned, deadpan, 'but we in the police cannot have that luxury.'

'You think I had something to do with Marcus and Robert's deaths.'

'We don't think anything.'

'Obviously.'

'Do you want a solicitor, sir?'

'Do I need one?'

'Not at this stage.'

'Then I will take your sage advice.'

'For the benefit of the tape, I'm showing Mr Stone exhibit EP 2, a plastic water container.' Preece pushed a plastic bag across the table. Inside it was a typical water bottle, with 'Estuary English' written on it. 'Now,' he leaned forward. 'Is this the bottle which Mr Spicer drank from?'

Mervyn barely looked down. He glared at Preece.

'Well, how should I know? A bottle is a bottle is a bottle. Yes. Probably. I don't know, do I?'

He was about to make a closer examination when Preece snatched the bag back. 'That's enough.'

Mervyn started picking chunks out of his polystyrene cup, putting the fragments in a neat little pile. 'I take it there's a point to this little charade?'

'There were three sets of fingerprints on that bottle,' Preece said. 'Mr Spicer's and Mr Trevor Simpson's were there. Understandable, of course. Mr Simpson put the bottles there, and Mr Spicer picked this one up and drank it. But the third set of fingerprints on this bottle...'

I can see where this is going, thought Mervyn. *I can see where I'm going if I'm not careful.*

'A bit of a mystery, as we'd fingerprinted the BBC staff present and it wasn't them. We were just about to round up the... ah... celebrities. Would you call them "celebrities", Sherwin?'

The constable grinned from his place by the door. 'Just about, sir.'

'We were just about to ask for some celebrity fingerprints, but first we ran it through our database and – hey presto! – your name pops out.'

'There must be some mistake.'

'Our computer's very reliable Mr Stone,' Preece said acidly, 'It's a proper one you know. It's not just a big cardboard box sprayed silver. It's real and it's proper and it does its job. Properly.' Mervyn couldn't be sure, but he swore he heard Preece mutter 'Our guns work too,' under his breath.

'I'm not doubting your computer, Inspector,' Mervyn hissed, rapidly losing patience. 'I'm just a little confused as to *why* you have my fingerprints stored inside your computer. I'm a law-abiding citizen.

Last time I looked this wasn't a police state.'

Preece glanced down at his notes. 'Do you, by any chance, remember a certain incident in 1989 in Soho, where you smashed the window of The Happy Pagoda Chinese restaurant?'

'Ah, well...'

'It doesn't say in our records that you were actually in a "police state" at the time...'

'Yes.'

'Just *a* state.'

'All right, all right,' said Mervyn hurriedly. 'So you've got my fingerprints. So what?'

'Would you care to tell me how they got on the bottle, Mr Stone?'

Mervyn's brain had started to sink slowly into the mire, but suddenly it spied a passing branch, and grabbed for it. A smile clicked on to his face.

'Yes, actually. I fiddle.'

'You fiddle.'

Mervyn pointed down, indicating the pile of polystyrene chunks that used to be a cup. 'When I'm nervous, I fiddle. I was nervous about doing the commentary, and I was fiddling with the bottles, turning them so their labels faced the same way. I'm sure if you check the other bottles, they'd all have my fingerprints on them too.'

Mervyn could tell it sounded sickeningly plausible to Preece. The Inspector's eyes narrowed. His eyes were lasers. 'That's as may be, but it isn't the point.'

'Then what is "the point", Inspector?'

The Inspector zapped him.

'The point being that raised voices were heard; a heated conversation between you and Mr Spicer in the toilet not more than 15 minutes before his death...'

But how do they...? The answer collided with the question before it had barely formed in Mervyn's head. *Joanna Paine. Of course. It had to be. She'd gone to the toilet at the same time, she must have been right next door. She couldn't have failed to overhear our little head-to-head.*

Preece continued. 'Another point being that a witness has mentioned that you were visibly tense and irritable the moment Mr Spicer arrived.'

Bloody Brian as well, fumed Mervyn. *With friends like these... I suppose he can't be blamed for blabbing. He's been on so many couches and at so many support groups he feels he's got to confess everything.*

Mervyn took a deep breath, and marshalled for a counter-attack. 'Yes. All this is true. I did quarrel with him. I was annoyed at him.'

'Why?'

'Professional reasons. Nothing more. Old writers' arguments. Nothing serious.'

'Nothing serious?'

'No.'

'You see, we know a lot more than you think, Mr Stone. We know that you once had a relationship with Mr Spicer's wife, before their marriage.'

What?

'Mr Spicer took her from you, Mervyn. Did that hurt? Did that eat away at you?'

How did he know?

'Did you resent him, Mervyn?'

Mervyn had nothing to say.

'And what about Robert? Mervyn? Was he getting close to Mrs Spicer? Was that why you killed him?'

WHAT?

'For the benefit of the tape, I am playing Mr Stone exhibit EP 3, a message left on the answering service of his mobile phone.'

He clicked a switch on a smaller, hand held tape recorder.

'Hello Detective Stone, Robert here. Yes, just thought I'd call you and tell you everything's under control. You don't have to get your magnifying glass out for Cheryl, I've sorted everything for her. I'm just going to push – aaaaaaaghh!'

Preece clicked the machine off. 'For the benefit of the tape, Mr Stone is staring at me with his mouth hanging open.'

'This is just bonkers. You are so barking up the wrong tree. You're barking up a tree which isn't a tree, which is just a pole... with "tree" written on it. That's what you're barking up.'

'It's not looking good for you, Mr Stone. You have motive, you were present on both occasions so you had the opportunity...'

'Opportunity? You still haven't explained to me quite how I managed to get the poison in the bottle. Or the marks on Robert's hands. Or how I got him to explode, come to that. It all sounds pretty impossible to me.'

'Mr Mulberry had a pacemaker. Which overloaded due to a massive electrical charge. There was no alchemy involved. And as for the poison in the bottle... I'm sure the great detective of...' he scrutinised his notes. 'Convix 15 wouldn't let a little thing like "impossible" stop him.'

How did he know all this?

'Yes, well, you're talking to an ex-script editor here, and I can easily see the myriad holes in your little narrative; you can frisk me if you like, but you'll find I don't carry a giant electric hand buzzer around my person, or a miniature chemistry set which turns water into cyanide.'

Preece just looked at him. Did the detective just say 'zap' under his breath? Mervyn must have imagined it.

'Look, I've had a lovely day, and I thoroughly enjoyed the coffee you got me out of your excellent machine, but this is all utter make-believe and you've concocted a preposterous story that would shame Andrew Jamieson.'

'Who?'

'He was a *Vixens from the Void* writer. And that's not a compliment. Can I go home now?'

CHAPTER FORTY-THREE

The hooded man watched Mervyn leave the police station.

It was dark now, and difficult to see, but the hooded man recognised Mervyn's distinctive slouchy walk.

He was worried that the police might have asked about the statuette. He sat in his car, tapping the steering wheel in irritation, not knowing what was going on.

He had to find out what they had talked about. He made a call.

'Hello?'

'Hi Eric. How's it going?'

'Oh, usual shit. Some smart-arse writer giving me a load of backchat.'

'Mervyn Stone?'

'You guessed.'

'Did he kill them?'

'You should know. You were there. Tell me how he did it. Let me in on the secret.'

'Can't help you, mate. Sorry.'

There was a withered sigh from the phone. 'Oh well. Just thought I'd ask.'

Mervyn was allowed to go home. Eventually.

He had been kept in the police station for hours, and it was now dark. The last tube meandered back to Uxbridge, containing only Mervyn and a very smelly tramp, who followed him from carriage to carriage with his dirty hand outstretched.

Mervyn finally put his key in the door on the stroke of midnight. Slumping on to his ugly, inherited sofa with a thankful sigh, he switched on the television set to watch News 24, and was greeted by the vision of Lewis Bream standing on a platform talking to a crowd of people. Lewis looked much better now. He had regained his confidence and his customary artificial grin.

'They have seen the vengeance of the Lord once more,' he barked. 'They did not take the Godbotherers' warnings seriously, and now look what has happened. This DVD must never be released, and any existing copies of old videos and masters of the episode must be destroyed, or the Lord's vengeance will be terrible to behold.'

The news item cut to small groups across the country making up piles of old videos on waste ground. Old copies of 'The Burning Time' which were promptly burnt, to cheers from the crowds clustered around the bonfires.

Mervyn rubbed his face wearily. *Well at least destroying all the old videos should help sales of the DVD*, he thought. *It's not much of a silver lining...*

The purloined bottle of water was still on the table, where he had left it. He felt like ripping it open and drinking it, to show the world he wasn't going mad. But no, he had to be strong.

He slowly became aware that something was poking into his bottom. It was the CD Robert had given him earlier that day, so very very long ago.

He decided he would do something positive; he would listen to the DVD commentary leading up to Marcus's death. He would examine it once again for clues as to how the poison got into Marcus's water.

He put the CD into his aged stereo, and pressed play. And was rewarded by a dull thumping and clicking sound. And an 'ERR' glowing on the digital readout.

It's not even going to play for me. I don't believe it. Someone up there's got it in for me...

This had not been a good day.

He threw the CD across the room.

CHAPTER FORTY-FOUR

'Is that Mervyn Stone?'

'Yes, who's this?'

'Wait one moment. I'm putting you through.'

There was a click and then a familiar voice came on the line.

'Hello Mervyn.'

'Oh. Hello Joanna.'

'I was hoping you'd kept the same mobile.'

'I have.'

'I've not rung you in a while.'

'No.'

'No reason to.'

'I suppose not.'

'Are you okay? Or is this call the only phone call you're allowed?'

'I'm not in prison. The police just wanted a chat.'

'Well that's policemen. They do get lonely.'

There was an awkward pause.

'Well that's the small talk out of the way. Look, I have to talk to you.'

'What about?'

'I'm not telling you over the phone, you idiot. The tabloids have all sorts of funny listening devices these days. Come to the agency. I have a lunch scheduled for one, before I go to the reading of Marcus's will. You can listen to me while I eat.'

'Paine Staking Literary and Theatrical Agency' was just off Tottenham Court Road, perched on top of a bookshop. He pressed a button and was buzzed up, entering a dingy hallway and picking his way up a rickety staircase as if to a shifty assignation with a West End working girl.

He once joked about it to Marcus when they paid a visit, way back when they were young writers starting out.

'Don't be fooled by appearances,' Marcus had said, a little patronisingly. 'It's the location these little agencies pay for, mate, not the building. They can afford to occupy a whole three-storey block in Archway for the rent they're paying for these few rooms – but who wants to rent a block in Archway?'

Marcus was patronising *and* snobby that day, recalled Mervyn. Not that he wasn't exactly right.

It looked a little better once he reached the top of the stairs, where there was a crowded office filled with young people making calls and tapping into keyboards.

He was asked to wait in Joanna's office, and a chair and a coffee was provided for him. He sat there, drumming his fingers on a box file and feeling self-conscious. The minutes stretched and he thought about making a discreet exit, but every time he began to leave, one of several secretaries appeared from nowhere and on the way to somewhere, offering him coffee or water as they passed, cutting off his escape. Once again, he was imprisoned by his own cringing Englishness.

Joy of joys, he spied a pile of out-of-date *Spotlight* books in Joanna's wastepaper bin. He could indulge in one of his favourite pastimes, flicking through actors' professional photos and working out how many decades ago they were taken.

He fished it out, and it immediately flopped open at an actor he recognised – a venerable whisky-sodden thespian called Roddy Burgess, who had been a regular on *Vixens*. It was a photo that pre-dated even his time on the show, some 20 years previous. The dark-eyed chiselled face topped with lustrous black hair bore little relation to the bewildered craggy lunatic he knew; the photo had clearly been taken when dinosaurs still walked the Earth.

It always amused him, how actors could convince themselves they were able to get away with such blatant fraud. He wondered if producers were fully wise to what they were getting, that when they picked a square-jawed thirty-something from these pages, they fully expected a bald, half-blind creature in a wheelchair, carrying his bladder around in a suitcase.

He thoroughly enjoyed himself, flicking through the book. The Bs gave way to Cs, and sure enough, up popped Brian Crowbridge, his impossibly young face engulfed in shadows. (Mervyn smiled: were they 'artistic' shadows, or was the photographic studio lit by candles due to Edward Heath's three-day week?) He sported a thin moustache that looked like it had been drawn on with an eyebrow pencil, and a clearly manufactured kiss-curl bounced playfully from his hair and rested over a quizzically raised eyebrow.

He picked up another volume, and allowed the pages to run through his fingers, letting the book fall open at a natural place.

It rested in the Ss, at a page which had been folded over, tucked into the spine. He flipped it out and, of course, there were more photos of actors; staring into the middle distance stroking their stubbly chins, leaning on trees, trying to look thoughtful and Shakespearean.

One of the photos was interesting. It was just a standard moody snap of a middle-aged thespian trying to age down – a Lear trying to look like a Hamlet or a Romeo. It was marked with a red pen, and the words 'NOT A VIC!!! RING MARCUS?' written along the side, an arrow sprouting from the words and pointing to the actor's face.

This wasn't unusual in itself – there were other notes and numbers scrawled around the pictures. It was a very old copy of *Spotlight* after all; but Marcus's name alerted him.

And there was something else. Something about the actor too, something about him tickled the back of Mervyn's mind. He was sure that face was familiar; no – it was more than that, he was certain the actor had swum into his head in the last few weeks for some reason, he'd actually seen his picture recently, but he was damned if he could remember where. He tried to place the face – he was certain it wasn't an actor who had worked on *Vixens*. At least, reasonably certain – it was usually the actresses' faces that found their way into his memory.

No, it wasn't *Vixens*, or any other shows he'd worked on, it was something different. No, he couldn't recall the name – Duncan Somerville – but the face...

'Having fun?' Joanna loomed over him.

Mervyn couldn't find any words for a few seconds, then he flapped the book and grinned like a cheeky schoolboy. 'Just, you know...'

'Flicking through *Spotlight*, laughing at the out-of-work actors?' She folded her arms with mock-severity. 'I don't know... How cruel. How many times did I find you two naughty boys gloating over the sad, the mad, the desperate and the unemployable? I remember you and Marcus sitting in that corner waiting for me, him picking up a volume and shouting to you, "Look Mervyn, they've turned Dante's *Inferno* into a flip-book."'

It was actually Mervyn's joke, and it was Mervyn who shouted it to Marcus, but Mervyn didn't say anything. He was used to stoically standing by and letting Marcus take the credit. It didn't look like he was going to be allowed to stop any time soon.

'How are you Mervyn?' Joanna air-kissed him, brushing his cheek with her pillow-soft skin.

'I'm fine. Apart from witnessing a dead body undergoing spontaneous combustion and getting interrogated by the police afterwards.'

'Oh, how did that go?'

'Great fun. I got coffee and everything. Thanks for mentioning my argument with Marcus to the police.'

Joanna shrugged. 'They asked me what I witnessed that day. I couldn't very well leave it out. You understand.'

Mervyn didn't answer.

'Okay, I'll make amends. How about lunch at the Ivy?'

Mervyn nodded his head vigorously. 'Sounds good.'

'Just wait there. I've got a few Post-it notes to write and stick on keyboards, and then we'll be out of this hell-hole.' Joanna disappeared into another glass-fronted office, and talked to a young man with horn-rimmed spectacles. 'Bryn, I'm taking lunch. If Max calls, they've upped the money to ninety grand, but they've made it very clear that he shouldn't make himself available to the BBC for any work.'

Mervyn stared at the picture. Damn. He wasn't going to rest until he'd worked out why that actor had found his way into his head. *(It was just like all those times he couldn't quite recall the name of that actor in the Hitchcock film. Why could he never remember the name 'Ray Milland' for more than 20 minutes?)*

Mervyn sighed. *Look, it's only an old copy of* Spotlight. *Sod it.* Coming to a sudden decision, he tore the page out and dumped the book back in the bin.

'Right, I'm ready. Let's go,' Joanna said.

She shrugged on a cashmere coat, and strode out the door without waiting for him. Mervyn moved alongside her, trotting to keep up with her brisk, lengthy stride.

It was just a short walk down Charing Cross Road to the Ivy. It hadn't occurred to Mervyn before, but as they came through the doors he noticed the restaurant was very like a church. They entered a kind of vestry affair and were greeted by a smiling man who was very happy to see everyone and very solicitous in asking how you were doing today – the epitome of a Church of England vicar. Then you passed into a large wood-panelled room, with long tables, bathed in the light cast by stained-glass windows. And there was the most important similarity of all. Once seated, people were there to be spotted by other people.

Mervyn raised the point to Joanna. 'This is very like a church, isn't it?'

Joanna peered around her and shrugged. 'I wouldn't know. I'm a Scientologist.'

'You're a what? Triangle power, lie detectors and souls from space? With aliens? You believe in all that?'

'Mervyn, I'd devoutly believe the human race was created by Jim Henson and the Children's Television Workshop and brought to you by the letter "B" if it meant me getting anywhere near Tom Cruise and Katie Holmes.'

'Ah.'

'Anyway – you can talk. You've based your whole life and career pretending aliens exist.'

'I've never pretended aliens exist.'

'Some of your followers do.'

'I don't have followers! I'm not a prophet! I do concede that some of the loonier fans of *Vixens* seem to behave as if it were real...' His mind leapt back to Mick, and her spangly bra, and her Vixens' codes. 'As for them... Whether some people appropriate what I've written and take it literally is nothing to do with me.'

Joanna grinned. 'Spoken like a true prophet.'

Joanna Paine was class. Mervyn always thought so. Underneath the trouser suit, the frown and the severe hair cut, there was a very attractive woman. Her silhouette reminded him of a cut-glass champagne flute. She was long-limbed with toned, almost manly shoulders tapering down to an achingly thin waist and exquisite legs that seemed about fifteen feet long from thigh to delicately shaped ankle. Her fingers were long and slender, very womanly, even though she kept her fingernails short. All the better to dance across her laptop.

She took off her jacket and draped it on the back of her chair. This meant that Mervyn could inspect her body, encased in a crisp white shirt. Even with Mervyn's obsession with (he would call it an appreciation of) the fleshier female form, he still thought her a fascinating creature; and even though her chest was shallow he still had to train himself not to peer into the spaces gaping between the buttons.

'A nice Merlot?' she said loudly, craning around to catch the eye of the waiter.

Mervyn jumped; he realised that, unbidden, his mind had wandered off to have a gossip with his libido. 'Sounds great.'

He also realised that they hadn't actually talked about Marcus's death; Marcus had been represented by Joanna for many years, and there had been a long and not completely unhappy professional relationship. And of course, the much shorter and more unprofessional relationship... Had anyone bothered to commiserate with Joanna about the loss of her client and ex-lover? Probably not.

'I'm sorry about Marcus,' Mervyn muttered, dutifully.

Joanna tapped her fork idly on the table. She looked almost embarrassed; Joanna was always a bit of a cold fish. Or perhaps she wasn't, and she just didn't like him very much. 'So am I. I'm gutted. The man made more for me in a day than most clients bring in for the year.' Typical Joanna.

She tapped her wine glass with her finger. If she had had longer fingernails it would have surely made a ringing sound, but her short nails only managed a dull 'clonk'.

'Okay, cards on the table. You probably heard Marcus and I had a... thing. It wasn't a wise thing, or a very long-lived thing – just a couple of pokes in Paris, and a handful of long weekends at Hambley Hall, but it was a thing, and it happened.'

Mervyn stayed silent; raising his eyebrows with polite interest.

'But that's not important. The important thing is that he confided in me more than you would your average agent. He talked to me a lot.'

'Oh yes?'

Joanna suddenly broke off and waved at the door. Mervyn turned and followed her gaze.

Oh no...

Such a pity he was in a nice restaurant; because he had suddenly lost his appetite. No, that was an understatement. His stomach had just shrunk to the size of a marble. Samantha Carbury was in the doorway.

'Hiya!'

Her bracelets clattered in the hush as she waved frantically. She scurried to join them, pushing past the waiters, her big canvas bag clonking against the back of heads of the great and the good. One diner, poised with a fork, got butternut squash risotto implanted in his left nostril. Samantha descended on them, sitting by Mervyn and pecking him on the cheek. Beneath the table, her hand scuttled along his leg, resting on his knee.

'Hi Joanna, hi darling. This is lovely here, isn't it? I haven't been here before...'

'Hello Samantha, glad you could make it.'

'Well no problem, I was just over the way, at the top of Carnaby Street. I was in Lush buying up soaps, and I got your message.'

She hefted her bag, to prove her story. Mervyn wondered whether the diners would feel better if they knew they'd just been dealt concussion by ethical products. Probably not.

'Are you all right Mervyn, my darling?'

'Hello Samantha. Yes I'm fine.'

'Are you sure? The police looked like they were taking you away to be arrested yesterday.'

'It was just a misunderstanding, that's all.'

'Oh, good. I hoped that's what it was. Have you both seen the newspapers today?'

Joanna and Mervyn nodded.

'It's just staggering, they're all talking about black magic, or the vengeance of some God. It's just ridiculous.'

'Absolutely,' said Joanna. 'Exactly what I think. Ridiculous.'

'Any sane person would tell them it's just the spiritual hole made by Marcus's death. Any creation of death through violence creates a link to a negative energy plane, which is basically a hole through which positive energy flows. Like a whirlpool, positive energy flows through the hole instead of flowing through us, denying those downstream the positivity to ward off negativity.'

'Right,' said Joanna, elegant eyebrows raised to the skies.

Samantha rested her head on Mervyn's shoulder. The muscles in his neck tightened with embarrassment, injecting a mild headache into his skull. 'Oh gosh, Mervyn, the karmic energy was so bad in there I could barely breathe.'

A handsome waiter, dark and stubbled, came up and took their order. Samantha took an age to decide, examining the small print of the menu. She hummed and hawed, asking about the origin and provenance of every vegetable on the menu, trying to guess whether they'd had a happy life before been uprooted, diced, chopped and steamed.

Mervyn let out a sigh through his nostrils, as Samantha hovered between the goat's curd salad and the fried courgettes. Joanna didn't seem to mind; her eyes were flicking up and down the waiter appreciatively.

The waiter finally left them and Samantha leaned forward, confidentially. 'Gosh, what a brilliant menu. And the waiter knew so much about the produce, didn't he? If he was right, and the courgettes were brought into Folkestone from Calais – that's the "wealth corners" of both countries. In Feng Shui terms, I'm inviting prosperity by eating them.'

'Anyway...' Joanna wasn't interested in Samantha's twitterings. 'As I was saying, I was pretty close to Marcus as an agent and as a friend. He talked to me a lot.'

'Talking is so important,' said Samantha.

'And there was one thing that was most uppermost in his mind in his final days. He was worried about Cheryl.'

'Oh.'

'Right.'

'He was very flip about it. He always was about things that were important to him. He called her his own "endangered species."'

'Awww,' Samantha made a gooey noise. 'That's so lovely, and sad, and cute, and sad.'

'But you could read between the jokes. He thought she was getting weaker. He was expecting something... final to happen quite soon.'

'Oh no...' Samantha clapped her hand to her mouth.

'I'm sorry to hear that,' said Mervyn. 'I like Cheryl a great deal, and I'd be very sad if she loses the fight... But she doesn't *seem* that bad.'

'Her spirit is sustaining her,' said Samantha, sagely.

Joanna ignored her. 'Cancer's a funny bastard. It lets you look like a trained marathon runner one week, the next...'

'It makes you look like an *un*trained marathon runner.'

'Nicely put. Now that he's gone, I worry about her. I'm wondering if we should help.'

Samantha tapped her chin with a long fingernail. 'I could talk to Megan and Raging Water. They could prepare the Way for her...'

Joanna sipped her Merlot. 'I was talking more about her welfare.'

Mervyn frowned. 'She's hardly living in a council flat, warming herself by a one-bar electric fire.'

'Things can change, Mervyn, someone should be there to watch out for her. Particularly when you've got these Godbotherers gunning for her. They're in danger of getting out of hand.'

'Oh gosh!' Samantha's voice had become a tense whisper. 'Has she had more threats? Hate mail?'

'Twice as many letters as usual. The publicity's really bringing them out of the woodwork. I'm not sure she can cope with it all.'

Their meals arrived, and they ate in silence. When they'd finished, Joanna dabbed her lips with a napkin and asked for the bill.

'Anyway. Thanks for talking.'

Mervyn was puzzled. Is this all she brought them here for? To talk about Cheryl's health? It didn't seem important enough for a power lunch. It was certainly not like Joanna to waste a dinner on a 'chat'. 'You're welcome,' he said, 'but I'm not sure what we've actually talked about.'

'I thought I'd made myself clear. I'm going to open a trust for her, which I'll manage. I was just wondering if you'd both like to be a director...'

'Oh, definitely.' Samantha nodded her head vigorously. 'Happy to help. I'm not good with budgets and things, but I can design your office for you.'

Mervyn stood up. 'I'd be happy to help Cheryl in any way I can, but as I said, she has enough money to buy my house a thousand times over. And I think Samantha has even less money than me.'

Samantha gave a helpless grin, confirming Mervyn's assumption with her silence.

'... So I really don't think Cheryl will need our help.'

Joanna smiled again. 'Just in case, eh? Good to prepare in case of emergencies. Acts of God, and all that.'

CHAPTER FORTY-FIVE

Joanna rushed back to the office to check her emails, leaving Mervyn and Samantha standing awkwardly on the street in St Martin's Lane.

Samantha spoke first. 'I... just wondered if you were going to the solicitors for the reading of Marcus's will?'

'I was planning to...'

'Because if you were, perhaps we could find a café, share a soy latte and a carrot cake?'

'I have a prior engagement. Sorry.'

'Oh. Okay.'

Samantha sounded slightly crumpled at this obvious lie. Mervyn felt like the biggest shit in the U-bend.

'See you at the solicitors, then,' she said, feebly.

'See you at the solicitors. Watch out for the negative energy.'

Mervyn loitered around the bookshops. It didn't seem long before it was time to go to the reading of the will.

The offices of Stoneleigh, Parsons and Williams were tucked away in a corner of Leadenhall. It was small, but tasteful. Paintings of men in whiskers and waistcoats glared down from the walls. The antique smell of money was everywhere.

Mervyn glanced around the well-padded waiting room. It was quite crowded. There was him, Samantha, Joanna, Cheryl, Cheryl's brother Barry who'd driven her there, Aiden the minder, a whiskery old man in a bow-tie who had introduced himself as Professor Alec Leman (Mervyn learned later he was a prominent humanist and director of the Spicer Institute), Marcus's American agent Dana Snow, Mark Langella (a director friend of Marcus who'd adapted his books for television), Andrew Jamieson (a writer friend of both Marcus and Mervyn), Siobhan and Carlene the personal assistants, George Jackson (an old school chum of Marcus) and a man Mervyn didn't know.

But, weirdly, he had a picture of the man in his pocket.

He unfolded the page of *Spotlight*, and sure enough, it was a photo of the actor standing in front of him. Duncan Somerville.

That was a strange coincidence.

Mervyn experienced a tidal wave of weariness as Samantha immediately moved seats and fastened herself to him. She slapped his knee and smiled at him. Mervyn flashed a tight, embarrassed grin back. Andrew Jamieson caught his eye and gave a playful wink.

'All right, Mervyn?' he grinned.

Mervyn just scowled at him.

Barry, Cheryl's brother, was pacing backwards and forwards, displaying the suppressed energy of a naturally aggressive man. 'I hope this don't take long. I was meant to be on the site at ten.'

'Sit down Barry,' said Cheryl. 'You're making the place look untidy.'

Barry owned his own building company, a business that had overstretched itself in the good times and was now groaning with debt.

'You don't have to wait,' Cheryl said.

'I do,' Barry grunted. 'I want to make sure he's dead.'

Mervyn remembered there was no love lost between Barry and Marcus. Barry took all the rumours of Marcus's affairs personally on behalf of his sister. He always seemed more upset than Cheryl ever was.

They were greeted by a young man swaddled in an expensive suit. 'Hello everyone, I'm Tim. Would you like to join me upstairs?'

'See you in a minute Barry,' said Cheryl. 'You'll be okay?'

They left Barry fuming and Tim led them upstairs. Joanna pushed Cheryl into the disabled lift and they all met up in a bare room filled with rows of chairs. Tim took a seat at the desk at the front and faced them nervously, like a student teacher.

'I am Tim Parsons, I represent Mr Spicer's estate, and I have been given authority to read his will which dispenses with that estate. Or rather, Mr Spicer will do that for me.' He opened a box file and produced a DVD. 'Mr Spicer recorded this one month ago, and this recording supersedes all previous wills he made.'

Mervyn heard a gasp, and a tiny 'Oh my god' from Samantha behind him. He didn't know about the negative energy implications, but by her response he could guess that they were serious. The whole situation was proving a bit ghoulish for him, too.

'Before I begin, Mr Spicer specified that you should all be given light refreshment.' He waved in some waitresses who glided among them, holding trays of sandwiches and glasses of wine. Mervyn took a sandwich as it passed. It seemed to be herring or something equally smelly.

As they ate, Tim slotted the DVD into his machine, chatting as he did so. 'We were worried that some of you might be unavailable, but thankfully all twelve of you managed to attend, thank you all so very much.'

Twelve people. Twelve disciples. The joke wasn't lost on Mervyn.

And guess what? They'd all been given bread and wine beforehand. This was Marcus's body and blood, given to them all. Loaves and fishes too. The man couldn't stop tweaking the nose of Christianity, even in death.

Joanna was counting. 'There's actually thirteen people here.'

Tim was distracted. He was fiddling with the remote control. 'Why isn't this thing playing? Yes, well. There *were* twelve invited to this reading, but I thought in the circumstances I should expand our little circle by one.'

Mervyn looked around him, wondering who the extra guest was. What an odd thing to say.

Tim pressed a button, and the picture sprang into life.

'Hello, playmates.'

There was Marcus, returned to life, two weeks after his death.

'Sorry about this bit of melodrama,' he said, not looking sorry in the slightest, 'but I thought I would do it this way so there would be no mistake that this will is mine, and there's been no tampering and no funny business.' He held up a newspaper and waved it. 'This is what people do when they're being kidnapped, don't they? As you can see, this newspaper is from September the fifth.'

September the fifth. One month ago.

'Anyway, it seems rather fitting in the circumstances. Okay, straight down to business. Let's do one disciple at a time. My very own doubting Thomas, Mervyn Stone. Because you helped me at the start of my career, and did a few tweaks on my *Vixens from the Void* episode "The Burning Time..."'

Cheeky bastard. Even in death, he's a cheeky bloody bastard.

'... I'm leaving you all future royalties to that episode. They will probably buy you a bag of peanuts, but they're yours now, fair and square. I leave the sums of £20,000 apiece to Siobhan Perry and Carlene Brown, my personal assistants. There you go girls, buy yourselves something nice.'

The girls grinned humourlessly; one flipped him the bird. They looked like they were used to being patronised.

'To Andrew Jamieson, I leave my cut-glass crystal decanters, and what's left of my Grey Goose vodka. I gave the drink up, and now I've given it up permanently, I will leave temptation his way.'

Andrew raised his glass and toasted the television.

'To Professor Alec Leman, I leave the flask of whisky in my desk at the Institute, and all my books. Perhaps both the books and the whisky will get devoured now.'

The man in the bow-tie smiled gently to himself.

'And I leave the house, and all bits and pieces therein, the country cottage in Wales, the cars, and blah blah blah, etcetera, etcetera –

basically, everything which is supposedly covered by that extortionate home contents insurance policy – all that stuff, and of course the sole rights to all my novels in perpetuity to my wife...'

He paused, savouring the moment. 'Samantha Carbury.'

CHAPTER FORTY-SIX

Tim switched the DVD off.

There was silence. Then there was a gentle cascade of muttered comments, one or two at first, then heavy and persistent, like raindrops on a window.

Comments like 'What?', 'Did I hear that right?', 'He didn't really say that...' Cheryl sat there, saying nothing.

Joanna stood in the corner, her face welded into a furious expression.

'There must be some mistake,' Mervyn said to Tim.

'Too bloody right,' said Joanna.

'There's no mistake,' said Tim, quailing under Joanna's hot temper. 'I'm sorry to break distressing news in such a dramatic fashion, but that was the way Mr Spicer specified...'

Joanna marched up to Samantha and stood there, so close their noses were almost touching. 'What the hell is this? What's he going on about. You were *not* married to that man.'

Samantha's eyes roamed around the room, looking for any kind of escape. 'Um...Well... I was... sort of...'

'What do you mean, sort of? Either you were or you weren't.'

'Joanna, please, you have to get out of my aura. I can't concentrate if you're standing in my head space.'

With a huge effort, Joanna took several steps back, folded her arms and glared at Samantha. 'Okay Sam. I'm out of your head space. What's this about "sort of" getting married to Marcus?'

'Weeell, we did kind of... sort of... get married. A bit,' said Samantha, using a voice a six-year old would engage when admitting to smashing a vase. 'It was on location, when we did "The Burning Time". Back in the 80s. It was such a confused point in my life...'

Every point has been a confused point in your life, thought Mervyn, ungraciously. *Up to and including now.*

'Marcus and I were having such a lovely time together we decided to get married and not to tell anyone, just as a bit of fun...'

Joanna crammed her hands on to her head. 'A bit of fun?'

Samantha scrunched up her face as she tried to think. 'To be honest, I forgot all about it. No, I tell a lie, I did remember a few years later, it all came back to me during a hypnotherapy session in Coventry. I asked Marcus about it, and he told me he'd fixed it.'

'He fixed it. He *fixed* it?' barked Cheryl's brother. All of a sudden, Barry was standing there in the doorway. He must have got bored and followed them up, heard the argument and wondered what was happening. He looked ready to thump someone. Samantha recoiled, anxiously gripping the back of her chair.

'Yes, he said he'd got us a divorce, or something.' She faltered. 'I guess he didn't...'

'And you didn't realise you were still married?' Barry swung round to her, hands bunched into fists. 'You stupid hippy!'

'Mervyn!' Samantha wailed, looking at him imploringly.

Mervyn found Samantha irritating. He found her sudden ownership of him annoying. She'd fastened onto him like an emotional leech. She'd initiated sex and broken the golden rule of television by demanding emotional commitment as a result. He felt no loyalty to this silly woman.

Nevertheless, he could not, in all conscience, allow a defenceless woman to get threatened by a large angry man, no matter what the provocation. He stepped in between them.

'I think it's best if we all calm down here. This isn't going to solve anything.'

'I think it's going to solve lots of things.'

'No it won't.'

Joanna appeared at their side.

'Well you would side with her, wouldn't you Mervyn?'

'I'm not siding with anyone.'

'Did you know about this all along? You were on location with them.'

'Of course not.'

'Of course you knew. It all makes sense now – that's why you've been canoodling with her this last week. Cosying up to the multi-million pound heiress.'

Mervyn's face grew hot. 'I've not been "cosying up" to anyone. And I didn't know!'

Joanna's mind was working at full speed, racing through the implications and making calculations. Mervyn guessed where Joanna was going to go next.

He was right.

Joanna made directly for Cheryl, falling to her knees and gripping the arms of Cheryl's wheelchair. 'Did you know about this?'

'Get off her!' said Cheryl's brother.

'Cheryl, what's going on?' pleaded Joanna.

Cheryl looked at Joanna wearily, but said nothing.

'Tell me you were married to Marcus. Tell me this is a joke.'

Tim cleared his throat. 'Perhaps, if you could retake your seats, Mr Spicer can explain the situation to you.'

They all sat down again. Mervyn thought the 'situation' very ironic. He'd already witnessed Marcus's death in a tiny room where a group of disparate people were all dragged together to watch a tiny television screen. Now he was witnessing Marcus's will in a tiny room full of people watching a tiny television screen. He wondered whether Channel 4 could be persuaded to televise the funeral.

The DVD was switched on again, and Marcus appeared once more. He wasn't even disguising the fact he was enjoying this.

'If you've quite finished shouting and arguing, mateys? Let me explain. Yes, it's true. Samantha and I got married while we were on location for "The Burning Time". We were young, in love, having a whale of a time, and we didn't give a stuff. And to be quite honest, we split up so quickly after, and it was such a spur of the moment thing, I never thought it that great a deal. I just felt like forgetting about it, so I never bothered with all the argy-bargy of getting a divorce.'

Typical Marcus, thought Mervyn.

'And before you start shouting, I was not a bigamist. Did any of you think for one moment while you were attending mine and Cheryl's wedding, why one of the most famous atheists in the country would want a huge church do, with hymns and prayers and flowers and an all-singing, all-dancing vicar? It was all nonsense. A sham. Cheryl and I wanted to make a statement. At that time, as some of you will definitely remember, if you wanted to get married in anything but a squalid little bare room, you were forced to ask permission from the Almighty. That was it. That was your choice. Get married in a toilet, or pretend to pay homage to a non-existent god. And even if you did believe in that rubbish, if you happened to be divorced, you still couldn't get married in a church – you weren't allowed to, according to a bunch of discredited boy-buggering old men.' Marcus leaned back in his chair, and laced his fingers together. 'So we wanted to show those Bible-thumping bastards. I found an old church that was in the middle of nowhere. It was closed down, condemned. I spruced it up, gave it a lick of paint, made it look functional again, just for the service. I printed up invites and you all came, just like it was a proper do. And as for the vicar...'

The man – the actor on the page from *Spotlight* in Mervyn's pocket – came forward and stood in front of them all. He took a swift bow and grinned.

'Meet Duncan Somerville, jobbing actor, cabaret singer, balloon sculptor, man of many voices and about as qualified to officiate at marriage ceremonies as my aunt's dog.'

Duncan gave another swift bow and retired to the back of the room.

'And no one checked, no one asked, and Cheryl called herself Mrs

Spicer for the next 20 years. So there you have it. I had one marriage in public, which was a lie; one in secret, which was true. Ironic. But those are the weird contortions that religion forces you to make. Cheryl's gone, we've got no kids, and so I'm making this gesture in remembrance of that fun time Samantha and I had in Dorking.'

Samantha gave a weak smile.

'Anyway, this is Marcus Spicer saying goodbye. I don't know where I'm going, but if it's heaven then – hey! Will *I* be the one with the red face! At least if there is a heaven, I might have the good fortune to be re-united with my darling "little Mary". My darling Cheryl. That might make being wrong all these years worthwhile.'

CHAPTER FORTY-SEVEN

There was a lot of anger, most of it directed at Tim the solicitor. Cheryl's brother grabbed him by the edge of his expensive lapels.

'What the fuck is this? You planned it with that bastard? When did you and that bastard decide to stitch up my sister?'

Tim was forced back into the room until the television was pushed into the small of his back. 'I'm sorry Mr... Limb, isn't it? Those were Mr Spicer's wishes. I have to carry them out. I'm sorry. I can't speak for Mr Spicer...'

'I thought that's what you *were* doing.'

'What I mean to say is, I can't interpret Mr Spicer's intentions when he made his last will, but I imagine he expected Mrs... er... Mrs... Miss... Cheryl, not to be, er, here, when he departed, due to er... Miss Limb's illness. Naturally, it's wonderful that she is still alive, but Mr Spicer wasn't to know she would outlive him.'

Barry bellowed in Tim's face. 'If you don't sort this out, you're not going to outlive me – and that's a promise, sunshine.'

'I can't do anything. His wishes, as you saw, were explicit. Perhaps as a wife she could contest the will, but as a common law partner she has much less "clout" in the eyes of the law, I'm afraid.'

'This isn't over. We'll contest this. She gave that bastard the best years of her life.'

'Leave it, Barry,' snapped Joanna.

A security guard entered the room. Barry had enough sense to know that he wasn't going to get anything done today. Not with threats. His hands dropped from Tim's lapels.

'Cher?' His voice was small. A little brother asking for guidance from his big sis.

'Take me home, Barry. We'll probably need to pack.'

'I don't understand this,' wailed Samantha. 'Are you sure you've played the right tape? I don't understand. The marriage didn't mean anything. I'm not a Christian either. It was just a bit of a lark. It's not as if it meant that much...'

Joanna slapped her, hard and full in the face. Samantha squealed, collapsed on the floor and held her face in her hands.

'Don't say another word,' said Joanna coldly. 'Just don't.' Then Barry wheeled Cheryl out, and Joanna followed on his heels. None of them said anything.

Mervyn moved to help Samantha, but Professor Leman beat him to it. *Quite a sprightly old buffer,* he thought.

'Are you all right, my dear?' said the professor.

Samantha nodded dumbly. 'Oh dear. Dear oh dear,' she sniffed. 'That didn't go very well, did it?'

'No, Samantha. It didn't go very well,' said Mervyn. He sat down by her and held her hand.

Tim was hanging around the doorway, unwilling to leave the room occupied. Mervyn looked over at him. 'You said there were only meant to be twelve here, but you invited another...'

'Yes. There were originally twelve people invited to the reading of the will. The one not invited was Mrs Spicer – I mean, Miss Limb.'

'Because she was meant to be dead by now.'

Tim flinched when Mervyn said 'dead'. Odd that a man who dealt in wills would have such a problem with the word. 'I imagine so. I wasn't privy to Mr Spicer's thoughts, but from what he said he didn't believe she would outlive him.' Tim flourished a weak smile. 'I felt Miss Limb had a right to be here for the reading, and Mr Limb insisted on joining her for moral support.' Tim collected his box folder and his DVD and walked past him with an apologetic smile. 'This is always a traumatic time for friends and family,' he said.

'Especially when the deceased's playing mind games with friends and family,' said Mervyn sourly.

'You can stay in here for a few more minutes, if you need to compose yourselves.'

Tim finally vanished. Now there were only the three of them left – Mervyn, Samantha and Professor Leman, who was sitting there with his arms folded over his chest. Oddly, the old man was chuckling to himself.

'Dear old Marcus, quite the Jesus complex...'

'Oh. You noticed,' said Mervyn.

'I knew Marcus well. I was well aware of it underpinning his life and work. And in death he's finally getting his wish, isn't he?' He waved his hand in the direction of the television. 'Dying and rising again... Allowing his twelve disciples to fall into feuding after his departure. I wonder if Cheryl will contest the will. I bet he's filed it in triplicate. Would that count as "denying him three times"? Oh, it's all beautifully orchestrated, don't you think?' The old man was practically hugging himself in joy.

'Can I have a hankie?' sniffed Samantha.

Leman remembered his manners, and sprang to his feet. 'Of course, my dear.'

He gave her an elaborate spotted hankie. Mervyn watched, fascinated, as Samantha dabbed her eyes. Then she stood up, perched on the arm of a chair, and flipped open a powder compact, looking at her face in the mirror secreted within. She tried to submerge the red mark beneath layers of foundation, but only served to make her face look even more crazed and artificial than usual.

'Oh dear, that doesn't look good at all...' She looked up at Mervyn, bewildered eyes full of tears. 'I don't know what's happening,' she sobbed. 'I always knew that most people didn't actually like me, but no one actually *hated* me either...'

'My dear...' said Leman, patting her shoulder. 'This was all Marcus's doing. No one is blaming you for this.'

'Joanna is,' she said, in a tiny voice. She touched her cheek with a trembling hand.

Mervyn looked down at her. Now he was angry.

'Right, that's it.' He fished out his mobile phone.

'What?'

'You're getting an apology from Joanna.' He checked his contacts. 'I've still got her number, thank God.'

'Oh Mervyn, don't. It's really not worth the bother...'

But Mervyn was already dialling. He listened for a very long time. 'Just the answering service. Don't worry Samantha, we'll find them. I'm sure someone knows where they've got to.'

'I do, sir,' said the Professor.

Mervyn's head snapped to the Professor. 'You know?'

'Yes, sir. They're going to the same place I'm going. To the Spicer Institute in Albermarle Street. It's our quarterly lecture on humanism. We've managed to grab Christopher Hitchens while he's in the country.' The professor straightened his bow-tie and picked up his waxed jacket from the back of the chair. 'Would you care to join me? I'm sure it's going to be fascinating.'

You said it, thought Mervyn.

CHAPTER FORTY-EIGHT

They piled into a cab, which lurched on to the congested London streets. They were soon stranded in traffic, not moving. Cars and taxis were crammed together like rocks in a dry stone wall.

'Oh dear,' sighed the professor benignly, twinkling at Samantha. 'We're going to be late. I'd say that someone up there doesn't like us, but I'm not supposed to say things like that.'

Samantha grinned uncertainly at him, and gave a huge, childlike sniff.

Mervyn's foot was tapping the floor of the taxi. 'I'll try Cheryl's phone.'

'Mervyn,' Samantha was pleading again. 'Let's not do this. I'm feeling we're heading into a huge crowd of negative energy. Let's go back to my little place in Richmond. You can have another foot massage, and some cleansing tea.'

Mervyn ignored her. He dialled Cheryl's number.

'Hello?'

Mervyn had the phone on speaker, so the voice flooded the cab. But it wasn't Cheryl's voice. It was Joanna's.

'Oh my,' whimpered Samantha.

'Joanna? I thought this was Cheryl's phone.'

'It is.'

'Oh.'

'I'm holding it for her, because that's what I do. I'm the one looking after her. Looks like you've chosen whose side you're on, Mervyn. I'm not surprised.'

'That's unfair.'

'If you'll excuse me, I'm rather busy. I have to make some calls myself. I need to organise Cheryl's removal from her house before Samantha moves in. I presume Samantha's going to live there, and not use it as a sanctuary for lesser-spotted tree-frogs from the jungles of South America or anything like that?'

'You can ask her yourself. I have Samantha with me.'

Samantha cringed, curling into a ball.

'Of course you do.'

'You need to apologise to her.'

There was a harsh bark of laughter from the phone. 'Do I, indeed?'

'Yes. Yes you do.'

'She's got all the money. She can employ someone to say sorry to her on my behalf.'

'Is Cheryl there? Can I speak to her?'

'She's busy. She's on stage. They've just introduced her to the floor...'

There was a huge whooshing sound, which consumed Joanna's voice. Mervyn realised it was a roar of applause, and a stamping of feet.

Joanna raised her voice over the din. 'They're giving her a standing ovation... Which I suppose might be in poor taste given as she's in a wheelchair... And... Oh... They're giving her the first of a new award they've just dreamed up, "The Marcus Spicer Remembrance Award". How bloody ironic, considering the sod completely forgot about her in his will.'

'We're coming over.'

'Don't bother.'

'You're going to apologise to Samantha.'

'God, you really do believe in miracles, don't you Mervyn?'

'I do. Get ready. We're not far away.'

CHAPTER FORTY-NINE

'Not far away' was a very elastic concept when it came to London. Their taxi stayed mired in traffic all the way, and the lecture had all but finished by the time they huffed up the stone steps that led to the indifferent Victorian exterior, fighting against the flow of people exiting the building.

And there were the Godbotherers again; the ever-present angels watching over Mervyn as he went through life. They were held back by a line of grim-faced policemen. He saw Lewis Bream barking into a megaphone but couldn't make out the words. He didn't need to.

They sidled round the crowds; Professor Leman showed his membership card to a policeman in a padded vest, and they were allowed inside. It was a big empty space that sent their footsteps echoing round a neo-Gothic ceiling. Chairs were being folded away. The last members of the audience were dribbling out of the hall.

'Oh bum,' sighed the professor. He ambled into the hall and stood, looking around him, spinning on his heels, wondering what to do next. He finally chose a direction and wandered into a side office.

Cheryl was near the stage. Barry and Joanna were with her. Joanna marched up to Mervyn. She folded her arms. 'Get lost.'

'Apologise to Samantha. She wasn't the one who did this. She's just caught up in Marcus's post-mortem mischief.'

'Tough.'

Samantha poked her head round Mervyn's shoulder. 'I don't want you to apologise, Joanna.'

'Good, because I'm not going to. Don't let me detain you.'

'I just want your help.'

'Of course you do. You always need help. That's just you. Do you want me to take the cash round to the shelter for deaf seals, or the Royal Society for the Prevention of Suicidal Lemmings?'

'Seriously, I really do need your help. I never wanted this.' She held out her hands imploringly. 'Help me give it all back. We have to give it back.'

Joanna's face creased with suspicion. 'I don't believe you.'

'I don't want any of this. I don't want it. I promise I'll give Cheryl the money back. I'll sign any bit of paper you like.'

Joanna untangled her arms. Her eyebrows unfurled. 'Are you certain?'

'We need to look after Cheryl. I was thinking about that trust fund thing you were talking about. Perhaps I can give it the money, so we can look after her.'

Joanna stroked her chin, thinking. 'Yes, that might work, let's do that...'

'Oh, thank you...'

'Come to my office tomorrow. I'll have our lawyers come in, and we can see if we can sort something out.'

Samantha flew into Joanna's arms, hugging her. 'Oh thank you! Thank you! Thank you so much!' She seemed pitifully grateful at the offer to have her money taken from her.

Realising that Samantha had a New Best Friend – at least for the moment – Mervyn took the opportunity to dodge past them and talk to Cheryl.

Cheryl was trundling into the side office. Mervyn stepped in front of her, and Cheryl stared at him murderously.

'Out of my way Mervyn.' She nudged a lever by her hand, and, with a sudden spasm, the chair lurched two inches towards him.

Mervyn smiled nervously. He felt like the lone student in Tiananmen Square, facing down a tank. 'What's going on, Cheryl?'

'It's our quarterly humanist lecture.'

Mervyn looked despairingly at her. 'I didn't mean that. You know that. About the will.'

'Bad timing, that's all.'

'Bad timing? Is that all you can say?'

'Don't have a go at me Mervyn.' She shrugged. 'Marcus remade his will a month ago, you heard. Everybody thought I was going to die long before. I had weeks, all the doctors said so. Why would he leave me anything?'

'But Samantha...'

'He had to leave it to *someone*, Mervyn. It was either that or a diamond-encrusted coffin. Don't forget; I was supposed to be dead by now. He'd never risk my brother getting his hands on any of his money by default. He hated Barry. Samantha was his latest charity. His hopeless case. His good cause. It was like giving money to retired pit ponies.'

Mervyn had to agree. Samantha had the knackered, bewildered look of a put-upon animal that had been worked half to death and then released into a field to frolic. She begged to be taken advantage of, and now she wasn't even worth taking advantage of any more she looked for anyone who could do it in tiny trivial ways; a thieving boyfriend, an internet scam merchant, an unscrupulous convention organiser.

'But all the other stuff. Was that all true? You invited me to your wedding. I bought you a wok,' he said stupidly. 'Was that all it was? A big joke?'

'Mervyn, you just don't understand.'

'You're right, I don't.'

'That's the trouble with you, Mervyn. You've never believed in anything... not even in the *absence* of belief. I believed in exactly the same things Marcus believed in. I still do.'

Mervyn's face felt hot; he'd been insulted by experts, but Cheryl's casual dismissal stung him.

She continued. 'Marcus made enquiries about getting married, and yes, before you ask, he told me about Samantha. We were both aware he had to get a divorce first. That wasn't a problem. But then we looked at our options – two atheists; one of us a potential divorcee. All we could get was one crappy room in a council building; no confetti allowed because they hadn't got anyone to sweep it up.' She looked at him, angrily.

There was a lot of anger there; but how much of it was at the world, and how much of it was at her condition, at Marcus for leaving her with nothing? *She's come a long way from that giggle in the production office*, thought Mervyn. *She's had a long, hard journey.*

'We thought it was a scandal there wasn't a decent secular marriage service. When Marcus suggested we just pretend to get married I thought it was a great idea. I thought it was funny. It was either we did a pretend service, or we had a shitty real one; us, the witnesses and a couple of quick photos in front of some post-war monstrosity. So we chose to fake it, and we were right to do so. It was a lot more fun. And if I had my time over again, I'd do it again.'

'But...'

'Let me pass, Mervyn, I've got things to do.' She glided into the office, leaving Mervyn alone with his thoughts.

For all of ten seconds.

A piercing scream came from the office.

Mervyn ran into the office. The first thing he saw was Cheryl, eyes wide, fist crammed into her mouth.

Pointing at the floor.

Professor Leman was lying there, face frozen in agonised death. There was a bottle of water on the floor, and a puddle of water by his head.

CHAPTER FIFTY

The police dashed in, but Mervyn sneaked out through a side door. He thought Detective Inspector Preece wouldn't look charitably on his continuing habit of turning up near dead bodies.

He grabbed a cab and disappeared into the crush of vans, cars and motorbikes. Once safely hidden in the middle of a traffic jam, he rang Mick and arranged a meeting.

They reconvened in the plastic motorway café.

'This is a huge headfuck,' said Mick, slurping on something thick, pink and creamy. 'And I've seen some pretty headfucky things in my time.'

Mervyn believed her.

'*This* time, the water in the bottle was just that – water. But it looks probable that the old geezer was *still* poisoned with cyanide.'

'Another miracle.'

'Could be.'

Mervyn picked up a chip and dipped it something called 'special sauce'. He ate it. He realised the makers used the term 'special sauce' the way education authorities used the term 'special needs'. This anaemic gloop on his chip was definitely a late developer.

'And we've still got work to do on Robert's body,' she said. 'Electrocuted and burnt to a crisp when his pacemaker exploded. Forensics are going mental trying to pick the bones out of that one.'

'Frankly, I have no idea what's going on,' said Mervyn. 'I can see why Robert was killed, he seemed to have made a discovery about Marcus's murder. But the professor? He was just a nice old man.'

'He was an atheist,' growled Mick menacingly. 'God hates atheists and fags.'

'Be serious.'

'Okay, 'Mick folded her huge arms. 'Rule one of police deduction: it's normally the wife that does these sorts of things.'

'Which one? The one who pretended to be his wife, or the one who really was his wife?'

'That's easy. The one in the wheelchair.'

'Cheryl.'

'Yeah. Stands to reason she did it. All people in wheelchairs are evil. Look at the facts. Davros from *Doctor Who*: evil. Blofeld from James Bond: evil. Makrol from *Vixens from the Void*: evil.'

'You're a policewoman, for God's sake. You cannot call someone evil just because they're in a wheelchair.' He picked at his chips. 'Besides,

Makrol wasn't in a wheelchair. That was his atmospheric support system.'

'He sat in it. It had wheels. It was a fucking wheelchair.'

'Let's be serious here. Let's look at some facts. Robert was absolutely certain that Samantha killed Marcus. He was sure of that just before he died. How could he think that? I couldn't. There's no way that she could plan an intricate and fiendish series of murders when she's so dizzy she can barely work her own phone. But he was pretty convinced.'

'Well, let's have a look in her file.' She got out her notes. 'Samantha Carbury, right?'

'That's right.'

Mick rustled through her papers. 'There's been background checks done on all those present at Spicer's death; phone calls, credit checks, bank account records, usual stuff. She's a bit of a fruit loop.'

'Hmm... More of a dried fruit segment nestling in some fairtrade organic muesli. But you'll get no argument from me. Yes, she does have her batty elements, does our Sam.'

'She earns less than my brother does on his paper round, and all she doesn't spend on pot-pourri she gives away to causes. Lots and lots of causes. The Actors' Benevolent Fund, Mencap, Amnesty, WWF, the RSPCA, the RSPB, the RSPCC...'

'That's the NSPCC.'

'No – she does give to the NSPCC, but she also gives to the RSPCC, which is "The Rubbery Society for the Prevention of Custard on Clowns". They're just on Facebook at the moment.' The list got longer: Mick showed no signs of stopping. 'Meditate for Climate Change, Feng Shui for Africa, Adopt a Ghost...'

'Wait a second, "Adopt a Ghost"? What does that one do?'

'Great website. That's a charity that's concerned that the number of ghosts in England is declining due to all the renovations of barns and old houses going on, and they want money to buy houses with known poltergeist activity and keep them derelict so the ghosts don't leave.' She continued reading. 'Slug Rescue, The Ley Line Restoration Trust... There's even one which promises to get psychics to send positive thoughts to dictators in the third world... And hiding in the middle of this list is something called "Hearts of Giveness", a charity which raises money to buy "faith books" and give them to schools. Guess who they're connected to?'

Mervyn was already ahead of her. 'Don't tell me. Is Hearts of Giveness a subsidiary of the Godbotherers?'

'You must be psychic, Mervyn Stone. Maybe she'll donate to you.'

'It could be a coincidence.'

'Could well be. The best thing you can say is she's a soft touch.'

'Yes...' Then he realised something. 'Of course!'

He scrabbled frantically in his jacket, turning out his pockets on to the table, one after the other. Bits of paper, credit cards, pens and loose change clattered on the moulded plastic, sliding and rolling to the six corners of the table. A tramp, sitting by the window and nursing a coffee, hungrily eyed up a stray pound coin that had rolled on to the floor.

'Mervyn Stone,' Mick muttered, with slow menace. 'You are getting crumbs in my coleslaw.'

'Here it is!' He unfolded the page of *Spotlight* he'd rescued from Joanna's bin earlier that day. 'Look at this.' He jabbed a finger at the red writing. '"NOT A VIC!!! RING MARCUS?" This is what I found in Joanna's office. This proves Joanna knew Marcus and Cheryl's marriage was a fake...' He slumped back in his chair, admiration blooming across his face. 'She manipulated us from the start.'

'Who?'

'Joanna Paine of course. She's been doing some investigating of her own. She must have gone through *Spotlight*, seen this actor's photo, recognised it, just like me, and made the connection...' Mervyn grinned. 'Do you know, I wouldn't put it past her to find out what was in Marcus's latest will. Agents have their ways. I bet she knew Samantha was the main beneficiary – that's why she met up with me! Because she was playing up the concerned citizen, worried about Cheryl... Then she pretends to act really outraged at the reading, slaps Samantha... It's all emotional blackmail, working towards a huge guilt trip, so Samantha gives up her inheritance to this "trust fund" Joanna's setting up.' Mervyn helped himself to another chip. 'I bet she's arranging to get control of all that money as we speak.'

'Clever bitch. She lives by the Vixens' codes. Like me.'

Mervyn didn't comment.

'Got you a present,' said Mick suddenly.

'Oh?' Mervyn flinched, instinctively. He had visions of Mick producing a photo album of her favourite tattoos.

'I thought this might be useful to Mervyn Stone's investigation,' she said, pushing forward a CD box with 'DVD COMMENTARY' written on it. 'They got copies made for the investigation, and I nicked one. I thought if you listened to it again, it might help.'

Mervyn grinned in what he hoped was a surprised and delighted fashion. He didn't let on that he'd already listened to the commentary recording, or attempted to get Robert to make a copy for him.

Well, he thought. *Robert's copy didn't work... At least this one will...*

Perhaps his luck was changing...

CHAPTER FIFTY-ONE

Mervyn picked up the CD case and slotted it into his pocket.

'Thanks. I hope it will help, because I'm none the wiser now. Joanna's scheme makes her clever and avaricious, but not a murderer. And Samantha, it turns out, had the most to gain from Marcus's death, but she doesn't seem interested in keeping any of the money. Who else? Brian? It can't be Trevor, surely. There's just no credible suspect with means *and* motive.'

'I keep telling you, it's the one in the wheelchair. She must be evil. Stands to reason.'

Mervyn gave her a long-suffering look.

'The henchman then,' said Mick. 'Henchmen are always evil.'

'Aiden?'

'Yeah.'

'But why? Aiden seemed pretty upset when Marcus was killed.'

'Emotions can be faked. Take it from me.'

'But again, where's the motive? We all knew what Marcus was like. He was no different from the moment he became rich and famous to the day he died. Insufferable – but annoying enough to kill? No. So what was new? What had changed in the past few months to make someone want to kill him?'

Mick impaled a chip, dipped it in some special sauce and dropped it into her mouth. 'I'll tell you what changed. That statuette got nicked.'

'Yes. The statuette. Cheryl thought it was all tied up with that statuette. She thought the Godbotherers were after it. She said Marcus thought it held some kind of secret that they would kill for. How are you doing with finding it?'

'You'd like to know how I'm doing with finding that statuette?'

'Yes.'

'Fucking terrible.'

'Oh.'

'Until last night.'

'Oh?'

'I did all the usual police stuff; went through Trace, Bumblebee, looked up the dodgy pawnshops. Sweet fanny fuck-all.'

'Oh.'

'Then I gave up and went on the fan forums. It was much easier. The fan network is much better at tracking down this stuff than any coppers. You've got hundreds of experts online, and they all know when something iffy is going on. Can't keep secrets from the fans.'

'So I gather.'

'There's a forum called Voices from the Void, and they've got a chatroom attached. I got told on the forum last night that some bloke called "SpikeL" had been in the chatroom a couple of nights ago, trying to see if anyone was interested in buying a choice piece of memorabilia, a statuette of the Virgin Mary.'

'Really? Oh fantastic. What's his name? Spike... Elle?'

'SpikeL. "Spike" with a capital "L" on the end. One word. That's his username.'

'Do you think he's selling the statuette so he can buy drugs?'

'"User" as in computer user.'

'Ah. I see. So how do we find him?'

'Only one thing for it; someone has to loiter around the chatroom waiting for him to turn up again.'

'Great stuff. Let me know what you find out.'

'I'm on nights all this week...' Mick leaned in and looked deep into his eyes. 'But I will pull a sickie and spend the rest of the week sitting in that chatroom. Because you are Mervyn fucking Stone.'

Mervyn flinched. He was in enough trouble with the police without encouraging an officer to waste time surfing the internet.

'Don't worry. I don't want you in trouble with your superiors.' He stuck his jaw out with grim determination, and stood up. 'I'll go into that chatroom, as myself, and I'll hang around there all night, as long as it takes. I will use my own name, and I will make small talk about *Vixens*, *Star Trek*, *Torchwood* or even that film with the teenage vampires until I find out what I want.' He made a dignified exit into the gents toilets, which was made slightly less dignified when he tripped over a mop that was being pushed across the floor by a bored employee.

Mick watched the toilet door close behind him. 'Mervyn fucking Stone. There goes a brave man.'

CHAPTER FIFTY-TWO

(Fnar) I don't remember that.
(Styrob) yes there eyes didnt glow at all
(Fnar) Ill have to look at my copy

User *Ed 69* has entered the room

(Ed69) evening all
(Fnar) evening
(Styrob) and there voices wer funny
(Primegurl) evening ed
(Primegurl) I had spicy sausage pizza from tecos for tea.
(Primegurl) tescos
(Styrob) its not out yet on DVD yet
(Ed69) what's occurring?
(Fnar) I have a copy recorded off-air
(Fnar) My dad kept his video he made in the 80s
(Styrob) cool

User *Daveboy* has entered the room

(Fnar) My dad fancied medulla
(Styrob) LOL ☺
(Styrob) who did'nt?
(Ed69) I fancied Medula
(Ed69) and so did my wife
(Styrob) LOL ☺ ☺

User *Mervynstone* has entered the room

(Fnar) Hy Mervynstone
(Ed69) Hi
(Primegurl) evening Mervynstone
(Mervynstone) Hello. Again.
(Styrob) wb Mervin
(Ed69) Hi
(Primegurl) I had a poster of Medula on my wall I fancyd her so much
(Styrob) Your a girl!!!!!
(Fnar) wa-hay! *waggles eyebrows at Primegurl*
(Primegurl) no im not

(Mervynstone) Sorry to bother all of you... again...
(Fnar) awww ☹
(Mervynstone) You're probably sick of me asking...
(Mervynstone)... But do any of you chaps know of someone called 'SpikeL'?
(Fnar) Mervynstone: no, still not heard of him. Soz. ☹
(Primegurl) Im primegurl cos im prime gurl material lol
(Fnar) u sed it
(Ed69) SpikeL? Yeah I know him

User *Daveboy* has left the room

(Primegurl) Fnar: LOLZ!
(Mervynstone) Ed 69: Really?
(Ed69) SpikeL. Yeah.
(Mervynstone) Thank god! I've been hanging around here for three whole nights!!! I feel like I'm ordering a meal in a Parisian restaurant. Everyone knows what I'm saying but no one wants to speak my language!
(Ed69) He was on a few nights ago talking about Vixens AFAIR
(Mervynstone) He had an affair with someone from 'Vixens'? Was it Samantha Carbury?
(Ed69) AFAIR. One F. Stands for – As Far As I Remember ☺
(Mervynstone) Oh, I see. And people saying LOL at me doesn't mean they're sitting comfortably and lolling about, right?
(Ed69) No ☺
(Mervynstone) What did 'SpikeL' say?
(Ed69) He wanted to sell his stature
(Ed69) statue
(Ed69) Said it was a collectors item from the series. Exclussive.
(Styrob) Primegurl: so u r a boy ☹
(Primegurl) Yeah sorry
(Styrob) This posting has been blocked by our obscenity filters.
(Ed69) was a Virgin Mary
(Mervynstone) Really? Did you buy it?
(Fnar) virginlol
(Ed69) NO WAY! Wanted five thousand for it
(Styrob) Were al virgins here I bet
(Fnar) lol
(Ed69) I told him 2 go 2 big collectors. They might want it
(Mervynstone) Did you tell him who might want it
(Mervynstone) ?

(Styrob) Not simon josh LOL
(Fnar) Bad karma Styrob ☹

User *Styrob* has left the room

(Ed69) Yes
(Ed69) E-mail me off list and I'll tell you who.
(Mervynstone) What?
(Ed69) Click on my name in the guest list. You'll get my e-mail.
(Mervynstone) Thank you so much. I'm so grateful for this, I am willing to pay you a little something.
(Ed69) No worries. Glad to help.
(Mervynstone) Perhaps a signed copy of a script book or something?
(Primegurl) r u realy Mervin stone?
(Mervynstone) I am. Nice to meet you, Primegurl. Well, I'm not really meeting you at all, am I? But you know what I mean.
(Primegurl) LOL
(Ed69) No need for payment
(Ed69) I'll take the statue when you've finished LOL
(Ed69) Signed script book wld b fine
(Mervynstone) Okay.
(Mervynstone) What does LOL mean?

User *Ed69* has left the room

User *Mervynstone* has left the room

(Primegurl) He didnt know what LOL ment
(Fnar) LOL

CHAPTER FIFTY-THREE

'Primegurl' sat back in his seat and removed his hands from the keyboard.

At last.

His mission was so sensitive he couldn't even risk asking about the statue in the chatroom. Anybody could have been lurking there, hoping to pick up information. After all, that's what he was doing.

He had to wait until 'SpikeL' blundered in again, so he spent his evenings flirting and talking nonsense, waiting. But 'SpikeL' never showed.

And then along came 'Mervynstone'.

It didn't take much to hack into 'Ed69's' account, look at all his postings and find out who he'd recommended to 'SpikeL' as a possible buyer for the statue.

Time to put the hood back on.

CHAPTER FIFTY-FOUR

Holland Park was a very nice area of London. There were long rows of Victorian houses lining the streets; none of them had clusters of bells by the door. None of them had been converted into flats.

It was very pretty. Nevertheless, Mervyn felt unnerved as he strode along the streets, walking slowly in the pools of light flung out by the streetlamps, glancing at his Google Earth map and dashing through the blackness in between. The map was a patchwork of pixels; as far as the view from space was concerned, most of the houses along this street didn't exist. A sure sign that Mervyn was in the presence of serious money.

He had a feeling he was being followed. No, it wasn't a feeling. He *knew* he was being followed. He'd heard the throaty roar of a motorcycle engine. He heard it come very close, and then stop. Then, minutes later, he saw someone illuminated by a streetlight; someone in leathers and a biker's helmet was walking about 40 yards behind him. Walking slowly, not hurrying.

The biker was off his bike. Why hadn't he taken his helmet off?

Mervyn tested a theory. He turned into a side street and picked up speed. He stepped into the drive of an eye-wateringly expensive house and peered around a stone pillar. The biker was at the junction, looking around, left, right and left again. Then the biker walked back along the main road.

When Mervyn was sure that the biker had gone, he slipped out of the drive and continued on his way. The opulent houses gradually gave way to ostentatious houses, and soon he found himself outside the gates of a house that was about the size and value of a small village.

He pressed the intercom, there was a chime, and the gates swung open.

'Greetings to you, Mervyn Stone,' said Graham Goldingay. He stood in the doorway, resplendent in an expensive dressing gown, monogrammed slippers decorating his feet. To Mervyn's mind, with his huge round head and jowly face, Graham looked like Orson Welles, bald cap on head, relaxing between takes on the set of *Citizen Kane*.

Mervyn was ushered into Graham's amazing house. He had never been in such an impressive foyer – not since he'd been to the Natural History Museum anyway. Just staring at the ceiling made him dizzy, it was so high. Wide windows decorated with coloured glass threw patterns across the floor.

There was another reason why it resembled the Natural History

Museum; the middle of the foyer also contained a dinosaur; a cheap flimsy creature hung up with strings and encased in glass.

'It's a genuine prop from the episode "The Salandrian Inheritance",' said Graham. 'It cost me £20,000. Simon Josh went up to £18,000, but I beat him. That was a great moment.' Graham looked sternly at him, bunching his features together in a tight wrinkled mass. 'Now, you said you had something important to ask me. I hope you have decided to end your self-imposed exile in regards to my independent productions...'

'Sorry Graham, I'm hard at work on my first novel.'

'Oh well, I'm sure you wouldn't deny my production company the first opportunity to adapt your book for the screen?'

'Let's talk about that when it's finished.'

They walked into the bowels of the building.

'I actually want to talk to you about something that may have "fallen into your hands" lately, or offered to you but turned down. Something *Vixens*-related. It used to belong to a friend of mine and I want to get it back... I don't know if you remember the item...'

'I remember everything. I can name and tell you the location and owner of every prop currently in the hands of a celebrity, collector, museum or exhibition.'

'You may have got it privately, from someone who approached you specifically...'

'Let me just say first, if we're talking about Samantha Carbury's underwear here, then I got them fair and square, with a certificate of provenance signed by the previous owner. I'm very shocked and saddened that an identical pair disappeared from her dressing room during filming in Studio 8 in 1991, but my pair is not that pair, and my ownership of them is completely legitimate and above board.'

'Don't worry Graham. I don't think you'd buy stolen knickers.'

'No.'

'That would be tacky.'

'I am very glad you think that, as they're one of my most prized pieces. Come and have a look at them and other prized pieces, and prepare to be amazed.' He waddled through wide, echo-strewn corridors and into more rooms. 'I take it this is in relation to your investigation into Marcus Spicer's death.'

'Now why would I be investigating anyone's death?'

'A simple deduction, Mervyn, I have read Andrew Jamieson's book, of course.'

'Of course.'

'Simon's loss was a great shock, I was delighted that you deduced his murderer.'

'Thanks.'

'But then, to be blunt, I'm also delighted that Simon Josh was murdered. I picked up a lot from his memorial auction. You don't mind me being blunt, do you?'

'You just do what comes naturally, Graham.'

'We are very much partners in this enterprise. I'm very glad we are both able to help the police with their investigations.'

'Both?'

'Indeed. The police contacted me, and asked me what I knew about the characters involved in the incident.'

'"Characters"... You mean us? Me, Samantha, Brian?'

'Yes, that is what I said, the characters,' retorted Graham, stroking his beard. 'I was pleased to say I was very helpful.' He showed Mervyn his lapel. 'I had this made, nice isn't it?'

Mervyn looked. Fastened to Graham's jacket was a badge with 'Police Adviser' printed on it. Mervyn's face suddenly grew hot. He'd made a connection. 'Did you tell the police about my relationship with Cheryl Spicer?'

'Of course I did. I told them everything I had in my files, the information I gave them on Samantha Carbury alone should keep them busy for weeks.'

Mervyn considered acting outraged and shouting at Graham, but just sighed and stayed silent. Explaining tact and discretion to Graham would be like the captain of the *Titanic* explaining shipping routes to the iceberg. As they approached a stairwell, Graham produced a plastic badge on a clip and gave it to Mervyn. 'You'll need to wear this.'

'Graham, I am not pretending that I'm in a science fiction convention. Much as it might give you a thrill. Sorry.'

'The badge stops you tripping my motion sensors. They're situated on all corridors adjacent to my museum of memorabilia. I have them sewn into every garment I own.'

Mervyn dutifully pinned on a badge, and they entered a huge wood-panelled library. Graham pulled a switch, and the lights plunged them into a deep blue, like they were suddenly at the bottom of a swimming pool.

'We have to switch to ultraviolet light. Normal electric light will fade everything.'

There were about a dozen glass cabinets glowing, illuminated by blue spotlights. The cabinets were beautiful; the contents were ugly. Shabby lumps of polystyrene. Warped bits of molten plastic. A crudely painted crash helmet with a shower hose attached to the back.

'You'll remember that,' said Graham as he passed it. 'That's the space helmet from "Day of the Styrax". The one Medula sabotaged. That... is television history. I got that from Simon's estate. He said I'd only get it from him if I prised it from his cold dead hands. And he was right.'

Mervyn was treated to an impromptu tour of tat. By the end of it he knew the history of two hairdryers, a kid's torch glued to a TV remote control and a shrivelled condom sprayed green.

'That was the larval stage of the Qu'arzal Wasp, believe it or not. It looks a bit different now. With some of my exhibits, it helps if you willingly suspend your disbelief.'

'I'm just about suspending my disbelief. Just don't tell me how much you paid for it.' He examined one of the hairdryers. 'Do you know, if I didn't know better, I'd say these "disappeared" from the set shortly after we wrapped. I always suspected Bernard Viner of taking them but we never found out –'

Graham jumped like a scalded cat. 'That's vicious slander.'

'Graham, I'm not saying...'

'If someone comes to me with merchandise and proof of provenance, then I don't ask questions. I always assume good faith.'

'You said. I'm sorry I mentioned it.'

'You will be. I attain lawyers like I collect merchandise. I have 23, and they're all very valuable, and very collectable.' Graham sat in a huge leather chair, and tapped his desk absently with stubby fingers. 'So, what is this piece you're so keen to track down?'

'Someone called "Spike" or "SpikeL" might have contacted you. You were recommended to him by a guy called "Ed69". God, I'm sounding like a footnote in *Lord of the Rings*. Anyway, it's a small statuette of the Virgin Mary from "The Burning Time".'

At the mention of the statue, Graham's piggy little eyes went cold. 'I don't know anything about any statuette.'

'But you just said you knew everything about every prop. Where they were, who owned them...'

'Let me rephrase that, I know nothing of the whereabouts of any prop that used to be owned by Marcus Spicer.'

'But I haven't told you who owned it yet.'

Graham stopped, blinking. He'd been caught out.

'Another simple deduction. The statuette was from "The Burning Time". You knew Marcus Spicer and you're investigating his death. It had to be the one which belonged to him.'

'Of course. How obvious.'

'It takes a lot to get past me.'

'I can believe it.'

CHAPTER FIFTY-FIVE

The hooded man pulled up some dustbins and clambered over the wall around Graham's house. It wasn't hard to circumvent the security cameras; they were stubbornly fixed on the side nearest the conservatory, daring any fortune hunters to break into the museum.

There were no cameras pointing at the entrance to the coal cellar; for the simple reason that the coal cellar didn't lead anywhere. It was just a featureless brick room completely cut off from the rest of the house.

The hooded man would soon fix that. He hefted a heavy hammer, ideal for breaking cement.

'I don't like your tone,' huffed Graham. 'Look around you. Is there a statuette of the Virgin Mary in any of these cases?'

'Of course I wouldn't expect it to be on display,' snapped Mervyn crossly. 'It's stolen property and you know it. You probably have it tucked away so you can take it out every night and stroke it.'

'How dare you! If you weren't creator of the best television show in television history, I would call the police here and now.' Graham switched off the UV lights, leaving only the desklamp to throw their shadows on the wall. 'As it is, I would like you to leave.'

'With pleasure.'

'I may never ask you to contribute to one of my videos, charity meals or documentaries ever again.'

'That's a risk I'm prepared to take.'

A BLEEH-BLEEH-BLEEH noise charged around the room, loud and unpleasant. Mervyn clamped his hands to his ears. 'What's that?' he shouted.

'It's the museum alarm,' bellowed Graham. He hauled his corpulent physique to the door with surprising speed. 'The motion sensors.'

The alarm was going, but the hooded man didn't care. He only wanted to get into the building.

Once he was in he had no intention of leaving. Not without the statuette. And he was willing to do whatever it took to get it.

Graham pulled a tiny handle, revealing a door which blended into the panelling of the wall; it was barely visible to the untrained eye. It opened on to a tiny cupboard-sized space crammed with television screens. Graham climbed in and Mervyn followed.

Graham gaped at one of the screens. There was a huge hole in the wall next to a pile of rubble. A lump hammer leaned nonchalantly against an antique hatstand. 'What's going on?'

A figure ran across one of the screens. It appeared on another screen, then it scuttled across a third, as if a mouse was loose inside the television sets. Then it appeared in close-up.

It was a man in a hoodie.

The figure stopped and looked up, directly into the camera. Mervyn shivered. The head was completely covered in a black balaclava and the eyes were shielded by sunglasses. It was as if the invisible man had decided to pay them a visit.

'Go away!' shouted Graham at the camera. 'Go away or I'll call the police!'

'Do your cameras have a public address system?'

'No,' muttered Graham, shamefaced. 'I always shout at the television. Force of habit.'

'I think we'd better think of something more practical we can do.'

They looked up and the figure was gone.

Graham pushed a button on the wall. Nothing happened.

'What was that supposed to do?'

'It's meant to lower the security walls. He's switched them off. How could he do that?' With shaking fingers, Graham prised his phone out of his shirt pocket. 'I knew I should have installed that panic room,' he said, flipping open the phone's carapace to reveal the buttons. 'I'm phoning the police.'

'Is there somewhere safe we can go in the meantime?'

'The study. We can lock ourselves in there.'

'Come on!' He pushed Graham in front of him, but the fat fan was too slow. He was grossly out of shape, and wasn't looking where he was going as he was trying to dial. Mervyn's brain screamed with impatience as he steered Graham through the house; the hooded man knew he had been discovered. He would have to move quickly.

Mervyn didn't realise quite how quickly, though, and only got the first inkling when something descended over his head, obscuring his vision, and his legs were pushed from under him. He made an unscheduled meeting with the floor below.

CHAPTER FIFTY-SIX

Mervyn couldn't see.

He was dragged into another room and his hands and feet tied to a chair. There was something on his face that smelt of fabric conditioner. A pillowcase, he guessed. There was also another odour. A sickly odour. A sickly, sweaty odour. A sickly, sweaty, meaty odour. A sickly, sweaty, meaty, curry-flavoured –

'This is appalling,' said a familiar voice.

Graham was directly behind him. From the feel of Graham's hands next to his, he was tethered to another chair facing in the opposite direction. Mervyn always felt he had a habit of ending up in the wrong place at the wrong time. He measured his location in degrees of wrongitude and crapitude. *Tied to a 20-stone man in a big dark house, empty save for a violent religious nut? I would put this at about 100 degrees wrong, 200 degrees crap.*

'What's going on?' wheezed Mervyn.

'I don't know,' trembled Graham. 'He tied you up, and then dragged us both in here.'

Mervyn shook his body vigorously, and found that by jerking his neck forward he could edge the pillow case from his head, one inch at a time. He finally dislodged it, and it fluttered down and rested on his knees.

They were back in the main exhibit room of Graham's pocket museum. The cabinets had been illuminated, their lights spilling eerily around them, like they were the star performers on a 70s TV variety show.

'My God,' whimpered Graham. 'He's switched on the normal electric lighting. The damage will be hideous...'

'Is he still here?'

'Oh yes. He's still here. He just came in a minute ago to have a look at us.'

Mervyn shook his head wearily. 'Why?'

'Probably to check we weren't escaping.'

'No I mean "Why have I ended up tied to you?"' Mervyn sighed. 'That settles it; there must be a God. This much vindictive hatred can't be the result of natural selection.'

'He could be back at any moment. You have to move fast.'

'Move fast? In what direction? What do you expect me to do?'

'When he tied me up I struggled a bit, so I could drop my phone in the confusion.'

'Good thinking Graham. Where is it?'

'Over there.'

Mervyn looked, and sure enough, nestled by the side of a pillar, was a small square of silver. 'Over there? What can I do about it?'

'Try to reach it.'

'You're joking.'

'I never joke about anything.'

Mervyn tried to push his legs against the ropes, but nothing happened. 'No chance.' But he had another go, harder. The ropes moved slightly, and he found he could move his leg about three inches away from the chair leg. 'I've got a leg partially released.'

'Well a partial release isn't good enough. You've got to release the whole thing.'

He pushed again. The ropes gave way. His leg came away from the chair so fast he almost kicked himself in the head. 'It's released.'

'Finally.'

He stretched out his leg towards the phone, but came up short. 'It's too far away.'

'You've got to get it,' babbled Graham, 'it's our only hope.'

Mervyn strained with all his energy. He found that, if he slumped low in his chair, he could slip the ropes a couple of inches further up his body and get more reach. His toes teased the edge of the phone, but it stayed stubbornly in the corner. 'Right,' gasped Mervyn. 'Third time lucky.'

He lunged, rocking the chair forward and almost tipping Graham on top of him in the process (that would not have been good). He slammed his heel dead square on the phone, and scraped it along the floor. 'Got it.'

'Good work.'

He dragged the phone until it was directly under his chair and eased it to where his fingers tickled the floor. They scuttled towards the phone and scooped it up.

'Okay guys, to business.'

It was a strange voice.

The hooded man was in the doorway. They hadn't heard him arrive.

Mervyn quietly slipped the phone in his jacket pocket.

'I'm not gonna beat around the bush. I just want to know one thing...' The voice was harsh, metallic, slurred. He was using something to distort it.

'... The statuette of the Virgin Mary and Child. I want to know where it is.'

Graham's eyes bulged. 'As I told Mervyn, I don't know what you're talking about.'

'Oh, you do.' He advanced on them with a crowbar. 'Where's the Madonna and Child?'

Mervyn raised an eyebrow. 'Don't you mean the Fallen Madonna with the Big Boobies?'

'You're funny. I hope Graham can laugh through the pain.'

Graham rippled with fear.

'You can torture us if you like,' said Mervyn. 'It won't make any difference.'

The hooded man shook his head emphatically. 'I'm not going to torture.. Well, not *you*, anyway.'

The hooded man dashed into a corner and brought the crowbar down on a cabinet, smashing the glass. Graham squealed in pain.

'Where's the Virgin Mary?' the hooded man demanded.

'I don't know!' wailed Graham.

The hooded man pulled out an artefact from the cabinet. It was nothing more than a piece of plastic guttering decorated with used disposable razors, glued to a lawn strimmer and sprayed a deep metallic blue. 'What's this?'

'It's Arkadia's bazooka. She used it on Magaroth's imperial robot guard in "Assassins of Destiny" episode two...'

'Not any more it isn't.' He threw it on the ground and stamped on it.

'Noooooo!' screamed Graham.

Grinding his hobnail boots on the prop until nothing was left, the hooded man went to another cabinet, smashing it with a swift jab from his crowbar. He picked up a tiny object. It was an air freshener painted black, with a telephone cord sprouting out of the side. 'What's this?'

'It's Medula's personal communicator,' sobbed Graham. 'It was featured in season –'

'Not any more.' The hooded figure threw it against the wall with all his might. It shattered on impact, and the bits cascaded down the wall. Graham wailed like his feet had been dipped in molten lead.

'You animal,' said Mervyn, casting worried glances at Graham's purple face. 'Can't you see what this is doing to him?'

'It's your choice, Graham,' grated the figure. 'The Virgin Mary and Child versus your entire collection. Is it worth more than all the other rubbish here?'

Graham shook his head, unable to speak. Barely able to think.

'Is it?'

'No!' he blurted.

'Then where's the Madonna and Child?'

Graham hesitated for a second too long, and he was rewarded with another crash, as a third cabinet felt the impact of the crowbar. The hooded man pulled out the crash helmet; the one Graham had proudly showed Mervyn earlier. He held it by the shower hose attachment and started to swing it, low and wide, like a priest swinging incense.

'It's in the wall! It's in the wall!'

'Where in the wall?'

'Behind the *Radio Times* cover!'

A *Radio Times* cover hung on the far wall, encased in a dark hardwood frame. Predictably, the cover featured the Vixens, firing their guns in all directions and heralding the second series of *Vixens from the Void* in 1987. The hooded man walked across and tugged at it. It clicked and swung smoothly open, revealing a small wall safe.

'Combination?' said the hooded man, still swinging the space helmet menacingly.

'It's the date of broadcast of the first *Vixens* episode.'

'Well how should I know that, you fat fuck? What's the bloody combination?'

'Eighteen left, nine right, 86 left.'

The hooded figure twiddled the dial and the door of the safe fell open, revealing a cheap plaster statuette of the Virgin Mary holding the infant Jesus. It was neither particularly pretty nor particularly well painted. It looked like a cheap prop, because that was what it was.

The hooded figure eased the statuette reverently out of the safe, behaving like it was the most important thing in the world. Mervyn knew the Godbotherers took their religion very seriously, but couldn't see why they would hold a lump of plaster of Paris in such high esteem.

'Goodbye, gentlemen. Do not be alarmed. I'm sure the police will be here before you know it.' He disappeared from the room.

They sat there, surrounded by glass and debris, listening to the silence.

'Can you reach that disposable razor with your foot?' said Graham at last, his voice thick with misery.

'Graham, that razor is 20 years old,' snapped Mervyn. 'There's no way it could cut through anything.'

'No...' snivelled Graham. 'I just wanted you to reach it, and push it over there, with the other disposable razor over there... Because they go together... And then you could try and put the third one there, and push the bit of drainpipe to go with them... Because they go together, you see...'

Mervyn realised that the large man was suffering from shock. They would have to get themselves released soon; before Graham started screaming and eating his own face.

We've got to get out of –

There was a 'thud' outside the door, and an almighty crash.

'My God, what's happening now?' whimpered Graham.

CHAPTER FIFTY-SEVEN

The leather-clad biker strode into the room. Hands reached up, straps were unfastened, and the crash helmet was pulled off.

It was Mick.

'Are you following me? That's harassment,' said Mervyn, angrily.

Mick produced a card. 'Here's the number of the Police Complaints Commission. Call it and make a complaint.' She proffered it, but of course Mervyn wasn't able to take it.

'Oh very good,' said Mervyn.

She stuck it back in her pocket and left the room, returning seconds later, dragging the hooded man in by the scruff of his neck. Mick was completely encased in motorbike leathers, and Mervyn could now make out 'HELL'S VIXENS' spelled out on her back in shiny pointy studs.

She grappled with their ropes. 'He's used good knots,' she said, grunting.

'Can you get us free?'

'Yeah. Just might take a bit longer than normal.'

Graham wobbled in concern. 'What do you mean "normal"?'

'What I mean.'

The ropes dropped to the floor, and Mervyn and Graham rubbed their wrists.

'Just walk about and touch your toes,' said Mick. 'My boyfriends find it helps their pins and needles.'

She dragged the hooded figure further into the room; like a caveman who had chosen a mate. She propped him up in Graham's expensive leather chair and swivelled him to face Mervyn and Graham.

'All right, let's see who this is.'

She pulled the hood back and rolled up the balaclava, tugging it off.

CHAPTER FIFTY-EIGHT

'Aiden?'

That wasn't what Mervyn expected at all. He was expecting some religious fanatic pursuing him in the name of the Godbotherers, as part of some *Da Vinci Code*-style plot.

'Who's that?' asked Graham.

'It's Aiden, Marcus Spicer's bodyguard.'

'I told you so, Mervyn Stone,' said Mick. 'Henchmen. They're evil. All of them.'

They tied him to the chair. Mick took the opportunity to go through Aiden's pockets. She plucked out his wallet and went through it, chucking out credit cards and making a shower of plastic confetti.

'Credit card... video club card... membership of the Spicer Institute... credit card... Hmm. Hello...'

Mervyn sidled up to her shoulder.

'Membership of a squash club in Kensington. Très mucho posho. But it's in the name of a Mr M. Spicer.'

'Why would he have Marcus's membership card?'

'Perhaps he used to pick up Marcus's sweaty kecks for him. You know how these types are with their burly butlers... Anyway, let's ask him, shall we?' She took off her glove and slapped his cheek with it. Aiden groaned. 'Come on, Mr Atheist. Time to come towards the light.' She glared at the unconscious bodyguard. 'Atheists,' she growled. 'I hate atheists.'

'I thought you'd hate the other lot,' said Mervyn. 'The Christians. You being a "Hell's Vixen" and all.'

'Me and Christians have more in common. We both believe in hell. The difference is, they see it as a bad thing.'

Aiden started to stir.

Mick's eyes narrowed. 'Not believing in hell is irritating. And rude.'

Mervyn would not have wanted to be in Aiden's shoes at that moment.

'Come on, Sleeping Ugly, wakey wakey,' growled Mick.

Aiden woke up, eyes rolling in bafflement. Before he could get his bearings, Mick grabbed each of his cheeks between a thumb and forefinger and forced him to look into her eyes.

'Okay, beautiful. You've not been very nice to Mervyn Stone. And that means you've not been very nice to me. If I were in full costume, I'd probably just hang you up on the wall and take your skin off with my electrowhip. Lucky for you it's at the menders.'

'Pshh uff.'

She let go of his cheeks.

'Piss off,' he repeated.

'You're going to be nice, aren't you?'

'Let me go, bitch.'

She wielded her glove again and slapped him hard across the other cheek. 'Don't tell me what to do. I only take orders from one guy here, and his name is decorating my arse. I don't think your name is on my arse, last time I looked. Unless your name is Harvey Nicks.'

Mervyn stepped forward. 'What's all this about, Aiden? What's so important about that statuette?'

Aiden didn't say anything.

'Look, I was Marcus's friend too. Surely we're on the same side here.'

'It's got nothing to do with you.'

'It would be easier on you if you talked to us. You're in a lot of trouble.'

'I've not hurt anyone. So don't even think of hurting me.' He nodded to Mick. 'What that cow's done is already technically assault. If you're very lucky, I won't press charges.'

'I'll call the police,' said Graham.

'Call the police,' sneered Aiden. 'Let them take me away.'

'Then I won't,' said Graham stubbornly.

Aiden gave a lazy smile. 'You can't keep me here. Just let me go. Give me the statuette and we'll say no more about it.'

Graham hugged the figurine close to his ample bosom. 'Absolutely not!'

'It's stolen property. It doesn't belong to you. I'll just come back with the police myself and take it back in the name of Mr Spicer's estate.'

'Mr Spicer's estate?' said Mervyn sharply. 'Who sent you. Was it Cheryl?'

Aiden kept silent.

'Was it Cheryl?' Mervyn said, slightly angry now.

'He said "estate",' said Mick. 'She doesn't own the Spicer estate anymore.'

'Oh no. So she doesn't. Did Samantha tell you to find this statuette? Was it Samantha?'

'I answer to no one. Just my boss, Mr Spicer.'

'You take orders from your dead boss?' said Mervyn, perplexed. 'That's a bit mystical for an atheist, isn't it?'

'I'm saying nothing.'

Graham was tiptoeing over the debris of his collection, his hands rubbing his huge egg-shaped head. 'I'll tell the police what you did to my beautiful collection! Not to mention my wall!'

'I'll tell the cops that I'm very sorry and I'm willing to pay for the damage... But you... I'll just tell them I was after stolen property, nicked from my boss. You'll have questions to answer too...' He strained around to look at the glass boxes. 'How much of this crap here is actually legit?'

Graham fell silent.

Aiden looked triumphantly at Mervyn. 'You can't keep the statuette and you can't keep me, so just let us both go, there's a good boy.'

'He's right. We can't. And he's not going to talk,' said Mervyn angrily. 'Give him the statuette, Graham.'

'No.'

Aiden grinned. 'Do you want to go to prison for receiving stolen goods?'

Mick stepped forward and wrenched the statuette out of Graham's arms. She held it out to Aiden. 'Okay beautiful, you win. You can have it.'

'At last, someone's got some sense round here. If you untie, me I'll say no more about it.'

'Only joking,' said Mick. She dropped the statuette on the floor. It smashed into a thousand pieces.

CHAPTER FIFTY-NINE

'NOOOOOO!' screamed Aiden and Graham. Graham's booming wail was a complete octave below Aiden's shriek; a perfect harmony of anguish.

The fragments skittered across the floor, sliding into corners and under tables. Graham fell to his knees amid the debris, staring at the pieces helplessly like a monkey trying to complete a thousand-piece jigsaw.

'Dat was irreplaceable,' sobbed Graham, his Irish brogue thickening with grief. 'Unique! The last ever cheap copy of an original statuette of its kind ever made.'

Something slid along the floor and rested against Mick's booted foot.

'Look,' said Mervyn, pointing.

Mick reached down amongst the fragments and picked it up. It was an ordinary piece of statuette but glued to it was a thick rubber bracelet. And attached to the bracelet...

'It's a key,' she said, holding it up so everyone could see. 'It was stuck inside. The hollow base was bunged up with white plasticine so it looked solid.'

'So it is,' breathed Graham, fascinated. He scrambled to his feet, the shattered statuette completely forgotten.

'Give me that key!' Aiden was struggling against his bonds furiously. The chair was dancing across the floor. 'That's mine! Give me that key!'

'It's small and fiddly,' said Mick, disappointed. Mervyn could imagine her saying something like that after a heavy-drinking Friday night, crushing the ego of many an amorous suitor.

'It's about the right size to open a safety deposit box,' said Graham.

'I don't think so,' said Mervyn.

'It's got a bracelet,' said Graham. 'Safety deposit boxes have bracelets.'

'Not rubber ones, they don't,' growled Mick.

'Leave it alone!' Aiden wobbled impotently on his chair.

Mervyn turned it over. It had '212' written on it in bold marker pen. 'There's a number. I wonder if it's from a luggage locker, like at a station?'

Mick placed something in Mervyn's line of vision. It was the membership card she'd fished from Aiden's pocket.

'Or a locker at a squash club?'

'Mick that's brilliant! I could hug you!'

'Wait until I've finished scabbing over. I'm still a bit tender.'

'Give me that key!' Aiden shouted. 'You'll be sorry! You'll be in a world of pain!'

Mick advanced towards Aiden, pulling something out of her pocket. Aiden grew alarmed. 'Stay away from me you bitch! I know you're police! I'll have your badge!'

She pulled out a thick roll of masking tape, unfurled it, pulled off the backing and stuck one end over his mouth. Aiden twitched this way and that, trying to avoid her, but she held his head firm in her huge hands, wrapping the roll round and round his head until the only evidence there was a human being inside was the tip of a nose poking out. Now he looked like the invisible man once more.

'Can you do that?' said Mervyn.

'Yes I can. You just saw me. Lucky I had the masking tape with me. Lucky I was planning to see my Jimbo tonight, or as he likes to be called, "Victim number seven".'

Mervyn didn't pursue the matter. 'I'll go to the squash club tomorrow and find out what he's looking for.'

Mick flashed the card. 'We can go now. It's open 24 hours.'

'Great. No time to waste.'

Graham scooted to the door, his slippers flapping on the wooden floor. He interposed himself in the doorway. 'You're not going anywhere. Not with that key.'

'Graham...'

'That key's mine.'

Mick placed her hands on her hips. 'Don't talk to Mervyn Stone like that, lardy, or I'll staple your stomach for you.'

'Don't threaten me. It's mine.'

'Look Graham, you should at least give the key to Mick. It's important evidence, and, would you believe, she's a policewoman.'

'I don't care. Neither of you are taking that key anywhere.'

'Graham...'

'It's mine. I bought it.'

'No it's not.'

'It's mine!'

'I don't think so.'

Graham pushed a button on the wall. An alarm honked twice, and heavy metal doors slammed into place around them. 'I've switched the security walls back on, as you can see.'

'You can't keep us here.'

'I don't intend to keep you here. I intend to phone the police and get them to arrest you both for trespass, vandalism and attempted theft.'

'Don't be silly, Graham.'

'I'm well within my rights. You're in my house, you've damaged my lawful property. And you're removing something that belongs to me.'

'It doesn't belong to you.'

'I bought the statuette, and what was inside it.'

Mervyn sighed. He knew Graham was going to wear him down. Graham wore everyone down, eventually.

Mick stepped forward, and stood a little too close to Graham. Graham looked nervous, but he held his ground. Eventually, she tossed the key at him.

'Okay doughboy. You can keep the key...' She produced the squash club card and held it in front of his face, carefully covering the details on the card with her thumb. 'But I've got this. Finders, keepers. So we know where that key belongs. You don't. Can't see you going round every squash club in London. You wouldn't know where they were, unless they were next door to a pie shop.'

Graham stared at her, eyes glaring mutinously. As the only Englishman in the room, Mervyn thought it his duty to calm things down. He stepped between them, hand upraised.

'Let's all go together,' he said. 'We can do that, can't we?'

Graham looked at the key in his hand, then he looked at the card in Mick's. 'Okay, he said. 'We go together.'

Mick picked up her helmet. 'Good. Can you ride pillion?'

'I'll try,' said Graham.

'I wasn't talking to you, Pavarotti. You can get there under your own steam. I was talking to Mervyn Stone.'

'A long time ago,' said Mervyn. 'But yes, I have ridden once or twice.'

'Good. Suit up, Mervyn Stone...'

Suddenly the heavy metal version of the *Vixens* theme sounded again, somewhere near Mick's left breast. She unzipped a pocket, pulled out a mobile phone, and flipped it open. 'Yeah?'

She listened.

'Oh fuck. You're fucking kidding me. Thanks Terry.' She folded the phone. 'That was Terry in CAD.'

'What did he say?'

'What did *she* say. Terry is short for Theresa. She thought her name was shit too.'

'Okay,' said Mervyn wearily. 'What did *she* say?'

'I rang her just before I got here, told her where I was. She's just sent a squad car over to this place. We didn't respond to the first alarm because someone answered the phone and told them it was set off accidentally...'

They all looked at Aiden's struggling form.

'But Pavarotti here's just set off the alarm again, and this time no one answered the phone. They'll be here any minute.'

They looked around at the debris. The broken cabinets. The shattered statuette. The struggling bodyguard.

'It don't look good,' said Mick. 'You and Porky Pig go and look in that locker. I'll stay here. I can tell them I was passing, heard the alarm and made an arrest. Which, luckily, happens to be true.'

Mervyn hovered in the doorway, looking warily at Aiden. 'But he'll talk. He'll say something.'

'He's not going to say anything. Even if he does, copper's word trumps burglar's word every time. Now piss off, and find what's in that locker. Catch.'

She threw the card at him. Mervyn was still hovering, but Mick was already on the phone, calling in a possible break-in and an apprehended suspect. Getting her story straight.

He finally turned, and ran after Graham, who was waiting by the front door, hopping from foot to foot with impatience.

CHAPTER SIXTY

The gym was on a quiet street in Kensington. It wasn't your average battered council building with graffiti on the walls and chipped paint, it was a beautifully polished building. Glass and steel. The reception smelled of lavender, and contained more marble than a mausoleum. This was where rich people got sweaty.

'Hello, we'd like to book a session on the squash court.'

The girl at the reception looked up. Looked at Mervyn. She looked at Mervyn's just-on-the-wrong-side-of-stout waistline. Then she looked at Graham. She looked at Graham's mountainous form slowly, eyes dancing up and down his body. Her gum-chewing, which until that point had been vigorous, slowed to a dull chomp and then stopped all together. 'Are you members?'

'I am,' said Mervyn quickly. He produced the card and gave it to her. Thankfully the card didn't have a photo on it.

'Okay...' Her fingers clattered on the keyboard, and she looked at her database. 'So you are,' she said, with a trace of incredulity. 'One of our platinum members. Okay Mr Spicer. When do you want your session for?'

'Right now,' said Graham, in a stentorian voice. He was already out of breath from the climb up the tube station steps and the short walk to the squash club door.

She looked at them both again, for slightly too long. 'Are you sure?'

'Oh yes.'

She picked up the reception desk phone and dialled a single number. 'Sean, are you going to be in the building for the next hour? Yeah. Can you see them?'

Mervyn glanced up at a CCTV camera, which was winking at them all with a little red light.

'Okay. Cheers. Thanks.' She put the phone down. 'Okay, that's fine. Sean says it's okay.'

'Good old Sean.'

'He's our senior qualified first-aid person. I just thought I'd check he was on hand...'

Graham was still breathing heavily, clutching the reception desk for support.

'Probably very wise,' agreed Mervyn.

They hurried through the white-tiled corridors of the squash club. MOR rock music was piped through tiny speakers, and mini fountains gushed feebly on every corner. It was certainly a better class of fitness centre;

the doughy smell of sweat and wet towels was refined with the odour of expensive aftershave.

They found the changing room. Thankfully it was empty. The walls were carpeted, with tiny, bright red doors. Lockers as far as the eye could see.

'212... 212... Where's 212?'

'19, 20... 48... Low numbers at this end.'

'The 200s are over there...'

'240... 232... 222...'

'212,' they said together.

They dashed over to the locker, jostling like boys in a dinner queue.

'Okay, here goes...' said Mervyn, more excited than he'd care to admit.

Graham pushed the key in the lock and turned it.

The door swung open.

CHAPTER SIXTY-ONE

'Oh,' said Mervyn, confused and disappointed.

Inside were documents, notebooks. Tiny tapes. A dictaphone to play them on. A shiny red briefcase with heavy gold locks.

Graham was impatient. He yanked out one of the notebooks. 'What's all this? What's it mean?' He flicked through it. 'It's notes for a story. Handwritten notes...' He pulled out another one. 'This is the same. I can read "Arkadia", and "Medula". It's notes about a *Vixens from the Void* story.' Graham peered ferociously at the scribbles. 'This handwriting's familiar.'

Mervyn plucked it out of Graham's protesting fingers. He looked at it long and hard. 'There's a reason why this handwriting's familiar,' he said finally.

'Why?'

'Because it's *my* handwriting,' said Mervyn.

CHAPTER SIXTY-TWO

Graham grabbed for the dictaphone, but Mervyn was too fast for him; he snatched it and pressed play.

Mervyn's tinny voice droned from the speaker.

'*Okay, here's a thought*,' he heard himself say. '*Big nuclear war, wipes out everything on Earth. What's left? Just statues. Statues of Christianity. Statues of women holding babies, and men being tortured on crosses. Perhaps that's why the Vixens' civilisation is what it is? I mean, what would any survivors think? That women are the stronger species, and they rule over men with an iron fist. Hmm. Could be controversial. Note to self: Don't go too heavy on the Biblical references...*'

He clicked the dictaphone off.

'This is my stuff,' said Mervyn, mystified. 'It got taken from my house years ago... I remember now. There was a burglary. I was more cross about the telly getting nicked than a box of old notes...'

Graham was staring at him.

'That's the story of "The Burning Time",' he gaped. 'That's your voice. You wrote it.'

'Well yes, I did.'

'You wrote "The Burning Time".'

'I know.'

Graham was still staring at him. The information had been lodged in Mervyn's brain for so many years he sometimes forgot how big a deal it would be for fans if they ever discovered he was the author.

'Hello?'

The voice was shockingly loud. Raised voices were rare in changing rooms, and Mervyn's heart gave a frightened flinch.

'That's him.'

The girl at the reception desk was pointing at Mervyn. Behind her were two men. They were obviously plainclothes policemen.

'Excuse me, sir,' said one. 'Can you come over here, please?'

Mervyn peered round the corner and reluctantly walked over to them with a sickly grin on his face, trying to look calm and normal, just an ordinary overweight man trying to get fit in the middle of the night.

'Can I have a look at your membership card, sir?'

Mervyn's stomach poured into his Chelsea boots. 'Of course.' He produced the card. The senior policeman, a man with a severe parting and shiny face, turned it over and over in his hands, not really reading it. He already knew what it said. He was just pausing for effect.

'So... you're Mr Spicer, sir?'

'Um... Yes...'

'I don't think you are, sir.'

'Well not exactly, you see... Mr Spicer is my friend, and he let me borrow his card because my own gym has been closed for renovation.'

'I believe Mr Spicer passed away some weeks ago. You might have read it in the papers.'

Mervyn's mouth moved, but no words were forthcoming. His brain finally caught up with his face, and he started to make noises.

'Well yes, and this is funny, but he actually was my friend...'

'I think you'd better come along with us, sir...'

'But... no. I can't. I've discovered something very important.'

'You can tell us about that at the station, sir...'

'I have vital evidence about Marcus Spicer's death, and it's right in that locker over there! Please let me show you! You're going to look very foolish if you don't let me show you locker 212!'

The senior policeman sighed. 'Fine, if it makes you happy.'

Mervyn guided them over to locker 212, which was ajar, the key still dangling from the lock. He pulled the door open.

It was empty.

It was only at that moment he realised that Graham had completely disappeared.

CHAPTER SIXTY-THREE

He was escorted out of the changing rooms, through the reception area (the girl was still staring bug-eyed at him, masticating furiously) and out of the squash club.

When they emerged, he saw a huge shadowy figure illuminated by the electric glare of a shopfront. Graham Goldingay, one arm full of documents, lumbering away as fast his legs could carry him, was huffing towards the Underground. The briefcase dangled from his other hand.

'Look, look there! That's the man who was with me! Graham Goldingay! The girl on the reception desk must have said I wasn't alone, surely!'

'Let's not worry about him for the moment, sir.'

'But he's stolen evidence, vital evidence!'

One of the policemen looked in the direction of Mervyn's pointing finger, but Graham had disappeared down the steps and was gone.

'Shouldn't one of you get after him? It doesn't take both of you to walk me to a car.'

'One thing at a time, sir.'

They didn't care. They were Just Doing Their Jobs.

Mervyn was being steered towards a couple of large black Volvos, and he could see someone waiting in the driving seat of one.

Detective Inspector Preece.

Preece opened his car door and got out, leaning on the roof. He looked directly at Mervyn, eyes unblinking, a faint smile skirting around his face. He actually took his hand out of his pocket and pointed it like a gun. He directed it at Mervyn, doing a comedy recoil motion while making a tiny explosive noise with his tongue.

That clinched it; Mervyn knew he wasn't going to get away in a hurry this time. He had used Marcus's card. Aiden was probably in a police station somewhere, making all sorts of accusations about him. It wasn't going to be a couple of hours in the grey room this time. He would be firmly squashed within the cogs of the justice system. And there would be no chance to clear his name.

Mervyn suddenly bolted, ducking from between the two policemen and running back the way he had come. But not into the squash club; he veered to the left, over the tiny manicured lawn that fringed the building.

He ran as fast as he could. He could hear the scrunch of police boots on gravel behind him, but he forced himself to close it out, concentrating on hurling his body across the grounds as far as he could go towards the cover of the trees.

He leapt over several walls, and didn't stop running until he was certain he could hear no one pursuing him; and even then, he decided to hide in a shed for an hour, listening to the noises of the night.

CHAPTER SIXTY-FOUR

Mervyn knew there was a sound from far away, and that there were shapes around him. Strange shapes. Everything else was just conjecture.

He had to stop the sound. That's what he had to do. Pick it up and stop it.

'Mervyn?'

What was this thing he was holding? A phone! Yes that was what it was. You had to speak into them. Yes.

'Cheryl?' he immediately woke up.

'You're alive. Thank God.'

'I think I am. It's a bit early to tell. What – is that? What time is it?'

'Half past five.'

'Half past five? In the *morning?*' There was no such time. If there were such a time, Mervyn would have heard about it by now.

'Where are you?'

'I'm in a...' He stopped.

He remembered where he was. He was in a grimy bed and breakfast near King's Cross. His eyes traced the cracks on the ceiling, starting from the corner of the room and ending at the naked light-bulb.

After he had given the policemen the slip, he rode the Underground in a befuddled daze until it was about to close. He picked a stop at random and emerged, blinking in the glare of the train station, and walked until he found somewhere to stay the night.

He also remembered he was on the run.

They could be using Cheryl to find out where I am. They could be listening in to our conversation right this minute.

'I'm staying with a friend in Surrey. He's just served up breakfast, so I can't talk for too long.'

'Is it true?'

'What?'

'I can't believe you didn't tell me. You've ruined everything. How could you do this? You've taken Marcus's good work and shredded it, and thrown it in the dust.'

'I've... What?'

'You've ruined everything. Why didn't you tell me? Take your phone off the hook. Don't speak to anyone until you've seen the newspaper.'

'What? Which newspaper?'

'*Any* newspaper.'

The story was on the inside pages of *The Telegraph*, *The Times* and *The Independent*. Even the middlebrow papers and the tabloids featured it – the link to recent deaths and possible juicy murders/religious sacrifices had helped them over their distaste with a highbrow story about publishing. *The Sun* had come up with 'Naughty Spice!' and *The Mirror* had responded with the also amusing but less pithy 'Fraud God Almighty'.

The Mail was having a predictable gloat in a long and badly-written 'Well What Did You Expect?' article, describing how such a loud-mouthed figure of godlessness was a lying charlatan all along. *The Evening Standard* was offering free copies of Marcus's old books to all its readers (just cut out the tokens this week) and the *Daily Star* inexplicably ran the story from the angle of '*Vixens* Actress Shocked at Writer Lie' – with made-up quotes from Vanity Mycroft saying how disgusted she was. Then again, considering the piece was accompanied by a huge colour picture from 1987 with Vanity wearing a basque and stockings while lying on a hearth rug with her bottom in the air, it probably wasn't that inexplicable after all.

The spread of articles across his floor made Mervyn's brain whimper. He picked up *The Daily Telegraph*, hoping that their article would be on the sober side and at least put things into some sort of perspective.

It did. Which didn't help matters at all.

Holy Ghost Writer
By Matthew Goode

The literary world has found itself in uproar, as it was claimed yesterday that the late novelist and polemicist Marcus Spicer, author of best-selling books such as *The Serpent on the Mount* and *The Last Sucker*, might turn out to be as big a fraud as he claimed Jesus Christ to be.

Strong evidence has come to light suggesting that he didn't write his controversial episode of cult classic science fiction *Vixens from the Void* and it was in fact the sole work of another writer, Mervyn Stone, the script editor of the series.

The episode, called 'The Burning Time', brought Spicer into the public eye with its bold and controversial religious themes. His follow-up novels sold tens of millions of copies and have become best-sellers in almost 40 countries, helping to catapult Spicer from relatively obscure television writer into a worldwide celebrity and a famous atheist, rivalling other noted secular humanists such as Gore Vidal and Richard Dawkins in terms of profile.

His wife, Cheryl Spicer, 45, also a television writer when she met Spicer, has refused to comment.

Spicer, 48, died at BBC Television Centre two weeks ago, recording a DVD feature for that very episode of *Vixens*. The death, which is being investigated by police and described as 'suspicious', has been taken as evidence of 'divine intervention' by certain fringe religious groups, proving that Marcus Spicer will be as controversial a figure in death as he was in life.

Mervyn Stone, the man who allegedly wrote the episode, was present when Spicer died and is now being sought by police who wish to question him. He is currently missing, and there are already concerns that he has committed suicide.

The evidence, including notes, papers and entire manuscripts in Mr Stone's handwriting, was delivered to Nigel Fox, literary editor of *London Book World* by an anonymous source. Fox said: 'If this is true, it's staggering. If this man really wrote this episode and killed Marcus in a final fit of jealousy, it could be the biggest story to hit the literary world since the Hitler diaries.'

Well at least they'd spelt his name right this time.

Mervyn stepped out into the sunshine and walked. And kept on walking. It was hard to find a payphone; Mervyn hadn't had cause to use one since the late 90s, so perhaps it wasn't that surprising.

He thought it was too risky to use his mobile; he'd seen films about fugitives on the run from the police. The moment he used his phone, satellites wandering in orbit would immediately turn their lenses in his direction.

He read the number off the screen; not without difficulty. The phone was filling up with texts and messages, interrupting his view of the number every few seconds. Finally, he made the call.

'Graham, what have you *done*?'

'I don't know what you mean.'

'You're a bad liar, Graham. You took those documents, and went to the press.'

'I thought you'd be pleased. After all these years, you get the recognition for writing a classic episode of *Vixens*.'

'Graham...'

'After all, it was much better than any of the other scripts you did.'

'Thanks a lot. Why did you do it?'

'I have a duty to the legacy of *Vixens from the Void*, I have spent the best part of 20 years exhaustively tracking down notes and documentation for posterity so that the history of this great show is exhaustively documented for all future generations.'

'Graham you have caused so much trouble! I knew you were irresponsible, but you have behaved disgracefully.'

'Don't get all moral on me, Mervyn, you lied to us, to all the fans, it is you that caused this by caging the truth all these years, and not allowing it to fly free.'

'It was none of your damn business!'

'Do you know how many of my programme guides and quiz books are going to have to be revised and reprinted?'

'I don't care!'

'I do.' A hint of glee oozed into his voice. 'Money in the bank. Everyone will have to buy new editions, after all these years, a new fact to add to add to the sum total of *Vixens* knowledge. Perhaps they'll bring back *Vixens from the Void* magazine for a one-off edition to cover it. Do you have any more long-standing lies that you could share? Is that what's in the briefcase?'

Mervyn hung up. Then he sighed, redialled and waited.

'Hello?'

'Graham, it's me again.'

'We seemed to have got cut off.'

'How about I give you an in-depth interview about how I wrote "The Burning Time".'

'Really?'

'Really.''

'You'll get me prison access to you?'

'Well, I was planning not to get sentenced for multiple murder, but if it comes to that then yes, you can interview me in prison.'

'That would be so amazing. Thank you so much.'

'But there's one condition.'

'Name it.'

'When you break into that briefcase – and I know your staff are probably attacking it with hacksaws and flamethrowers as we speak – you let me know what's inside.'

'It's a deal.'

'I will be the first person you ring. Promise.'

'Promise.'

'I'll give you the number of a pay-as-you-go mobile, which you will keep utterly secret, and you ring that as soon as you find out.'

CHAPTER SIXTY-FIVE

It was an idiotic thing to do; but he had to do it.

Mervyn waited until the street was completely empty, and leapt over the low wall, running over the tiny ragged lawn. He crept around the side of the house until he was by the kitchen. Wrapping his hand in a rag found in the shed, he lightly punched a pane of glass in the back door. Thankfully, the glass gave way with a tiny tinkle and Mervyn was able to snake his hand inside and turn the big metal key.

The door creaked open. He was in.

It was quite an odd sensation, breaking into his own home.

It was a mess. The police had pulled out all his books, turned his chairs upside down and disembowelled his sofa. They'd obviously assumed he wouldn't be returning home soon, so they'd felt no need to tidy up.

The bottle of water was gone. *What a pity,* he thought. *I was looking forward to drinking that once I'd solved the case.*

The broken CD Robert had given him had gone, too. No doubt both water and CD were inside little plastic bags and lying in a drawer in a police station somewhere, labelled 'evidence'. He noticed his laptop had been confiscated too; it looked like he'd never finish that bloody novel.

It didn't look good.

Not only was Mervyn present at the scene of three murders; he had two clear motives to kill Marcus; his 'relationship' with Cheryl and Marcus's 'theft' of his script, the details of which were now decorating the insides of every newspaper in the country. A picture of him was being manufactured, of a bitter and jealous man. Unfortunately the picture wasn't entirely inaccurate. And that wasn't the half of it. He'd used Marcus's pass to break into his squash club locker in the middle of the night. They'd discovered a bottle of water and a CD with 'Burning Time commentary' written on it inside his house.

They'd throw away the key.

What if they fixed the CD and found Marcus's last moments on it?

They'd throw away the key *and* the spare.

What if they'd discovered cyanide in the bottle of water?

They'd throw away the key, the spare, the padlock and seal him in with a welding torch.

He'd made a stupid mistake. He'd started to run, and now he couldn't stop running. He was a fugitive; he had no idea where to go, or what to do. More importantly, he had absolutely no idea how to clear his name.

He went upstairs, pulled out a duffle bag and filled it with clothes. He was in the process of chucking in the contents of his sock drawer when his jacket pocket started vibrating.

He reached inside and pulled out Graham's mobile. He'd forgotten he'd picked it up. The screen was glowing. He put it down on the table. Every 30 seconds it scuttled forward angrily, demanding to be heard. Then it stopped. The screen displayed 'MISSED CALL'.

Mervyn leaned down, and then it jumped again, like a rattlesnake playing dead to snare unwary rodents. This time the screen said. 'MESSAGE RECEIVED'.

Should he?

Mervyn wrestled with his conscience. Well 'wrestled' was too strong a word. He kicked it and it ran away, whimpering.

Sod it. Of course he should. That would teach Graham a lesson. *'The truth should be allowed to fly free', should it? Well, he can't complain if I listen in on his phone messages, can he?*

Mervyn dialled the 'message' number, and put it to his ear.

'You have – one – new message,' said the phone. 'Press one to hear it, two to erase it, three, to –'

Mervyn pressed 'one'.

'Hello Mr Goldingay. You don't know me. My name is Lionel Bickerdyke. I gather on the grapevine that you like buying up "exclusive merchandise". Well, I've got something for you. Something really special. Some merchandise you do not want to be without. The most amazing thing ever.'

Lionel Bickerdyke?

'Everyone's going to want this, fans, collectors... And the police. Particularly the ones investigating Marcus Spicer's murder, if you know what I mean.'

What?

'How much for material evidence in the murder of an actual *Vixens from the Vortex* writer? If that isn't the ultimate merchandise, I don't know what is. Anyway that's all I'm saying. For now.'

A woman's voice came on the phone. 'End of messages. Press two to repeat, three to delete, four to save, five to call the person back –'

Mervyn pressed 'five'.

The phone barely started ringing before a loud voice surged into Mervyn's ear. 'Yeah?'

'Mr Bickerdyke?'

'Is that Graham Goldingay?'

'Yes,' said Mervyn, amazed at his own audacity.

'That was quick. You just got my message.'

'Yes.'

'You interested?'

'Very.'

'Well, things move fast in this game, Graham. I've just had another offer, so I'm expecting a bit of a bidding war on this.'

Another offer?

'Whatever's on the table, I'll beat it,' said Mervyn. 'In fact I'll double it.'

'I like the cut of your jib, Graham. I look forward to meeting you to discuss this further.'

'You want to meet?'

'I'm not doing this over the phone, Graham. I'm not stupid. I'm currently meeting the other party at Hambley Hall, near Dorking. You know it?'

'I know it.'

'I knew you'd come. I've reserved you room 79. Get here as fast as you can, and there might be merchandise left to sell. The other potential buyer is very keen. Hurry Graham, you haven't much time.'

The phone went dead.

CHAPTER SIXTY-SIX

Mervyn didn't want to use his Visa card; he'd also seen that film where the hero used his credit cards and they lit up the police computers like Christmas trees. He used the last of his cash to buy a train ticket for Dorking.

As the train lumbered out of Waterloo, Mervyn pressed his head against the window and thought.

It all seems to lead back to Hambley Hall, doesn't it? he thought. *It was where Marcus stayed while we were filming 'The Burning Time'. It was very likely the place where he seduced Samantha. Didn't Joanna say Marcus took her there a few times? It was where Marcus had held the reception for his fantasy wedding to Cheryl, and it's where I'm going back to now.*

Why?

Why had Lionel picked this particular place? He doesn't seem that much of a fan of Vixens from the Void *– he didn't even get the name of the show right – so the irony of it all won't be very apparent to him...*

It only took an hour before Mervyn was alighting at Dorking and falling into a minicab. Hambley Hall was just a stone's throw from the station, and adjacent to the quarry where they'd filmed 'The Burning Time'. It was a big hotel that sat in the middle of acres of lush greenery. Instead of a safari park, Mervyn's taxi took him through rolling greens, where he could watch savage golfers prowling in their natural habitat.

Inside the hall was a mixture of antiquated class and comfy familiarity; Hogwarts for adults. Friendly staff breezed around carrying plates of sandwiches and coffee for the guests, who were chatting in front of open fires, reading *The Telegraph* or discreetly tap-tapping away on laptops.

As soon as Mervyn entered the front doors, his duffle bag was wrestled away from him by a jolly, pink-cheeked porter who escorted him along wood-panelled corridors, past the gym, swimming pool and games room and out into a small courtyard. A fountain gushed in the centre, and a clock tower looked over the square. The clock hands were stubbornly stuck at 11.33. This was where the more modest rooms were tucked away, further from the main house.

The porter took him into a long corridor, interrupted by a row of identical doors, and left him outside room 79.

He was slightly disappointed with what he found. After the majesty of the house, these rooms were modest, functional. There was no four-poster bed or portraits of men with huge moustaches, just a desk, coffee-making facilities and tasteful paintings. It was comfortable and clean, but it was just like any room in any hotel by any motorway. He may as well have been attending a sci-fi convention.

He didn't want to waste any time. Dusk was falling, and he didn't want to spend the night here. He pulled out Graham's phone again and dialled. It rang once, then a voice said 'Hey Graham.'

'I'm here,' said Mervyn.

'Quick work. Did you get room 79?'

'Yes.'

'Great. I don't want to go tramping round the hotel.'

'I can understand that.'

'Look outside the door.'

Mervyn didn't go to the door straight away. He was pretty certain that Lionel Bickerdyke didn't know what Graham looked like. Whether he knew what Mervyn looked like – that was less certain. He mustn't forget that this Lionel Bickerdyke character had recorded and sold footage of Mervyn sitting on the toilet. So at the very least he must have seen Mervyn's face and found out who he was. Then checked out whether the film he'd made of the tubby guy straining and making notes on the loo roll was of anybody famous.

But more importantly, Mervyn's face had now appeared in all the papers, and even though the photo they all used was the same blurry shot (the one taken with a huge smelly fan at last year's science fiction convention that made him look small and sinister and his face wrinkled in polite disgust) he was taking no chances.

He'd only shaved his chin, and left the beginnings of a moustache on his lip. Even though it looked feeble, it helped to disguise his face. Last night he'd dyed his hair black and gelled his tousled locks into a severe back-comb. For the final touch, he crammed cotton wool in his cheeks and put on his sunglasses.

He went to the door and pulled it open. Facing him was a man. Not a particularly striking man; he had a straggly ginger moustache that merged into a scrappy beard. His face was pale and pink-eyed. He wore a ragged checked shirt over a T-shirt. His saggy belly rolled over the belt on his battered jeans.

'Good to meet you, Graham,' said Lionel, proffering his hand.

'Likewise, Lionel,' said Mervyn, in his best gravelly voice. 'You were quick.'

'I'm in room 81, next door. So...' He pushed past Mervyn and sat down on his bed. 'Let's get down to business. The other party has currently made a bid of £50,000.'

What?'

'Any advance on that, Graham? The clock's ticking...'

Mervyn tried to think about what Graham would do in this situation.

'Wait, wait, wait a second,' growled Mervyn. 'I'm asked to spend over fifty grand on something and I don't even know what it is?'

'I told you what you're buying, Graham. What you're buying is information. It's an item of exclusive merchandise that proves beyond a shadow of a doubt who killed Marcus Spicer. Something only my buyer will know. Along with me and the killer, of course. Just think. You can take that information with you to the grave.'

'Well,' growled Mervyn, 'I don't know about that. You have to let the truth fly free. I'll have to tell the world, because I'll need to update my programme guides, and my fact files...'

Lionel shrugged. 'Fine. Do what you like. Throw the murderer to the police. It's all the same to me. I can see why you'd want to. I mean, from now on, you'd be the one – on record – who caught Marcus's killer. They wouldn't be able to write a book about Marcus Spicer without mentioning you.'

Mervyn imagined that if he were Graham Goldingay, he'd be salivating so hard he would be leaving puddles on the carpet.

'I didn't realise it would be quite so much.'

Lionel shrugged again. 'If you don't have the money, then it goes somewhere else. No hard feelings and all that.'

'I didn't say I couldn't pay. I can pay a lot more than a mere £50,000. I do have a considerable fortune. I just need to call my accountant. I will have a definite offer within the hour.'

'Make it half an hour, Graham. I'm a very busy man.'

Lionel stood up to go. Mervyn followed him into the corridor. He could hear the slam of Lionel's door behind him as he wandered off pretending to make a phone call. 'I don't care, Nigel. If you're worried, I'll just sell the Picasso!'

'Look I'm sorry your mother's got sores, Nigel, but you can bathe them later. This is business. Ring up Sothebys and put the Chippendales in the crate.'

Mervyn wandered along the corridor, continuing his imaginary call. He was so engrossed in developing this scenario with his fictional lackey (who had developed an ailing mother and an overly needy girlfriend in the last few seconds) that he collided with someone walking just as aggressively in the opposite direction.

They both ended up flat on the floor.

Mervyn pushed himself up into a sitting position just as the other person did the same. Their eyes met.

It was Brian Crowbridge.

CHAPTER SIXTY-SEVEN

'Very sorry,' Brian mumbled. 'Didn't see you there.'

Brian didn't recognise him.

He stumbled to his feet and carried on. Mervyn stared after Brian's retreating figure; he was walking down the corridor from which Mervyn had just emerged.

Brian? Here? Was he the 'other party' bidding for this evidence?

Mervyn turned back and followed him. But Brian didn't go to Lionel's room. Instead, he headed for room 67, just along the corridor, took out a pass key and entered. Mervyn knocked on the door.

'Hello?'

'Room service,' said Mervyn.

There was a pause. A scuffle. 'I didn't order any room service.'

'Just restocking the mini-bar.'

Brian couldn't resist. The chain rattled and the doorknob turned. Brian stood in the doorway dressed in a fluffy dressing gown and slippers.

Mervyn removed his sunglasses and spat out his cotton wool.

'Mervyn?' Brian's face twitched.

'What's going on Brian, what the hell are you doing here?'

Brian's eyes flicked back inside the room. He looked scared. 'I could ask you the same question!' He wedged his hands in the doorframe, obscuring Mervyn's view of the room. 'You're on the run! They say you murdered Marcus!'

'Oh come on Brian, think! You know that's not true!'

'Do I? You were pretty cross at him on the day of the DVD commentary!'

'Oh the day of...? But his murder must have been planned weeks in advance! That's exactly why I'm here. There's a man here who says he has evidence of who killed Marcus, and I'm trying to get hold of it.'

'I don't believe you.'

'I'm telling you I can prove it! Just look!' He pointed down the corridor. 'He's just down there. His name is Lionel. He's a tubby bloke with a beard and ginger hair and a check shirt...'

Brian just gaped at him.

'Come on. We've got to get to him before he destroys the evidence!' Mervyn took Brian's arm and dragged him down the corridor. Lionel's door was on the latch and it 'ker-chunked' open.

But the room was completely empty, save for a puddle of clothes on the floor.

Mervyn walked into the middle of the room, his arms outstretched idiotically, as if expecting to feel an invisible presence. He dipped his head inside the bathroom, found nothing. He looked behind the bed and in the wardrobe. The room was pathetically small, and there was nowhere else to look.

'Where's he gone?' He tried the windows, they were locked. 'He's completely vanished.'

Brian held his hand over his mouth, his eyes wide. 'It's the Rapture,' he gasped. 'It's the time when we're taken up to heaven, leaving our earthly garments behind! It's another sign, just like Marcus and Robert... Mervyn, the end of the world is nigh! We're fast approaching the end of days!' Brian's eye started twitching again, forcing the wrinkles above his cheeks to pulse like gills.

Mervyn grabbed Brian by the shoulders and looked directly into his good eye. 'Listen to me Brian. You are a good man. A man of faith. Just because we've witnessed two impossible deaths – three if you count me finding the professor – doesn't mean there's not a simple explanation for it all. And it does not give you the excuse to start fainting and speaking in tongues like some straw-sucking hick in Overbite County USA.'

Brian seemed to calm down. 'But...'

'He's not here, but he's not been taken by the Rapture. Trust me, Brian, from what I know about Lionel, he's not the type the Good Lord would want sitting at his right hand.'

'If you say so...'

There was something odd about the room. On the ceiling. Someone had tampered with one of the ceiling tiles. It had been moved, leaving a tiny hole about three inches square above the puddle of clothes.

'Look up. Perhaps he got out through there,' joked Mervyn, and Brian barked with hysterical laughter. 'Come on. Let's see what's in your mini-bar. I think we both need a drink.'

Brian stopped laughing. 'Well actually, I'd rather you didn't go into my room,' he said nervously.

Mervyn blinked. 'What?'

'If it's all the same to you.'

'Why not?'

'Ah... I don't have to give a reason.'

'Lionel said there was someone else bidding for this "evidence". I might reasonably assume that that someone else might be the murderer. Are you the other bidder?'

'No, of course not!'

'Then why don't you want me in your room?'

Brian suddenly turned and ran out of Lionel's room, dashing back down the corridor to his own. But Mervyn was ready. He was running too, and as he was marginally younger and fitter, he overtook Brian, and barged the door open with his shoulder.

The room was also empty, save for two suitcases arranged neatly at the end of twin beds. An ironing board had been erected by the bathroom door, with a pile of shirts folded on one end.

'Okay Brian, what's the deal? Out with it, why exactly are you here?

Behind him, a man left the bathroom, also submerged in a big fluffy dressing gown and monogrammed slippers, towelling his hair.

Lewis Bream.

CHAPTER SIXTY-EIGHT

Lewis saw Mervyn, and the colour bled from his face. It became as white as a shroud.

'What... What's *he* doing here?'

'I just popped in for a drink. Do you have some water? Bottled will do,' said Mervyn cheerfully. His eyes danced from Lewis to Brian, and then back again. 'Obviously I'm intruding. You have to forgive me my trespasses.'

'It's not what it seems,' said Brian, feebly. 'We're just sharing a room to save money.'

'I see. You and the Chief Godbotherer bunking up together, just saving money. That makes sense. Rooms are so expensive. Very sensible. You both obviously have so much in common.'

'Oh God,' said Lewis.

'We do have a lot in common, Mervyn. We're both Christians, despite our differences. We sit and we talk about scripture. We pray together.'

'Not together, surely. Surely you take it in turns to get on your knees?'

'Oh God,' said Lewis again.

'Mervyn, that's beneath you...'

'And what's beneath you, Brian? Brian, I'm not a religious expert, but I think "Thou shalt not bear false witness" roughly translates as "Thou shalt not lie".'

'Oh my God,' said Lewis again.

Mervyn looked at Lewis. 'Are you taking His name in vain, Lewis, or are you calling on Him to spirit you out of here?'

'Mervyn...' said Brian.

'He's just spirited away someone in a room down the hall,' said Mervyn to Lewis. 'Maybe He could do the same for you.'

'Mervyn...' Brian pleaded. 'Just listen for a second.'

Mervyn went silent. Brian sat on the bed and sighed wearily. 'Okay, fair enough, fine. We're lovers.'

Lewis clutched the bathroom door. He gave a whimper.

'Don't worry Lewis,' said Brian. 'It's for the best. If I learned one thing from my AA meetings, it's that lies are the cracks in ourselves we fall into. I met Lewis a few years back, at a prayer meeting in Maida Vale, when I first heard the call of the Lord. We were both fallen wretches, and we discovered Him together.'

'And a lot more besides.'

'Mervyn, don't do the holier-than-thou bit, please, it doesn't suit you. You know me, old chap. I don't believe in any form of discrimination in religion. I am a proud gay Christian. There's nothing hypocritical about me.'

'And Lewis?'

'Lewis can speak for himself.'

From the expression on Lewis's face, it was obvious he couldn't speak for himself. He couldn't speak at all.

Brian continued. 'Lewis decided to take a different path. Our pastor said there was nothing to be ashamed of regarding our... preferences, but Lewis became convinced that what we did was wrong, and tried to turn his back on his sexuality. But I always thought he would realise the error of his ways.'

Mervyn understood. 'He's the friend you were talking about. The one who you were encouraging to get back on the right path.'

'Yes. It was Lewis. He's a good man at heart, aren't you Lewis?'

Lewis remained in the doorway of the bathroom, a hysterical grin fixed to his face, eyes wide in frozen terror.

Mervyn shook his head. 'You're a fool, Brian. You always fall for the wrong types. Your wife was a bitch. Tarquin was just a young bastard who humiliated you, and Lewis is... just a bigot with a megaphone.'

Brian shook his head with a smile. 'You're wrong Mervyn.' He smiled at Lewis with obvious affection. 'He's just been trapped by his position and his role as head of the Godbotherers to take an extreme view. He just needs to free himself from his earthly cage.'

'And you seriously believe you can change his position? To coin a phrase?'

'Oh yes. I'm very hopeful. We talk for hours about scripture, and I believe he understands that we're not doing anything wrong. Why would he be here, otherwise?'

'Why indeed?' Mervyn flashed a cynical smile.

'The angels always rejoice when a sinner repents. He's not completely turned his mind against –'

Lewis grabbed the iron from the ironing board and thwacked it, full force, across the back of Brian's head. Brian was propelled forward, past Mervyn, landing on the carpet. He lay motionless, flat on his back. A deep red stain bloomed from his head, soaking into the carpet. Lewis stood there, bug-eyed, staring at Brian's body. His mouth was moving, but no words were coming. A tear sprang on to one cheek.

'Oh my God... Lewis! What have you done?' said Mervyn.

Lewis dropped the iron, which thudded on to a chair. He looked at Mervyn, then at Brian, then his mouth opened again, and he finally found his voice. 'Oh my God!' he screamed. 'Mervyn Stone is here! He's just killed someone! Help! Help!'

Mervyn fled out of the door, turned to run into the hotel, and came face-to-face with the rosy-cheeked porter, who was huffing bags to a room. The porter was cutting off his escape.

'Help! Murder!' screamed Lewis again.

The porter dropped the bags and dived for Mervyn's legs, attempting to rugby tackle him to the ground. Mervyn went down but kicked himself free. He ran down the corridor and hurled himself into Lionel's room, locking it behind him.

This time it wasn't empty.

Lionel had mysteriously returned, and this time he was dead. *Obviously God threw him back.* He was lying on the floor, fully dressed, next to the pile of clothes. His eyes were bulging up at the hole in the ceiling. A telephone flex was embedded in his furry neck. *This gets better and better.*

There was a window open – *Surely that wasn't open before?* – and Mervyn ran to it, looking out. A figure in a trenchcoat and hat was running away.

Mervyn heard the 'ker-chunk' of a pass key in the lock behind him. The porter.

Mervyn struggled out of the window and fled into the night, away from his pursuer and towards the real murderer.

He ran into the darkness. He could almost hear the distant whine of police sirens floating across the grounds, frightening the deer.

'Mervyn!'

That was a woman's voice. He recognised it. Or thought he did. Who was she? Was she part of a search party, a hotel guest being a have-a-go hero on behalf of the police? Or was she all in his head?

He was nearer the trenchcoated figure now. The figure was running towards a battered wire fence decorated with 'KEEP OUT' signs. He seemed to know where he was going, because when Mervyn caught up, he found a tangled hole ripped into the mesh. The figure had obviously slipped through.

Mervyn struggled through the hole, knowing he was being insane, but enjoying the insanity nonetheless; there was wind in his hair, rain in his face and wet grass under his

– feet? Something was wrong. There was a scream; a woman was in trouble.

No she wasn't – the scream was his, and he was screaming because he had run off the edge of the world, or maybe the world had tipped the ground over and shaken him out like grit from one of its shoes. He realised something important.

The quarry where they'd filmed 'The Burning Time' was closer to the hotel than he remembered.

For a split second, he tried to doggy-paddle his way to the clouds. Then physics gave a wicked grin, and gravity was punching him in the face with a rock.

Soil, stones and rocks attacked his face like angry bees. He blindly put out his hands to slow his fall and was rewarded with dead plants that came away in his fists.

All he was able to see was a mad collage of images, rolling and swerving and jerking past him. His vision shook and juddered as he ploughed downward, not resting his eyes on anything for more than a split second. It was as if he'd become the cameraman of a particularly pretentiously shot documentary, investigating the terrible unforeseen dangers involved in falling into quarries.

The moon winked in and out of his line of sight, as he half-rolled, half-fell down something steep and painful.

What was it Duggie 'Don't lean against that window' Fletcher used to say about falling down a sheer drop? Oh yes. Don't even try it. Leave it to the professionals. Wise words, Duggie.

It was five whole seconds before he found something flat and hard he could lie on. He let out a shuddering breath, rolled over, realised he'd only landed on a tiny ledge halfway down, and continued his descent all the way to the bottom. The only thought rattling around his head was one of relief, that no one had seen him doing his little comedy intermezzo; he'd even let out a strangulated yell.

He felt oddly at peace lying there, the rain pummelling his face with refreshing pin-sharp droplets. He hoped he hadn't broken his spine, it felt so comfortable. Shouldn't he be in pain? He waggled his fingers. Nothing wrong there. He flexed his feet. Fine. He moved his head – and whimpered with the pain.

A figure swam into his vision. He heard the woman's voice. A low voice. She pulled out a bottle of Estuary English water and *Click-click-click-click* opened it. Pouring the contents gently on to him.

Mervyn could feel a cool wetness hitting his face, mixing with the rain. He screwed his face up tightly, thrusting his face to one side. He knew what was in the water, and he knew what would happen if he swallowed any. All he could see was the rain and the water flying towards him, and the moon glowing at him, giving a huge conspiratorial grin.

And then nothing at all.

CHAPTER SEVENTY

Mervyn woke up in heaven.

At least, he assumed he was in heaven. It didn't look like heaven, but it had to be. Stood to reason.

He said some words out loud, testing the heavenly acoustics. 'As I mentioned some time ago to a blonde policewoman with interesting tattoos, "When you eliminate the impossible, whatever remains, no matter how improbable, must be the case."' He had fallen into a quarry in Surrey, someone had drenched him with poison, and now all of a sudden, he had woken up in his own house. That couldn't have happened. That was utterly impossible. Therefore, he must have been poisoned. He must be in heaven.

There was other evidence to suggest he was in heaven. The house was spookily clean. The mess that the police had left had been tidied away. The bottle of water had been returned to its place on the middle of the table. The CD Robert had given him had also been neatly put back.

He was either in heaven, or he'd hired himself a cleaner. Heaven was more likely.

If this were heaven, then it was a bit disappointing. If he'd have to spend eternity in a perfect facsimile of his own house, God should at least have the decency to give him some nicer crockery.

After a few minutes, he convinced himself it wasn't exactly heaven, more a waiting room for heaven. A little piece of cosy purgatory. A familiar-looking annexe so the freshly deceased could acclimatise themselves to their lofty new surroundings. He'd been scuba-diving once, and he knew the dangers of getting the bends when coming up too fast. Mervyn approved of God's very sensible nod to health and safety.

More minutes passed. Mervyn tried the television.

He decided that this wasn't a waiting room for heaven after all. God may be vengeful at times, but He wouldn't allow property shows on the television.

He turned it off and wondered how he'd got home.

Now he realised he wasn't in heaven, earthly worries like being caught by the police became uppermost in his mind. He sat in the dark on his hideous sofa, afraid to turn the lights on. His neighbours weren't the friendliest at the best of times, and he had visions of them tapping out 999 the moment the house looked occupied.

He couldn't switch the television on again. He was aching to hear the news, but he daren't risk it. Instead, he found some headphones and listened to Radio 4, hoping to catch a bulletin; but no. It was just a programme about how thimbles were making a comeback. Instead, he just sat in the gloom and stared at the bottle of water.

He ended up doing that for quite some time.

He wondered if it was the same bottle. He turned it around and, yes, there was the tear on the label from where it had bounced around inside his bag. It was definitely the same bottle – only it wasn't just a bottle any more, it was a symbol, and he didn't have to ask the Godbotherers to find out how important symbols were.

He picked it up, then he put it down again.

He reached into his pocket. There was the CD of 'The Burning Time' commentary that Mick had given him, still there. Well, he could listen to that at least. He had to keep investigating. He had to keep thinking.

Find out what happened to Marcus. It's the only way I can clear my name.

He put it into the CD player, and put his headphones back on. Marcus's self-satisfied lecture filled his ears. He listened right through, from his own stumbling introduction to the death of Marcus Spicer.

'... Mark my words, we're heading back to a new dark age, where people are once again put to the sword for simply saying the world is round, and it was created a few thousand years ago; those are the stakes we're playing for... And I for one don't want to be tied to one just yet...'

Then there was a harsh KLAK-LAK-LAK-LAK as Marcus opened the deadly water bottle, and a pause as Robert silently told them in their headphones that they were stopping because of the noise. Then Marcus said 'Sorry,' and then Mervyn's own voice turned up. Mervyn was surprised how tetchy he sounded. He always thought he had a gentle voice.

'I know all that, I wouldn't have... commissioned the story if I didn't believe that. But there are plenty of moderate people of faith in the world who despair of extremism just as much as we do. Being thoughtlessly provocative doesn't help anyone's case. All it does is leave a nasty taste in the mouth.'

'Oh! This can't be what I...'

Then there were the terrible noises of Marcus dying. The gasping, the choking, the retching.

'Marcus? Are you all right?' That was Samantha's voice.

And then the 'flumpf' of body on carpet. And the glog-glog-glog as the upturned bottle leaked poison on to the floor.

Then it ended. Either Robert or Trevor must have pressed a button and rushed into the sound booth. He couldn't remember which.

He turned off the CD.

He kept looking at the bottle.

He realised he was being intimidated by it. No, not just intimidated, he was in *awe* of it. He was *frightened* of it. He'd given it its own special place. He'd eaten his meals around it. He had been depressed to find it missing. Now it had returned, and he was in awe of it.

He was treating it with the same kind of reverence that the Godbotherers had for their narrow beliefs, with which Graham Goldingay treated his props, that Marcus Spicer reserved for himself.

Well sod that. He was Mervyn Stone, and he didn't believe in anything. He had no time for magic talismans, graven images or objects of worship.

He picked up the bottle, held it aloft, twisted the lid. It opened with a muted *click-click-click-click* and he defiantly guzzled the water down.

Nothing happened.

Of course it didn't. There was no way Lewis could have poisoned one of the bottles. Perhaps he'd prayed over them, asking for the water to magically transform after it had left the building?

But nothing had happened. There was no miracle. Mervyn felt exactly the same as he was seconds before.

Or did he? Something was different. He felt different. What was it?

It was something in his head. The ghost of a realisation.

He listened to Marcus's final moments again. And then he realised what it was. He got very excited. He pulled out his mobile.

'Hi Mick.'

'Hello, Mervyn Stone.'

'I'd like to ask you something...'

'I see I got "unknown number" on my phone when you called.'

'Yes. It's a new phone. Pay as you go.'

'Very wise.'

'Mick. I know I shouldn't bother someone like you at this moment...'

'At this moment'?'

'Er... Yes.'

'"At this moment"... by which you mean that "at this moment" you're on the run from the police. And by "someone like me" you mean "the police". Am I right?'

'Um... Yes. You put it very succinctly.'

'I do succinctly.'

'I quite understand if you don't want to talk to me, me being an escaped murder suspect and all...'

'Nah. Don't worry about it. I'm off duty.'

'Oh great. I just want to ask a question about Marcus.'

'Yeah?'

'About what he had in his pockets.'

'Nothing special. Keys, wallet, cards...'

'This is very important. Was he on any medication?'

'No.'

'Oh.'

'But he did have aspirin in his pocket. He complained of a headache that morning, and Joanna Paine gave him a bottle of pills.'

'She gave him a bottle of pills? Fantastic! That's just... Fantastic. That's just what I thought you might say.'

'The pills were checked, Mervyn Stone. They weren't poisoned or anything like that.'

'No, I didn't expect them to be. Thanks very much, Mick.'

'Pleasure.'

Now he knew he was on to something. The bottle of pills was the first pebble in an avalanche, and now connections were raining down on his brain. Things started to make sense.

And then he heard the noise.

The noise was a dull thud. Mervyn had a forlorn hope that it came from outside, or next door, but the next, louder thud was utterly unmistakable. It came from upstairs.

'Mick, there's someone upstairs...'

'Upstairs where?'

'I'm in my house.'

'Go and look then.'

'I can't. I'm scared.'

'Listen. Mervyn fucking Stone is not scared of anything. Mervyn fucking Stone wrote "The Burning Time". A man who had the balls to put that on prime-time telly is not scared of some kid going through his bedroom drawers and shitting on his duvet.'

'You're right.'

'I know I'm right.'

'I'm going to look. Will you stay on the phone?'

'Yes.'

Let it go, Mervyn, he thought to himself. *I don't have to stay in this house.*

But curiosity was a powerful thing, and Mervyn found his feet on the stairs; one step at a time. *It's a burglar. Mick's right. It must be. A violent insane ratboy burglar, defecating on my bed, ready to pull his trousers up and bash my head in with my own hairbrush.*

'I'm going up the stairs now.'

'Good for you.'

He pushed open the door.

The woman was completely naked, standing in front of the mirrored door of his wardrobe, examining herself. She was holding a mobile.

She heard the creak of the door and turned round.

'Hello Mervyn Stone,' she said into the phone. 'Have you found your intruder yet?'

'That wasn't funny.'

'Yes it was.'

'What are you doing in my house?'

'Waiting for you.'

She stood there, unashamed. The dragon lurking by her abdomen looked sinister in the half-light. There was a brief spasm of realisation in Mervyn's brain. A flash of Stuart in his luminous bib, saying with a grin, *'Am I Hannibal Lecter to your Clarice Starling?'* Mervyn had read those books many times. The story of a jailed mass-murderer leading the detective to the lair of a tattooed psychopath...

Don't be ridiculous.

'Okay, I'll rephrase that. What are you doing – naked – in my house?'

'Checking out my new tattoo. What do you think?'

Her bottom was pointed at him. Mervyn flinched. 'Very good.'

'A bit scabby, but it's come out well. Really clear. Well, as clear as your handwriting gets. You could authorise your cheques with my arse, Mervyn Stone.'

'I'll bear that in mind.'

'Don't mention it. Oh, yeah. About the tattoo I'm getting of you...'

'The one of me fighting your salivating dragon?'

'Yeah. Well I hope you don't take this the wrong way, but I'm going to wait a bit until I get it done. Just in case you did kill Marcus and Robert and that old guy. I don't want a multiple murderer on my inner thigh. It might get a bit embarrassing in the showers at Hendon.'

'I quite understand.'

She walked to the bed and (thank God) tugged her jeans on.

'I found you lying in a quarry,' she said, pulling her belt on, and fastening the skull-like buckle tight. 'I poured water on your face to wake you up, but you were dead to the world. When they started coming out of the hotel, I carried you to my car and stuffed you in my boot. Harder than it looks – lucky I've come across a few types that stuff bodies in cars for a hobby. You've got to put the legs in first and let the head rest on the wheel arch. I drove you back to London. Managed to give the police the slip.'

'Mick... You *are* the police.'

'Not the Surrey police I'm not.'

'Fair enough.'

'I saw the news. Your expedition with Pavarotti didn't go to plan. So you wrote "The Burning Time"? I'm impressed. Mervyn fucking Stone is the man.'

'You really smuggled me from the police? For all you know, I could be a mass murderer.'

'Yeah. But you wrote "The Burning Time". That's huge. Great works can forgive a lot of bad things. I bet they would have let Charles Manson out long ago if his poems weren't so shit.'

Mervyn didn't know what to say.

Mick moved forward and gripped his shoulders. 'Listen. You are a creator, not a destroyer. You are not a murderer. I believe in you, Mervyn Stone.'

'Thank you. Thank you for believing in me, for whatever strange reason you have. And thank you for saving me... Twice.'

'I am your guardian demon, Mervyn Stone. It's like a guardian angel, but with a more interesting basement. How's your head?'

'Sore,' he felt it tenderly, thinking about the events of last night. 'Oh God. What about Lewis? And Brian? Lewis Bream attacked Brian, you know.'

'Dunno anything about that. Just drove through the night. It's only been a couple of hours since we left.'

'Did you clean up my house?'

'Yeah. Sorry about the mess before. Dave and Gerry are good police officers, and good girls, but they can get a bit carried away.'

'Where did the bottle come from? And the CD?'

'I knew your house was going to get searched. I broke in before to make sure you didn't have anything incriminating in your house. And you did.'

'Yes I know.'

'It would have looked very bad for you, so I took it. I thought you might need the stuff to complete your investigation, so I took it and hid it. I've got your laptop too. It's on your bedside table.' Sure enough, there it was, powered up and ready to use.

'Well thank you; you've done far too much for me, Mick.'

'I have to. You're –'

'I know. I'm Mervyn fucking Stone.' Mick pulled out some scary thigh-boots from behind the bed and zipped them on. 'So, that stuff about Marcus having the aspirin? That's useful is it?'

In the excitement, Mervyn had forgotten. 'God, yes, the pills. Absolutely. Really useful. In fact I think I know who the murderer is.'

'You're fucking kidding me.'

'Yes. And it's all thanks to you. If it wasn't for that commentary CD you gave me, I'd never have worked it out.'

'Really?'

'Oh yes.'

'Fuck, what a result. But you already had a CD of the commentary. I found it downstairs.'

'No, Robert gave me that, but it didn't work...'

Oh.

'It didn't work. No... Why didn't it work? Robert was Mr Technical. He filmed and edited documentaries for a living, and restored old TV programmes. Why would someone as technically minded as that give me a CD that didn't work?'

Mick shrugged.

Mervyn was already running back downstairs. 'I always wondered why Robert was so certain Samantha was the murderer. He said something like he bet the CD would bring me to the same conclusion.'

There was the CD Robert gave him, on the table where Mick had put it. He took it out and examined it. He put it back in the CD player, but the machine clicked and complained and vomited it back out. 'ERR' came up in pretty digital letters.

Mick thumped down the stairs. Mervyn waved the CD at her. 'It says "Commentary" on the case. But supposing it wasn't? He said something about "putting me in the picture," which I thought was a bit of an idiotic thing to say. Unless...'

On a sudden impulse, he switched the television on and put the CD into the DVD machine.

CHAPTER SEVENTY-ONE

'Hello?'

'Did you make it back okay?'

'What? Who is this?'

'From Hambley Hall. I hope your encounter with Lionel wasn't upsetting.'

'Who is this?'

'Allow me to introduce myself, I am Graham Goldingay.'

'How did you get this number?'

'I know a lot of things. Phone numbers are the merest tip of my information iceberg.'

'I don't know how you got this number, but I'm putting the phone down. Please don't call again, or I'll call the police.'

'I wouldn't hang up if I were you. I'm ringing to inform you that I have opened the red briefcase.'

'Red briefcase? What red briefcase?'

'I think you know what red briefcase. The one Mervyn Stone and I found in the locker of a squash club in Kensington. The same locker that was opened by a key hidden inside a statuette of the Virgin Mary and Child. Stop me when you work out what red briefcase I'm talking about.'

Silence.

'I made a deal with Mervyn Stone that he would be the first person I would ring when I got it open. That I would tell him what was inside.'

'And did you?'

'No.'

'Why not?'

'When I got the briefcase open, I thought better of it. I thought I should contact you and ask you if you wanted it.'

'I see.'

'And do you?'

'Yes.'

'I thought you'd say yes. I think we should meet somewhere private.'

'Where do you suggest?'

'I have a production company. The BBC leases me rooms and equipment for certain projects. I have a room booked tomorrow which would otherwise not be used.'

'And where is this room?'

'I think you might find it amusingly apt.'

CHAPTER SEVENTY-TWO

In Recording Suite 4, everything was exactly as it had been on the day of the DVD commentary. Bowls of chocolates were placed enticingly on the table.

And there were bottles of water; a dozen of them on a silver tray, all in rows like soldiers standing to attention.

Marcus Spicer's murderer came in.

'Hello?'

The room seemed empty. The murderer walked up to the table. Picked up one of the bottles. Put it down again.

'Hello?' the murderer said again, wandering into the studio.

Mervyn's head popped up.

'Hello there!' Mervyn said.

'Mervyn?' said the murderer.

'Sorry, you were expecting to meet Graham Goldingay, weren't you?' Mervyn grinned. 'That was a bit of a fib. Sorry. I'm getting better at impersonating him, I think. Practice makes perfect.'

'What's all this about?' said the murderer.

'The bit about him having the red briefcase wasn't a fib. Graham has got it, as far as I'm aware. I don't know if he's got it open yet, but I don't really need to know what's inside. I've got a pretty shrewd idea anyway.'

The murderer looked puzzled, suspicious. 'Look, what's going on Mervyn? It wasn't easy for me to get in today.'

'Oh don't get me wrong. I'm really glad you could make it. I know you're busy. I've arranged another DVD commentary recording. I want you to help with it, you're my special guest. I hope you don't mind.'

'What?'

'Did you go to the toilet before you came in? I wouldn't want you to be uncomfortable before we start.'

'Seriously, Mervyn, if you don't explain yourself, I'm leaving.'

'I'll do better than explain myself. I'll show you.'

'Show me what?'

'Marcus Spicer's killer, in the act of murdering him.'

'What?'

'Just put the headphones on.'

'No.'

'Why not?'

The murderer looked nervous, scared. 'Because I don't want to.'

'You want the murderer caught, don't you? Then this will clear it up.'

The murderer backed to the door, but Mick appeared from nowhere. She shut the door and leaned back on it, arms folded.

'No way, cupcake.'

Trevor appeared too, from the recording suite. He looked cold and angry, not a cringing apologist at all.

'Sorry, but you're not going anywhere,' said Trevor. 'Just a few words of advice. While you're watching the screen, try not to just describe what you're seeing. We can all see what's on the screen. Use what you see to remind yourself. If you have any anecdotes, keep it light and friendly.'

The murderer looked very afraid.

Trevor continued, a hint of menace creeping into his voice. 'Don't worry about revealing how it's going to end. You're not spoiling it for us, because we've seen it before.'

'Bollocks to this,' said the murderer. 'I'm leaving now. Get out of my way.'

'So keep the chat going, keep the energy up, and don't swear or make defamatory remarks,' said Trevor. 'You are being recorded, remember.'

The murderer tried to get past Mick, but she wasn't moving.

'Get out of my way!'

Frustrated, the murderer tried to prise Mick's hand from the door handle.

'Give it up, Ironside,' said Mick. 'You're not going anywhere.'

'Cheryl, please...' said Mervyn, sadly. 'The police have the recording too. You might as well talk me through what you did and why.'

Cheryl smiled; a dead humourless smile. She walked up to Mervyn, who was sitting at the desk in front of the screen. It was such an odd feeling, Mervyn thought, to be staring up at Cheryl's face.

She put her hands on her hips. Mervyn proffered a spare pair of headphones.

'You're ridiculous,' she said.

'Humour me. You played me like your own personal detective. You put me in a hamster wheel and made me run full speed on the spot. It's only fair. You owe it to me to tell me.'

She sighed, and took the headphones. 'Okay Mervyn. For old time's sake. I'll play it your way. Now what are we going to watch? As if I didn't know.'

Cheryl and Mervyn put on their headphones. Mick and Trevor assumed their positions on the other side of the glass. Mick crossed her arms just like Joanna had before, a fearsome genie from a dark fairy tale.

Trevor pressed some buttons on the console in the studio, and the screen in front of them flickered into life. On it was a steady image, like a CCTV camera picture. The camera was high up, showing an aerial view of the inside of a toilet cubicle.

Cheryl nodded. 'Lionel's recording. I might have known. I'm going to appear any moment, aren't I?'

Trevor's voice buzzed in their headphones. 'Don't describe what's on the screen, and don't get ahead of yourself.'

Despite herself, Cheryl laughed. So did Mervyn.

Sure enough, someone appeared, creeping stealthily. A figure buttoned up inside a trenchcoat, a wide-brimmed hat.

The figure locked the cubicle door, but did none of the usual things people did when they were inside. The figure stood on the toilet and wrestled with the grille in the roof. Long manicured fingernails scraped against the grille, pushing it up. After some nudging and scraping, it was edged to one side. The figure reached into the hole and brought down a small dusty hip flask.

'So, Cheryl,' said Mervyn. 'The floor is yours.'

'Okay, this is me putting cyanide in Marcus's hip flask. The hip flask he stashed in the roof. The hip flask at the moment is full of vodka. Marcus always said he'd given up the drink, but of course he hadn't.'

On the screen, the figure opened the lid of the toilet and poured the contents of the flask away. Then she fished in her shoulder bag, took out a clear plastic bottle, and poured all of it into the flask until it was full again.

'Like a lot of alcoholics, Marcus was a secret drinker,' she continued. 'First, he hid booze all over the house; in pot-plants, books, under floorboards. But of course, being Marcus, he got more ambitious. He hid bottles everywhere he went. He hid them in Joanna's office, at the gym, in his club... And he hid them in the toilets of the BBC, as you can see.'

Mervyn looked at the screen sadly. 'He loved parading his secret alcoholism in front of other people, pouring vodka into his orange juice at the BBC club. I never realised how extreme it had got.'

Cheryl gave a cold smile. 'He knew it was naughty, Mervyn. He knew he wasn't supposed to, but he loved to do it. He loved the deceit. He loved the idea of walking out of the house knowing he'd have a "secret supply" everywhere he went. So when I decided to kill him, I went around all his haunts doing a little treasure hunt, looking for his secret flasks in their secret places, replacing his booze with liquid cyanide. I nipped into the BBC using Joanna's pass, which I nicked. The flask was easy to find. Marcus was so predicable.'

Mervyn shook his head in admiration. 'It was a stroke of genius. It was just a matter of time before he pulled out a flask from one of his hiding places, drank the cyanide, and you would be nowhere near him at the time. A perfect alibi – because you, as the murderer, had the perfect accomplice. The victim himself.'

'It was a perfect crime, Mervyn. Shame about Lionel and his filthy little toilet camera. You wouldn't have worked it out without this bloody recording.'

'As a matter of fact, I did work it out,' said Mervyn, tetchily. He was stung at being dismissed so casually. 'I worked it out just before I saw this footage, actually, and I did it with the help of the commentary of "The Burning Time".'

'That bloody thing.'

'Yes, that "bloody thing". On the recording of the commentary, the sound of Marcus opening the bottle was really loud, like a collection of pistol shots. It was so loud Robert had to stop the commentary.'

He cued Trevor, who pressed a button. Marcus's final seconds echoed through their headphones .

'... those are the stakes we're playing for... And I for one don't want to be tied to one just yet...'

KLAK-LAK-LAK-LAK-LAK

'Sorry, just opening my water.'

Mervyn picked up a bottle from the table. 'I've opened two of those Estuary English bottles since Marcus's murder. I saw Joanna open one in this very recording suite, and I saw Mick over there open one last night... And each time they all sounded like this...'

He twisted the top, and a timid *click-click-click-click* emitted from the bottle.

'But Marcus's bottle sounded exactly like this...'

He took out a bottle of pills and twisted the childproof lid.

KLAK-LAK-LAK-LAK-LAK.

'That was another nice touch of Marcus's,' said Mervyn. 'Very him, showing off his own cleverness. Actually using the noise of the pill bottle he'd got in his pocket to make it sound like the water bottle's seal was breaking; to make it look like he hadn't opened the bottle in the toilet beforehand and filled it up with what he thought was vodka. He made it look like a miracle.'

'A bloody miracle,' spat Cheryl. 'It was bloody annoying.'

'Why?'

'Isn't it obvious? I didn't plan it to be a bloody miracle. I just thought he'd pull out a flask from a hidey-hole and neck it down straight away. I didn't expect the bugger to wander into a crowded room and poison himself in front of everybody. I'd spent weeks waiting for that phone call, to hear about him being found dead in some corner of a room with a flask of cyanide in his hand; I had a ready-made forged suicide note, all sealed and ready to send off to Joanna in the post; Marcus complaining about the pressures of being a fraud. Of living a lie. Admitting that I'd written all his books and he'd taken all the credit.' Cheryl smiled sadly. 'And I would come forward – reluctantly – as the real author of his books, and carry on the legacy.'

CHAPTER SEVENTY-THREE

'I should have realised,' said Mervyn. 'I should have realised that someone like Marcus would never have the dedication or concentration to even read a novel, let alone write one.'

'I was young and keen,' sighed Cheryl. 'And in love. Marcus was making a name for himself on the chat show circuit, but he wasn't capitalising on it. He wasn't thinking of the future. I could see what needed to be done, so I just rolled up my sleeves and wrote the books.'

'And Marcus let you?'

'Of course he did. He was lazy.'

'And you let him?'

'Of course I did. I was in love.' Cheryl rubbed her forehead. 'But Marcus and I had a deal. An agreement.'

'You agreed that you would do all the work, and he would take the credit.'

She laughed. 'Yeah, I suppose that's right too. That's why he called me his "Little Mary". Not after Mary the Madonna; after Mary Magdalene. The woman who did the work, but got no credit. The one that got airbrushed out of history. Marcus thought that was very amusing.'

'Marcus would.'

'But we had an agreement. I forced him into it, while he was pissed. We agreed that if one of us became ill or died, then we'd come clean to the world. And I would get my moment of recognition.'

'And then you got cancer. And Marcus had second thoughts.'

'Of course he did. He dithered, he argued, he persuaded me that the time wasn't quite right. He took long trips away. I had a nasty feeling that he was waiting for me to die.' Her face hardened. 'And then I became sure of it. All my notes. All my research, all evidence that I'd written the books disappeared from the house overnight, while I was away in hospital having chemo.'

'I presume he put all the notes in a red briefcase with gold clasps?'

'I don't know. I suppose. He did have one like that. It was then I finally woke up to the fact that I would never get the credit for my books.'

'So you decided to kill him.'

'I knew that spineless bastard wouldn't have the courage to destroy my notes. He'd need them some day, if he was interviewed by a newspaper, and the poor sap needed to be reminded of what he was supposed to have written.'

'Crib notes. Like the summaries they give us for DVD commentaries.'

'If you like. So I just had to work out where he'd put them. Another little hiding place to find. Once I'd worked that out, I could kill him.'

'And then the statuette got stolen.'

Cheryl nodded. 'And then the statuette got stolen. He went frantic. He spent more time looking for that fucking statuette than we'd spent together during our fake marriage. He sent Aiden out to every bring-and-buy sale in the country. He was about as subtle as a fucking brick. When my spies in Stoneleigh, Parsons and Williams told me I'd been cut out of his will and replaced by that congenital airhead Samantha Carbury, everything slipped into place.'

'What slipped into place?'

'Haven't you worked out why he did that, Mervyn? I realised the instant I heard.'

'Please enlighten me. It's fascinating.'

'Thanks, I will. My darling fake husband, as you can probably guess from his photo displays, his ridiculous Spicer Institute and his silly tricks with his will, was a man obsessed with his legacy. He wanted to be known as Mr Best-selling Novelist and Godhater-In-Chief long after he'd died and ascended to a non-existent heaven. Everyone has a Jesus complex to some extent, Mervyn; to be remembered after we're gone. It's why you and me, we're both writers. It's why I wanted credit for my work, after all these years. It's why you do these DVD commentaries.'

Mervyn said nothing. He didn't have to.

'Everyone has a Jesus complex, and Marcus had a bigger Jesus complex than most.'

'I noticed.'

'He knew there was the tiniest chance that I might outlive him. Not a huge chance, but the teeniest tiniest chance that I might. He got death threats all the time. It wasn't beyond the realms of imagination that a religious freak might stab him through his minuscule heart with a sharpened crucifix.' She looked at him with her huge green eyes. 'So what happened if he'd died and the statuette got recovered? It would come right back to me of course.'

'Or worse, your brother.'

'That would have been bad, too, for Marcus. I'm not an idiot, and he knew I wasn't an idiot. Obviously, the statuette was important to him in some way. If I ever got it back, I'd examine it. My brother certainly would. He'd smash it to bits with his hammer first chance he got. So Marcus transferred everything he owned to Samantha, with some bullshit justification that she was his first love blah blah blah. What he was thinking was, if the statuette got recovered, it would get sent off to some dizzy cow who always left her front door open because she wanted positive spirit energy to flow up her skirt. Easy for Aiden to burgle.'

Despite himself, Mervyn choked up a smile. Cheryl shook her head disbelievingly. 'It was so idiotic of Marcus. The fool. He took away the inheritance. The fact I wouldn't get any money took away the most obvious motive to kill him and gave the motive straight to Samantha. He practically signed his own death warrant. Arsehole.'

'I would imagine that Marcus gave Aiden instructions to find the stolen statue, get hold of the key, get hold of the notes and destroy them. He didn't stop carrying out his master's orders, even though his master was dead. Did you think Aiden knew Marcus was a fraud?'

'I'm not sure. I don't think so. Aiden's a simple soul. He can't stop being loyal to his master, like a dog sleeping by his dead owner. I'm certain Marcus wouldn't have told Aiden what the notes actually were. Marcus would want to keep it between himself and poor little me, his dying wife.'

'So that was your plan. Marcus dies from apparent self-poisoning, a suicide note is discovered, Marcus confesses he's a fraud by letter, you find the proof that you wrote the books and emerge as the real Marcus Spicer.'

'Exactly.'

'But things didn't go quite as planned.'

'Too bloody right,' she snapped. 'Marcus's quiet little "suicide" becomes the Vengeance of the Lord and the world's press goes mental. Not that I didn't think it was funny, the God squad having a collective orgasm over his death, but it turned it into a murder hunt. So, before his death I was hunting for the notes to prove I wrote the books... *Now* I was hunting for the notes to shred them. To make sure no one knew I had a motive to kill Marcus.'

'You used me to find that statuette.'

'I did. Sorry.'

'You pretended that Marcus had said something to you about the statuette, about its great significance to the Godbotherers, but he hadn't.'

'No.'

'You used me.'

'Yeah, but I'm sure you had fun, running around like something out of a Dan Brown novel. But I told you the truth didn't I? I bet the Godbotherers would have loved to find out what Marcus had done. A mysterious secret. A cover-up. Just this time, it was us atheists with the dark secret.'

CHAPTER SEVENTY-FOUR

Mervyn sipped his bottled water. He didn't feel nervous about drinking it any more, now he knew how the poison got in the bottle.

'Then there was your other problem. Lionel.'

'Oh yes. Lionel and his bloody covert filming,' she gestured to the screen, which was still playing the footage on a loop. 'Filthy little bastard. Who does this kind of thing? Some people...'

'So... I'm guessing Robert found the footage first, on Lionel's laptop.'

'Can you believe that idiot?' she shook her head disbelievingly. 'Robert contacted me, telling me he knew how Marcus was killed, had footage of the murder, and yet he couldn't even work out it was me who'd done it.'

'He thought it was Samantha.'

'Yes. He was very proud of his deduction. He could see it was a woman on the recording, but he assumed it was Samantha, because of the long fingernails. Joanna didn't have long fingernails. I did, but he never thought it was me, not for a second. He was so keen to catch the killer for me. He even invited me into the gents toilets to show me his discovery. Useful, because it saved me climbing up there.'

'And you were ready for him. How did you kill him?'

'It was simple, really. Death by wheelchair,' she gave a sour grin. 'I stripped the edges of the rubber from the handles, so anyone who went to push it would automatically touch the metal. Then I rigged up the car batteries that power my chair so they were feeding current into the metal.'

'Oh! That's why you didn't power the wheelchair that day. The batteries were needed for something else.'

'Robert showed me what he'd found, brought down the flask from the ceiling, rang you to gloat and then started to push me back to the recording suite. The charge knocked him across the room. I didn't know if it was going to be enough to kill him, but I was in luck. I didn't know he had a pacemaker, and the charge overloaded it, blowing up and taking him with it. Now that was something else I didn't expect. Can you believe it Mervyn? Another miracle! Stigmata on the hands and spontaneous combustion! Jesus!'

Mervyn smiled, a very tired smile, and looked at the screen, on which the figure in the trenchcoat was endlessly filling the flask with a never-ending supply of poison. 'I knew it was you on the tape. The moment I saw it.'

Cheryl smiled bashfully. 'Really, Mervyn? How did you know?'

Mervyn pointed at the screen, where the tape was still playing. 'The mark by your thumb.'

Sure enough, when the hand reached up to push the grille back, there was a little mark on the hand, stretching over the knuckle.

'Awww. The mark you gave me, Mervyn. That day in the production office, when you caught it in the photocopier. I've always loved that little mark. It always reminded me of you, Mervyn. Of happier times.'

Mervyn's heart gave a jolt, as though it had been shocked by an electrified wheelchair.

Cheryl got up from her chair and waved cheerily at Trevor and Mick. Mick, to her credit, waved cheerily back. Mick caught Mervyn's eye and mouthed something. Something he could easily lip read. *Told you so. Henchmen. Evil. Wheelchair. Evil.*

Mervyn gestured to Cheryl to sit back down. Cheryl obliged. It was obvious they were both enjoying this. Perhaps too much.

'Let me guess what happened to Professor Alec Leman,' said Mervyn.

'Okay Mervyn. The floor is yours.'

'I would say that, after Marcus's death, you needed to go back to the hiding places where Marcus stashed his booze and empty out the poison you put in. You couldn't risk them being discovered.'

'Too right. Bloody impossible though, with Aiden watching the house, pining for his dead master, and me having to pretend I needed a wheelchair. I got a few flasks. Not all.'

'In his will, Marcus left Professor Leman the flask of whisky he kept in his desk drawer in the Spicer Institute. When Leman got to the lecture with us, he went into Marcus's office. He must have had a quick drink, which you'd presumably poisoned.'

'Exactly.'

'You went in there first.'

'Yes.'

'You needed to act fast.'

'Oh yes.'

'So you grabbed the flask, stuffed it in your chair, grabbed a bottle of open water and threw it on the floor, just as I came in.'

'Exactly right.'

'Another miracle.'

'Another bloody miracle. Can't get away from them, can I?'

'And there was another flask you'd forgotten about. The one in Marcus's book, on your own bookshelf. I discovered it, and the moment I did you realised I'd found it. You had to think fast then, didn't you?'

'I'm sorry, Mervyn.'

'You snogged me just to get the poisoned flask out of my pocket. You accused me of being a drunk... And I fell for it. What an utter booby I am.'

'I'm so sorry Mervyn. Playing you along... The murders. I didn't mean any of it to happen. Once the rollercoaster started I just couldn't get off. I was doing what I had to. But... I thought that was nice too. I wish we could have stayed like that, but I was in too deep. Anyway. Happy times, Mervyn.'

Mervyn's heart jolted again.

CHAPTER SEVENTY-FIVE

Cheryl's face creased in thought. 'Where was I. What happened then?'

'Lionel.'

'Oh yes. Lionel. He was very pleased with himself because he worked it out... eventually. He didn't make a lightning deduction like you, Merv. Or get it hopelessly wrong like Robert. He guessed it was a woman who knew Marcus well. He had the date and time I'd entered the BBC toilets imprinted on the tape. He was an ex-security guard, so he knew what he was doing. He slowly eliminated all the suspects, one by one. Joanna was in America at the time, Samantha was at a convention in Newcastle, Carlene and Siobhan might have had the opportunity, but neither were married.' Cheryl waggled her ring finger. 'The woman on the tape wore a wedding ring. How bloody ironic, seeing as I wasn't even married. Once he started to suspect me, he blew up pictures of the hand on the tape, looked at old newspaper clippings and – finally – noticed the little mark you gave me.'

Mervyn couldn't help seeking out the mark on her hand.

'So the old perv contacted me,' she continued. 'He'd watched me fill the flask on his grubby little toilet tape, and now he wanted money. I pretended to go along with his demands, arranged to meet him in the hotel. I had to do something about him – another one I had to get rid of. I only wanted Marcus gone, but the whole thing was just becoming a nightmare that I couldn't wake up from.'

She looked up at Mervyn, but he refused to catch her eye. She sighed and carried on.

'I made sure Lewis Bream was there too, so I had someone to frame. But that wasn't too hard. I sent him an anonymous gift; three nights in Hambley Hall. All paid for. Well, I thought, if the Godbotherers wanted to take the credit for all these murders, I'd let 'em.'

'That wasn't the only reason you chose Hambley Hall to meet Lionel,' said Mervyn.

'God no. I never waste my precious energy. Hambley was where he used to take Joanna for their naughty weekends. Not that I have anything against Joanna; she was welcome to the little shit. But it was another place he hid one of his flasks, and another one which I'd substituted with cyanide. It was the furthest away one I'd done. I'd thought I'd take a trip, kill Lionel, frame Lewis Bream and dispose of my incriminating evidence.'

'All in a day's work.'

'Exactly. Lionel had booked rooms 81 and 83 like I'd asked him to, but just my luck in a classic fuck-up, he'd taken room 81. The one I wanted – with the flask in the ceiling. And I certainly wasn't expecting him to book room 79 for Graham as well. And then you turned up instead of that fat idiot... Jesus! After Lionel had talked to you, he came into my room to talk. To try and up my price. I knew I had to work quickly.'

'Of course,' said Mervyn. 'I didn't see what room he'd gone into after he left me. I just heard a door shut and assumed he'd gone back into his room. When Brian and I went to find him, the door was open, and all we could see was his clothes lying on the floor!'

'Well, he was hardly what you would call a neat man, Mervyn. What did you expect him to do? Unpack his clothes into the hotel wardrobe and use the hangers provided?'

'You had to... work... quickly?' Mervyn's brain started to catch up with what Cheryl had been saying. He knew what she meant, of course. He just needed her to say it herself.

'Well, pretty quickly. All the time you were talking to Brian about the Rapture, Lionel was in the room next door, getting strangled by me. When you and Brian left, I dragged him back into his room, retrieved the flask from the ceiling, and left by the window.'

'Another miracle.'

'Another bloody miracle. You nearly caught me that night, Mervy.'

'You move fast for a wheelchair-bound woman on her deathbed.'

'Yeah...' She looked at the screen, at herself. The figure in the trenchcoat leaping nimbly onto the toilet and retrieving the flask. 'Another bloody miracle...' Her mind was a million miles away.

'Cheryl? Are you okay?' said Mervyn.

It seemed an odd thing to say to a woman who'd killed three people and caused the death of a fourth, but the niceties of polite behaviour never left him, even in situations like this.

'All that bollocks, about Marcus being killed by God. About being killed by a miracle. I asked you if you believed it, Mervyn. Remember?'

'I remember.'

'You were surprised I asked the question.'

'I was.'

'Mervyn. Marcus would have got everything he wanted. He'd got my notes taken away from me. Just like he stole your notes from you, even though we were both too decent to let the cat out of the bag. We do all the work, he gets all the credit. We're two of a kind, Mervyn, you and me. We should have stayed together, but Marcus was very persuasive. Yeah, we should have been together you and me, got married properly.'

Mervyn's heart suddenly put on a lot of weight. It sank into his stomach.

'Well, maybe not,' she continued. 'Maybe it's not good for writers to be happy. Certainly not with each other.'

Mervyn nodded, but he didn't want to. He really did not want to nod.

'So Marcus had it all. He had our notes, he had me trapped, literally and figuratively. And I would be gone soon. His legacy was assured, his fame and his notoriety secure. He'd never have to write another book, just shout on television and opine at book festivals to damp old maidens from the shires. Perfection. His idea of heaven in fact... It was assured. Except for one thing. I recovered.'

'You...'

'I got better. I was so gonna die, Mervyn. Everyone said so, all the experts. And then the cancer went away. Something happened, and I don't know what. I didn't tell anyone. I swore my doctor to secrecy and kept shaving my head. Made Marcus think I wasn't going anywhere but the grave.' She stood up again. Stood over him. 'Something gave me my health back, my strength to walk, to move about incognito and poison those flasks. Vengeance was mine.' She looked at him with her big green eyes. 'So they were right. The Godbotherers were right. A miracle did kill him, Mervyn. A miracle killed him in the end.'

CHAPTER SEVENTY-SIX

Mick called for back-up.

Inspector Eric Preece arrived. After Mick gave him a very forceful account of what had really happened to Marcus, Robert and the others, complete with murderer's recorded confession and evidence, he grudgingly gave up the ghost and stopped trying to arrest Mervyn.

When Preece left the room, he could swear that Mervyn made a tiny 'zap' noise at him, when his back was turned.

They took Cheryl away, and she was charged with murder. There was a predictable media circus that grew into a carnival the nearer she got to trial.

While she was waiting to go into court, she went to the toilet, escorted by a female police officer. The officer, waiting outside the door, didn't notice that Cheryl happened to go into the gents rather than the ladies.

Cheryl never came out alive.

Mervyn remembered how Marcus was always ending up in court; being sued by this pressure group or that pressure group for blasphemy, libel or whatever they tried to throw at him that week. He relished it. Every trial gave him publicity for 'his' next book.

Obviously, he had liked a drink while he was waiting.

Brian survived Lewis Bream's attack, and was instantly plastered over the pages of the tabloids. His glum, bandaged head looked out from the news-stands. The headline was 'Beware of the God-Botherer'.

The Godbotherers fragmented. A small proportion of them stayed loyal. A much larger proportion, disgusted by Lewis's behaviour, went away to form another group, called the Jesus Peepers.

Marcus's Spicer Institute also fragmented. The atheists found themselves in the shoes of the theists they once ridiculed; their titular head was in disgrace, a fraud. Their philosophy, however laudable, was shrouded in deceit. Some lived in denial, and declared that Cheryl hadn't written the books at all; it was all a theist conspiracy to discredit them. Like the Pope, Marcus had to be infallible or it was all for nothing.

Others, quite rightly, looked over the immediate scandal and said that whatever the individual failings of their heroes, the institution wasn't at fault. Both the Spicerists and the Godbotherers fell into the predictable patterns of damage limitation, denial and survival.

Samantha found herself still with a huge amount of money, and she was free to indulge her desire to heal the world. Joanna gave up being an agent and joined her, becoming the snarling counterpart to Samantha's drippy benevolence. Joanna actually seemed to enjoy doing good works for a change. Beneath the trouser suit and the business hairstyle, there was actually a beating heart. Thanks to Joanna, the money actually went to people who needed it.

'The Burning Time' was slipped out in a season four box set, with no DVD commentary. There was a documentary tribute to Marcus on the disc and a sketch about God from *The Kenny Everett Show*.

Anyway, for Mervyn it was back to the novel.

Well, not quite. There were the inevitable distractions that went with being a bored writer stuck at home with a magical typing machine that had access to the world's pornography.

Mervyn didn't think of himself as a dirty old man. Oh no.

His mind wandered to the possibilities that might be conjured up by his search engine, and he was reminded of the Peek-a-Boob site. Just curious, mind. He wasn't a D.O.M.

Yet.

Finding the site was easy. He hacked his way through the jungle of pop-up ads, insisting he take detours to this dating site or that saucy webcam, until he found himself facing the cartoon naked lady lounging on the logo.

He was somewhat relieved to find the pictures of him on the toilet gone; he guessed the flare of new publicity surrounding Cheryl's arrest and the role Lionel's candid footage played in her capture must have scared the few remaining sites into removing the offending material.

That was a relief.

His relief was short-lived however, when he clicked on a section marked 'NEW BOOBS!!!' and was rewarded with the photos of the cleavage of Mervyn Stone.

There was a sword in his hand. He was stripped to the waist and fighting a non-existent dragon. He should have known.

Never trust a man called Judass...

AUTHOR'S NOTE EXTRA

A quick round-up of what's real and what isn't in this book...

Betchworth quarry sort of exists. There is a hole in Dorking called Betchworth Quarry, but it's been largely filled in, so you're perfectly safe to visit it.

Hambley Hall definitely doesn't exist, so you're not safe to visit it. Don't try staying in one of its rooms, because you'll just catch cold.

At the time of writing, BBC TV centre exists, but at the time of reading, it could well be a hole in Dorking for all I know.

The Godbotherers don't exist, neither does the Spicer Institute, and Estuary English water. The Godbotherers' headquarters, nestling in amongst the naughty shops in Soho is very not real. Don't try visiting it, or you'll just catch something far worse than a cold.

God may exist, but I think that's down to an individual's 'personal canon'.

The Mervyn Stone Mysteries Book One

❖

GEEK TRAGEDY
by Nev Fountain

Mervyn Stone does not look like a special man. However, he is special in one very important respect. He has *Vixens from the Void* on his CV. This is why, 20 years later, Mervyn reluctantly finds himself at ConVix 15.

It's a funny thing... everywhere Mervyn's dormant career takes him, there are murders. Here's another funny thing. Mervyn, with his script editor's eye for sorting out plot holes, seems to be the only one able to solve them.

❖

The Mervyn Stone Mysteries Book Three

❖

CURSED AMONG SEQUELS
by Nev Fountain

It's the announcement all the fans have been waiting for! After 17 long years, they're bringing back *Vixens from the Void*. But Mervyn Stone is not sure it's a good idea. And to make matters worse, someone is trying to kill him.

Is it the incompetent director who hates Mervyn from way back? The mad fan who wants the relaunch stopped? The producer with a guilty secret? Mervyn is learning something important. Perhaps the past should stay in the past...